P9-EMH-171

BATHSHEBA

CH

BATHSHEBA
RELUCTANT BEAUTY

A DANGEROUS BEAUTY
NOVEL

ANGELA
HUNT

BETHANY HOUSE PUBLISHERS
a division of Baker Publishing Group

Published by Bethany House Publishers
11400 Hampshire Avenue South
Bloomington, Minnesota 55438
www.bethanyhouse.com

Bethany House Publishers is a division of
Baker Publishing Group, Grand Rapids, Michigan

Printed in the United States of America

Library of Congress Cataloging-in-Publication Data
Hunt, Angela Elwell.
Bathsheba : reluctant beauty / Angela Hunt.
    pages ; cm — (A dangerous beauty novel)
    Summary: "Bathsheba, a beautiful woman forced to become one
of King David's wives, is committed to protecting her son while deal-
ing with the dynamics of the king's household in this biblically based
novel"— Provided by publisher.
    ISBN 978-0-7642-1696-1 (softcover)
    1. Bathsheba (Biblical figure)—Fiction. 2. David, King of
Israel—Fiction. 3. Women in the Bible—Fiction. 4. Mothers and
sons—Fiction. 5. Bible. Old Testament—History of Biblical events—
Fiction. I. Title.
PS3558.U46747B38 2015
813'.54—dc23   2015015263

Cover design by Paul Higdon
Cover photography by Olena Zaskochenko
Interior design by Paul Higdon and LaVonne Downing

Author is represented by Browne & Miller Literary Associates

15 16 17 18 19 20 21   7 6 5 4 3 2 1

Angela Hunt Presents
The DANGEROUS BEAUTY Series

"The Hebrew text has two words that are typically used to describe personal appearance. One, *yapeh*, is rather mild and means 'good looking.' The other, *tob*, when applied to women's looks, conveys sensual appeal. This woman is so beautiful that she arouses the desire of men who see her."

—Sue Poorman Richards and Larry Richards,
authors of *Every Woman in the Bible*

Beauty does not always benefit the woman who possesses it. On occasion it betrays her, and at other times it endangers her, even to the point of death.

These novels—*Esther*, *Bathsheba*, and the upcoming *Delilah*—are the stories of three *tob* women.

Everybody, soon or late, sits down
to a banquet of consequences.
—Robert Louis Stevenson

Chapter One

BATHSHEBA

Spring, 996 BC

THE FIRST TIME I SAW KING DAVID, I was sixteen and he was behaving like a man possessed. The procession carrying the holy Ark of the Covenant was moving slowly down the street where we lived, and the pageantry of the parade mesmerized me. Scores of musicians preceded the Ark—trumpeters, harpists, men who played the lyre, and singers with fine voices—and dozens of somber priests walked alongside them, their faces a study in reverence and sobriety.

Then I caught the glimmer of sunlight on a cherubim's golden wing. I clutched my father's arm and wondered if I should hide my face from such a sacred sight, but before I could ask, a rising cloud of dust caught my attention. Behind the two priests who guarded the ark, between the Levites who were blowing shofars, I spotted an auburn-haired, bearded man who leapt and spun and whirled in reckless abandon. He wore the linen ephod and robe worn by the priests of Israel, but as the day was warm and the sun hot, he stopped spinning long enough to shrug off the outer robe and toss it to one of the guards. Then, clad only in the light linen shift, he continued to leap and twist, all the while grinning like a man who had been caught up in a holy rapture.

I glanced at my father, certain that I would see him frowning. In a moment he would call out a rebuke to the guards; he would command one of his friends to haul the madman away.

Instead, my father smiled, and in his eyes I saw the same look of fond indulgence with which he regarded me when I had done something foolish.

I tugged on his sleeve. "Father, who is that man?"

Reluctantly, he tore his gaze away from the energetic dancer. "Did you say something, daughter?"

"That man—who is he?"

His smile broadened. "That, Bathsheba, is David, the king of all Israel."

"Behaving most inappropriately," my grandfather grumbled.

"If you knew him better, you would not criticize him." Father elbowed Grandfather and grinned. "That free spirit you see serves us well in battle, for the man is fearless and Adonai is with him. There's no other way to explain how he always manages to elude his enemies."

Grandfather did not respond, but pressed his lips together and crossed his arms in stony disapproval.

I stared at the leaping king. I had heard many stories about the youngest son of Jesse, but I had never been so close to him. To think that those sweaty hands killed a Philistine giant, that tongue devised praises to Adonai, that bushy head received the holy oil of anointing from HaShem's prophet, Samuel . . .

I watched, fascinated, as women from both sides of the street broke blossoms from their shrubs and threw them at the dancing

king's feet. I did not know much about kings in those days, but even
I was shocked to see the irreverent interest the women displayed.

"Is—is that quite proper?" I asked, feeling ill at ease. "Won't the
king be offended by their behavior?"

My father chuckled, then slipped his arm around my shoulders
and guided me back into the house. "David is a man after God's
own heart," he said simply. "He lights up every room he enters;
he elicits love from nearly everyone he meets. Do not judge him
harshly, Bathsheba, for one day you may meet him again. Then
you will love him, too."

I did not argue with my father, but something in me doubted I
could ever love such a man as that.

⚜

According to family history, when my parents presented me
to Samuel at the time of my mother's purification, the *Ruach Ha-
Kodesh* touched the ordinarily coherent prophet in such a way that
the torrent of words from his lips resembled nothing so much as a
stream of gibberish. Though my parents strained to understand the
prophet's words, they caught only a few. My father recalled hearing "mother to a great man" and "affect the future of Isra'el." My
mother, on the other hand, caught only two words: "*tob* woman,"
a phrase that pleased her very much.

At only eighty days old, I retained no memory of my encounter
with the prophet, but in the years ahead I came to understand
that a river of foretellings and curses had carved out the events of
my life, a torrent of words with the power to rip me from people I
loved and settle me on unexpected shores.

Because the prophet Samuel declared that I would be mother
to a great man, my father stressed my duty to marry well and
provide my husband with sons. Because my mother heard that I

would be not merely *yapeh*, pleasant-looking, but *tob*, highly desirable, even in my childhood she urged me to keep my nails clean and my hair smooth. Because I would be blessed with the gift of beauty, she often reminded me, any man Father chose would be blessed to marry me.

I was an obedient daughter who wished to please my parents and Adonai, so I wanted nothing more than to marry a good man and have as many children as the Lord allowed. The most important duty of any woman, my father intoned nearly every night, was to accept a husband and bear sons and daughters. Once the children were weaned, my husband would teach my sons a trade and I would teach my daughters how to be dutiful wives. Together my husband and I would teach our children to reverence Adonai, King of the Universe, and the king of Israel, whom God had anointed through His prophet Samuel.

A constant theme echoed through every lesson my parents taught: I was special because I had been chosen to bear a son who would greatly influence Israel.

HaShem had every right to exercise His sovereign will through choice. He had chosen Aaron and his descendants to be His holy priests. He had chosen the Levites to be His special servants. He chose Saul to be our king; then, after Saul displeased the Lord, HaShem chose David, son of Jesse, to reign over us.

When the spring of my eighteenth year arrived, on a day not long after Passover, my father announced that I was about to commence the journey Samuel had foretold. For the past year I had been betrothed to Uriah, a soldier in the royal corps known as "the Thirty." The marriage document had been signed, the dowry paid, my future home made ready. All that remained was for the bridegroom to appear at my father's house and escort me to the home we'd share for the rest of our lives together.

When the agreed-upon day arrived, I was more than ready to

marry the broad-shouldered warrior who'd caught my eye during a harvest festival. I knew I was unusually blessed, because the brave warrior had earned my father's approval, as well.

"Amaris!" About to panic, I turned to the corner, where my ten-year-old sister sat on a soft pillow and strummed her harp. "Do you remember where I put my veil?"

She scrunched her nose, then pointed to the basket beneath the window. "Elisheba had it. She embroidered it for you."

My alarm melted into appreciation as I pulled the rectangle of blue fabric from the basket. Elisheba, the loyal servant who had been Amaris's wet nurse after our mother's death, had embroidered tiny gold blossoms along the rectangle's edge—a lovely touch and quite fitting for a wedding.

I ran my fingertips over the tiny stitches. "It's beautiful."

"I'm glad you like it." Elisheba's throaty voice caught me by surprise. I turned to find her standing behind me, tears glistening in her eyes. "Child, I cannot believe you are old enough to have a family of your own."

"More than old enough." Smiling, I pressed a kiss to her cheek, then pulled back to look into her dark eyes. "How old were you when you married?"

She sighed the way she always did when we asked about the life she'd led before coming to us. "Fifteen."

"See? I feel positively ancient in comparison."

Elisheba shrugged. "I was ready to be married almost from the moment I was born. But you are special, child. Your father did not want to rush. After all, he had a prophecy to keep in mind."

I resisted the youthful impulse to roll my eyes, for Samuel's oft-repeated foretelling seemed a world away from the excited flutterings in my chest. "Why should an old prophecy worry him? If Samuel was a true prophet of Adonai, nothing could nullify his words. Adonai is not a man that He could change His mind—"

"Hush, I'm not going to argue with you today. Are your nails clean?"

I smiled at the familiar question. "They are."

"Your hair—did you rinse it with the scented water I mixed for you?"

"I did." I caught a handful of hair and brought it to my nose, inhaling the mingled aromas of flowers and herbs. "I did everything you told me."

She stood in front of me, her keen gaze traveling from my new sandals to my emerald-green tunic. She studied my face, her expression still sharp and assessing, and then our eyes connected and affection softened her countenance. "A *tob* woman," she whispered. "That you are, my dear. Uriah will be the envy of every man in Jerusalem today."

I looked away as an unwelcome warmth crept up my cheeks. "I think I will be the envy of every woman. I have seen them watching Uriah when he walks with me. Even the grandmothers smile at him."

"Silly fools." Elisheba tucked a stray strand of hair behind my ear. "I wonder how you will like being a soldier's wife. You will spend many days alone."

"But not for at least a year." I smiled again, confident in my happiness. "Uriah cannot go to war in our first year of marriage, and a year feels like forever. I have waited a year for this day, and I thought it would never come."

"But it did, child. And when you are my age, you will look back at your days as a girl and wonder how the time could pass so quickly."

"Bathsheba?" My father's rough baritone stilled our conversation. Elisheba stepped aside so I could see him in the doorway—tall, oiled, and dressed in his best tunic and cloak. "Are you ready, daughter? I hear the sound of approaching revelers."

"Ready and eager, Father." I pulled the embroidered scarf over my hair, then dropped a sheer fabric square over my face. I would

go to my groom veiled like Leah and Rachel, but this groom would
know who waited beneath the sheer fabric.

I turned to face him, and for a long moment my father stood
as though he were rooted to the floor. Without being told, I knew
he was remembering the past. He might have been reliving the
moment he first glimpsed my mother as his bride, or perhaps he
was remembering the day Samuel placed his hand on my head and
uttered a prophecy instead of a blessing.

"Daughter . . ." Father's voice clotted with emotion. "You are
more beautiful than ever."

I whispered my thanks, but he had already begun to stride across
the room. "Climb aboard, little monkey," he told Amaris, kneeling
beside my younger sister. "Today you shall sit at your new brother's
table and eat as much as you want."

Though Amaris could walk with a crutch, we traveled faster when
she rode on Father's broad back. She threw her arms around his neck.
He stood and waited while Elisheba playfully tucked my sister's thin
legs into the spaces beneath his arms. Once Amaris was securely
aboard, Father moved to the door and opened it to a flood of noise—
laughter and clapping and rattling tambourines. Someone blew a
trumpet, and my new husband's ruddy face appeared in the doorway.

"Bathsheba." His eyes moved into mine, sparing not a glance
for the household furnishings or my father or even for the veil that
stood between us. His gaze filled an emptiness within me, the space
that yearned for a good man who would love me and give me the
child who would fulfill my destiny. Surely Adonai had created me
for a man like Uriah.

My heart sang with delight as I stepped forward and slid my
hand into his. He gave me a look of unmistakable gratitude, then
together we moved through the courtyard on our way to the place
he had prepared—a lovely stone house on the heights of Jerusalem,
a dwelling that lay in the shadow of the king's grand palace.

Chapter Two
Nathan

All the events of King David's reign, from beginning to end, are written in *The Record of Samuel the Seer, The Record of Nathan the Prophet,* and *The Record of Gad the Seer.*

1 Chronicles 29:29

IN THE SETTLED AREA BEYOND THE WALLS of Jerusalem, in the last house before the land surrendered to wilderness, I lay on my sleeping mat and stared at the ceiling. Despite my wife's gentle snoring, I had not rested the previous night. Bizarre images and disturbing sensations troubled my sleep, causing me to toss and turn on the thin mattress. At one point I awoke, completely alert, and sat up, expecting to hear Adonai's voice in the darkness. But the Lord did not speak, so I stretched out again and closed my eyes, wondering if my dreams and discomfort had more to do with indigestion than the will of God.

I dozed until the ribald cackle of Ornah's rooster roused me from sleep. Though bright sunlight gilded the elevated City of David and poured through my window, an unsettled feeling haunted me. Trouble stirred somewhere, and I couldn't help wondering if HaShem was about to stretch out His hand in judgment . . .

On me? I sat up and searched my conscience, but could find no transgression other than the sin I confronted daily. My parents had assured me I would grow to love my wife after marriage, but though I had been faithful and Ornah had borne me two daughters, only compassion and pity stirred my heart when I looked at her sturdy form. My wife's name meant *cedar*, and like a mighty tree she had provided me with shelter, shade, and companionship. But my passion did not ignite when I looked into her small eyes, and my blood did not race when I kissed her wind-chapped lips. We remained friendly with each other, and I did not seek out harlots, but at night when I turned to Ornah in response to a manly urge, I painted someone else's face on the darkness.

The thought of that face pulled a wistful sigh from my lungs before I lifted my head and looked at the two little girls sleeping a few feet away. Nira, age two. Yael, age four. Two precious souls who looked like their mother and considered me their best playmate. If they were awake, they would be standing on my thighs, pulling my hair, and trying to climb my back.

I sighed again. For a prophet, mine was a good life. Every day I woke, then looked and listened for a message from Adonai. If I saw and heard nothing, I focused on my responsibilities to my family. Even prophets had to eat.

I was blessed to have a wife, two girls, a goat, and a lamb. We farmed a small plot of land in the Kidron Valley, and we worked and prayed beneath the shadow of the Ark of the Covenant, which rested in the Tabernacle atop Mount Moriah. We lived beneath the king, who with his wives and concubines dwelled in a grand cedar palace next to the Ark of Adonai.

I closed my eyes and cocked my head, listening with my ears and my heart. Had Adonai been the reason for my restless sleep? I waited, but heard nothing. I saw nothing. Apparently, all was well in Jerusalem.

I waited a few moments more, then rose and went outside to splash water on my face. If Adonai was not ready to speak, I would feed the lamb and goat and clean myself afterward.

Because I had been invited to a wedding.

Chapter Three

Bathsheba

The house at our journey's end was far nicer than I had expected, and evidence, I realized, of Uriah's commitment to my happiness. The structure sat nestled among a row of homes that bordered a winding street leading to the king's palace. Since most of the streets within Jerusalem's walls ascended to the higher elevations, the homes on our street were situated near the highest point in the city; only the king's house and the Tabernacle stood higher.

Uriah and I entered our new home on a tide of celebrating friends and relatives, who pushed and jostled their way through the courtyard and into the house. There my gaze took in the many bowls of fruit, jugs of wine, and stacks of linens that friends had arranged in gift baskets to celebrate our marriage. More than a few guests laughed or made good-natured jokes as they surveyed our elaborately decorated marriage bed, but I ignored them, not wanting to behave like an embarrassed virgin. Elisheba had told me what to expect when I was finally able to lie with my husband, so I was trying not to dread my first intimate encounter with a man.

I was rendered speechless, however, when Uriah led me through a doorway at the back of the house. Outside, with only the blue sky for a ceiling, lay a second courtyard, a lush garden paved with stones and enclosed by slender cypress trees. A large *mikvah*, a trough for watering our animals, stood at the center of the exquisite space.

"Nights will be beautiful here." Uriah caught my hands as we stood face-to-face. "I look forward to lingering in this garden with you. The moon and the starry host will be witnesses to my devotion."

I blinked, startled by this decidedly unwarrior-like declaration. I would have risen on tiptoe to kiss him, but my father had begun to urge others to vacate the house and move into the front courtyard. "They are married, so let us leave them in peace," he said, tossing Uriah a sly glance. "Let them consummate the marriage, and *then* we will celebrate!"

Grumbling good-naturedly, the celebrants left us alone. They would wait outside, feasting and drinking, until we emerged, as wedded in flesh as we were in law.

After watching them go, Uriah gripped my hand and led me into the house, but one man remained inside the front doorway—my tall, stern grandfather.

"Uriah, I pray you will allow me one more moment with my granddaughter," he said, moving toward me. "I would like to say a few words to her."

Uriah flexed his jaw, silently signaling his frustration, but Grandfather was not the kind of man who could be easily dissuaded. "Bathsheba"—he tugged at my sleeve—"I would give you my blessing."

I swallowed over the lump that had risen in my throat and allowed myself to be pulled from my husband's side.

"Listen well." Grandfather's dark gaze pinned me to the floor. "You must not heed anyone who would think less of you for marrying outside your tribe, for Uriah is a good and faithful man. He has pledged his allegiance to David and to Adonai, and both your father and I trust him completely."

With difficulty I restrained my impatience. "I know."

"Now let me bless you." Grandfather placed his broad palm on my head. "Blessed are you, Adonai, our God, King of the Universe, who created joy and gladness, groom and bride, mirth, glad song, pleasure, delight, love, brotherhood, peace, and companionship. Adonai, our God, let sounds of joy and gladness echo in the streets of Jerusalem, the voice of the groom and the voice of the bride. Blessed are you, our God, who causes the groom to rejoice with his bride, and blessed are you, Bathsheba. May Adonai make you like Rachel and like Leah, who between them built up the house of Israel. May the fruit of your womb change the course of history and bring blessings to Israel."

Content to have executed this grandiose and ceremonial gesture, Grandfather pressed a kiss to my forehead, then left the house and closed the door behind him.

❧

Outside the house, revelers shouted and clapped while pipers played and tambourines jangled. But those sounds faded to a dull roar as Uriah strode toward me, desire flushing his complexion. His steady gaze bore into me in silent expectation, and I took a step back, unnerved by the way my heart fluttered. I thought I knew what to expect in our coupling, but all my preconceptions vanished as the man for whom I had waited removed my veils with one hand. As I struggled to catch my breath, he caught my head and pressed his lips to mine in a kiss that sent the pit of my stomach into a wild swirl. I wrapped my arms around his neck, a half smile twisting my mouth. Would I ever be able to deny him anything?

When he pulled away and whispered my name, I trailed my fingertips across the oiled tendrils of his beard and searched his dark eyes. A wave of tenderness swept through me, but I had no time to explore that feeling, for my tall husband's hands cupped my face and pulled me toward him. I stretched on tiptoe, wondering if he would lift me off the floor.

My impatient husband picked me up and lowered me onto our rose-covered bed. A fresh linen sheet had been spread over the blanket to gather the proof of my virginity, but Uriah paid it no mind as he stretched out, scattering red and pink petals onto the floor. I closed my eyes and breathed in the sweet scent of the flowers, and as his left arm encircled me, I realized that I had never lain so close to any man, not even a brother.

"Bathsheba?"

I opened my eyes to see him peering at me. "Yes?"

"Are you . . . all right?"

I nodded, then forced myself to speak. "I am fine." I caught his free hand and pressed my lips to his palm, then met his gaze again. "I am fine, husband."

He pressed his lips to the pulsing hollow at the base of my throat. With his left hand he stroked my hair, and then, as a trembling thrill raced through me, his fingers trailed down my arm and over my breast. I clung to him, kissing his neck, his shoulder, his strong jaw, the tiny curls near his earlobes—

I do not need to write of the private moments that followed. Any woman who has ever surrendered to a man who loves her knows about the pain and the passion of those first private moments.

When the storm of our desire finally subsided, I whimpered in his arms, then exhaled a slow, steady breath.

I had been vanquished. I had become flesh of this man's flesh.

I finally understood how it felt to utterly belong to a beloved man.

CHAPTER FOUR
NATHAN

THE CELEBRATION HAD OVERFLOWED the newlyweds' courtyard by the time I arrived. I threaded my way through the throng and found Ahithophel, the king's chief counselor, talking to the bride's father near the courtyard gate. Since both men were close to the king, I wondered if David himself might appear.

"Greetings." I nodded to each of them. "Congratulations on this wonderful occasion. I know the bride is beautiful and the groom a good man."

A small frown appeared between Ahithophel's brows, as if he were struggling to place my face, but Eliam had no trouble remembering me. "Nathan! How good it is to see you." He gripped my shoulders and kissed both my cheeks. "Have some wine. Elisheba will bring out food as soon as the bride and groom reappear."

I took the cup he offered, lifted it in a silent salute to the newlyweds, then took a hearty swallow. Lowering my cup, I surveyed the merrymakers in the street. "So many of David's mighty men are here: Ashel, Zelek, Gareb, and Benaiah. Will the king celebrate with us today?"

Eliam and Ahithophel cast each other a look, and the bride's father burst out laughing. "Considering the many wives in David's harem, I doubt he has the strength to even attend another wedding. We were just joking that the king needs to enlarge his palace to make room for all his women."

"Seven wives kept him busy in Hebron," Ahithophel said, lifting his cup, "and one would think a woman for each day of the week would satisfy any man. But David has quite an appetite for beauty."

"An uncommon appetite," Eliam said with an arched brow. "But then, he is the king. Who are we to deny him?"

I sipped from my cup, then politely turned my attention toward the older man, whose reputation for wisdom and virtue was legendary. "Have you more than one wife, sir?"

A muscle twitched at the corner of the counselor's eye. He shook his head. "Adonai blessed me with a virtuous woman, but she died years ago. Unfortunately, my son is also a widower."

The bride's father heaved a sigh. "My wife died in childbirth, leaving me with two daughters, both of whom are beautiful. But Amaris, my youngest . . ." He shifted his attention to the musicians in the courtyard. "I have a feeling she will remain under my roof for the rest of her life."

I followed his gaze and spotted a child of ten or eleven years sitting near a trumpet player. A pretty girl, she sat on a pillow and slapped a tambourine in time to the music. Only when I looked down did I see her misshapen foot.

I turned back to her father. "Can she walk?"

He shrugged. "Slowly, with a crutch. In the house, she finds it easier to crawl on her hands and knees. And I know few men who would want a wife who crawls to his bed every night."

"She looks happy and content," I said. "Surely such a pleasant girl would not be an imposition."

"Not an imposition"—Eliam tugged on his beard—"so long as I have a nurse to care for her. Years ago the widow Elisheba stepped into my late wife's place, and she has cared for both my daughters. But I am no fool and I've accepted that Amaris will probably never marry." His eyes narrowed as he shot me a pointed look. "Unless *you* might want a pretty wife who can play the harp and sew for you. She's young, but she'll be of marriageable age in a few years."

The thought of marrying Bathsheba's sister scraped against the scar on my heart, but I refused to let the pain show on my face.

I shook my head. "Thank you, but I have a wife and two daughters. My little house already overflows with women."

Eliam grinned. "I have heard that you are wise, Nathan, and now I know the stories are true. No man should have more wives than he can honestly love."

With great difficulty I summoned the courage to speak of Uriah's new wife. "Your eldest daughter, is she a happy bride?"

"Our Bathsheba?" Ahithophel's voice rang with pride, and I saw the same emotion mirrored in Eliam's eyes. "Our treasure is completely happy to be marrying the man we have chosen. We had good reasons for not accepting just any man for her, and would never have accepted a Hittite, no matter how skilled a soldier—"

"Yet I convinced him Uriah was the right man," Eliam interrupted, leaning toward me. "I have fought beside him long enough to know Uriah is among the best of his people—strong, bright, and skilled. His father was a metalworker, and I hope Uriah will take up the trade one day. Such a trade—such skills—might change the course of Israel's future."

"In peacetime," Ahithophel added, staring at the ground, "when we need more plows than swords."

Eliam and I lifted our drinks. "May peacetime come soon."

I had just emptied my cup when the door to the house opened. Uriah stepped through the doorway, his face gleaming with a sweaty smile. He lifted a linen sheet dotted with bright red drops.

A collective cheer rose from the assembled guests, and pitchers of wine traveled through the crowd again.

Holding tight to my empty cup, I ignored the passing vessels and adjusted my position to see around Uriah's bulky form. Standing behind him, but firmly gripping his hand, stood Bathsheba . . . still the most beautiful woman I had ever beheld.

My teacher, Samuel, had taught us that prophets must be skilled with language to frame God's truth in the most powerful words possible. But language failed me as I beheld Uriah's wife, leaving my tongue thick and awkward. The woman in the doorway possessed all the proper parts—two eyes, a straight nose, full lips, a delicate pair of ears, thick, lustrous hair—but the arrangement of those elements was more pleasing than sinuous Egyptian vases and the colorful painted works of Canaanite artists. She had grown into the embodiment of female perfection. Yet not only did her form leave me breathless, but her countenance radiated kindness, compassion, and virtue. Her father and grandfather had not been exaggerating when they referred to her as their treasure.

"Nathan?" Eliam gave me a curious look. "Did you hear me?"

I redirected my gaze to my host's face. "I'm sorry, I was distracted. It's . . . noisy out here."

"The feast will continue for at least another day," Eliam said. "I was inviting you to stay at our home if you don't want to leave the city tonight. If you want to remain—"

"You are most generous," I interrupted, "but I do not think I should stay. For me to remain might be"—my thoughts returned to the beauty standing beside the groom I'd come to honor—"unwise."

Eliam didn't seem to mind my reluctance to enjoy his food and wine. He clapped my shoulder, thanked me for coming, and smiled while I said my farewells to his father.

When I turned to make my way back to the road that would lead me through the gates and away from the City of David, I felt a small, obscure twinge of unease.

What did it mean?

Chapter Five
Bathsheba

On my first morning as a married woman, I woke long before I found the courage to open my eyes. I lay next to Uriah in an otherwise empty house, the silence broken only by birdsong and the distant tramp of passersby on the road outside our courtyard.

Our courtyard. I smiled, loving the idea of being linked to a husband.

The wedding guests had dispersed shortly after sundown. Though many would return to enjoy more food and wine, for a few moments I would have my husband all to myself.

Peering through a half-opened eye, I studied the hulking form next to me. Uriah's long, deep breaths seemed to indicate that he was still asleep, though I had heard that the king's warriors slept with one eye open and their hands on their swords. When I shifted on our straw mattress and Uriah didn't move, I rolled onto my side to better study the man I had married.

He lay facing me, one hand stretched out and curving over my head. My gaze followed the slope of his broad chest as it narrowed to a trim waist, the straight edge of male hips and the flare of thighs above thick legs that could run for hours beneath a blistering sun. His skin was the color of warm honey, his hair dark with golden strands. Black curls dotted his chest, his arms, and even the backs of his hands, but I found an elegant perfection in their symmetry and texture. His chest was firm and well defined, his belly flat, his arms strong enough to carry me with ease. Two scars marred the perfection of his torso, both, he had told me the day before, were the result of sparring with comrades.

I tensed when the rhythm of his breathing changed. His brown lashes fluttered, then his hand rose to support his head as he smiled and whispered my name.

I stared at him, not knowing what a husband might expect from his wife when they woke together for the first time.

I managed to croak a timid response. "Do you want something, husband?"

"Only you." His arm swung around to draw me closer. "Bathsheba. Daughter of an oath. And now my wife."

I tipped my head back to better see his dancing eyes. "My mother gave me another name at my birth—Bathshua, daughter of a cry."

"So you were a squalling baby?" Uriah's mouth curved with merriment. "One of those infants who screams morning, noon, and night?"

I pretended to pout. "My father says I was pleasant enough. My grandfather says I was perfect."

"Grandfather Ahithophel is always right." My husband's smile stilled as his hand curved around my jawline. "You are perfect for me, daughter of an oath."

His lips sought mine, making my senses spin, but before surrendering I pulled away and placed my fingertips across his mouth. "Uriah, I want you to know something."

"What?" He kissed my fingers, then looked at me with a wry but indulgent glint in his eyes. "I'm listening."

"I don't know if you've heard about Samuel's prophecy—"

His eyes twinkled. "Your grandfather might have mentioned it a time or two."

"My father believes it with all his heart. The prophet said I will have a son who will greatly affect Israel's future, but I am not with you because of the prophecy. I am with you because I want to be your wife. I want to give you children, as many as HaShem wills. You are a good man, so no matter what my father or grandfather says about that prophecy, know that I came to your house and to your bed willingly . . . even happily."

His eyes remained fixed on mine for a long moment, then he tapped the tip of my nose. "I wouldn't have a wife who came to me in any other way."

His words, spoken so simply and sincerely, echoed in our small house and warmed my heart. "It's just—" I hesitated, searching for truthful words that would not shame my parents—"when I was growing up, my mother and father did not seem happy. I never saw them laugh together. They did not seem like two people who loved each other. Despite my father's conviction that I had to marry a great man, I have always wanted to marry a man I could love."

His fingers tightened around mine. "And have you done that?"

"Uriah." I nestled closer to him and tipped my face to his. "I have spent the year of our betrothal watching you. I have noticed you are dependable and that you serve the king for long hours without complaining. I have observed you care deeply for our laws and traditions. My grandfather, who is not quick to accept an outsider, has assured me that you will be a good father and provider. But more than anything, husband, I have seen how you cared for me . . . how you were careful never to do anything that might cause anyone to question my virtue. So yes, I love you. And I am certain that the old women who sit at the well were right when they said I would learn to love you more with every passing sunset."

He pulled me to him, his lips gentle and searching. As his kiss sang through my veins I closed my eyes, eager to love him forever.

NATHAN

I HAD JUST BROKEN MY FAST with cheese and bread when I heard footsteps on the gravel outside the house. I opened my door and stared at a pair of men wearing leather armor and the red mantles favored by the king's royal guard.

The tallest man, a broad-faced Pelethite, squinted at me. "Nathan the prophet?"

I squinted back. "Who asks for him?"

"If you're the prophet, the king summons you. We are to escort you to the palace."

I glanced at my tunic, stained with goat's milk and scattered bread crumbs. I ought to change, but if the king sent for a prophet before the morning chores were finished, he should accept the prophet as he was.

"I'll be back." After nodding to the guards, I went inside the house and pulled my cloak from a peg in the wall. I ran my hands through my hair, rinsed my mouth with a swish of water, then spat against the stone wall.

Bent over her mortar, Ornah stopped pounding grain long enough to glance over at me. "Up the mountain, then?"

"Apparently." I gave her a nod, briefly placed my hand on my youngest daughter's head, then I stepped outside and peered up at the guards, both of whom towered over me. "I'm ready."

We walked the pebble-covered path that led through houses scattered around the approach to the City of David, passing shepherds with their flocks and children who scrambled between buildings as they played. Since the guards and I traveled in relative silence, I lifted my gaze and studied the sky, a cloudless blue bowl overhead. Did this royal summons have anything to do with the disquiet that had been troubling my sleep? Adonai had not spoken to me in many days, but His presence felt like an arm across my shoulders, a hand that pinched my neck now and then to make certain I had not fallen asleep.

As always, my heart beat faster when we approached the eastern gate of Jerusalem. Important men sat under canopies here, waiting to be seen by those who wanted to buy or sell property, settle inheritances, or propose business. We slowed our pace to navigate the congestion at the gate, and one of the guards scowled at me as if I might break free and run. He needn't have worried. Running was the last thing I wanted to do.

Once we entered the city, we followed the winding streets and passed courtyards where women milked their goats and scattered feed to their hens. A merchant nearly ran into me, so intent was he on counting the wrapped cheeses in his basket. He looked up, mumbled an apology, and hurried on in his rush to reach the market.

I averted my eyes when we passed the tidy house where Bathsheba lived as the wife of Uriah the Hittite.

I had been serving as an apprentice to the prophet Samuel when a young couple brought their baby to the Tabernacle. The infant had been swaddled tightly and the face covered with linen, but when the prophet moved to bless the child, he lifted the linen and gasped. I edged closer, curious about what sort of startling deformity lay beneath the veil, but Samuel startled all of us by opening his mouth and releasing a river of words. Taken aback by my teacher's unusual prophecy, I gaped at the child—and instead of a monster I found a baby so pleasing that my eleven-year-old mind wondered if someone had painted an image on a child's toy.

I remained interested in the little family, often spotting them near the Tabernacle. As I moved into adolescence, I looked for the girl and wondered why my teacher had been so taken with her. As far as I could see, she was only a girl, and everyone knew that girls were merely HaShem's afterthought.

In my mid-twenties, I encountered the family again. When I spotted Eliam and his father making a sacrifice at the Tabernacle, I waited outside the tent of meeting, hoping to see if the girl had developed into something unusual. I waited until wise Ahithophel led his son out of the Tabernacle, then I gaped like a boy who knows no better. The girl had become . . . breathtaking. Struck speechless, I stared at hair that flowed like black glass over her shoulders and down her back. Her eyes were dark pools, her skin the smoothest alabaster. She carried herself modestly, with quiet confidence, apparently indifferent to the many appreciative glances cast in her direction.

And as she passed by, she lifted her gaze and smiled at me.

We did not speak, not even when we were so close I could have reached out and touched her. Her father's scowling face was more than enough to discourage any inappropriate gesture, and her grandfather's position in the king's court was enough to intimidate a young prophet. But that day I gave her my heart, and her smile gave me the hope I needed to wait for as long as her father demanded.

My feelings of love deepened as the weeks passed. I would have given anything to marry her, and if called upon, I would have happily sacrificed my life for her. *She* was no mere afterthought; she was one of HaShem's most beautiful creations. I came to believe that Adonai had willed our long-ago first meeting, because the Lord wanted me to watch out for her and protect her . . . but from what, I could not say.

I planned to wait until I was twenty-seven and she sixteen before approaching her father. As the months passed I refused to consider any other woman, but continually pled my case before Adonai, hoping He'd give some assurance about my wedded future.

When David moved his court from Hebron to Jerusalem, I moved as well, knowing that Ahithophel and Eliam would certainly follow the king. Finally reaching my twenty-seventh year, I went in search of Eliam and found him in the courtyard of the king's half-built home. He was lifting a cup to mark the completion of the palace wall, and one of his warrior comrades asked if he ever planned to arrange a betrothal for his lovely daughter.

The earth shifted beneath my feet at the sound of those words. I stood like a post, my legs rigid, my proposal of marriage stuck in my throat. While I waited, tongue-tied and helpless, Eliam said he wouldn't give his daughter to just anyone, as important prophecies must first be considered.

Prophecies? Hope infused my veins, for prophecies were my livelihood. As Samuel's student I had studied the prophecies of Moses and Miriam, Joshua and even Saul. I was prepared to discuss any foretelling or forth-telling that had ever been uttered by anyone who spoke for Adonai, but I couldn't understand what prophecy had in common with Eliam's beautiful daughter.

Before I could ask what the man meant, I heard Adonai's voice as clearly as if He had shouted in my ear: *Eliam's daughter is not for you*.

A spasm of panic shot through my body like it always did when the voice reminded me that my thoughts were not mine alone. For although Adonai did not speak often, He was always listening, always aware of my every inclination. His voice was firm and final; to ignore it would be unthinkable.

I turned and stumbled away. My disappointment was so heavy, so palpable, I felt as though I carried a dead man on my back. Perhaps I did—the man who wanted to marry Bathsheba had died, crushed beneath Adonai's uncompromising hand.

I mourned for the better part of a week, sorrow a painful knot inside my chest. I remained indoors, cloaked by shadows in my windowless hut, terrified to venture out and risk glimpsing Bathsheba before my heart had hardened to the point where I could bear the knowledge that she would never be mine.

Months later, I approached the father of a girl who lived nearby. Ornah's dowry was small, enough for a goat and materials to build a small house at the outskirts of the cleared land outside Jerusalem, but a hardscrabble life would suit me well. It would force me to focus on working to establish a household and family, leaving me little time to think about Bathsheba.

"Just," I whispered as my escorts led me up the street to where she lived, "as I do not think about her now."

I looked up when the guards led me to the wide entrance to David's palace. Stout stone walls spread to our left and right as we passed through the gate with little fanfare. The king lived securely here—any murderous intruder would have to wend his way through the city's inhabitants and dozens of sharp-eyed warriors before he ever reached the king's doorway.

I thought I might have to wait on the king's pleasure, but my escorts marched me to a wooden structure, where the tallest man rapped on the door. A masculine voice bade us enter, and I found myself standing in the presence of Adonai's anointed king—David, celebrated musician, renowned giant-killer, and storied guerrilla warrior. We had met before, when a younger and more desperate David sought refuge from Saul with my master Samuel, yet I doubted the king would remember me as a lad.

I followed the example of the guards and bowed before the king, who had somehow united the often-fractious tribes of Israel.

"Nathan the prophet?" The red-haired man who reclined on a fur-covered couch appeared to be in his late thirties. Laugh lines creased the corners of his eyes, and a smile darted in and out of the thick tangle of his ginger-colored beard.

I straightened to meet his gaze. "I am Nathan, student of Samuel, formerly of Ramah."

The king sat up. "I knew Samuel well—in many ways he was like a second father to me." His expression sobered. "I was sorry when we lost him. All Israel mourned, of course, but I felt his loss keenly. He was a true friend and a man of God." The king glanced around, then pointed to a table where a tray of bread, fruit, and cheese lay beside a bowl of honey. "Are you hungry? I know you've had a long walk. Please eat something."

I inclined my head in a gesture of appreciation. "Thank you, but I have already broken my fast."

"An early riser, then. Good." The king slapped his hands on his bare knees, pressed his lips together, and looked at my escorts. Without a word, they departed as silently as ghosts.

"Please, Nathan, have a seat." Standing, the king pointed to a cushion on the floor. Still not certain why I'd been summoned, I sank onto the pillow, giving the king time to gather his thoughts.

"My seer, Gad, told me to send for you." David paced through the narrow space between me and his couch. "Apparently this matter is something I should discuss with none other than Nathan the prophet."

He looked at me, seeking some kind of confirmation, but I had none to give. "I am happy, my lord and king, to be of service."

He stopped pacing. "How long have you been in Jerusalem?"

"I came here along with the king's household."

"Then you are as much a newcomer as I am. Because, Nathan, I've been thinking about this city. We've accomplished so much over the past year. We've filled in the Millo, enforced the city walls, erected the Tabernacle, built the foundation of my house. I was considering our accomplishments when I realized something—here I am, a mere man, living in a cedarwood palace, but the Ark of God, throne to the King of the Universe and Creator of all, remains in a frail tent. This should not be! I want to build a house for Adonai on this mount. I want to erect a temple worthy of the God of Israel."

I blinked, surprised by the passion in the king's voice. I had heard that David was a man given to extreme feelings and emotional outbursts, but in my few encounters with him I had seen no evidence of that temperament. Yet David appeared to be sincerely concerned about what could be viewed as disrespect for Adonai. Since I could not conceive of any reason to dissuade him from his plan, I uttered the first words that sprang to my lips: "Go then, do everything that is in your heart, for Adonai is with you."

The king's eyes widened. He clapped, the sound like a burst of thunder, then dropped to the floor in front of me and sat cross-legged, propping his chin in his hand. "I've much to consider." He narrowed his gaze as he stared past me. "I've plans to make, supplies to gather, men to enlist in the work. Hiram of Tyre helped build this palace, but now I want to work on the Temple. The people of Israel should build a home for their God."

He looked up, seemingly distracted, but his eyes cleared when they focused on me. "Thank you, prophet, for this assurance. I am pleased to know I'm doing the right thing."

As if by magic, my escorts reappeared in the doorway, so I stood and joined them for the long walk home.

That night, as the sun sank behind the western horizon, Ornah put the girls to bed and then stretched out next to me. After a moment, she timidly tapped my arm. "Nathan?"

"Not now," I whispered, making an effort to keep my voice gentle. Ornah was a kind woman, a good mother, and a hardworking wife, but she had never excited my imagination or my loins the way Bathsheba had. But Bathsheba now belonged to someone else, and my thoughts had no business trespassing in another man's home.

The straw mattress rustled as Ornah rolled onto her side. A few moments later I heard the deep, regular sounds of her breathing, a soft rhythm punctuated by the quicker, lighter breaths of our daughters.

I got up, opened our door, and sat in the doorway, staring into the night. The moon, only two days from full, lit the ragged landscape to my right and David's namesake city to my left. My surroundings vibrated softly with the skittering movements of nocturnal animals, and I waited, poised to hear from Adonai.

On the walk back down the mountain, a sense of conviction had gripped my heart, assuring me that I had given the king *my* words, not Adonai's. When the king asked my opinion, I had taken quiet pride in my logic and inherent pragmatism. I had given him a solid, practical answer.

But Adonai had not approved, and since the king had asked for a *prophet's* opinion, I should not have spoken until I heard from the Lord.

Samuel had taught me to pay attention to small things, to nudges and whispers and prickles that crept across the back of my neck. Adonai had spoken to him when he was a child, on the dark night the Lord whispered that He was about to reveal something that would tingle the ears of every listener. HaShem was about to execute judgment against the high priest and his family for the many evils they had committed.

In the days that followed, Adonai fulfilled His promise, bringing about the deaths of Eli and his irreverent sons. Samuel grew up to take Eli's place, and though my teacher died when I was only thirteen, no one had yet risen to take Samuel's place. Occasionally I wondered if I might pick up the torch my mentor had dropped, but Israel had many prophets, and Adonai used us as He saw fit. The prophet Gad had been David's personal seer since the days of King Saul, and only lately had the king sent for me . . . apparently at Gad's request.

Why had Gad sent for me? Had the Spirit of Adonai directed him, or had He some other reason for wanting to involve me in the king's affairs? Perhaps it had been a test. If so, I had failed miserably.

I closed my eyes, regretting that I would have to ask the king's forgiveness for doling out my wisdom instead of the Lord's. I waited in my doorway, knowing I must soon climb the hills of Jerusalem again, this time alone and with a confession on my lips.

I don't know how long I sat—long enough for the moon to climb and cast its silver radiance over the summit of David's city—but my eyelids were beginning to droop when the night noises ceased and the hairs on my arms stood at attention. I straightened as a current tingled my limbs, and then, like blood out of a vein, a thick silence slid toward me, enveloped and filled me until all I could hear was the voice of Adonai.

When He had finished speaking, I bowed my head in submission and sat motionless until the silence ebbed and the night noises returned.

"So be it," I whispered. Then I stood, closed the door, and went to bed.

⊱✤⊰

The next morning I rose early, dressed with care, and climbed the hill to Jerusalem with a great deal more apprehension than the day before. If I could get an audience with the king, I would speak, yet this time I might snuff the light of joy from his eyes.

After entering the palace courtyard, I walked to the wooden building and gave my name to a guard at the door. After a few moments of tedious waiting, the guard returned to usher me into the king's presence. David was not in his throne room or the more casual space I'd visited earlier, but in what appeared to be his bed-chamber. An ornate bed dominated a distant corner, while the king stood beside a large table spread with parchments.

He appeared far more relaxed than he'd been at our first meeting. He wore a brilliant blue tunic embroidered with stars, and his hair and beard had been freshly oiled. At one end of the table, a pair of men, one old and one young, studied parchments and occasionally scratched at them with the burnt end of a stick.

I knelt on the floor and bowed, and this time the king met me with a welcoming smile.

"Nathan the prophet." He stepped out to greet me. "Have you a suggestion for Adonai's house? As you can see, I have summoned the best architects in Israel."

"I have—" I swallowed hard—"something to tell you. Today I must confess that I have seriously wronged you and sinned against Adonai. I have come to confess my sin and to ask your forgiveness."

"What is this about?" David's eyes narrowed, but he leaned against the table and folded his arms, ready to listen.

I lowered my face to the floor. "A prophet of Adonai must not offer his own opinion when asked for guidance; he should speak for Adonai alone. Yesterday I gave you an answer from my own mind, my own logic. Adonai had not given me a message for you, so I was wrong to speak from my own wisdom, small that it is."

David tilted his head. "And today?"

"Today I bring you a message from the Most High God and Master of the Universe. He spoke to me last night and bade me give you His words." I stood and drew a deep breath. "Adonai says: 'You want to build me a house? I do not need a house, but I will build a house for you.'"

I broadened my stance, feeling the heavy import of the message I'd been sent to deliver.

"'Are you the one to build a house for me to live in?'" I continued. "'I have never lived in a house, from the day I brought the Israelites out of Egypt until this very day. I have always moved from one place to another with a tent and a Tabernacle as my dwelling. Yet no matter where I have gone with the Israelites, I have never once complained to Israel's tribal leaders, the shepherds of my people Israel. I have never asked them, Why haven't you built me a beautiful cedar house?'"

I glanced at the king, but David had not stirred. He had, however, lowered his head so that I could not read his eyes.

"'Now go and say to my servant David,'" I continued, "'This is what the Lord of Heaven's Armies has declared: I took you from tending sheep in the pasture and selected you to be the leader of my people Israel. I have been with you wherever you have gone, and I have destroyed all your enemies before your eyes. Now I will make your name as famous as anyone who has ever lived on the earth! And I will provide a homeland for my people Israel, planting them in a secure place where they will never be disturbed. Evil nations won't oppress them as they've done in the past, starting from the time I appointed judges to rule my people Israel. And I will give you rest from all your enemies.'

"'Moreover, Adonai declares that he will make a house for you—a dynasty of kings! For when you die and are buried with your ancestors, I will raise up one of your descendants, your own offspring, and I will make his kingdom strong. He is the one who will build a house—a Temple—for my name. And I will secure his royal throne forever. I will be his father, and he will be my son. If he sins, I will correct and discipline him with the rod and blows, like any father would do. But my favor will not be taken from him as I took it from Saul, whom I removed from your sight. Your house and your kingdom will continue for all time, and your throne will be secure forever.'"

I stopped, out of words and breath, and looked to see what effect my message had wrought in the king. David stood motionless for a long moment, then he straightened and walked toward the doorway as if he had completely forgotten about me and his architects.

Along with a pair of bodyguards, I trailed after him, following him through the palace, out the northern exit, and over the sandy path that led to the Tabernacle. He hesitated for a moment at the outer curtain before going inside. He sat before the altar of burnt offering.

I sat in the dust behind him, content to be a spectator and a mouthpiece should Adonai desire one.

David sat without moving for a while. Then he tipped his head back and let out a joyous, agonized, surprising wail. When he finally found words, the king cried to Adonai in an awe-filled voice, "Who am I, Adonai Elohim, and what is my family that has caused you to bring me this far?"

His voice cracked, and his shoulders trembled as he lifted his face toward the Holy of Holies. Overcome by the feeling that I was eavesdropping on a personal conversation between a man and the Most High God, I lowered my gaze, content to listen.

"Yet in your view, Adonai Elohim," David continued, "even this was too small a thing; so you have even said that your servant's dynasty will continue on into the distant future. This is indeed a teaching for a man, Adonai Elohim. What more can I say to you? For you know me intimately, Sovereign Lord."

I struggled to resist an urge to lift my head and watch the king address his Lord, for the expression on a man's countenance spoke volumes about the desires of his heart. But I did not need to know. HaShem knew David better than I did, and His opinion mattered more than mine.

Samuel, my teacher, once told us about how he initially balked when the Spirit of God told him to anoint the youngest and scrawniest of Jesse's sons to succeed Saul as king. When Samuel hesitated, Adonai answered, "The Lord doesn't see the way humans see. Humans look at the outward appearance, but I study the heart."

That scrawny shepherd had grown into a man, who now knelt before God with outstretched hands and an open heart. "Because of your promise and according to your will, you have done all these great things and have made them known to your servant," David cried. "How great you are, O Sovereign Lord! There is no one like you. We have never even *heard* of another God like you! What other nation on earth is like your people Israel? What other nation, O God, have you redeemed from slavery to be your own people? You made a great name for yourself when you redeemed your people from Egypt. You performed awesome miracles and drove out the nations and gods that stood in their way. You made Israel your very own people forever, and you, O Lord, became their God. So now, Adonai, God, establish forever the word you have spoken to your servant and his house. Do what you have promised."

I blinked, and in a sudden burst of clarity I realized that David must have wondered if his reign would end like Saul's. Would he be king for only a short time, then be cast away because of some failure? Even I had been surprised when Adonai gave me this message for David, for what man had ever been worthy of an eternal heritage? Saul had been a good king until he disobeyed, but he was human, with a man's weaknesses and failures. From what I had heard, David was every bit as human and in some ways even more erratic than his predecessor.

But I could not plumb the king's heart, and I was not Adonai. My task was not to judge but to speak the truth of God.

"May your name be magnified forever." David's voice dissolved into a thready whisper. "So it will be said, '*Adonai-Tzva'ot* is God over Isra'el, and the dynasty of your servant David will be set up in your presence.' O Lord of Heaven's Armies, God of Israel, I have been bold enough to pray this prayer because you have revealed all this to your servant, saying, 'I will build a house for you—a dynasty of kings!' For you are God, O Sovereign Lord. Your words are truth, and you have promised these good things to your servant. And now, may it please you to bless the house of your servant, so it may continue forever before you. For you, Adonai Elohim, have said it. May your servant's family be blessed forever by your blessing."

We sat there—the king, his bodyguards, and I—covered in dust from the rising wind, awestruck by the presence of HaShem and the king who worshiped him with wholehearted enthusiasm. The wind lifted the curtains around the Tabernacle, sending dust skimming over the ground, but David did not seem to notice. He sat a long time in silence, his eyes focused on something beyond my field of vision, until one of the priests walked over and laid his hand on the king's shoulder.

David stood slowly, clinging to the priest's arm for balance. As he turned, I saw his face. Above his beard, his cheeks were coated in desert sand and streaked with the runnels of tears.

CHAPTER SEVEN
BATHSHEBA

I HAD BEEN MARRIED A FULL MONTH before Elisheba and Amaris came to visit. Uriah went to fetch them from Father's house, and when he returned Amaris was riding on his back, waving joyfully as he shouldered his way through the crowded street. After ducking through the doorway and depositing my little sister on a cushion by the fire pit, he gave me a shy smile and departed, leaving the three of us to talk of womanly things.

"My sweet sister!" I bent to give Amaris a hug and then hugged Elisheba, as well. "How are you? I miss the voices of other women in the house."

Elisheba rolled her eyes, then gave me a sly wink. "How are you enjoying married life? Uriah seems like a happy man."

"I hope he is." I picked up a bowl of water to wash their feet, but Elisheba waved the bowl away. "Don't worry yourself, we won't stay long. We don't want to get in the way of newlyweds."

"You could never be in our way." I sank onto a cushion between my guests and grinned at my sister. "Are you managing to stay out of trouble?"

Amaris's mouth curved in a smile. "I'm never in trouble. Father says I'm a little angel."

"If only that were true." Elisheba gave Amaris a playful pinch. "I can never understand how such a small girl makes such big messes. This morning she spilled the water jug right after I'd returned from the well. Then she lost my sewing needle and let the cook fire go out."

"You found the needle, though." Amaris's nose crinkled in an impish expression. "When you sat on it."

"For that I should be grateful?"

"Never mind." Amaris shifted her attention to me. "I have a question for my sister."

The gleam in her eye made me wary. "A question?"

"Are you going to have a baby?"

"No—yes—well, I hope so." As my cheeks burned, I turned from my sister to Elisheba, my fount of womanly wisdom. "Honestly, I want to fill this house with babies. But I don't think it's possible for me to know if I'm having a baby just yet."

"You'll know." Elisheba lifted a brow. "First, you'll feel tired for no reason at all. Then you'll begin to smell things you never smelled before, and the sight of food will make you sick. And if those things haven't convinced you, your breasts will become tender and your monthly *niddah* will cease."

Amaris tugged on Elisheba's sleeve, her eyes brimming with questions. "Have *you* had a baby?"

"Once. Long ago."

"What happened to him?"

"He died."

Elisheba spoke calmly, with no outward trace of sorrow, but pain squeezed my heart at the thought of her unspoken grief. Elisheba had lost a husband, and then a child, shortly after his birth. How could any woman survive such pain? I could not even imagine such anguish.

I reached for her hand and patted it. Amaris was too young to understand the depths of a woman's emotions, but I was beginning to explore those cavernous places. Loving Uriah had opened my heart and expanded my capacity to love. Since being married, I found myself loving so profoundly, intensely, and lavishly that I couldn't imagine the equivalent quantities of loss.

Elisheba tapped Amaris's knee. "Enough talk of babies. We came here to see your sister, not to talk about private things."

I would have gladly heard more on the subject of reproduction. My education in such matters had come only from Elisheba and whispered conversations among the women at the well. Married women tended to lower their voices when virgins wandered into their vicinity, and Elisheba's instructions had been more about my wedding day than procreation.

"Are you faring well, then?" Elisheba's eyes searched my face. "Is Uriah a *gentle* man?"

My face reheated, but I couldn't stop my grin from broadening. "He is most gentle and kind. In our first days together, he was . . . quite considerate and tender with me. Sometimes, in the early morning before anyone else has ventured out, we stay in bed and talk. We laugh together. About all kinds of things."

Elisheba's eyes sank into soft nets of wrinkles as she smiled. "You are among the most blessed of women, Bathsheba. I thought Uriah would be a good husband, and apparently your grandfather was right to advance his cause. Your father misses you, but he is terribly proud of his new son-in-law. He has nothing but good to say about Uriah."

"I love being married." The words came out in a rush, but I'd been dying to say them. And who better to hear this news than the two women I loved most?

"I am happy for you. And I will always be proud of you, child."

Amaris eyed the plate of figs and goat cheese I had set near the fire, but the plate lay beyond her reach. Seeing her predicament, I picked it up and let her take some figs, then offered the dish to Elisheba.

"My only regret," I said, lowering the dish, "is that this first year of marriage will pass all too quickly. Soon Uriah will have to rejoin the army, and then he'll be away fighting for the king. Who knows when I'll be able to see him. I asked Uriah if wives ever traveled with the army, and he said any army with women along would be an ineffective force, as any man who slept with his wife would be ceremonially unclean and unfit for battle the next day."

"Then enjoy this year while you can." Elisheba's eyes twinkled above the fig she held near her lips. "Your husband sounds like a young man in love. Truly, it does my heart good to hear you say these things. Some say husbands and wives fall in love over time, but I am happy to hear that you have found love at the beginning of your lives together. Adonai has richly blessed you."

I hugged my knees in an overflow of happiness, unable to believe that the union of a man and woman could result in such delight and joy. There I sat, talking with women I loved in a home of my own, a dwelling that would one day shelter sons of the man I adored, miniature olive-skinned Uriahs, sturdy little boys who would march around the fire pit with pretend spears and bows and slingshots.

"I can help you with those long days alone." The thin line of Elisheba's mouth clamped tight for a moment, and then she looked at me, a smile lifting the wrinkles on her cheeks. "The secret of contentment in hard times is to collect a bountiful store of memories and set them aside like treasure. Life is made of seasons, child, and they will not always be as sweet as the one you are enjoying now. When pleasant days are hard to find, pull out your memories and live in them until happiness returns."

"Then this"—I draped one arm over Elisheba's shoulders and the other over my little sister's—"is one of my most precious memories.

I will never forget this day, the sight of you eating figs from my new plate, the scent of sweet fruit, and the sound of your voices."

And to prove it, I leaned toward each of them, pressing a kiss first onto a lined cheek, then onto a rounded, youthful one. Life was beautiful, and in that moment I was as happy as I had ever been.

～※～

Days stretched before me like a golden cord, one morning as bright as the next. I loved my husband more with each passing sunrise, for every day I discovered another of his unique characteristics.

I learned that Uriah was a wonderful teacher. Though the Law forbade him from going to war during the first year of our marriage, he still spent many hours at the palace, training with his weapons and mingling with the king's royal guard. I had never understood the difference between one man in armor and another, but Uriah taught me a lot about Israel's military.

Israel not only had soldiers, we had *divisions* of soldiers. Israel had a national army and the king had the *salisim*, a group of warriors devoted to him alone. The *salisim* were composed of David's famed mighty men and an army of six hundred foreigners who had been allied with him since his days of running from King Saul.

"Why doesn't the king dismiss these foreigners?" I asked, perplexed. "He has finally united the tribes of Israel, so surely there is no need for him to employ outsiders."

Uriah laughed and tapped the tip of my nose. "My sweet, have you forgotten that I am one of those foreigners?"

I stammered in confusion. "Well . . ."

"Who would dismiss men whose loyalty has been proven in battle? And don't forget, the mortar holding your twelve tribes together has not fully set. The king needs trustworthy men, and the *salisim* have fought alongside him for years. They would die for the king, but others in Israel's army"—Uriah shrugged—"who can say where their loyalties lie? Some men fight for Judah, some for Saul, some for David. They are held together now only by the power of Adonai."

The first of David's elite men, Uriah explained, was Jashobeam, the Hacmonite, leader of *the Three*—the three mightiest warriors among the close-knit team David considered his personal force. The other two members of the Three were Eleazar, son of Dodai, and Shammah, son of Agee. Both were famous throughout Israel for their feats of might and courage.

After the Three came *the Thirty*, the renowned group that included my husband and my father. Abishai, son of Zeruiah, led the Thirty along with Benaiah, son of Jehoiada. Benaiah also commanded the king's bodyguards.

Outside the *salisim*, Joab, the king's nephew, commanded Israel's field army. He had been instrumental in conducting the surprise raid against the Jebusites that resulted in David's claiming Jerusalem. The Jebusites had considered their city unassailable until Joab led a band of warriors through a horizontal tunnel from the Gihon Spring and then up a vertical water shaft. Stunned by the resourceful and clever invaders, the city quickly surrendered to David.

Uriah's lessons in history and military divisions sometimes left me bewildered, but I could have listened to him talk for hours. He did not speak of fighting or battlefield activities, nor did he describe the gruesome injuries and deaths suffered in the course of combat. He talked instead about his friends, men who were so devoted to David that they would risk their lives and travel behind enemy lines just to fetch water from one of his favorite wells.

In those days I did not understand the realities of war, though I had always liked my father's soldier friends well enough. My father cut an imposing figure when dressed in his armor, yet he had often crawled about our house on his hands and knees, pretending to be a horse so Amaris could ride on his back. And Uriah, who intimidated most men even when not wearing armor, was among the gentlest of creatures when not focused on duty. Because I was acquainted with good-natured warriors, I had come to think of war as an exercise in swordplay, big men clashing and wrestling, then patting each other on the back before the journey home.

Uriah might have thought it odd that a soldier's daughter knew so little about the nature of combat, but Father and Elisheba had always sheltered us from life's brutalities.

My husband's military service offered me an unexpected feminine pleasure. After each trip to the palace, he brought home stories I would never have heard otherwise. He shared palace gossip, telling me about the king's wives—Michal, Ahinoam, Abigail, Maacah, Haggith, Abital, Eglah, and others Uriah could not name—and the king's concubines, most of whom remained tucked away in the special compound constructed for the royal harem.

"Are the king's wives very beautiful?" I asked, alarmed that my husband's remarks about other women could ignite a spark of jealousy in me.

Uriah shrugged. "Some men say so. But they do not have Bathsheba waiting at home. If I were inclined to compare the king's wives with you, the royal women would be found wanting."

I giggled as my husband's lips touched a sensitive spot at the side of my neck. "I know our king is not like other kings, but are his women like other women? Do they cook and sew and clean?"

Uriah ran a rough finger down my forehead and the length of my nose, then gently traced my lips. "I don't know what they do all day," he said, his voice growing hoarse. "And I don't care. My thoughts are occupied with one woman who is more beautiful than most, and more precious than any."

I gazed deep into his eyes and saw currents moving there. "Of whom do you speak, husband?"

"Of my coy little wife." The corner of his mouth quirked in a smile just before he kissed me.

CHAPTER EIGHT
BATHSHEBA

I HAD BEEN MARRIED ONLY NINE MONTHS when an unexpected disaster upended my life. On a warm afternoon in which I had planned to bake bread, a messenger from my grandfather stood outside our courtyard and shouted that I should run to my father's house at once. I dropped a damp cloth on my kneading bowl and hurried away, jogging over the cobbled street until I reached my father's home.

I found Amaris and Elisheba huddled together in the courtyard.

"Elisheba?" I darted through the gate and dropped to her side. "What's happened?"

"Your father is ill." She dabbed at her watery eyes. "He has been sick for two days and he didn't want to alarm you. But today he took a turn for the worse, and the physician says he will not survive."

My mind reeled in confusion. My father and grandfather were

rarely sick and never weak. They worked when other men took to their beds, and they never complained about anything.

"Not survive *what*?" I searched her eyes. "Did he fall? Did he cut himself? Has he an injury?"

"Nothing like that." She swiped at her nose with a cloth. "Three days ago he came home and said he wasn't hungry. Then he vomited up his food. Later he said his gut hurt, and when he took to his bed I knew something was terribly wrong. The physician gave him a tonic to purge his system, but it didn't help."

I turned at the sound of crunching gravel. Grandfather trudged through the gate, his eyes as red and watery as Elisheba's.

"Bathsheba."

He held out his arms, so I stood and embraced him, comforted by the solidity of his strong frame. But when I lifted my gaze, I saw tears on his cheeks.

I had never seen a man—*any* man—cry.

"Grandfather, I am so sorry."

Amaris began to sob. I stood in the center of the courtyard, unable to comfort my sister or my grandfather while grief constricted my own heart so tightly that I could barely breathe.

Fortunately, I did not have to flounder for long. Uriah came into the courtyard, red-cheeked and breathless from haste. With one glance he took in the scene before him, then strode into the house to ascertain my father's condition for himself. Grandfather followed him.

I sank to the bench beside Amaris and slipped my arm around my little sister's shoulders. She was weeping silently, a quiet shadow beside Elisheba's hunched form.

After a long while, Uriah came back outside and shook his head. I rose and went to him. He wrapped me in the circle of his strong arms, then released me so he could address the other members of my family. "Elisheba, Amaris," he said, his voice raw and rough, "from this day forward your home will be with us. Eliam has joined his fathers."

My knees turned to water. My father had always been a highly visible figure, a man with a dauntless air, yet he had died before Grandfather and in the prime of his life. I sat beside Amaris, too stunned to speak or cry.

The physician and his assistant filed out of the house. Grandfather appeared in the doorway then, grief emphasizing the dark pockets beneath his eyes. "Elisheba," he said, not lifting his bowed head, "fetch other women to prepare the body. I will gather the mourners. We must bury him before sunset."

Like a man in a trance, Grandfather crossed the courtyard and entered the street, walking with stiff dignity toward the well where men often gathered in the cool of the day. Uriah gave my shoulder a final squeeze and followed him.

When the men had gone, Elisheba rose and caught me in a fierce hug, and then she helped Amaris to stand. As I slipped an arm beneath my sister's shoulder, Elisheba caught my gaze. "Go inside and prepare the body for washing. I will bring spices when I return with the other women. We must work quickly, for the hour is late."

I nodded, then took Amaris's full weight as Elisheba hurried out of the gate.

The hired mourners sat outside, their keening wails an eerie accompaniment to our work. Because she was too young to help, Amaris sat on a stool in the corner while Elisheba and I sponged my father's body. I had never bathed a corpse before, and the comparison between Uriah's healthy glow and my father's diseased form struck like a blow. Though only a few years separated the two men, Uriah's body was golden, warm, and supple, while death had transformed my father's into something mottled, cold, and stiff. Three days earlier my father had been a handsome man, but nothing about his appearance now appealed to the eye.

Death, I realized, left no beauty unspoiled.

Elisheba had been washing the body with strong, horizontal strokes, but she paused to point at a dark shadow on my father's groin. "Here." She pressed a finger to the lower right side of his abdomen. "The flesh here is like granite. The illness came from this spot."

I was no physician, but neither was I prone to doubt Elisheba's truth. In all the years I'd known her, she had never led me astray.

Two other women joined us, quietly entering the house with baskets of rags and spices. After murmuring condolences to me and Elisheba, they set about helping us prepare my father for the grave.

After cleaning the corpse, two of us managed to lift the body high enough for one of the women to slide a linen cloth beneath it. When the corpse lay on the smooth fabric, Elisheba dropped a fabric square over the face while another placed sprigs of fragrant plants beneath his arms, on his chest, and along his legs. When they had finished, we wrapped one side of the fabric over the other, then tied his shroud with strips of cloth.

Finally, my father was ready for burial.

Elisheba went to fetch Grandfather while I sank to the floor next to Amaris. She looked at me, her chin quivering. "I'm sorry," she whispered. "I know you probably don't want me living with you. You've only just married Uriah—"

"Hush." I squeezed her bony little knee. "Of course we want you to live with us—you are family. You will love Uriah, and you will keep me company when he has to leave with the army."

Fresh tears sprang to her eyes. "But I may never leave your home. I know, Bathsheba, that I may never marry. What man would want a wife who cannot walk or take care of his house?"

"We will not worry about that." I strengthened my voice. "Whether or not you marry is Adonai's decision, not mine or even yours. When the time comes, Uriah or Grandfather will negotiate the bride price for you, and if that time does not come, Uriah will be the brother you've never had. Don't worry about tomorrow, little bird. This day has brought us more than enough grief; we don't need to borrow from the future."

We fell silent as six men entered the house. Without speaking they surrounded my father's body, and together they lifted Eliam, son of Ahithophel, and carried him from the house.

If we had been burying Grandfather, my father would have followed the procession with Amaris on his back. I saw that realization flit across my sister's face, but before it could elicit more tears, Uriah strode through the doorway, knelt beside her, and lifted her as if she weighed no more than a bag of feathers.

Weeping in silent gratitude and grief, I walked behind my husband and followed the procession that wended its way out of Jerusalem and down to the valley where we buried our dead. As we walked, I studied my husband's broad shoulders and remembered how Grandfather had once hated all the pagan nations, including the Hittites. In Moses's day, Adonai had marked the Hittites, Girgashites, Amorites, Canaanites, Perizzites, Hivites, and Jebusites for destruction. "Make no treaties with them and show them no mercy," Moses told my ancestors. "You must not intermarry with them. Do not let your daughters and sons marry their sons and daughters, for they will lead your children away from me to worship other gods."

But though Joshua and his army did claim much of the Promised Land, they never completely eradicated the territory's inhabitants—and we never reckoned that some of them might assimilate *our* ways. Such had been the case with Ahimelech the Hittite, who aided David during his struggles against Saul, and such was the case with my husband. Abraham had transacted business with Ephron the Hittite, who sold him land for Sarah's tomb. "So how," my father had one day asked Grandfather, "could any man refuse to betroth his eldest daughter to a worthy man like Uriah?"

At first, Grandfather had been adamant in his refusal to bless my betrothal to a Hittite. I suspected the real reason had nothing to do with Uriah's race and everything to do with his work. In light of Samuel's prophecy, a soldier did not seem likely to produce a son who would affect the destiny of Israel, but who could predict how Adonai would work? After all, He had chosen a shepherd boy to be a giant-killer and a king.

And the City of David was far from homogeneous. Jerusalem was home to all kinds of foreigners, including many of the conquered Jebusites, so a Hittite who followed Adonai had to be vastly preferable to a Jebusite who still filled his home with carved idols.

As for me, I would forever be grateful that Father had found a way to soften my grandfather's granite opinions. And as we placed my only remaining parent's body into a narrow tomb, my chief sorrow lay in the realization that he would never see the fulfillment of Samuel's prophecy in a grandson from my beloved husband.

CHAPTER NINE

BATHSHEBA

My newlywed happiness faded immediately after my father's death. Grief draped a shroud over our small house, every bit as tangible as the cloth Elisheba had dropped over my father's face. I went about my daily routine, but I felt as though I moved through thickened air on feet as heavy as iron. I wanted time alone to weep and cry, but Amaris and Elisheba had joined us in the house, and I did not want to weep in front of them.

I had no idea that solitude was a luxury I would never know again.

I could not blame Uriah for the black grief that welled in me at odd moments, nor could I blame my father. I could only blame Adonai, though I knew I had no right to do so. Who was I, a mere woman, to question the Creator of the Universe? But if HaShem held the fates of kings and nations in His hands, if He controlled the winds and the rain, why couldn't He give my father enough time to see the grandson he'd dreamed of for years?

The sense of immortality I'd always taken for granted evaporated like the morning dew. The grave had taken my mother and father; now it waited for the next family member in line. Since Grandfather had proven himself invincible, the grave yawned for me.

Faced with the inevitability of death, my desire for the promised son intensified to desperate longing. I fixated on stories of soldiers who perished from their wounds and strong men who came home, lay down, and died from some unknown disease. Uriah was both a strong man and a soldier, but he was mortal, so I wanted a child in my belly before he left to join the king's military campaign.

Because my husband's newlywed furlough was nearly over, I begged him to tell me all the details of the king's current war. I yearned to understand the conflict, as though knowledge could help me keep my husband safe. Within a few minutes of Uriah's explanation, I realized the king's current military action had begun because of an insult.

How like men to go to war over wounded pride!

Several months before our wedding, King Hahash of the Ammonites had died. To express his condolences, King David sent ambassadors to Hahash's capital. But Hahash's heir, Hanun, did not trust David's emissaries, imagining that they were spies intent on surveying the Ammonites' weaknesses. So instead of welcoming the men of Israel, Hanun treated them disgracefully, holding them captive until he had shaved off the right half of each man's beard and cut off the back of each man's tunic. Deeply humiliated, the bare-bottomed and half-bearded ambassadors retreated to Jericho, where a messenger carried the awful news to Jerusalem.

Mercifully, King David allowed his ambassadors to remain at Jericho until their beards grew out, but Hanun's brazen affront galvanized the king for war. At David's command, Joab deployed Israel's troops to fight, and Hanun hastily assembled a coalition of his Ammonite warriors and Arameans. Under Joab's capable command, Israel's army killed seven hundred charioteers and forty thousand foot soldiers, including the Ammonite army commander. Hanun's men fled into the fortified capital city, Rabbah, and the Arameans sued for peace, agreeing to become vassals of the Israelites.

Winter came and the Israelite army returned home. But the chilly winds that whistled around Jerusalem did nothing to cool the king's battle fever. As soon as the weather warmed, David again dispatched Joab and his warriors to Rabbah, but Hanun and his army remained out of reach behind the fortified city walls. The Ammonites no longer possessed a functional army, but since the king had not capitulated, Joab laid siege to Rabbah, preparing to maintain his position until Hanun surrendered.

Soon Uriah would have to return to his duties in the king's fighting force. He would not return home until Israel's army had either conquered Rabbah or suffered defeat in battle.

Knowing that Uriah would soon leave me, I watched the days float away like leaves from a dying tree. Each month I had held my breath and prayed I would not see the flowing of my monthly courses, and each month my prayers went unanswered. From my retreat to a cushion in the corner of the house and the forlorn expression on my face, Uriah knew when I had entered the time of my *niddah*. He bore the disappointment better than I did, always assuring me that Adonai would bless us at the proper time.

But he was not a woman, so how could he understand? Adonai had *created* me to bear children. If I could not bear children, why didn't Adonai make me a man? If I was not meant to bear children or do manly things, why did He create me at all?

When the time of my uncleanness was done, I would go to the Tabernacle, make my offering and pray, reminding Adonai that He had chosen Israel out of all the nations, the Levites out of all the tribes, David out of all the sons of Jesse, and me, his humble servant. As my parents had often reminded me, I reminded HaShem that I had been assured of my role by the word of Samuel, a true prophet, and a true prophet could not lie. Then I would return home . . . to wait.

I think Elisheba wanted a conception almost as desperately as I did. She always greeted the signs of my monthly *niddah* with an audible sigh, and though she took pains not to mention babies or children during the week of my uncleanness, when the seven days were finished, she drew water for my bath with an almost tangible optimism. After sunset on the seventh day, she would take me by the hand and lead me into the courtyard at the back of our house, helping me disrobe by lamplight and then pouring fresh, clean water into the *mikvah*.

My little goat would stand off to the side and nicker as I soaked in his water trough.

One night as Elisheba massaged oils into the skin at my back, I protested that she worked too hard. "I am a grown woman," I reminded her. "I can bathe myself."

"Nonsense." She clicked her tongue against her teeth. "I have been bathing you for years, child, and I'll draw your bath as long as you have need. Besides, no woman can properly reach her back, so lean forward, think happy thoughts, and let me do my work."

Truth to tell, I was always eager to surrender to her strong, ministering hands. And as weeks passed and the anniversary of my marriage approached, my despair at remaining childless and thoughts of Uriah's departure evoked the old feelings of abandonment that had haunted me when my mother died. Anguish plunged me into a deep well of depressing childhood memories.

Uriah did not know what to make of my tears, my variable moods, and my deep silences. How could I explain such womanly things to a man who meant what he said and said what he meant without undergirding each word with some emotion?

More than once I snapped at him; more than once I apologized.

I tried to explain that he had done nothing to cause my distress, but my own words—*you've done nothing*—accused him yet again. Was I barren because of something he hadn't done?

I wanted to be patient. I wanted to believe that Adonai would bless us in due time, but how was I supposed to conceive a son who would influence Israel if my husband went away to war?

During the month before Uriah's departure, I went into his arms every night, urging him to love me with all his might, tempting him with mandrakes and perfumed garments and his favorite foods in case the failure for conception lay in a lack of effort or desire on Uriah's part.

And in case the problem lay with Adonai, I did my best to earn His favor, too. Recalling the story of how Hannah prayed fervently in order to win the Lord's favor and conceive a son, every morning I climbed the steep path to the Tabernacle and sat outside the tent of meeting, praying that Adonai would hear and grant my petition. I prayed in the blazing sun, determined to show HaShem that my desire was sincere and my intention pure. I prayed aloud whenever a priest appeared, hoping he would remark upon my prayers and assure me that God would grant me a son in the coming year.

I poured myself out in every way I knew and still my courses flowed, even on the day of Uriah's departure.

Elisheba and Amaris remained in the house while I walked my husband to the courtyard gate. I tipped my head back to look into his eyes. "I wish you didn't have to go."

"But you know I must."

"Be careful." I locked my arms around his waist. "I have just lost my father. I can't lose you, too."

Uriah gave me a warrior's confident smile. "I am skilled, Bathsheba. I can handle myself."

"I know, but . . . well, sometimes unexpected things happen."

"Do not fret yourself." He ran his broad hand over my head,

smoothing my hair. "Joab is a wise commander, and Adonai is with him. This battle, when it finally comes, will be ours. Right now the army is only laying siege, and that means many hours of sitting and waiting. So don't worry. Be well."

I studied his eyes, searching for any sign of regret that he was leaving or sorrow that we hadn't yet conceived, but all I saw was love, confidence, and conviction. So I pressed my cheek to his chest and prayed that Adonai would keep him safe from harm. Then, finally, I released him.

I don't know what Uriah thought of my tears. He might have thought them an extravagant display of how much I would miss him, but we had become so entwined that I'm sure he read the truth in my eyes. I would miss him certainly, but my barren belly had become my overarching concern. If something happened to him, I might never bear a child, unless some other man took pity on me and married me. If I never had another husband, I would become a woman like Elisheba, a nurse to other women's children, a servant with no family of her own.

Worst of all, if something happened to Uriah, the prophet's words would be proven false and HaShem a liar. And that I could not bear.

≈❖≈

Five months passed, long weeks of waiting and praying and fretting over my husband's safety amid the stupidity of war. At the end of yet another womanly cycle, Elisheba extended her hand and helped me from the cushion where I had spent the past week complaining. The time of *niddah* always frustrated me, because my courses normally flowed for only three days, yet the Law constricted my movements for a full week.

"Time to relax," Elisheba told me, placing her arm on my shoulders.

"I can't relax." I chafed under her gentle touch. "Uriah remains away from me, and another month has gone by. How am I supposed to bear a son when my husband is never here?"

"Do not fret, child. HaShem knows the desires of your heart, and He knows what is best. So come with me—we will let Amaris play her harp while I draw your bath. And while you soak in the *mikvah*, you will resign yourself to the will of Adonai. You will pray for your husband's safety and smile in the sure knowledge that you will have a son when the time is right."

I exhaled a heavy sigh and pretended acquiescence, though my heart groaned within me. I was not yet twenty and I yearned for my dreams with the frantic impatience of youth. Though something in me knew Elisheba was right, my strong will was not ready to surrender.

The house felt empty without Uriah, and so did my bed. I missed his company and his warmth, and every four weeks I felt nothing but frustration and sorrow during the time of my uncleanness.

"Why couldn't Uriah have stayed home a few more months?" I asked, my voice tinged with whining. "No one would have blamed him if he tarried until I conceived. Grandfather is an important man in the king's court, and he could have asked permission for Uriah to remain in Jerusalem. I should have gone to Grandfather in tears. I should have begged him to make sure Uriah remained at home another month—no, six months more."

"And what would your husband have thought of all this tearful begging?" With an effort, Elisheba lifted the large pitcher we used to haul water from the well. "He would have resented your interference, and in time he would have resented *you*. A man like Uriah does not want special favors; he takes pleasure in doing his duty. He would not want to remain at home, living at ease and in luxury while his comrades slept on the battlefield."

I thrust my lower lip forward in a pout. "But if he loved me, he would have asked. No man wants to leave an unhappy woman at home—"

"That's where you're wrong, child. *Any* man would choose to leave an unhappy woman at home, because no man wants the sound of a whining wife in his ears." She braced her free hand on her hip. "So tell me—why has the happiest young wife in Israel become the most miserable?"

The question hammered me. Why? Because I wanted the son I'd been promised. And I wanted my husband. I was tired of waiting for them.

My blood ran thick with guilt as those thoughts took shape in my mind. My husband was attending to duties that both fulfilled and defined him. I had fallen in love with a warrior, a man just like my father. I knew what being a soldier's wife entailed.

So why had I become more concerned about my own happiness than my husband's? I had been telling myself that Uriah wanted a child as much as I did, but the desire to hold a son clearly tormented me more than it did him, and something in me resented the inequity.

I turned, not wanting Elisheba to see the guilt on my face, and heard the soft groan of the leather door hinge as she went for water. Amaris leaned on her crutch and studied me, her head tilting as her gaze met mine. "Are you all right?" she asked. "You don't seem at all like yourself."

"I'm not," I snapped, too frustrated to exercise my usual patience with my sister. "I want a baby, but everything and everyone seems to be working against me. My husband has gone away without a word of complaint, Adonai is deaf to my prayers, the priest at the Tabernacle ignores me, and Elisheba insists on lecturing me."

I knew my accusations were unfair, but rather than listen to a rebuke from a child, I turned and walked into the garden at the back of the house. The air was sweeter outside, perfumed with flowers, and something in the quiet helped calm the thunderstorm in my heart. I gulped deep breaths and then looked up. The sunset had spread itself like a peacock's tail, bright and brilliant, across the western skies. Golden rays feathered across the balustrade on the roof of the royal palace, then streamed out to paint the tips of our cypress trees with yellow light.

Uriah had said we would stand together in this garden, so why wasn't he with me when I needed him?

"Are you in a better temper now?" Elisheba joined me, the water pitcher on her hip and a forgiving smile in her eyes. "Let me rub your shoulders, child, and let the *mikvah* wash away your sorrows. You're only upset because you miss your husband, but in time you'll feel better. Besides, who's to say he won't be home as soon as the victory is won? The siege may not last nearly as long as you fear. And if a child is part of Adonai's plan for you, then a child you will have, and do not doubt it."

Her words patted my heart like soothing raindrops, and the clean, cool water sloshed into the trough with a bracing sound.

Perhaps she was right. Perhaps I would feel better with the start of a new month. And each passing day was one less I would have to wait for my beloved to come home.

I gave Elisheba what I hoped was a repentant smile, then unbelted my tunic as the gentle sound of Amaris's harp streamed through the window.

Chapter Ten

NATHAN

I HAD NO SOONER SAT TO SHARE THE EVENING MEAL with my wife and daughters when I heard Adonai's voice: *Come outside.*

No warning this time, no premonition or sense of approaching disaster. Only a clear and insistent voice.

I gave Ornah an apologetic look and stood, then walked out of the house and waited. The voice gave me no further instruction, so I walked over to the spindly fig tree and sat in its shade. I leaned against its narrow trunk and waited for Adonai to tell me what He wanted me to know.

A communication from the Lord of Hosts almost always sent a tremor scooting up the back of my neck, so I waited with heightened senses and a thumping heart. Within a moment of being seated, an inky blackness crept over my field of vision, blocking out the familiar sights of my neighbor's house. I blinked, but could not dispel the darkness or focus my eyes.

So this time Adonai would not speak with words, but with images. I was about to see something the Lord wanted me to see.

I sat motionless and waited for the vision to unfold.

The blackness moved, re-forming itself into a familiar landscape. Though I could feel solid earth beneath me and the fig tree against my spine, my eyes informed me that I had been swept up by an eagle, a cormorant, or the very hand of Adonai. We flew over the Kidron Valley and the hills of Jerusalem, the city walls passing beneath my dangling legs. We did not zig and zag along the established paths, but flew straightway to the summit. Looking to my right, I saw the Tabernacle's fluttering curtains. Beneath me, the rectangle of David's stone palace. To my left, the twisting streets where the residents of Jerusalem had built their homes. Then Adonai lowered me until the flat rooftop of the royal palace sprawled only a short distance beneath my sandaled feet. Servants had erected a tent there, and after a moment the king stepped out from beneath that tent, yawning as if he had been asleep.

HaShem lowered me until my eyes were level with the king's, but though I hovered directly in front of him, he did not acknowledge me in any way. By some working of the *Ruach HaKodesh*, I must have traveled in spirit only.

I glanced around, but no one else stood near the king. So why had I been brought here? Would I appear before the king in a moment, or would he never see me? If I materialized, how was I supposed to explain my presence?

Adonai offered no answers, so I breathed deeply and waited. The king yawned again before calling an order to a servant standing near the doorway. The man quickly disappeared, then returned with a cup of wine.

Sipping from his cup, David walked to the edge of the rooftop and studied the city, where buildings were springing up like mushrooms. Many houses on the palace's south side were still under construction, and the sound of hammering reached my ears even though the hour was late. Something in the sight must have pleased him, for he crossed his arms in a pose of great satisfaction.

Then he shifted his position and turned slightly, peering down at a row of homes within shouting distance of the palace wall. I studied David as he studied his city. Why was the king in Jerusalem when his army had gone to Rabbah? David was known for courageous military exploits, and I had every reason to believe he thrived on the challenge of battle strategy. So why had he remained behind?

An image focused in my memory—on my last visit to David I had relayed a message from the Lord, a promise that Adonai would secure David's kingdom forever. Was the king now so confident in his success that he no longer felt the need to personally invest in Israel's military campaigns?

I frowned and considered the question. If David considered Adonai's last message an eternal reprieve from a king's duties of work, worship, and righteous war, he had forgotten the nature of HaShem. The Lord of Hosts loved David, but like a good father He chastened His children when they went astray. Surely Adonai had not given His promise in order to lull David into complacency. A complacent man would eventually neglect the Lord, because he would depend upon HaShem's promise and not HaShem himself.

I bit my lip and scrutinized the king's countenance. From where I watched, the rays of the setting sun tinted his hair with red-gold highlights, painting him like a man ablaze. He had aged since claiming the throne of Israel, and looked as if he had lived hard in each of his thirty-nine years. Laugh lines radiated from the corners of his eyes like cracks, and time had etched deep grooves from the edges of his nostrils to his red beard. But his hair had not yet gone white, nor had it measurably thinned.

David's posture shifted abruptly as he bent from the waist and lowered his forearms to the balustrade. He leaned into open space, and for an instant I feared he would fall. Then I glimpsed his face and saw this was no careless king. He wore the expression of a man who has not eaten in days, and his eyes had gone from dreamy and contemplative to black and dangerous. His expression—dare I say it?—was that of a man overtaken with the mindless fervor of a stallion in rut.

Alarmed, I looked down on the city to see what had caused this abrupt change in his countenance. My gaze skimmed rooftops and gardens, houses and pathways, and then I spied two women in a tree-lined courtyard. One sat in a *mikvah*, her back to me. Her hands gripped the sides of a stone trough while her servant poured fresh water over her hair and shoulders. But even though the younger woman's face was not visible, the glimpse of slender shoulders, the gentle tapering of ribs to a narrow waist, the flare of feminine hips . . . my own loins began to stir. I turned away, realizing I had no business gazing at any woman in that manner. I looked at the king and saw that he had not averted his gaze. Instead of turning aside or closing his eyes, he remained focused on the tantalizing sight. He then straightened and signaled for the guard at the door.

My hope—my confidence—in Israel's anointed king shriveled as the guard hurried to answer his master's command.

"See that house?" David pointed to the courtyard below. "Make note of it, go inquire, and return straightway to tell me who that woman is."

With only a brief downward glance, the guard jogged away while David bent again, devouring the sight of the woman as she stood, accepted a robe from her servant, and left the garden, her long wet hair streaming over her back like silk ribbons.

My viewpoint abruptly shifted, as if the giant hand or bird holding me aloft had jerked me to another position. I saw the guard hurrying down the rooftop stairs, crossing the paved courtyard, and exiting through the palace gates. I lowered my heavy eyelids, not needing to see anything else.

What was I supposed to do with this knowledge?

My stomach clenched as my heart overflowed with angst and despair. "Why have you shown me this vision?" I asked the darkness. "What am I to do with this knowledge? Is this something that might happen, or is it something that *has* happened? And if it has happened, how can I confront the king? He holds the power of life and death in his hands, and I saw the look in his eyes just now—he is not in a mood to be reasonable."

When I lifted my head, I found myself sitting beneath my spindly tree with only the whisper of fig leaves to disturb a stillness as deep as a Sabbath morning.

CHAPTER ELEVEN
BATHSHEBA

I HAD JUST SLIPPED A PLAIN TUNIC OVER MY HEAD when we heard a pounding at the courtyard gate. Elisheba's wide eyes met mine, then she hurried to the front door and opened it, reflexively ducking when she saw the tall guard standing outside the house. With one glance the man took in Elisheba, me, and Amaris, then his gaze settled on me. "The king summons you," he said, gesturing with a hairy hand. "Do not delay, but come at once."

"The king?" My heart filled with fear as I turned to Elisheba. "Do you think something has happened to—?"

"At once!" the guard repeated.

"I have just dressed for bed," I tried to explain, "yet if the king wants to see me, I will dress properly. I can't go to him like this, with wet hair and no shoes—"

"Now!" The guard stepped forward and crossed our threshold, something he would never have done if Uriah had been home. While

Elisheba stared in disbelief, with trembling fingers I lifted a cloak from a wall hook and threw it over my shoulders. My thoughts scampered in such panic that I couldn't remember where I left my shoes, so I slid my feet into a pair of tattered papyrus sandals. They were not fit for an audience with the king, but at least I wouldn't have to lace and fasten them.

When I reached the doorway, the guard gripped my arm with surprising force and half led, half dragged me along the cobbled street toward the palace. The sun had hidden itself behind the horizon, so we scurried through shifting shadows as my neighbors gathered around their cook fires to enjoy the evening meal. I found myself grateful that few of them would witness my frantic journey to the king's house. Something terrible must have happened to Uriah, something so horrible that the king had returned to Jerusalem to personally explain how my husband died.

My escort glanced at me when we reached the palace gate, then whispered to the guard on duty. Without a word, that man stepped aside and let us pass.

We walked across the large paved courtyard, past a building with several doors, and finally through a long passageway that ended in a flight of narrow stairs. The guard gestured for me to precede him, so I did, carefully lifting my tunic so I wouldn't trip.

When we reached the top of the stairs, I found myself standing on the wide roof I'd observed from my garden. A colorful canopy had been erected against a wall to provide shade from the slanting sun. Potted plants stood around the periphery as a sort of screen, I supposed, to offer a measure of privacy from the servants and guards.

Was the king here? If he had news of the battle, I would have expected him to meet me in his council chamber or the great hall.

I did not have time to ponder the odd setting, for the guard placed his hand in the small of my back and prodded me forward, his touch altogether too rough for a man who'd been sent to fetch a

warrior's widow. I glanced back to rebuke him with a look, but his
dark eyes remained impassive and unreadable. Instead of speaking,
he pointed toward the canopy.

With no other choice, I walked past the line of potted palms and
caught my breath when I recognized the red-bearded man seated
on a couch. Since the return of the Ark, I had seen King David
only from a distance, and on those occasions he had always seemed
regal, strong, and impressive. Now, softened by twilight and with
no more space between us than was proper for an ordinary man
and woman, he looked far less royal and more like the man who
had danced in the dust.

Only when he lifted his gaze did I fully realize where I was.

"O King, live forever." I collapsed on the floor as my quivering
knees gave way. I stretched my hands toward the king of all Israel
and struggled to find breath to speak. "If I have found mercy in
your sight, please tell me what news you have of Uriah the Hittite."

Keeping my gaze downcast, I heard him utter two words to the
guard. "Leave us."

Was the news so dire he could not bear to share it before a
guard? A tumble of confused thoughts and feelings assailed me,
but I knew I ought to remain bowed and submissive until the king
gave me permission to rise. Grandfather had taught me about of-
ficial protocol, but at that moment I had neither the patience nor
the discipline for royal rules. Desperate for news of my husband, I
raised my gaze to study the king's face, searching for some hopeful
sign. Perhaps Uriah had been captured, or perhaps he had been
injured while on patrol. As long as his body hadn't been discovered,
I could hope, the king could negotiate, and others could search for
him. Together we could find some way to bring my husband home.

My stomach dropped, however, when I beheld the king's expression. The eyes I had never examined at close range were not cloudy
with grief or soft with compassion; they sparked. They burned, in

fact, with the same heat I saw in Uriah's eyes when he came home after a long day and wanted to take pleasure in his wife. I delighted in that look when I discovered it in my husband's eyes, but seeing it in the king's . . .

Cold panic bloomed between my shoulder blades and ran down my spine.

"By all that is holy, you are the most beautiful thing I have ever seen." The king leaned forward and grinned, his hot gaze searing my skin. "When I looked out and saw you bathing, I knew I had to have you."

I covered my ears, unable to trust what I'd heard. This could not be happening. The king possessed a harem of women, many of them famous for their beauty, and all of them righteously belonged to him. He ruled over an entire kingdom of families with beautiful virgin daughters, any one of whom would willingly leave her home to become a royal wife. He could have any unmarried woman he wanted, so why did he send for me?

"My lord and king." I lowered my head in the proper posture of submission. "I am honored you sent for me, but I came because I thought you had news about Uriah, my husband. He has been at Rabbah with the army these past five months—"

I did not have an opportunity to finish. Without warning the king loomed over me, his hands clasping my wrists like iron manacles. I gasped as he lifted me to my feet, and his mouth smothered mine before I could remind him yet again that I belonged to another.

Somehow, even as his hands gripped my wrists, he found the cord that tied my cloak and loosened the knot. My mantle slid away from me, leaving me exposed and vulnerable in my light tunic.

I stood, stiff and still, as urgent thoughts pushed and jostled in my head. The king tasted of wine, he smelled of perfumed oils, and his mouth felt hard and demanding. What was I to do? For a moment I considered slapping him in the hope of bringing him to his senses, but he still held my wrists, and who was I to strike the king? I thought about screaming when he finally pulled his mouth from mine, but even if someone heard, who would take action against Adonai's anointed ruler? Not the guard who had brought me to this place, and surely not the servants. No one would come to my aid. The king was the king, and he could do as he pleased with his people.

Familiar words from a long-dead prophet whirled in my head. *"She will be a* tob *woman."* One who possessed intoxicating beauty. One who would be desired. Coveted. Craved.

The king's mouth traveled down my neck, over my thin linen tunic, and pressed against my breasts. In that moment I would have given my life to be ugly.

"My lord, please." My voice trembled. "You are a far better king than this. I am your servant, but I am another man's wife—"

"If the king cannot take what he wants, why is he king?"

The words were a warning growl. The inner trembling that had begun when the guard appeared in our courtyard now spread to my limbs. I shuddered as he pushed me onto the couch and gasped when he planted his knee, forcing a space between my legs. "My lord and king," I begged, openly weeping, "please let me go. I will say nothing of this. I will go home and remain silent like a good soldier's wife. You have other women. You have but to send for them, and they will come. You are king of Israel; nothing righteous will ever be denied you—"

"Be quiet now, and do not resist." A feral light gleamed in the depths of his eyes as he stared down at me. "I will not hurt you if you do not struggle. And no one ever need know."

No one? I would know. I would never forget this horror, nor would I ever hear his name without reliving these moments. How was I supposed to face my husband, who adored the king? How was I supposed to listen to my Uriah *praise* Adonai's anointed one?

What could I say to the man above me? He had not listened to reason, and I had run out of words. I neither wanted nor welcomed his attentions, but he was a king and I a mere woman. All I could do was surrender . . . and trust him to keep his word about keeping this secret.

Because greater than this sin would be the sin of hurting my honorable, loyal, and trusting husband.

In reluctant acquiescence, I stopped struggling. The king loosened his grip on my wrists, apparently satisfied that I would not strike or claw at him.

As my arms went limp, I closed my eyes and felt my heart turn to ice as the king of Israel used me for his personal pleasure. During the assault, I focused my thoughts on Uriah and promised myself that I would remain silent to protect the man I loved. I would not speak of this to Elisheba, or Amaris, or even Adonai, because I could not understand how HaShem could know everything and do nothing as I suffered.

When the king had finished, he sat on the edge of the couch without looking at me, poured himself another cup of wine, and then summoned a guard. "A new tunic," he told the man, jerking his thumb toward me. "The other is ruined."

The guard glanced at me, then removed his cloak and held it open, silently indicating that I should stand and wrap myself in it. Ignoring him, I darted toward my own cloak, then wrapped it around me. I waited, silent and shivering, until the guard returned a few moments later with a tunic to replace my torn garment.

When I had again made myself presentable, I left the king sitting in a chair, sipping from his cup and gazing into the darkness. The guard led me down the stairs, then escorted me home.

But I did not go inside the house. Unable to face Elisheba and Amaris, I curled up like a wounded animal on the gritty stones of our courtyard and wept until daybreak.

Chapter Twelve

NATHAN

The sun seemed to rise reluctantly the morning after my vision. Weak, gray light seeped into my house, announcing an end to my sleepless night and the beginning of a dreaded day. I stared at the rugged ceiling beams as the darkness thinned, unable to look at my wife or daughters lest they wake and see the distress on my face.

I had not seen everything in my vision. In His mercy, Adonai had spared me the violence of what must have happened after David learned the woman's identity, but I had seen enough to know that the Lord's anointed king had coveted a beautiful woman and sent for her. If David had only lusted, Adonai would have forgiven him, and the Lord would not have shown me the event. If the king had learned that the woman was married and put thoughts of her aside, again, Adonai would have forgiven and forgotten the offense. But the God who knows past, present, and future had known what would happen after David lusted for that beauty, and Adonai wanted me to see the result of a darkness that had entered the king's heart.

Our beloved king, who had been anointed to replace disobedient Saul, had also disobeyed the Law and the moral instruction given to Adonai's chosen people. Why? Because he believed he could get away with sin.

I closed my eyes as Ornah stirred beside me. I had not yet regained my composure, and better that she should think me asleep than to know what troubled my thoughts.

What did Adonai expect me to do with the knowledge He'd given me? I could go to the palace and confront the king, but few men relished being caught in their crimes, and fewer still handled rebuke with gracious repentance. David might say that a king had the right to take whatever he wanted, and most of his counselors would support his position. I would look like a fool, and for what? If the woman had not been injured, some would say no harm had been done. To my knowledge, the king had not violated a child or committed any unnatural act. He had simply seen a lovely woman and sent for her, practicing the same right held by the kings of the many peoples around us.

But David . . . I had held such hope for him. I had placed such faith in him. He was a better man than the king I watched last night.

Unable to remain motionless a moment longer, I swung my legs off the mattress and rested my head on my knees as my heart filled with despair. Was Israel doomed to be led by men who allowed power to corrupt their minds and hearts? Could *any* man be trusted with the authority and responsibility necessary to govern the affairs of a nation?

HaShem had warned us that our cry for a king would result in misery. Samuel told the people that a king would draft our sons and assign them to his army, making them run before his chariots. Some would be generals and captains in his military forces, some would be forced to plow in his fields and harvest his crops, and some would make his weapons and chariots. He would take the best of our fields and vineyards and olive groves and give them to his officials. He would take a tenth of our grain and grape harvest and distribute it among his officers and attendants. He would take our male and female slaves and demand our finest young men; he would take our donkeys and force them to carry his loads. He would demand a tenth of our flocks, and we would be his slaves. And he would take our *daughters* . . .

But Israel did not listen. We insisted that we wanted to be like the nations around us, and now we were. Our king was as prone to evil as their kings, and last night David had been every bit as predatory.

I slid onto my knees and asked HaShem if I should go to the king and admonish him for his misdeed. But I heard no response.

I exhaled slowly, grateful that Adonai had not told me to confront David. This sin would remain hidden until Adonai chose to reveal it, yet one small detail gave me hope. In my vision, as the guard hurried down the palace stairs, I saw Ahithophel, the king's chief counselor, pause in the courtyard to watch the guard rush by. With his brow crinkled, the counselor followed the guard to the gate as the man exited, then Ahithophel crossed his arms and leaned against a pillar, apparently eager to see for whom the guard had been so speedily dispatched.

I was not the only one who witnessed last night's events at the palace. Servants had seen, and at least one guard knew what the king had done. Ahithophel, reported to be the wisest man in the king's court, had been alerted that something might be amiss. None of those people were likely to confront the king about his unrighteous behavior, but neither were they likely to deny my vision should Adonai command me to reveal it.

I lifted my head and opened my eyes in time to see Ornah prop herself on one elbow and regard me with a speculative gaze.

CHAPTER THIRTEEN
BATHSHEBA

I ROSE BEFORE DAYBREAK, stumbled through darkness to the courtyard gate, and walked to the well in the gray gloom of a dawning day. After reaching the well, I leaned on the edge for support as my legs began to quiver. My thoughts kept drifting into a fuzzy haze, a mishmash of memories, sensations, and pain.

I gripped the stones beneath my palms and forbade myself to tremble. Nothing moved in the stillness but a wayward chicken, so no one was around to notice that I was dirty and terrified. That I was not myself.

Quietly I pulled the rope and drew water. When I had splashed the last traces of sand and grit from my face, I smoothed my hair with wet hands and walked home, firmly placing one foot in front of the other until I reached our courtyard. Then I slipped inside the house and pulled a pat of resting dough from my bread bowl.

I was desperately kneading it when Elisheba's hand dropped

onto my shoulder. The unexpected touch caused me to flinch and draw back in terror.

"Sorry." Elisheba's eyes widened. "And I'm sorry I fell asleep before you came in last night. I tried to stay awake, because I was desperate to know—how is our dear Uriah?"

I avoided her gaze. "He is well."

"The king summoned you to say *that*?"

Fresh tears stung my eyes as I struggled for words. The king had not only forced me to lie with him; now I would have to lie to my dearest friend. "The king—" I punched the dough—"wanted to tell me that Uriah was a fine soldier."

Elisheba said nothing, but from the corner of my eye I saw her cross her arms and lean against the wall, her appraising eye focused on me. The intensity of her gaze scalded my skin.

"I don't mean to upset you," she said, her voice low and controlled, "but the king does not send for a soldier's wife to share such mundane news. So what did he really say?"

My hands clawed at the dough. How could I do this? But better, surely, for Elisheba to believe a hundred lies than to know one horrible truth.

"Apparently"—my voice sounded strangled to my own ears—"there was some sort of ambush outside Rabbah. Uriah risked his life to save others. His act was unusually brave, the king said, so he wanted me to know my husband was a hero. He said we should be proud of him."

Panic flitted across Elisheba's face. "Was Uriah hurt? Poor man, charging into the fray like that. If he was injured, he ought to come home and mend here—"

"He wasn't hurt." I gave her a tight smile. "He could have been, but he wasn't."

Elisheba clasped her hands. "May Adonai be praised. HaShem has sheltered our Uriah."

"So it would seem." I kept my attention on my bread, working the dough as if I had to beat it into submission.

"Did the king give you that new tunic?"

I clenched my jaw as memory filled my ears with the sound of tearing cloth. A scream rose at the back of my throat, but somehow I transformed it into words. "Yes. A gift."

"It's lovely."

"Is it?"

"Of course. But you would look lovely in anything, child."

I snatched a quick breath. "It really doesn't suit me. I don't think I want it."

"Really?" Elisheba tilted her head. "All right, then. Give it to someone else." She turned away, then hesitated. "You were out very late. Did it take so long for the king to give you this news?"

"One cannot simply walk into the palace and see the king." Exasperation clipped my voice. "Others demand his attention, too. I had to wait."

"Oh." She spoke in a quiet, wounded tone. My sharp reply had hurt her, so again my conscience smote me.

"Elisheba, I am sorry." I lifted my sticky hands and met her gaze straight on. "I didn't sleep well last night. Please forgive me for being short with you. I am exhausted."

"Of course you are." Elisheba stepped forward to squeeze my shoulders, then moved to the corner where Amaris slept. "How is our little bird faring today? I know *she* slept—even in my dreams I heard her snoring."

As Elisheba woke Amaris and helped her roll her sleeping mat, I patted my dough into a rectangle and set it on the coals smoldering in our fire pit. I washed my hands in a basin and looked around, eager for something else to do. If I could stay busy with ordinary things, maybe I would be able to convince myself that nothing had happened. The king had stolen only a few hours of my life, so if I put my troubling thoughts aside, I ought to be able to resume living at the point where my ordinary life had been interrupted. I would fill our pitchers at the well while the air was still cool. I would speak to the other women and laugh at their stories. I would milk the goat and make cheese. I would take mature cheeses to the market and haggle with visitors to Jerusalem. In time, if I kept working and talking and haggling, I would forget all about my encounter with the king.

"Elisheba . . ." I pulled a scarf from a basket and wrapped it around my hair. "I am going to fetch water."

"I'll go for you," she answered. "As soon as I help Amaris dress—"

"I would like some fresh air," I assured her, lifting an empty pitcher. "I'll be back soon."

With the pitcher on my hip, I stepped outside and again followed the road to the well. How many times had I walked this path with a smile on my lips? Until last night I had generally been a happy bride. I'd experienced a few frustrations, of course, but I had celebrated my love for my husband with every bucket I pulled to the surface. I worked eagerly, happy to be serving my family, and smiled "me too" smiles at other women with husbands and families.

How could I face Uriah after last night? Would I ever be able to think of him without a hollow feeling in the pit of my stomach?

I reached the well, waited for another woman to finish filling her jar, then caught the bucket. Lowering it into the well, I stared down the length of the rope, and every detail came flooding back—the king's scent, the oily feel of his beard against my cheek, the drops of perspiration that dampened the hair on his chest . . .

I groaned and closed my eyes. No matter how sincerely I wanted to forget, I couldn't think of Uriah with bruises on my wrists and the smell of the king's perfume on my skin.

"Well met, Bathsheba." I lifted my head to see one of Elisheba's friends approaching, her brow raised. "A new tunic? The color suits you very well."

Abruptly realizing that I hadn't noticed the color, I glanced at my sleeve. The fabric was royal blue, a shade far too rich for my station. I gave the woman a polite smile and another lie. "My grandfather is most generous."

The woman bobbed her head in appreciation. "You should wear that color more often, though I've never seen anyone but the king's women wear it."

I tried to smile again, but my lips wobbled precariously and my gorge rose. I turned to the side and vomited, then stood, panting and weak-kneed, as my companion stared with wide eyes. "Are you ill? Should I fetch Elisheba?"

I pressed my hand to my forehead as fresh memories of the king's burning gaze rose in my memory. "Please. Tell her to come quickly."

⁘

"I need a bath. Please."

Elisheba chuckled and helped me sit on a small stool by the front door. "You need to sleep; that's why you are sick. But Amaris is at her friend's house, so you'll have lots of time for a nap."

"I don't want a nap. I need a bath." I looked at her, hoping she could read the desperation in my eyes. I didn't want to spill my secret, but I needed to be clean, I needed to wash every trace of the king from my body.

Elisheba's brow wrinkled, and something moved in her eyes as she studied me. "All right, then. I'll draw a bath, and soon you'll feel as good as new. Let me fetch some water and fill the trough outside—"

I caught her arm in a death grip. "Not there. Never again out there. I need . . . to be clean, but I must bathe inside the house . . . where no one can see."

"Where no one can—" Elisheba's smile faded, and she nodded

and eased my hand from her arm. "We'll have you feeling better in no time," she said, filling a basin with water. "Almost ready. There. Lift your arms now." She pulled the blue tunic over my head and began to fold it.

"Don't." I crossed my arms over my nakedness. "Throw it away. I never want to see it again."

A line appeared between Elisheba's brows. She dropped the tunic and placed a hand on her hip. "Enough," she commanded, her voice gentle but firm. "I'm going to give you a sponge bath, and you're going to tell me what's troubling you."

I buried my face in my hands. How could I tell her that I had lost control over my own life? That the king had stolen my dignity, even my sense of self? I didn't know who I was anymore. Was I the esteemed daughter of Eliam and the virtuous wife of Uriah, or was I a street prostitute? My life had become a confused tangle of fears and insecurities.

"Bathsheba." Elisheba stepped closer and lowered her voice. "You can tell me anything. Did someone insult you on your way back from the palace? Did someone . . . accost you?"

I burst into tears. I had hoped I would be able to keep my secret forever, but Elisheba knew me too well. And I knew her—she would not rest until she had the entire story. So now she would have the truth whether or not she wanted to hear it.

"I will tell you, but you cannot look at me. Please, turn away and let me speak to the wall."

I could see Elisheba's mind working behind her eyes. She looked at me with a perplexed expression, as if she'd formed a question but lacked the courage to ask it. Then she nodded and moved behind me, sliding the basin to my side.

I drew a deep breath as she dipped a sponge into the water.

"That guard," I began, flinching beneath the cool touch of the sponge, "took me to see the king. I thought . . . I was afraid he had bad news about Uriah, so I hurried. If I'd known what would happen, I would have sat in the road and refused to take a single step."

A small strangled sound came from Elisheba's throat, but she asked no questions. "Go on," she whispered, swishing her sponge in the bowl.

So I told her everything. I told her about my protests, and I told her how the king had answered and what he had done. As I hugged my knees and shivered beneath her gentle ministrations, I heard her tongue click against her teeth as she ran the sponge over bruises on my arms.

"He did not otherwise hurt you?" she asked when I had finished. She stepped in front of me, and when I did not look up, she put her hand under my chin and lifted my head. "Did he strike you? Did he force you to do anything . . . unnatural?"

I stared, bewildered, then made a face. "No, no. He promised not to hurt me if I didn't resist."

Elisheba breathed out a sigh. "I have heard of worse things done to women," she said, her voice heavy with dread. "Among the Philistines and other nations, women are often subjected to unspeakable practices."

"I cannot imagine anything worse—"

"Then bless Adonai for His mercy, child, and know that you will survive this. My heart breaks because this happened to you. I would have given my life in order to prevent it. But now you must go forward. You should obey the king, remain silent, and try to forget about what happened. Our king is as much a man as any other, and though I do not condone what he did, you had no choice. You are not to blame for this."

"But if Uriah finds out—"

"Uriah is not here, nor will he be for some time. So rest, daughter, and put it out of your mind. In time, Uriah will come home, you will create a family, and you will forget everything that happened in the palace. Give yourself time to heal, child."

Elisheba slid the basin forward, then bade me step into it. As I crossed my arms and shivered, she climbed onto the stool and poured a pitcher of water over me, living streams that should have made me ritually clean.

But when I stepped out of the basin and dried myself, I realized the bath had not washed away the king's sin. A leper could not have felt more unclean than I did at that moment.

After I put on a tunic and curled up on my sleeping mat, Elisheba draped a blanket over me and urged me to rest. I didn't believe I would ever forget what had happened, and something in me wondered if I would ever be able to welcome my husband's caress without thinking of how the king had touched me.

As I drifted into drowsiness, I remembered how much pleasure my mother derived from the prophecy that I would be a *tob* woman, and I wished the prophet had cursed me instead.

But Elisheba knew more about life than I did. Hoping she was right, I finally slept.

CHAPTER FOURTEEN

NATHAN

FOR DAYS I HEARD NOTHING FROM HASHEM. I fasted and prayed and went about my daily work with an ear cocked for Adonai's voice, certain the Lord had a reason for showing me what the king had done. I went to the palace and mingled with other men in the king's courtyard. I watched counselors and courtiers and priests when they spoke openly and when they whispered in dark corners. None of them displayed any outward concern about the king's character, and after a while I wondered if they would even care if their anointed king fornicated with a woman who was not his wife.

Adultery was a grievous sin in Israel, resulting in a death penalty for both the man and woman. As a married man and woman were meant to be faithful to each other, so Israel was meant to be faithful to HaShem.

But we had not executed anyone for adultery in years, perhaps generations.

One afternoon as I visited the palace, I spotted Ahithophel crossing the courtyard. My spine stiffened. If my vision could be trusted—and I had no reason to believe it could not—this righteous man either suspected or knew that the king had transgressed. What, if anything, had he done about it?

I stepped out of the shade where I had been standing and greeted the king's counselor. "Well met, Ahithophel."

He hesitated, then nodded in return. "Good day, prophet. I trust you are well?"

I gave him an honest answer. "I have been greatly troubled of late. I have difficulty sleeping, and when I do sleep, I wake to find my pillow watered with tears."

Ahithophel tilted his head slightly. "For whom do you weep?"

"For the king. And for Israel."

The old man's brows flickered. "Why would you weep for our king?"

"I have had a vision." I lowered my voice to reach the chief counselor's ear alone. "I saw the king looking out from his rooftop balcony. He spied a young woman at a house below and sent for her—a woman who did not belong to him. For all I know, she may have been another man's wife."

"And for all you know, she may have been a virgin the king plans to marry next month." The old man showed his yellowed teeth in an expression that was not a smile. "Why have you approached me about this matter?" His eyes narrowed. "In this vision of yours, the woman lived near the palace?"

"She did."

"Could you identify this woman? Did you see her face?"

I lifted my gaze to meet the older man's. "I did not."

"Ah. Well." The counselor looked away and pressed his lips into a thin line. "I would not worry about the matter. The king has always had a keen appetite when it comes to beautiful women. Good day."

Without another word, he turned and walked away.

I stared after him, speechless. In my vision, Ahithophel had been clearly suspicious of the king's activities. He spoke to David nearly every day, so had he said anything about the king's actions on that night? The counselor was known as a virtuous man, so why hadn't he said something to David?

Perhaps he had, and the king had repented. If so, why had Adonai allowed me to glimpse the king's lust? The Lord did not reveal hidden things for His own amusement. He expected something of me, but what?

Perhaps Ahithophel had determined that the king intended no harm by sending a messenger to the woman at that late hour. But only a fool would come to that conclusion, and the king's counselor was no fool.

If Ahithophel had been suspicious, if he had witnessed the arrival of an innocent woman intended for the king's pleasure, and if he had said nothing to the king, my mind could form only one conclusion: perhaps the counselor was hoarding his knowledge, holding it close to his breast, either out of love for David or out of personal ambition.

Which was it? I waited, hoping Adonai would grant me some insight, but the Spirit of Adonai did not answer.

CHAPTER FIFTEEN
BATHSHEBA

THE TRUTH ARRIVED, not as an exhilarating burst of mental illumination but as a sliver of understanding that connected to a moment of revelation and an inescapable feeling of guilt. Willingly or not, I had enticed the king to commit the act that haunted my sleep and filled me with disgust. Because I was a *tob* woman, I had to bear the blame and the shame for everything that happened.

My emotions vacillated from one extreme to the other after that fateful night. For Amaris's sake, and for Elisheba's, I tried to pretend nothing had happened and I had not been changed. But in the midst of my daily activities I would close my eyes and see the patterned canopy over the king's couch. I would wake feeling nauseous with memory, so my appetite waned. Often in the course of a day I would inhale a scent I had breathed on that rooftop—a honeysuckle vine, or a perfumed oil—and my stomach would churn.

I cried easily. I wanted to sleep longer than usual, and little annoyances infuriated me to the point that I once picked up Elisheba's favorite oil lamp and flung it against the wall, shattering it.

Though Amaris gaped at my uncharacteristic display of temper, Elisheba did not rebuke me, but picked up the broken pottery and urged me to lie down. I had never spent so much time sleeping, but what else could I do with the rest of my life?

As the time for my monthly courses drew near, I dreaded the thought of my ritual bath. Elisheba would not want to move the heavy mikvah into the house, but I would never again be able to bathe in the back garden. The goat might not care if the king spied from above, but in the past month I hadn't even been able to go out and milk her. Amaris had taken over the chore after Elisheba said I missed Uriah too much to spend time in the courtyard, where we used to watch the stars together.

Though my bruises had faded, my wounds remained. Exacerbating them was a growing fear that I would not be able to greet my husband without giving away my secret. How could I let him hold me without feeling the king's hands on my arms? How could I let him look at me without remembering the king's scorching stare? My future looked hopeless, and I dreaded the day I would see Uriah again. How could I welcome him, soiled and shamed as I was?

Days passed, and yet my courses did not flow. I told myself that my emotional upset had confused my body. I thought I would eventually return to normal, but until then I would continue to sleep like a dead woman and sicken at the slightest memory of the king.

After seven weeks had passed, Elisheba sent Amaris out to milk the goat, then she caught my arm. She had been watching me with wary eyes, and with a firm voice she bade me sit.

"You have not bled this month," she said, her tone matter-of-fact. "I fear you are with child."

For the briefest instant, my heart expanded with exhilaration. I'd been praying for a baby, and Adonai had finally answered.

But Elisheba's sober expression reminded me of what I had momentarily forgotten. I wanted *Uriah's* baby, and this child wouldn't be his. I had been bleeding when he departed, so when my husband learned about this pregnancy, he would have every right to turn me out or have me stoned for adultery. Serious consequences, but more awful than death was the realization that my beloved Uriah would believe I had willingly gone to another man's bed.

"Elisheba, what shall I do?" The words broke from my lips in an agonized cry. "Uriah will know, and the news will kill him."

Elisheba pressed her lips together and dipped her head in a decisive nod. "I have been thinking about this, and I believe you have only one recourse. You did not willingly commit this sin against your husband; the blame belongs to another. So you must send word to that person and tell him what has happened. If he possesses even a shred of righteousness, he will do the right thing."

"But what is the right thing? Will he ask Uriah to divorce me? I don't want Uriah to know about this. I love him. I don't want to hurt him. I want to have *his* babies."

Elisheba sucked at the inside of her cheek for a minute, her brows working over her eyes. "I don't know what the king will do. But the blame is his, so he should shoulder this responsibility. You must send word to him at once."

"I'm to blame." I paced in front of her, clenching and unclenching my hands. "I should not have been bathing when the king was outside."

"How were you to know he was on the roof?"

"If we'd placed the trough in the *front* courtyard—"

"Then some other man might have seen you. Where else were you supposed to put the water trough, in the house? You were bathing inside your own courtyard. You were not exhibiting yourself."

"But I must have done something. I am a *tob* woman—"

"Stop." Elisheba grabbed my hands and held them as if she could still my frantic thoughts. "Do not do this. You are innocent; he is guilty. You are a beautiful woman, but he is a king who should follow Adonai's Law. Do not take his sin upon yourself."

I wanted to believe her, but the rock of guilt in the pit of my stomach had not eroded with the passing days. "But Uriah is also innocent, and he will suffer for this. He will believe I was unfaithful. He will think I didn't love him, that I wasn't willing to wait for him—"

"Not if the king confesses the truth." Elisheba reached out and smoothed my tear-stained cheek. "I don't know what possessed our king in this moment of folly, but your father always said that David truly fears the Lord. So trust the king to do the right thing, child. Trust your husband to know how much you love him. And trust in Adonai. His ways are far above our ways."

I chewed my bottom lip. I *wanted* to trust, but how could I be sure I wouldn't be cast off or forsaken? The only completely trustworthy person I knew was Elisheba.

Slowly, I met her gaze. "Will you come with me? If I go to the palace?"

"I will, child."

After a long moment in which I fought for self-control, I squeezed Elisheba's hands, plucked my cloak from the hook by the door, and called to Amaris in the back courtyard, "We are going out, sister. We'll return soon."

With Elisheba by my side, I walked to the palace and waited outside the gate until I saw the guard who had escorted me to the rooftop. After catching his attention, I pulled him to the side of the road and gave him a message for the king. "Tell no one else," I finished, glancing around to be sure no one watched us. "And tell the king I'll be waiting for his reply."

The man glanced from me to Elisheba, whose face had gone fierce with protective love, then he left us.

Without the surge of courage that had propelled me to the palace, my knees went weak. I clung to Elisheba's arm and prayed she was right about the king's virtue. Though I couldn't see any way to salvage the situation with my honor and dignity intact, I would be content to safeguard my husband's love. If the king would summon Uriah and accept the blame for this pregnancy, Uriah might be able to forgive his king and accept this child as his own.

And in time, perhaps I could do likewise.

⁂

The next day I wandered restlessly through the house, my nerves as tight as harp strings. Every time I heard a voice in the street I hastened to the window, but hours passed with no sign of the guard who'd carried my message to the king. What if he had ignored my request? What if the king had ignored my message? How long should I wait before I took some other action?

I quietly decided that if the king did not respond within three days, I would leave the city. As a pregnant adulteress, my life in Jerusalem would be destroyed, my husband shamed, and my grandfather humiliated. So I would rise early and slip out of the city as the sun rose, walking north until I could walk no farther. I would be like Hagar and plan to die alone in the desert, but no merciful angel would appear to me. I would perish, and my shame along with me.

The second day passed like the first, and my pacing did not go unnoticed. Amaris asked why I was so jumpy, and Elisheba stared at me with speculation in her eyes, but I did not respond to either of them. If I had to leave Jerusalem, the less Elisheba and Amaris knew, the better off they'd be.

On the morning of the third day, I heard the creak of our courtyard gate. I hurried outside and met the guard, who regarded me not with the respect due a soldier's wife, but with a smirk.

Embarrassed, I drew my mantle closer. "You have a message for me?"

The smirk deepened. "No message, but something else. This." He held out a basket covered with a white cloth.

I stared at it, bewildered. The king had sent a basket, filled with what—an adder?

"Take it, woman."

I accepted the odd gift, cautiously peeking under the covering. I saw a salted roast, a loaf of bread, and a few *lebibot*, delicate heart-shaped cakes. "What is this?"

Again the sly smile. "A gift for you and your husband."

"But my husband is at Rabbah."

"Not anymore." The guard rested his hand on the hilt of his sword. "The king sent word to Joab yesterday, commanding him to send Uriah the Hittite back to Jerusalem. My guess is he'll show up here later today."

I blinked, baffled by this turn of events. At that moment Elisheba stepped out of the house. From the expression on her face, I knew she'd heard everything.

"Thank you," she told the guard, gripping my arm. "Thank you for letting us know. We'll prepare a good dinner for him."

As the guard strolled away, I turned to her. "I don't understand what any of this means."

Elisheba slipped her arm around my shoulders and led me back into the house. "Child, you are far too inexperienced. The king has decided to send your husband to you. Uriah will come home and you will sleep with him. When the child is born, everyone will believe the babe is your husband's. No one need ever know the truth."

Relief and regret warred in my heart as I stared at the basket. "That . . . makes sense," I admitted, grateful the king had found a way to prevent Uriah from knowing I'd been with another man. "But the king . . . well, he's lying."

"Would you rather your husband know what happened?" Elisheba gave me a sharp look, and I had to admit she had a point. I didn't want to believe our king would prefer to cover his sin rather than confessing it, but for Uriah and me the consequences of a lie would be infinitely less painful than the truth.

"So, let's see what we have for dinner." Elisheba peered into the basket, her smile broader than it had been in days. "A nice roast. The bread looks fine. And *lebibot*—how romantic. I have some vegetables I can add, then perhaps we could have a stew. Would you check to see if we have enough oil to fry some barley cakes?"

Still numb with shock and confusion, I moved to the corner where we kept jars of flour and oil.

"The bread smells wonderful," Elisheba said, sniffing the loaf's crusty exterior. "I wonder what kind . . ."

She cracked the loaf, and I flinched when I recognized the bright yellow fruit inside: mandrakes, a plant believed to stimulate a man's passion and aid in a woman's ability to conceive. Did even the king's cook know about my shameful predicament?

"Throw it out," I whispered, my voice trembling. "I will make another loaf, but throw out that one."

Four hours later, we had a lamb roast, fresh bread, and a bubbling pot of vegetables ready for dinner, but Uriah did not come home.

Chapter Sixteen
NATHAN

A DELICIOUS WARMTH SPREAD THROUGH MY LIMBS as I left the house and walked the road to Jerusalem. Above me, a hawk scrolled the updrafts, mindlessly circling, doing what Adonai had created him to do. Just as I was.

Nothing in the setting or the landscape signaled that the day would prove to be a turning point for David and the kingdom of Israel.

I passed the houses of my neighbors, most of whom were already at work clearing their fields, and waved at their distant figures as I took care to avoid stones that might cause me to turn an ankle on the road. More mothers than fathers worked those fields, for many of the men were still at Rabbah, enforcing the siege. Had they engaged the enemy at all? Perhaps I would hear news at the palace.

After reaching the king's house, I walked through the gate and approached the well, where I could wash off the dust from the journey. I had no sooner finished splashing my feet when I glimpsed a familiar face.

I turned, my jaw dropping. I expected all of David's elite soldiers to be hunkered in the hills outside Rabbah, so a shiver of shock rippled through me when I saw Uriah the Hittite striding across the courtyard. I stared as the warrior embraced Bathsheba's grandfather and kissed him on both cheeks.

Why wasn't the man with Joab?

Adonai had not spoken to me in days, so I moved closer to eavesdrop. By the time I positioned myself in a pillar's sheltering shadow, Uriah and Ahithophel had finished exchanging greetings. "The king sent for you?" I heard Ahithophel ask. He pinched the end of his oiled beard and twirled a portion of it between his fingers. "Do you know why?"

Uriah shrugged, his face shining with his customary good nature. "He wanted to know how the siege progresses."

"And how does it progress?"

Uriah laughed. "A siege doesn't accomplish anything unless the enemy surrenders or attempts to fight. So we have been sitting and waiting, reserving our strength for when the enemy emerges. We do not expect the Ammonites to surrender without a struggle."

Ahithophel's eyes narrowed even as his lips curved in a smile. "I suppose you will go home now. Bathsheba has been unbearably lonely since you've been away."

"The king also urged me to go home," Uriah acknowledged, grinning, "but a night with her would leave me unfit for anything but singing her praises. Then what good would I be to the king?"

Ahithophel continued to study his granddaughter's husband, but I couldn't tell what the older man was thinking. His smooth face remained utterly unreadable, a quality that undoubtedly served him well in the king's court.

"Good-bye, son." He clasped Uriah's shoulder. "May God keep you until we meet again. Serve the king well."

"I do my best."

"I have never questioned your devotion to David. And I know how deeply you are committed to my family's welfare. You have been kind and generous to both Bathsheba and Amaris."

A shadow crossed the younger man's face. "I've been wanting to tell you . . . we feel your son's absence most keenly. I wish Eliam was still with us."

Despite an obvious effort to retain control of his features, a spasm of grief knit the counselor's brows. "We have our plans, and Adonai has His. I have stopped trying to predict what HaShem, blessed be His name, will do. Go in peace, son, and remain safe."

The two men parted. Ahithophel moved toward the palace gate while Uriah hailed another soldier across the courtyard.

I turned toward the stone wall to sort through my thoughts. Uriah and Ahithophel, Ahithophel and Uriah—two men united by their service to a king and by the woman who had haunted my heart for years. Bathsheba had been the center of my youthful dreams, the sun around which I orbited, the answer to every longing of my heart . . .

In a flash that was barely comprehendible, I saw the truth as if it had been painted on the stones in front of me. When I spoke to Ahithophel a few days earlier, he had not only asked if I'd seen the woman's face in my vision but if her house was near the king's palace, a house he knew well because his granddaughter lived in it.

A whimpering sound escaped my lips as my knees buckled. Down I went, my hand slamming against the cobbled stones, my knee scraping the rough edge of a rock.

The king hadn't summoned just any woman to his bed that night, he had called for beautiful Bathsheba. Ahithophel must have lingered in the shadows until he saw his own granddaughter being escorted to the king. He could not have been happy about David's lechery, but even now he managed to maintain a countenance smooth with secrets.

Now I knew what he knew, yet this knowledge had not come

from Adonai, but from an undeniable reality—men who looked upon Bathsheba wanted her, and not even the sanctity of marriage could protect her from those lecherous gazes.

"Prophet, are you all right?" One of the king's guards hurried over to assist me. "Here, take my arm and let me help you."

I pulled myself into a sitting position and sat on the ground, knees bent, head bowed, and eyes filled with tears. Around me, voices flowed like water over a rock: "Is he ill?" "He has been out in the sun too long." "Should we send for the physician?" "Perhaps HaShem struck him down."

The last comment elicited a wry chuckle from me. I had been hard on David for lusting after Bathsheba, but hadn't I been guilty of the same sin for years? I had not gone so far as to take her to my bed, but I had never had the power to do so. If I were king and David a prophet, would the situation be any different from what it was?

I shaded my eyes and looked up, then saw Uriah peering down at me, compassion stirring in his eyes.

"Do you need help?" He extended his broad hand. "Come sit in the shade. We have water and bread—"

"No, thank you." Using my own hand for support, I pushed myself off the ground. Once upright, I looked around the circle of concerned faces and waved them away. "I'm fine. Let me be, please."

I stood in awkward silence as the onlookers reluctantly walked away. At least Ahithophel had not been among them. I did not think I could bear to look in his eyes and see the confirmation of what I had just intuited. The king had taken Bathsheba to his bed. So what did the wise and powerful royal counselor intend to do about it?

I didn't know, but before Uriah could rejoin his companions in the courtyard, I caught his arm and looked directly into his eyes. "I'm going home to comfort my wife," I told him. "You should do the same."

Chapter Seventeen
BATHSHEBA

I WAITED, MORE NERVOUS THAN A CAT, until the sun set and oil lamps glowed in my neighbors' windows. Amaris and Elisheba waited too, and when the knock finally came, all three of us jumped.

I wanted to fly to the doorway to greet my much-loved husband, but shame and guilt weighed me down. Elisheba must have guessed what I was feeling, for she went outside to the courtyard gate. She returned a moment later, not with my husband but with a parcel.

"From your grandfather," she said, her voice flat and passionless. She set the parcel on a table and cut the string around it. When I unfolded the fabric cover, the three of us stared at the gift: a new tunic. In royal blue.

"Grandfather sent you a tunic?" Amaris squeaked in the silence. "Whatever for?"

I had not believed my humiliation could grow any deeper, but in that moment I knew my shame would never be alleviated.

When not at his farm in Giloh, my grandfather lived and worked in the king's palace, and lately he had been staying in Jerusalem to advise the king. Grandfather was in Jerusalem now, and so was my husband.

Grandfather sent the tunic as a message; he knew what happened to my old one. He sent it now because he'd seen . . . and he knew.

A wail rose within me. I pressed my lips together and tried to imprison the sound, but failed. I began to sob in earnest, keening over the knowledge that Grandfather knew of my shame, and not even Elisheba's frantic shushing could comfort me.

"Bathsheba?"

Through my tears I saw Amaris's wide eyes.

"Won't someone tell me what's wrong?"

"Go to bed, little one." With her arms wrapped around me, Elisheba could only nod toward the corner where our sleeping mats waited. "Your sister is fine, she's just . . . overcome."

For once, Amaris did not argue, but hobbled to the corner and rolled out her mat. She stretched out beneath a blanket, yet I knew she wouldn't sleep until we did.

"Come, child." Elisheba drew me to the far corner of the house, then stood me against the wall and looked up into my eyes. "Tell me. Why has this gift upset you so?"

I hiccupped a sob, then swiped the back of my hand over my cheeks. "Grandfather knows."

"How could he?"

"He knows, I tell you. He's never sent me a tunic in his life, and now this? He knows, and he sent it because he saw my husband today. He's going to tell Uriah what happened."

Elisheba gasped. "He wouldn't. He couldn't know about the baby—"

"Maybe he does and maybe he doesn't know about that. But he must have heard that the king sent for me, and he's going to tell."

My voice cracked as I clung to the possibility that my instincts were wrong. But I knew Grandfather, and I knew that men took inordinate delight in staking out their territories. Grandfather wanted Uriah to know he'd been betrayed by the king he served so selflessly. This tunic was a battle flag, a warning that Grandfather was about to avenge me. He was sure his news would enrage Uriah, and then my husband would—what? Strike the king? Murder David on his throne?

My eyes welled with fresh tears, and I trembled at the thought of my husband killing the anointed king to defend my honor. He would scarcely have time to thrust with his sword before the guards would strike him down.

"Come now," Elisheba whispered. "It's a tunic, child, nothing more. Your grandfather spoils you because he loves you."

I shook my head, realizing that Elisheba might never understand. But I had grown up in my father's and grandfather's shadows. Grandfather wielded powerful words in the king's court, and Father had wielded a strong sword in the king's elite corps. They were strong men, proud men, and Uriah was cut from the same cloth.

How could Grandfather do this? Why hadn't he talked to me? Did he care so little for me that he wouldn't ask how I felt about what had happened or what should be done?

Or . . . merciful heaven, did he think I had gone to the king *willingly*? Did he suspect me of trying to attract the king's attention?

Avoiding Elisheba's confused gaze, I drew a deep breath and struggled to make sense of my whirling thoughts. No matter what Grandfather believed, he would never have talked to me because I was female. In his eyes I was a woman destined to have a great son for Israel, not a woman who would be raped and set aside. Grandfather could have only one reason for telling Uriah about what the king had done—he wanted to make David pay for his crime.

Grandfather wasn't thinking about the prophecy; he was thinking about our family's—about *his*—honor. He wanted revenge.

And as a woman, I could do nothing about his intentions.

Some time later, after the lamps had been doused and Elisheba and Amaris slept, I stood at the window and searched the darkened street for any sign of Uriah on his way home. Nothing stirred but a stray dog in search of scraps. For a moment I considered throwing him the fertility bread from the king's cook, but the last thing the city needed was another litter of puppies.

A cock had begun to crow by the time I crept to my mattress, my eyes sandy with fatigue. No one had come to the house, no one at all. I couldn't know if Grandfather had spoken to my husband, but with every passing hour I became more certain that I would never see Uriah again.

Chapter Eighteen
NATHAN

My feet felt heavier than usual as I trudged to the palace the next morning. Something in me wanted to learn if Uriah had torn himself away from his comrades and followed the king's suggestion to go home, but something else in me was certain I'd find the man exactly where I'd left him.

I entered the palace courtyard with a growing sense of trepidation. The guards had cleared away their blankets and packs, and several stood at a basin where they drank and splashed their faces. I was beginning to think Uriah *had* gone home, but then I spotted him eating breakfast with another soldier. They were sharing bread and cheese, a soldier's typical morning meal. Uriah had already laced up his sandals and put on his mantle.

Was he preparing to go back to Rabbah?

While I watched, Ahithophel came from the direction of the throne room and tapped Uriah on the shoulder. The warrior finished his bread in a great hurry, dusted his hands, and followed his wife's grandfather through a hallway. I trailed after them, but when I saw the two stop to converse in a small alcove, I knew I could go no farther without being noticed.

I returned to the courtyard and sat, only half listening to the conversations around me. The area filled with the bustle of a new morning—merchants bringing their wares to the king's steward, guards changing shifts, donkeys loaded with fabrics and trinkets to tempt the king's women and children. Zadok, one of the priests at the Tabernacle, caught my eye and nodded in greeting, but did not stop to talk. He was probably looking for Gad, the king's seer, to inquire about the king's daily sacrifice.

A good thing he wasn't looking for the king's counselor.

I drew a deep breath and exhaled it slowly, then from the corner of my eye I saw Ahithophel approaching. The counselor smiled at Zadok, then took the priest's arm and led him away to discuss whatever counselors discussed with priests.

I didn't care about the old man; I wanted to know about Uriah.

I did not see the soldier for several moments, when finally he emerged from the hallway and staggered to a bench against the wall. He fell onto it, staring at nothing while wearing a look of deep preoccupation. His face had gone deathly pale except for two red spots, one glowing in each cheek, as if cruel fate had slapped him again and again.

I could think of only one conversation that might have such an effect on Uriah the Hittite.

I sat stock-still and listened for the voice of Adonai. Would I be given words to share with this loyal soldier? Or should I remain silent?

My heart roiled with emotions I wanted to express. Part of me disliked Uriah because he had married the girl I adored, but another part of me felt compassion for what he must be feeling if my instincts were true.

For a long while I sat and watched Uriah on his bench. More than once another soldier approached and attempted to talk to him, but Uriah rebuffed them all.

As midmorning approached, one of the king's young messengers entered the courtyard. He rose on tiptoe, peering through the crowd, then walked directly toward Uriah. He said something to Bathsheba's husband, and to my surprise, Uriah stood and followed the lad into the king's house.

Overcome by curiosity, I rose and entered the great hall. A small group of men stood in the vestibule, but when the doors to the throne room opened, they shuffled inside. I brushed dust from my tunic and moved forward as well, hoping I would be permitted to remain and observe. After all, I was a prophet of Israel and personally acquainted with the king.

I whispered my name to the guard at the door and was quietly surprised when he allowed me to enter the long, rectangular room. At the farthest point of the chamber, David sat on an elevated throne surrounded by his counselors, several of his sons, and a great many guards. The king slouched casually, but a muscle in his jaw tensed as Uriah neared the dais.

I drew closer, threading my way through the others who sought an audience with the king.

"Uriah the Hittite," David called, his voice resonating in the high-ceilinged space. "What's this I hear? One of my guards has reported that you spent the night with your comrades in the palace courtyard. After being away from home so long, how could you do that?"

Uriah stepped forward, but instead of prostrating himself, he inclined his head in the slightest of bows. "I had to think of my comrades, O king. The Ark and the armies of Israel and Judah are living in tents, and Joab and my master's men are camping in the open fields. How could I go home to dine and sleep with my wife?"

His husky voice solidified to a tone as hard as iron. "By your life, by your very life, I will not do this thing."

I blinked in astonished silence. I had quietly observed Uriah for months, and I had never heard him use a harsh tone with anyone. Furthermore, no one spoke to the king without addressing him as "my lord and king," yet Uriah had just spoken not as a subject to his king but as one man to another.

If the king noticed any change in this steadfast soldier's attitude, he didn't remark on it. His lips curved as his chest rose and fell in a deep sigh. "Stay here today," David said, giving the man a smile that did not reach his eyes. "Enjoy yourself. Dine at my table tonight so that I may honor a true warrior. And tomorrow I shall send you off."

I tugged on my beard, suspecting that the king had not been truthful about his motivation. Dozens of courageous soldiers served in the armies of Israel, and David had never summoned any of them for such vague reasons. Uriah had not saved his commander's life or killed a giant or captured a city. The only thing that connected him to David was Bathsheba, but why would the king want to unite a cuckolded husband with the woman he'd victimized?

I stared at Uriah, fascinated by the question, and watched as the soldier dipped his head in icy acknowledgment of his king's request.

Unless I had completely misjudged the Hittite's character, I did not believe he would go home no matter how much food and wine David forced on him. So what would the king do tomorrow? And how would Uriah respond?

I bit my lip, curious, but not at all eager to find out.

❧

The next morning, Ornah rose before I did. After waking, I propped myself on my elbows and studied her as she squatted to care for our little girls. Her shape was more solid than sensual, composed more of straight lines than curves, but she had never been anything but a loyal, virtuous wife.

My heart flooded with gratitude that Adonai had not given me a beautiful woman.

Without speaking, I tossed off the blanket, then bent and wrapped my arms around my wife. She squealed in surprise while my daughters' eyes rounded to full moons.

"Nathan? What ails you?"

I spun Ornah around and kissed her, then grinned at Nira and Yael. "Your mother is a wonderful woman," I told them in an overflow of gratitude for Adonai's blessings. "Be nice to her today."

As Ornah stared, I pulled a clean tunic from the wall peg, put it on, and then grabbed my mantle and staff. "I'm going up to Jerusalem." I reached for a hunk of bread in the table basket. "I should be home by sundown."

Ornah looked at me like a woman who had just been knocked over by a charging goat. "You're going again? Is everything all right?"

"All is well with us."

"Are you sure?"

I didn't answer but opened the door and breathed in the clean scent of fresh air. When I looked back at my wife, a small smile trembled on her lips.

I hadn't seen her smile in a long, long time.

I left my family and began to climb the ascending path. I had barely traveled one hundred paces when I met a caravan of soldiers. Walking in pairs, most of them led donkeys that carried baskets, water jugs, and other goods—surely supplies for the army at Rabbah.

My pulse quickened when I recognized Uriah among the men. He walked with a spear in his hand and his head down, as if he were deep in thought.

Without thinking I stepped into his path and was nearly run

over for my trouble. He looked up, blinking in surprise, then his face lit with recognition. "You're the prophet."

"Well met, Uriah the Hittite." Turning, I scrambled to keep up with his long stride. "When I saw you yesterday, you were on your way to the king's dinner."

Uriah groaned. "Never drink too much of the king's wine. My head is pounding even now."

He looked at me, awaiting some kind of response, and I didn't know what to say. I was desperate to understand what had happened with the king, but Uriah was not a man who liked to chatter.

"Please." I tugged on his cloak. "Please stop a moment."

Uriah looked at the man beside him, then shrugged and stepped out of formation.

While I stood beside the road, the voice of Adonai thundered so unexpectedly that I staggered backward. Uriah must have heard nothing but the wind whistling among the rocks, because his only reaction was a subtle frown. "Are you well?" His eyes ran over my form, taking in the unadorned tunic, the mantle, and the walking stick. "You'll never reach the city without water. It's too hot to ascend without it."

"It's not thirst that makes me tremble," I whispered, struggling to speak and listen at the same time. The familiar light-headedness had settled in my brain, and the world had gone soft, without edges.

"What . . . ?" I struggled to hear the words Adonai rumbled in my ears. "What is that you carry at your belt, Uriah?"

Uriah startled, clearly surprised, and I understood the reason for his reticence. "I know you are carrying a message from the king," I said, "for Adonai has told me so. If you would tell me what it says . . ."

"If you are a prophet, ask Adonai to tell you." His face split in a grimace. "As for me, I do not know. And I will not open a sealed message from the king."

No sooner had he uttered those words than the *Ruach HaKodesh* revealed all, and the weight of the revelation was enough to make me stagger.

Uriah caught my arm. "What is it?"

I shook my head, then lifted my hand to shield my face from the bright sunlight. Aided by this small shade, I studied the Hittite's face, knowing I would never see him again.

"I am grateful," I whispered, my heart welling with sympathy for the man who had given his all to a friend who had betrayed him. "I am glad that you did not kill the king. And I am so very sorry for what must happen at Rabbah."

"Do not fret on my account." Uriah's eyes gleamed in a moment of clean, transparent truth. "My life is the king's to command. David is the Lord's anointed and I—"

"You are a loyal soldier," I interrupted, unable to stop myself.

Uriah shrugged. "Yesterday a wise man told me that HaShem has His purposes, and we need not try to understand them. No matter what my heart feels, no matter who implores me to act, I am sworn to serve the king. And so I shall."

I lowered my gaze from his compelling eyes and spied the leather satchel at his belt. Inside, I knew, lay a missive written in David's own hand, a letter commanding Joab to put Uriah in the front of the fiercest battle and draw back, leaving the Hittite to die.

With Uriah out of the way, David would be free to claim Bathsheba . . . and the unborn child.

Comprehension emerged from confusion, and the *Ruach Ha-Kodesh* confirmed my intuition. Bathsheba was pregnant. Uriah had not gone home to sleep with his wife, and now the king wanted him out of the way.

And the Hittite knew it.

"I should not detain you." I stepped aside, leaving the pathway open, even though we both understood where it would lead. I looked again at the man who loved Bathsheba and asked a simple question: "If you knew this road would lead to your death, would you continue on it?"

For an instant, a laughing light filled Uriah's dark eyes. Then he sighed and gave me a grim smile. "Others may not fulfill their vows, but I will. I could not live with myself otherwise."

"Even for *her*?" My eyes searched his. "Because she does love you deeply."

He hesitated, and only his eyes revealed the torment within his soul. He flexed his jaw and stared at the road ahead. "I love her, and I *know* her. So I will not torture my wife by making her choose between a hard truth and an easy lie."

I stepped back, my soul filling with admiration. Uriah the Hittite was a better man than I . . . and a far better man than his master.

I cleared my tight throat and clasped my walking stick. "Go then, my friend. And may HaShem grant you peace."

⌒⋇⌒

The next day I presented myself at the king's court to witness events as they unfolded. For Uriah's sake, I wanted to watch the king's scheme play out to its bloody conclusion. I also wanted to study David's countenance when he learned that his loyal servant was dead.

My walk into Jerusalem had not been pleasant. A stinging wind had come up, riding the edge of an approaching storm, and sharp sand had invaded every crevice of my clothing by the time I reached the palace. I could not close my mouth without feeling grit between my teeth, and I knew I was leaving a trail of sand in my wake as I entered the king's throne room.

The court bustled with the usual couriers, attendants, royal children, and guards. Content to watch and wait, I stood against the back wall and listened to various proposals, reports, and disputes that had been brought before the king.

The day was about half spent when a pair of couriers, dusty and perspiring, entered the king's chamber, shouldered their way through the throng, and bowed before the man on the throne.

In a gesture that seemed overly theatrical, David gripped the gilded armrests of his royal seat. "Do you bring word from Rabbah? How goes the battle?"

I lifted a brow. He should have asked about the siege, but the king had slipped. Would anyone else catch his mistake?

One of the couriers stood and pressed his hand to his chest. "My lord and king."

My vision misted over, and the scene shifted before my eyes. Leaning against the wall for balance, I saw Uriah hand the king's letter to Joab. I saw the commander's face twist with consternation as he read it. The king's clumsy plan to leave Uriah alone at the front would leave no doubt that the man's death had been arranged, so Joab would have to improvise. In order to successfully carry off the charade, more than one man would have to die—not only Uriah but other innocents, as well.

Though a vision of a field outside Rabbah filled my eyes, I heard the army courier's voice echo in the throne room: "My king, the enemy came out against us in the open fields."

I saw Uriah striding across a sunlit field, where a corps of valiant men waited. They welcomed him, slapping him on the back, then they crouched behind a stand of scrubby brush. Behind them, Joab stood with other soldiers, who faced the city and watched for any movement of the gates or along the stone walls.

The gates of Rabbah opened, and a group of defenders rode out on mules, spears and swords at the ready. Uriah and his companions sprang forward and attacked, unseating the men from their mounts and driving the city's defenders back toward the walls.

A sour taste rose in my mouth. Every man in Israel's army knew the danger of fighting next to a fortified wall, for during the time of the judges a tribal ruler had been killed when a woman leaned over a tower wall and dropped a millstone on his head. Joab knew of that danger, and he knew he ought to sound a retreat when the fighting drew near a city's fortifications.

I watched, transfixed, as the previous day's events continued to play before my eyes. I saw Uriah and his men strike at the Ammonites, who steadily retreated toward their stronghold. Step by step, blow by blow, Uriah fought his way forward, sweat streaming into his eyes, blood running down his arms, his sword flashing in the sunlight. Every ounce of his energy went into the fight; he was not looking for landmarks or keeping track of his position.

I saw one of Joab's captains pick up a ram's horn, ready to sound retreat and call the warriors back. He lifted the horn, but Joab put out his hand, stopping him.

A line of archers appeared on the top of the wall. I watched them knock their barbed arrows and pull their bowstrings, and then a rain of deadly missiles fell on the men of Israel. Undaunted, Uriah and his four companions continued to cut and slash and parry the enemies' blows, until one by one they dropped outside the thick stone walls. Uriah, roaring with every effort, struck a death blow to the commander of the Amorite army. As he pulled his sword from his enemy's corpse, an arrow sailed straight and true and struck the center of his forehead.

Uriah fell, wide-eyed, to the earth and lay silent, his hand wrapped around the hilt of his sword, his gaze blankly regarding the heavens.

I closed my eyes as tightly as I could, unwilling to stare disrespectfully at a hero of Israel.

And in the king's throne room, lifting his voice in a dramatic crescendo, the courier finished his accounting: "As we chased them back to the city gate, the archers on the wall shot arrows at us. Some of the king's men were killed, including Uriah the Hittite."

My vision cleared, the city of Rabbah fading as my eyes focused on David's face. The lines of tension that had marked his mouth and eyes melted away, and the faint suggestion of a smile twisted his lips. "I am sorry to hear this report," he said, leaning back on the cushions of his throne. "Tell Joab not to be discouraged, for the sword devours this one today and that one tomorrow. Tell him to fight harder next time and conquer the city."

Almost as an afterthought, David lifted his hand in a fist, a weak attempt at a call to arms, but I did not think the retreating couriers even noticed. They had turned to leave, their faces masks of relief. They had delivered a tragic report of their commander's foolishness and hadn't had to endure the royal tongue-lashing their report deserved.

I sank to the floor, overwhelmed by this brutal evidence of our king's treachery. Was this why Adonai did not send me to upbraid the king for taking another man's wife? HaShem had not been content to expose a mere thread of David's sinful nature; He wanted to uncover the entire tapestry.

CHAPTER NINETEEN

BATHSHEBA

I HAD JUST HELPED AMARIS TO BED when I heard the squeak of our courtyard gate. Alarmed by the thought of a guest at this hour, I hurried to the door and found my grandfather pacing in the courtyard. He walked with trepidation, his hands behind his back, his head lowered and his brows tight with fury.

Through the gathering darkness I peered at his face. "Is there some trouble, Grandfather?"

He stopped pacing and spun to face me, then took a breath and lowered his voice. "Your king," he said, his words clipped, "has murdered your husband."

The words struck like a slap. I stepped back and felt the rough plaster of the house against my arms. "That can't be true."

"I only wish it weren't." With a glance to the left and right, Grandfather inched closer and shook his finger in my face. "I *know*, Bathsheba! I saw you leave the king's palace that night, and I know

David brought Uriah back from Rabbah in an attempt to cover his sin. I talked to your husband myself."

"And you told him . . . what?" A thread of hysteria entered my voice as thoughts tumbled in my head. Uriah couldn't be dead. As far as I knew, he was still in Jerusalem. The king was probably trying to find the right time to tell him what had happened, and then he would send Uriah to me.

A gleam of resentment entered my grandfather's eyes. "I told him everything. He had to know that the Judean upstart we call *king* had stolen his wife. You should have seen his face when he heard. I've seen dying men look happier."

Faced with the confirmation of my worst fear, I brought my hand to my mouth and choked off a scream. Pressure bloomed in my chest, tightening my throat and cutting off my breath.

"I told him, but my words didn't have the effect I intended," Grandfather snapped, his gaze falling on my still-flat belly. "It wasn't difficult to understand why David kept insisting your husband return home. You are carrying the king's child, and for that your honorable husband had to return to Jerusalem. I told Uriah to kill the king before he was killed himself, but instead he went off to war as if nothing had happened." Grandfather shook his head. "Apparently he is less a warrior than I thought, and today's news proved it. He is dead, killed at Rabbah. How convenient for your lover."

Each pointed word felt like a stab in the heart. I released a strangled cry as my knees gave way. I sank to the ground, buried my face in my hands, and wailed for my murdered husband and my nonexistent future. As a pregnant woman with no husband in sight, I had no hope of survival. People would whisper as soon as my belly began to show. They would count months on their fingers, and I would be cast out for being an adulteress or a harlot. I had shamed my sister, my dead husband, and my esteemed grandfather.

Worst of all, I was to blame. If Uriah had not married a *tob* woman, he might have lived a long and happy life.

"Bathsheba." Grandfather's voice held a note of impatience. He bent and gently helped me to my feet. "Shh, do not carry on so. You are not to blame for any of this."

I tried to control myself, but my eyes overflowed despite my efforts. "Uriah did not deserve to die."

"You are right to weep and mourn him, for he was a good man, even a better one than the shepherd who sits on the throne. Weep for your husband, observe the full mourning period, but do not say anything to anyone about the child."

With much effort I looked up at Grandfather's face. His stern expression was enough to silence my sobs, but what could he do to preserve my reputation?

"The king has committed a great evil, but I'm sure he does not wish to harm you," Grandfather said. "If he cared nothing about you, he would not have bothered to have Uriah killed. Since David is responsible for your condition, I will make certain he protects you. And if it takes the rest of my life, I will make him pay for what he has done to this family."

I stared in confusion as Grandfather's words piled atop each other. I had no idea what he meant or what he would do, yet I understood his anger. In that moment I would have shared it had my heart not been so heavy with grief.

As always, I had no control over the powerful current that was dragging me away from the life I loved. I had to trust my grandfather or leave Jerusalem.

But for the next seven days, I had to mourn the husband I had unwillingly betrayed.

We grieved for Uriah throughout the next week. Grandfather hired professional mourners who sat cross-legged in the courtyard and filled the air with keening. We had no funeral, for my husband had been buried in the blood-soaked earth outside Rabbah. Our parting five months ago had been our last kiss, our last embrace, our last exchange of words. Uriah walked out of my life to serve our king, and our king had deliberately taken his life.

I moved like a woman in a trance, nodding to those who came to comfort me, weeping with those who wept, thanking those who brought food or gifts to honor my husband's memory. Elisheba and Amaris were nearly as inconsolable as I, but they were better able to converse with guests and smile at happy memories.

My lips had turned traitorous; I could not smile. Knowledge of the king's treachery and his child within my belly overshadowed every thought, and when I wasn't grieving for Uriah I trembled in fear of my own future. Grandfather said the king would take care of me, but what if the sight of my face reminded him of the horrible evil he'd committed? What if I were nothing more than an entertainment that ceased to amuse once it had been explored and vanquished?

In our crowded community, where homes adjoined their neighbors and words carried easily from one household to another, my pregnancy would not remain a secret for long. In another month, maybe two, my belly would begin to grow and everyone would know. The women first, followed by their men. The priests . . . and Nathan the prophet. Since Adonai often revealed things to him, perhaps he knew already.

I bowed my head as fresh tears began to flow. I did not know the prophet well enough to speak to him, but he had been a fixture in my youth, the boy who visited the Tabernacle with Samuel and often stopped to share a meal with my father and grandfather. As a child, I had admired Nathan's open countenance and dedication to his teacher, and even as a woman I would rather walk across burning sand than do anything that might cause him to think less of me. I had always wanted him to like me, but he would be shocked and disappointed if he learned I was pregnant by a man who was not my husband.

The day after Elisheba and I put away our sackcloth and swept the courtyard, a pair of messengers arrived from the palace. "King David would have you be his wife," the tallest messenger announced as he eyed me from head to toe. "And our lord the king will take care of your household from this day forward."

I turned my back to them, surprised and more uncertain than ever. "But I don't want to be his wife," I whispered in Elisheba's ear. "I hate him."

"You must go." Elisheba slipped her arm about my waist, then gave me a squeeze. "Don't hesitate, and don't worry. Surely the king knows what is best."

"But how am I to do this?" I clenched my hands in frustration. "He might command my body, but he will never command my heart."

"Shh." Elisheba placed her fingers over my lips. "Be careful, child. Speak little. Look much. And plead your case before Adonai, who pays special attention to the prayers of widows and children."

For the first time in my life, I doubted Elisheba's wisdom, but what choice did I have? I turned and saw Amaris staring at me, her wide eyes about to overflow. I walked over to her, knelt to wrap her in my arms, and whispered a gentle farewell. "I'll still see you," I promised. "You'll always be my little sister."

I felt the sting of tears behind the smile I gave her. I stood, straightened my shoulders, and stepped forward as Elisheba looked on with approval. Though Amaris wept with confusion, Elisheba wore relief like a garment.

I wish I could say I found the courage to walk away from the home my beloved husband had built for me, but in truth, my walk to the palace was precipitated more by resignation than bravery. A walk to David's house, difficult as it was, was infinitely preferable to a suicidal trek into the desert.

So between two unfamiliar messengers I climbed the path to the palace, preparing to live with a man I did not know and most assuredly did not love.

⁂

After entering the palace gate, my escorts led me through the large courtyard, where more than a few scorching glares followed us. Those who knew me must have wondered what business Uriah's widow had with the king's household. Those who did not know me must have considered me another concubine sought for the king's pleasure. Such thoughts, I have since learned, are routinely ascribed to *tob* women.

The escorts did not linger in the open space but led me to another enclosure, a series of rooms belonging to the king's wives and concubines. These royal rooms were less lavish and more crowded than I had expected, for David had many wives and even more concubines in his harem. Many children too, I noticed, as I glanced at the little ones scurrying to their mothers as we approached.

I steeled myself not to flinch beneath the gazes of the women, who seemed intent on evaluating my face, form, and even the cut of my tunic. Though I had little experience with female competition and only a little knowledge of royal protocol, intuitively I knew I was being judged according to some sort of comparative scale. I did not speak to anyone but followed my escorts to a small room that had been furnished with a narrow bed, a wooden table, a trunk, a chair, a basin and a pitcher of water.

A room with everything I needed, but as impersonal as a harlot's roadside hut.

After seeing me safely inside, one of the escorts inclined his head and pressed his hand to his chest. "Be well, my lady. A servant will bring you dinner."

"Wait." I took a step toward him, not sure what was expected of me. "Is there some sort of . . . do I need to *do* something?"

The man's brow lifted. "Everything has already been done. The king has proclaimed that you are his wife, so you will be granted the respect due a royal wife. Your family is now his responsibility, so he will care for those who remain in your household. This is your room; the harem is your domain. You may wander freely in it and you may go to the king when summoned. Otherwise, you are not to leave the palace without an escort, for now you belong to the king."

Overcome by the swift efficiency of the royal household, I sank onto the bed and stared at the stone floor as my escorts closed the door and departed. In the space of an hour, the king had made me his wife, removed me from my family, and stolen my personal freedom. The procedure was altogether clean, quick, and loveless.

How different my marriage to Uriah had been! We had feasted with family and friends, we had lain together, we had laughed and loved and received congratulations and good wishes from everyone who knew us.

I might have married a king, but instead of congratulations from friends, I received cold looks from the king's other wives. Instead of feasting, I would dine in solitude. And instead of lying next to a loving husband on a straw-stuffed mattress, I would lie in this cold and lonely bed.

Would I always sleep alone? I had no idea if the king had any intention of sleeping with me again. This effort might only be the result of a guilty conscience.

I ate lightly of the meal a servant delivered and then paced in my room with nothing to do. Then, as the sun lowered in the west, someone knocked on my door. I opened it to find a guard waiting. The king, he announced, had sent for me.

I swallowed hard. Should I go to him as I was or should I ask for a change of clothes? I didn't know if he wanted to speak to me or sleep with me, and the thought of either caused a riot of panic in my chest.

Since I had no other clothing and no servant to help with my appearance, I smoothed my hair, girded up my courage, and followed the guard out of the harem, down a corridor, and into another chamber much larger than the small space reserved for a royal wife. There the king reclined on a couch, eating his dinner. At my approach he wiped his fingers, pushed his tray aside, and stood. He gave me an uncertain, crooked smile as he waved the guard away.

I tilted my head, studying the man who had haunted my sleep for the past several weeks. He seemed smaller than I remembered, ruddier, and less physically powerful. Uriah had definitely been the more attractive man.

"I have sent for you, Bathsheba," the king said without preamble or apology, "to tell you how deeply I regret what has happened between us thus far. Yet I will take care of you, so you need not fear for your safety." His gaze sharpened and ran over my form, then for the first time it met mine. "Are you still with child?"

At first I could not speak over the boulder in my throat, but I pushed the words out. "Do you think I would have come if I were not?"

His face twisted, then he turned so I could not see his eyes. "I deserved that." He moved to a standing tray and plucked a few grapes from a stalk. "In that case—" he tossed a grape into his mouth—"because Uriah did not avail himself of my kindness and go home as I commanded, the world must believe the child you carry is mine."

"Which it is." Forced through a tight throat, my words sounded hoarse.

"Yet for the child's sake, you must remain with me tonight," the king continued, turning to face me again. His mouth curved with the faint beginning of a smile. "I will sleep with you, the child will be known as a prince of Israel, and I will not disturb you again."

The shivering at my core erupted into violent trembling. I closed my eyes, unable to bear the thought of touching the man who had brought me such pain and heartache and shame. But I was his wife, his property to use or ignore as he chose.

Braced for his caress, I waited, but nothing happened. Still terrified, I opened my eyes and found him standing directly in front of me, his smile twisted and his forehead creased with apparent concern.

"I don't want to hurt you," he said, not knowing I'd heard him say those very words in my nightmares.

"If it please my lord the king," I managed to whisper, "you do not have to touch me in order to establish that you are the child's father. As long as we pass the night together, every wagging tongue will be stilled. No one would dare doubt the child's paternity."

His eyes narrowed as though he were weighing the motivation behind my suggestion. "I have done you a greater injustice than I realized," he said, his tone apologetic, "and I have gravely wounded you, though that was not my intention. Please, lady, sleep in my bed, and I will pass the night on the floor. And in the morning, as you have said, no one will have reason to doubt that you carry a royal child."

"I will lie on the floor." I took a half step back. "The king should not be deprived of his bed."

He exhaled softly and chuckled. "I have spent many a night on ground harder than this. Take the bed, daughter of Eliam, and sleep in peace. You may find this hard to believe, but I am not a complete monster. I am—" he shrugged, and when his eyes met mine again, they appeared to shine with contrition—"only a man."

A common shepherd, my grandfather would have said. As common a man as could be found in Israel.

What could I do but take the king at his word? I moved to the far side of his bed and slipped out of my sandals, then crawled beneath the blanket in an effort to disappear. Experience had taught me that David took what he coveted, and I did not want him to wake in the night and covet me yet again.

I huddled beneath the stifling blanket for what felt like an eternity and listened to him move about the room, shuffling parchments and squeaking the chair. Finally I heard him blow out the oil lamp. When I gratefully pushed the blanket away from my perspiring face, I drank in gulps of fresh air and saw nothing but shifting shadows.

I could not see David where he lay, but after a while I heard soft snoring from the far side of the room. I remained awake, anxious and alert, until the cock crowed and servants began to shuffle in the hallway.

Careful not to wake the sleeping king, I slipped out of his bed and hurried back to the safety of the harem and my small space within it.

And so ended my second wedding night.

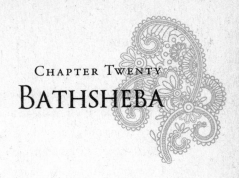

Chapter Twenty

BATHSHEBA

Months passed. Except for brief visits from Elisheba and Amaris, I spent my days in solitude and seemed to be David's wife in name only. The king did not call for me during those long weeks, and most of the other wives avoided me as much as possible. When I chanced upon them in the palace garden, the wives with children tended to speak to the air above my head, especially Maacah, the princess of Geshur, who had given David two children, beautiful Tamar and handsome Absalom.

The other wives ignored the growing bulge beneath my tunic. I would have ignored it myself if I'd had a choice. If not for the bulge, Uriah would be alive and I would be living contentedly with Elisheba and Amaris in my little house. If not for the ill-begotten bulge, I would be free to come and go as I pleased. If not for the bulge, I would be able to sleep without nightmares.

One night I dreamt that a lion chased me through the streets and finally pinned me to the earth. I felt his massive weight on my arms as a growl rattled in his throat and his hulking body loomed over me. He lowered his head and sniffed at my neck while I turned my face away and clamped my teeth together, trying not to scream. He roared, and I braced myself for death—and then I woke up.

I lay motionless, my heart pounding, my skin slick with perspiration. For a long moment my dream world felt more real than the bed beneath me. Then my room slowly made its way back into my consciousness. I pulled the blanket to my chin and searched the darkness, lit only by a sliver of light at the bottom of my door. As my eyes adjusted to the gloom, I spied my table, my cloak, my shoes on the floor. In another apartment a child cried, sandal-clad feet whispered in the hallway, and in the distance, guards laughed at a ribald joke.

In the shadowy world-between-worlds, I pressed my hand to the bulge at my belly and felt a responding kick. I stiffened, somehow certain that the child wanted his first contact with me to be as violent as the act that had conceived him. I removed my hand and turned my head, not willing to encourage any further communication between us.

In that moment I wanted to be with Uriah, curled up next to him in a grave somewhere outside Rabbah.

None of the king's women seemed willing to befriend me, nor the king himself. So why shouldn't I resign myself to a life without joy, purpose, or meaning?

In the quiet of my chamber I yearned for the companionable conversations I used to enjoy with Elisheba and Amaris. We had spent so many years sharing close quarters that at times I found myself snatching a breath to speak to Elisheba, then realizing she was no longer with me. I would have given anything to keep Amaris by my side, even though she was too young to comprehend many of the thoughts that troubled my heart.

I could not understand why the king's other wives ignored me. I had done nothing to steal his affection, and he spent very little time in my company. One afternoon, as a servant swept my room, I happened to remark that the other wives did not consider me a friend. The servant, a stout Jebusite woman, chuckled under her breath.

"Did I say something funny?" I smiled so she would not think I was angry. "Please, if you know why the other women avoid me, please tell me."

She narrowed her eyes and studied me, then gave me a small grin. "They are jealous because of the story whispered throughout the palace, my lady. Throughout Jerusalem, in fact."

A thrill of panic shot through me. *What* story was being whispered? The story of how I came to be the king's wife, or the story of how David murdered my husband?

I swallowed to bring my heart down from my throat. "And what story would that be?"

"The prophecy, my lady." She leaned closer. "They say that when you were born, one of Israel's greatest prophets took a look at you and said you would be one of the most desirable women in the land. And that you would marry a king and have a son who would be the greatest ruler in the world."

The rumor wasn't exactly accurate, but at least it wasn't one of the stories I'd feared. "*That's* why they avoid me?"

The servant nodded. "They'd never admit it, but all the other wives are working to make sure it's *their* son who inherits the throne. Michal is no problem because she hasn't got a son, unless you count the five nephews she's raising for her dead sister. But that Ahinoam—her son is Amnon, the firstborn, and she gives herself airs because she fancies herself mother of the crown prince. Yet she's nothing compared to Maacah, Absalom's mother. Since she was a princess before she came to Israel, she thinks her boy should be king. And frankly"—the woman lowered her voice—"sometimes I think the king agrees with her. He'd never admit it, but he dotes on Absalom more than the others; anyone can see it. I guess sometimes you can't help having a favorite, and Absalom is the most gorgeous child in the palace."

She stopped and lifted a brow, waiting for my reaction, so I thanked her for her honesty. My hand moved to the bump beneath my tunic. Windows in my mind blew open, reminding me that I carried a child too, perhaps a son. The prophecy was real enough, and its certainty guaranteed. Had Adonai allowed Samuel to look into the future and see that this baby would be the king of Israel?

The more I considered the possibility, the more it made sense. Ahinoam might have given birth to the king's first son and Maacah might have borne his favorite, but the king *owed* me. To atone for Uriah's murder, David ought to name my son his heir. The prophecy guaranteed that he would.

The idea brought a small smile to my lips. Though I abhorred the memory of how this child was conceived, I knew that Adonai often worked His will through tragic situations. Didn't Abraham have to endure the trauma of placing Isaac on the altar of sacrifice? Didn't Joseph have to withstand slavery and imprisonment before HaShem brought him out and placed him on a throne?

I had borne a horrific assault and I'd been treated like chattel. My beloved husband had been murdered. But HaShem had given me a promise . . . and I carried the son who would influence Israel forever.

I dared not speak of my new understanding, but in my prayers I begged Adonai to protect my unborn child.

❧

Servants were not my only visitors to the palace. The royal midwife checked on me often and assured me that she would deliver a healthy baby. After she left, I stroked my rounded belly and knew I'd been wrong to resent the child. How could I resent a child God meant to be our next king?

By my reckoning, I was a month away from delivering when a messenger informed me that I had guests. Leaving my little room for the first time in days, I went to the harem courtyard and found Elisheba and Amaris waiting.

Amaris's eyes went wide when she saw me. With the artlessness of a young girl, she gaped at my belly. "You are getting so big! Are you going to have a girl?"

I smiled. "I am carrying a son."

I hugged each of them, then bade them sit on the bench near the fountain. As usual, Amaris lost all custody of her eyes and stared at everyone who walked by, probably eager to spot one of the princes. Yet Elisheba held my hand and studied me intently. "How are you, child?"

I gave her the brightest smile I could manage. "I am well fed, and the midwife says the baby is fine."

"That's not what I asked." Elisheba leaned closer. "How is your heart? The last time we visited, you were still grieving over Uriah and sick with worry about how you would live with the king's women."

I stared into the fountain's rippling water and sought words that would neither alarm her nor be untruthful. "The king has not been unkind to me," I finally said. "Neither have the other wives. I have lots of time for sewing, so my life here is not unpleasant."

Elisheba turned my hand and studied my soft pink palm. "You've not been grinding grain or hauling water, anyone can see that."

"No," I admitted. "The king's servants make life easy."

"But not everything is easy." Elisheba's dark eyes probed mine. "Our neighbors have been full of talk about you. Most of them believe the king took you as his wife out of generosity, and word of the child has also become common knowledge. Some of your father's friends know about Samuel's prophecy, so they expect your son to be our next king."

"Adonai chooses kings," I reminded her, though I had quietly come to the same conclusion.

Elisheba dipped her chin in a firm nod. "Samuel was Adonai's prophet. And if he speaks God's words, a true prophet cannot lie."

We continued to share stories. Elisheba told me about the latest happenings on our street, about the bird that had nested in the garden, and the neighborhood girl who had recently been betrothed to a shepherd from the tribe of Benjamin.

"And she was only thirteen," Amaris added, smiling a gap-toothed smile. "Almost as young as me."

"Don't be in such a hurry." I wagged a finger at my overeager little sister. "I was seventeen before Father arranged my betrothal. I have a feeling Grandfather may want you to wait, too."

A frown crept into the space between Amaris's brows. "Will my marriage be arranged by Grandfather or the king? The king is my brother-in-law, isn't he? And with Father dead . . ."

I blinked, startled by her question. She was correct in her assumption, but I couldn't imagine David taking an interest in my sister's marriage. He hadn't yet done anything to arrange marriages for his own children.

"I don't know." I gave her a smile. "But I know you shouldn't worry. These things tend to take care of themselves at the right time."

Elisheba patted my hand, then leaned forward to kiss my cheek. "I know you are trying to paint a pretty picture, child, but I see loneliness in your eyes. Know that I am praying for you to have an easy birth and a healthy child. But most of all, I will be praying that you will find love. If ever a woman deserved it, Bathsheba, you do."

She stood and gestured to the guard who had escorted them into the harem, and then she and Amaris hugged me and said good-bye.

The first birth pangs came just before dawn. I bore them quietly, not wanting to draw attention, but by the third hour of the day I was pacing the width and breadth of my room as sweat ran down my face and my chest.

The midwife came as soon as she heard the news. "The king knows," she announced when she entered my room. "Now take off that shawl and walk with me to kill the pain. Hold my hand if it will make you feel better."

I wanted Elisheba, but I didn't want her around if something went wrong. Despite Samuel's prophecy, I knew how often women and their children died during childbirth. Despite my faith in the prophecy, I wondered if the nameless bulge at my belly would be the end of me, freeing me to join Uriah, my mother, my father, and a host of ancestors whose names I didn't even know.

I cried out and bit my fist during the worst pains, and paced in my chamber when they eased. I felt as though my body would burst. My loins burned, my back ached, and all the while the midwife told me to keep walking. How could a woman *walk* when her legs felt like water?

I walked—or stumbled—throughout most of the afternoon. A pair of servants brought fans to move the air in my small space, and during the worst pains the midwife wiped my forehead with a damp cloth. A serving girl brought a plate at midday, but the midwife shooed her away, saying that I shouldn't eat until after the child had come.

By sunset I had become convinced I would die with the child inside me. Because as a *tob* woman I had enticed the king, HaShem intended to punish me.

With no strength left, I collapsed on my bed, my tunic saturated with sweat, my hair drenched, and my life ebbing away. Like the bleating of a goat, the midwife's voice blended into the sounds of the palace. Then, without warning, a ripping pain tore at my flesh.

"Get up!" the woman commanded, taking my hands and pulling me off the bed. "Lift your tunic and squat! Now! To the floor with you!"

My legs barely supported me as I lowered myself, pressed my hands to the floor, and leaned forward. I gritted my teeth and pushed . . . as a child slid into the world on a bloody tide.

Dazed, I turned in time to see the midwife wrap a linen square around the child, then use a corner of the cloth to wipe the mucus from its nose and eyes.

"A boy," she said, smiling at the infant. "The king has another beautiful baby boy."

I sank to the floor as the room spun around me. Was it possible we had both survived?

Another servant stood by to catch the afterbirth, but I was beyond caring about what happened to me. But we were both alive—me and the son I'd been given. Perhaps Adonai did hear the prayers of a *tob* woman.

The servant helped me onto my bed as the midwife washed the baby, rubbed salt over his skin, and wrapped him. When she had finished, she placed the swaddled child in my arms. He lifted pink eyelids and caught my gaze for a second, then rooted around for my breast.

I found myself smiling through tears.

"I will tell the king," the midwife said, washing her hands in a basin. "Have the servants comb your hair, lady, and prepare you for your husband. I daresay he will soon be on his way."

I wanted to correct her, for the king had never darkened my door, but thought it best to remain silent. This baby might always remind the king of unpleasant circumstances, so I would understand if he never wanted to see the child.

But since Adonai heeded the prayers of a shamed *tob* woman, I could—and would—love this baby boy, this promised prince.

⌀⌀⌀

The first day of my son's life was very nearly perfect. By the time the king heard that my son had arrived, the servants had combed my hair, washed my face, and dressed me in a fresh tunic. They eased me into a chair with the baby nestled in my arms, so I must have looked fairly presentable when the king arrived.

I didn't know what to say when he came through the door, so I simply sat there, tongue-tied and exhausted. The king hesitated at my threshold only a moment. Once he glimpsed the child, he strode forward and fell to his knees at my side. With only a smiling glance at me, he thrust a finger toward the baby's curled hand. The boy, intent on my breast, nonetheless wrapped his tiny digits around the king's finger, eliciting a broad smile from the man next to me.

Something in my heart softened at that simple sign of joy. The king's delight was as real as any emotion I had ever seen on a man's face, and in that moment I realized I need no longer fear him. He was a man like any other, and as prone to sin when not focused on pleasing Adonai. But this baby delighted the king, and when David lifted his gaze to meet mine, in his eyes I saw a wordless appeal for forgiveness.

I looked away, unable to forgive or forget . . . yet.

We sat together until sunset, marveling at the beauty and perfection of our child. We talked about possible names, though the decision wouldn't be final until the baby's circumcision on the eighth day, and we argued gently about whether he had my nose or his father's. I watched as the king gingerly lifted the child in his rough hands, and I marveled that a man who had fathered so many children could still be exhilarated by the miracle of birth.

As my son dozed on his father's bare knees and my eyelids drooped with exhaustion, the servants entered to light the lamps. The king—David—stood and apologized for being selfish and keeping me from my rest. He gently placed the baby in the nurse's arms, touched my cheek, and left my room.

But while the door stood open, I glimpsed him in the hallway, where he stopped to say something to Abigail, one of the older wives. She lit up with an answering smile, then threw her arms around him. He drew her into an embrace, and then the door closed and blocked the sight.

Odd, that the thought of David with another woman had the power to rouse a spark of jealousy within me. But exhaustion doused it as I crawled into bed and curled up on my side.

I was not in love with David, so why should I care if he loved Abigail? I should be grateful that he had other wives to satisfy his needs. I had a prince and the prophet's promise, and I needed nothing else.

CHAPTER TWENTY-ONE

NATHAN

OVER THE COURSE OF SEVERAL MONTHS, I watched several significant events unfold. I stood outside Uriah's house and heard the ululations of mourning for the Hittite warrior. His wife, his wife's nurse, his sister-in-law, his wife's grandfather, and his neighbors keened mightily for the murdered soldier. I did not know how sincerely Bathsheba grieved for her husband—did she mourn him out of true sorrow or out of some secret guilt?—but her eyes remained red and swollen throughout the seven days of mourning.

At the end of that week, I watched as David's emissaries came to the house to escort Uriah's wife to the palace. Hidden in a sheltered alcove, I saw Bathsheba embrace the older woman and her young sister before surrendering to the guards and walking up the hill to her new home. Word spread like a wildfire: David the king had taken Bathsheba, widow of Uriah the Hittite, to be his wife. Some people said he married her to honor Uriah's sacrifice and provide for the warrior's widow. Others said he only wanted to honor his counselor Ahithophel, the woman's grandfather. Widows subsisted on charity unless they had sons or brothers to support them, and Bathsheba had neither. But as one of the king's wives, neither she nor the two women she left behind would have to worry about being fed, clothed, and sheltered. David, the people assured themselves, was a most generous king.

Seven months later, two days after the birth of Bathsheba's child, Adonai woke me with a command. The time for confrontation had come.

I dressed in a clean tunic, picked up my staff, and walked the road to the palace, my steps heavy with trepidation. On many occasions I had made the journey with no greater intention than observing the king's court, but this time Adonai had given me a message and a mission. This time I would speak HaShem's words, and the result would depend upon the receptivity of David's heart.

I found the king's throne room filled with the usual mix of travelers, dignitaries, supplicants, and counselors. A festive air permeated the gathering, for the king was accepting gifts and congratulations on the birth of his newborn son. I shouldered my way through the center of the assembly, then stopped before the king and brought my staff down, hard, on the stone floor. David looked up from the parchment he'd been reading, and his eyes widened when he recognized me. "Prophet?" His gaze flicked at me, then he smiled at young Absalom, who sat on a cushion at the king's feet. "Have you come to congratulate us on the most recent son born into our household?"

I slammed my staff down again. In the past, David had sent messengers to fetch Bathsheba, to recall Uriah, and to escort his new wife to the palace. Now God had sent a messenger to David, and I would not be taken lightly. "Adonai has commanded me to speak to you."

Confusion flitted in the king's dark eyes. He set his parchment aside and gripped an armrest of his throne. "I am listening."

Praying that I had chosen the right approach to the hard rebuke I had to deliver, I drew a deep breath and tightened my hold on my staff. "In a certain city there lived two men, one rich, the other poor."

At this innocuous beginning, as I spoke of ordinary men in ordinary circumstances, David relaxed and slouched into a more comfortable position. He crossed one leg over the other and watched me, his eyes alight with speculation. As king, he was obligated to settle disputes and administer justice, so he probably thought I had disrupted the festivities in order to present a case for judgment.

"The rich man had vast flocks and herds," I continued, sensing the invisible circle that had formed around me, a holy space no man would dare crowd. "But the poor man had nothing except for one little ewe lamb, which he had bought and reared. It had grown up with him and his family; it ate from his plate, drank from his cup, lay in his lap—it was like a daughter to him."

"I had a lamb like that once," the king interrupted, smiling at his son Amnon, who leaned against the back of his father's chair. "When I kept the lambs for my father, one became quite attached to me."

I shot the king a reproachful look. If he had only taken Bathsheba into his harem, my story would have ended with the rich man placing the ewe lamb in his own flock. But David had done far more, and Adonai was about to reveal his sin to the world.

I drew a breath and continued: "One day a traveler visited the rich man, and instead of choosing an animal from his own flock to cook for his visitor, he stole the poor man's lamb, slaughtered it, and boiled it for his guest."

Gripping my staff, I waited for the story to take hold. A lamb was only a lamb, but the context of the tale should prick David's repressed conscience.

I did not have to wait long. Almost immediately our shepherd king's face flushed with fury. David sat upright and uncrossed his legs. "As Adonai lives, *doomed* is the man who has done this! And because he had no pity, he shall pay the poor man four times as much as he stole."

Four times? I sighed in regret, knowing that David had just pronounced his own sentence.

Every eye in the room swiveled toward me. The onlookers probably expected me to bow and thank the king for his righteous verdict, but I had not entered the king's chamber to invoke a judgment against other men. David had rightly responded with rage, but he had missed the truth in my tale.

My gaze locked on David's. "*You* are the man."

Adonai's words filled the hush, and every man present, even the king's young sons, remained motionless as my voice reverberated in the room. "Here is what Adonai, the God of Israel, says," I said, not taking my eyes from the king's. "'I anointed you king over Israel. I rescued you from the power of Saul. I gave you your master's house and your master's wives to embrace. I have given you the house of Israel and the house of Judah. And if that had been too little, I would have added to you a lot more.'"

David stared, his face as pale as a death mask.

"So why," I continued, "have you shown such contempt for the word of Adonai and done what He sees as evil? You murdered Uriah the Hittite with the sword and took his wife as your own; you put him to death with the sword of the Ammonites. Now, therefore, the sword will never leave your house because you have shown contempt for Adonai and taken the wife of Uriah the Hittite as your own wife. Here is what Adonai says: 'I will generate evil against you out of your own household. I will take your wives before your very eyes and give them to your neighbor; he will go to bed with your wives, and everyone will know about it. For you did this secretly, but I will do this before all Israel in broad daylight.'"

Someone behind me gasped as the guard nearest David raised his spear. All the king had to do was nod in my direction, and I would be murdered as surely as Uriah had been.

I waited, a chill in the pit of my stomach, until David lifted his hand and glanced at the guard, wordlessly commanding him to lower his weapon. Emboldened by this positive sign, I walked forward, climbed the steps, and came within inches of the king's ear. "Through the power of the Spirit," I whispered, staring at the guard stationed behind the king, "I watched you spy on her."

"I wanted her," David said.

"*Every* man wants her," I answered, barely able to bridle the resentment in my voice. "But they do not take her."

I backed away, leaving him with his head propped on his hand, his eyes closed.

I returned to my original position and waited to see what effect my words would have on the king. After a moment, amid a silence that was the holding of a hundred breaths, David shuddered. "I . . . have sinned against Adonai."

The hush in the room deepened as the king's words echoed over the assembled court. I could almost hear the snap of breaking hearts and the crack of shattering illusions.

David had committed his sin in private, but within hours all Jerusalem would know about it. From this moment on, the king who had been much loved and much celebrated would be viewed with wariness. With this murderous act, David had proven himself to be like any other man—and worse than many. But with his confession, he had demonstrated that he remained a man who loved and revered HaShem.

I drew a deep breath and softened my voice. "Adonai also has taken away your sin, so you will not die. However, because by this act you have so greatly blasphemed the Lord, the child born to you by Bathsheba . . . must perish."

I bowed my head as the awareness of God's heavy judgment descended on the crowd. I felt the heaviness too, but in a different context: David deserved judgment in his sin, but Bathsheba, the ewe lamb, had not transgressed against Adonai or her husband.

Yet she, too, would suffer.

My throat ached with unhappiness as I turned in a circle of stunned silence and left the palace.

CHAPTER TWENTY-TWO

BATHSHEBA

I WAS NOT PRESENT when my childhood acquaintance confronted the king, but I felt the effects of the prophet's pronouncement almost immediately. I caught servants whispering to each other in my presence, and when I looked up, they fell silent. From my doorway I spotted several concubines buzzing while they stared toward my chamber, though no one would tell me what had set their tongues to wagging.

Later that afternoon, while the baby napped, I strolled into the harem courtyard and approached Michal, Saul's daughter and David's first wife. My handmaid had told me that Michal lived for her children, five strapping boys who had been born to her sister, Merab. When Merab died giving birth to a sixth son, who perished as well, her grieving husband, Adriel, brought her five surviving sons to Michal, knowing they would lack for nothing if reared in David's household.

Michal was several years older than me and appeared about as friendly as a porcupine, but since she did not seem close to any of the other wives, I thought she might be willing to engage in conversation.

I found her by the fountain with a harp in her lap. Though she had to sense my presence, she did not look up right away. Finally she lifted her head and took in the paunch at my soft belly with one raking glance. "So you are Bathsheba," she said, turning her attention back to her harp. "The woman so irresistible that David was willing to earn a curse from Adonai in order to take her."

My heart began to pound in an unsteady rhythm. "Did you say *curse*?"

"Have you not heard?" A twisted smile crept to her lips. "Half the kingdom is whispering the news. David the king, who has more wives than he could possibly handle, stole the wife of Uriah the Hittite and murdered the inconvenient husband. For his sin, Adonai has cursed him with violence and"—she looked again at my swollen belly—"other unfortunate events."

I sank onto the empty bench next to her. "So everyone knows?"

"Everyone knows, everyone is horrified, everyone grieves for the poor, cursed king." She pressed her hand on the vibrating harp strings and eyed me with a sharp look. "I will always be mystified by David's ability to triumph over dire circumstances. He can walk through a river of cattle dung and smell of blossoms on the opposite shore. He will pay for his sin, of course—Adonai's prophet has declared it. You will pay, too. But a month from now the people will have forgotten about David's sin and feel nothing but compassion for him. The common people will always love him, because he behaves more like a shepherd than a king."

Her words evoked the memory of David dancing in the streets as priests carried the Ark to the Tabernacle. Soon after the event, my father had confided a corollary to the story. Michal, who observed the king from a palace window, had upbraided him for behaving like an exhibitionist in front of twittering servants and slave girls. Infuriated, the king retorted that Adonai chose him over her father, so if he wanted to make himself even *more* contemptible, the slave girls would honor him for doing so.

At the time I heard the story, I wondered if Michal and the king would ever mend their relationship, but one look in her glittering eyes informed me they had not.

"Everyone loves David, but David does not love everyone." Michal lowered her harp and propped her chin on her hand. "Tell me, do you love David? All the other wives seem to."

I caught my breath. Lately my emotions had veered crazily from grief to fear, from loneliness to joy over the baby's birth, but I had spent so much time mourning that I could scarcely remember the happiness of love. "In truth—" I struggled for the right words—"I do not know him."

Michal lifted a brow, then pressed her lips together. "He sleeps with you but does not speak to you? He is even more brutish than I realized."

"He has never been brutish," I hastened to add. "When . . . the child was conceived, he promised he would not hurt me. And he does not sleep with me. Not anymore."

"Ah, the singular vanity of men. They take you for their pleasure, thrust and stab, and then walk away without realizing they've left fatal wounds on your heart." She sat silent for a long moment, her eyes focused on the fountain's flowing water. At last she turned to me. "I know you have been wronged—and no one else will tell you, especially not the king—but this morning the prophet not only predicted violence for the house of David, but some are saying the king's action will result in four deaths."

Her words tumbled and twisted in my thoughts. "Why would anyone say such a horrible thing?"

Michal managed a tremulous smile. "Because after the prophet told his story, David declared that the guilty party should repay the debt fourfold, and the king's word is law. The reparation for one murdered husband equals four deaths from David's household . . . including your son, I am sorry to say."

A confusing rush of panic and dread whirled inside me, but Michal's eyes were open and honest, her countenance free from malice.

She reached for my damp hand and held it tight. "I know," she whispered, leaning closer. "I know how it feels to suffer for a man's foolishness. My father could have established a dynasty, but he disobeyed Adonai and forfeited his future. David could have given me children, but when I rebuked him for behaving like a fool, he shut me out. Now David can't stand to look at me. But better to remain barren, I think, than to have a son and watch him die because his father sinned against HaShem."

My lips parted in horror. Through all the sadness and pain, I had dared to trust the prophecy, to believe that my child would be a special blessing from God and a gift to Israel. But if my baby died . . . had all my pain and grief been for nothing?

My hand fell to my empty belly.

"The king loves children, as do I." Michal's gaze moved to some interior field of vision I couldn't see. "Though he ignores the sons I am raising, he adores his boys and dotes on his daughter. I have never been able to bring him much joy, but the other wives have succeeded remarkably well."

My thoughts continued to jostle and shove, pushing aside opinions I'd formed long ago. I used to believe that HaShem never repented of His decisions, but now . . . "Isn't it possible," I sputtered, "perhaps . . . couldn't Adonai change His mind about my baby? Could the prophet return and tell us that HaShem has reconsidered? If the king confesses and repents, perhaps—"

"David has confessed," Michal said. "He confessed his wrong-

doing before the entire court. The prophet said Adonai has taken
away David's sin, yet forgiveness comes at a price. Without the
shedding of blood . . ." She shrugged, then gave my hand a final
squeeze.

As I sat in stunned silence, Michal lifted her harp and ran her
nails across the strings. "I remember another time the prophet
Nathan paid David a visit. He said many things that day, but I
particularly remember him saying that if David strayed from the
ways of the Lord, Adonai would punish him with a rod and blows."
She cut me a quick glance. "Welcome to the king's house, where
we all bear David's bruises."

Strumming her harp, she began to hum a melancholy tune. Tears
flowed over my cheeks as I listened. Finally I stood and went back
to my room, where the baby had begun to cry.

Chapter Twenty-Three
NATHAN

THE MAN ON THE DUSTY PATH was no mere messenger; the cut and ornamentation of his garment signaled an officer of some distinction. As he drew closer to the spot where I sat under my fig tree, I recognized the sharp features of the king's chief counselor.

"Greetings, Nathan." Ahithophel stopped on the path and granted me a dignified nod. "I trust you are well?"

I tilted my head to study him. The king's counselor had never stopped at my house, even though he passed it whenever he journeyed to his farm in Giloh. What could possibly have motivated this visit?

I stood to show respect. "I am well. Are you?"

Ahithophel pointed toward an empty stool under my fig tree. "May I?"

"Far be it from me to deny any man a bit of shade on a hot day."

Ahithophel sank to the stool, then exhaled and wiped a trail of perspiration from his forehead. "I am sorry to trouble you," he said, pulling a scroll from the leather bag hanging from his shoulder, "but I wanted you to read this and tell me if Adonai might be swayed by these sincere words from a repentant heart."

I frowned, not understanding, but after unwrapping the scroll I recognized David's handwriting. I had seen his writing before, on parchments for the priests. The king had an exceptional talent for poetry and music.

I sat on my bench. "I cannot speak for Adonai unless He speaks to me first."

"Understood."

"And I have already proclaimed the Lord's judgment on David's household."

"Indeed. I was in the throne room when you spoke to the king. But the king and his wife love their new baby, and I would have you read this and tell me if Adonai might be willing to honor a truly contrite heart."

I skimmed the text. "The king wrote these words himself?"

"With his own hand." Ahithophel crossed his arms. "I will wait while you read."

I lifted the scroll.

> God, in your grace, have mercy on me;
> in your great compassion, blot out my crimes.
> Wash me completely from my guilt,
> and cleanse me from my sin.
> For I know my crimes,
> my sin confronts me all the time.
>
> Against you, you only, have I sinned
> and done what is evil from your perspective;
> so that you are right in accusing me
> and justified in passing sentence.

True, I was born guilty,
was a sinner from the moment my mother conceived me.
Still, you want truth in the inner person;
so make me know wisdom in my inmost heart.

Create in me a clean heart, God;
renew in me a resolute spirit.
Don't thrust me away from your presence,
don't take your *Ruach Kodesh* away from me.
Restore my joy in your salvation,
and let a willing spirit uphold me.
Then I will teach the wicked your ways,
and sinners will return to you.

Rescue me from the guilt of shedding blood,
HaShem, God of my salvation!
Then my tongue will sing
about your righteousness—
Adonai, open my lips;
then my mouth will praise you.

For you don't want sacrifices, or I would give them;
you don't take pleasure in burnt offerings.
My sacrifice to God is a broken spirit;
God, you won't spurn a broken, chastened heart.

How blessed are those whose offense is forgiven,
those whose sin is covered!
How blessed those to whom Adonai imputes no guilt,
in whose spirit is no deceit!

The writing continued, but I lowered the scroll and turned to
my companion. "The king wrote all of this?"

Ahithophel nodded. "He has been in mourning since your visit.
That evening his baby became ill, and the king retired to his chamber when he heard the news. He spent the night on the floor in

prayer. We encouraged him to rise the next morning, but he would not be persuaded. He remains in his bedchamber, eating nothing and drinking only water, but he writes. I'm sure he's written other things, but these are the writings he gave me to share with you . . . in the hope that Adonai would change His mind and save the child."

I drew a deep breath and turned the scroll, closing it. "It would seem our king has been thoroughly chastened. You must be happy to know he has repented of his sin. He had grown complacent in his relationship with Adonai, but I don't think he will take the Lord's favor for granted again."

Ahithophel's frown deepened as he took the scroll from me. "But he caused Uriah's death, and the Law demands that anyone who murders must die. For HaShem made men in His own image—"

I lifted my hand, cutting him off. "Adonai has also said that David will *not* die, but will feel the consequences of his actions. It is not for us to second-guess what HaShem will do."

"It is not enough." Ahithophel leaned forward and looked at me, dark fury glowing in his eyes. "If a star should fall from the sky tonight and destroy all the king's wives and children, it would not be punishment enough to atone for what he has done. He killed a loyal servant and ruined a virtuous woman."

I recoiled, startled to discover such a depth of anger in the older man. In the king's court Ahithophel was a model of rectitude, with steady nerves, a humble attitude, and an implacable disposition. I had never seen this aspect of his nature . . . nor, I suspected, had the king.

"Adonai judges the heart," I said quietly. "And the words written in that scroll seem to indicate that David's repentance is sincere. You should accept the will of Adonai and support our king, for HaShem has promised him an eternal dynasty."

A thunderous scowl darkened the counselor's brow, and he looked away. His anger resonated in the space around us, and only after several moments of silence did he manage to calm himself enough to speak again.

"Now you understand my dilemma," he said, staring into the distance. "The prophet Samuel gave our family a prophecy: Bathsheba's child will be a great man who will do great things for Israel. This infant boy ought to be our king, not that murderous son of Jesse. With a wise counselor to guide him until he reaches the age of maturity, this baby boy could be the greatest king the world has ever known."

I stared wordlessly at the king's counselor, my heart pounding as a memory washed through me, pebbling my skin like the touch of the *Ruach Kodesh*. I remembered my master's voice and a baby girl, but had not considered the prophecy in years. Yet here it was, rising as a threat to David and the throne of Israel.

Ahithophel did not understand. But he would.

I closed my eyes, waiting for some word from Adonai, and finally it came: *Send him away.*

I lifted my head. "Adonai wants you to return to your home. He has already spoken in this matter, and His word will be fulfilled."

Ahithophel looked at me, astonishment on his face, then snorted softly and stood. "Thank you for your opinion."

He dropped the scroll into his leather bag and walked away without once looking back.

Chapter Twenty-Four
BATHSHEBA

ON THE THIRD DAY OF OUR SON'S LIFE, only a few hours after Nathan's visit to David's throne room, the king and I sat together in my room. Without warning, the baby at my breast stopped nursing, vomited, and turned blue. In a cold panic I screamed for the midwife while David sent for his physician. As we waited, I patted the baby's back, trying to force the sickness out of him. David prostrated himself on the floor, then stretched out his arms and prayed aloud, begging Adonai to have mercy on our son.

The king's attendants urged David to return to his own chamber, but the midwife remained with me, holding a nearly silent vigil over my pale son, who struggled for every breath.

Over the following days, my baby's skin grew bluer and blotchier while the whites of his eyes turned yellow. I remained by his side, letting him clasp my finger or holding him close to my breast in the hope I could bring some comfort to such a small and vulnerable soul. More than once I caught him watching me, silent and helpless, with his increasingly yellowed eyes.

Servants who visited my chamber reported that David, the king of all Israel, lay on the floor of his room, already mourning the death of our son. His counselors pleaded with him to rise and eat, but he refused. The business of the kingdom stalled while the king remained in his chamber, and his advisors worried that he would be too grief-stricken to govern if the child perished.

By the seventh day, our precious son had little life left in him. I held him in my arms and gently ran the back of my finger over his cheek until his breathing slowed and stopped. When I was certain he would never breathe again, I sent my servant to tell the king.

With my sad vigil at an end, Michal later told me, the royal advisors huddled outside the king's chamber, afraid to give him the terrible news. "He wouldn't listen to reason while the child was ill," they murmured, "so what drastic thing will he do when we tell him the child is dead?"

But David heard them whispering. He opened his door and regarded them with a weary look. "Is the child dead?"

As one, they nodded.

David closed his door, washed himself, put on lotions, and changed out of his rumpled clothing. Leaving his stunned officials in a bewildered huddle, he left his chamber and walked to the Tabernacle. After offering a sacrifice of praise and thanksgiving, he returned to the palace and asked for his dinner.

"His advisors and servants were amazed," Michal said. "They couldn't understand why David was inconsolable while the baby was sick, and calm after he died. David told them that he'd wept and fasted because he hoped Adonai would be gracious and let his son live. But once a child has died, what more is to be done? David told them, 'I shall go to him, but he will not return to me.'"

I must have looked shocked, for Michal squeezed my hand.

"David is the most pragmatic of men. Prone to intense mood swings, yes, yet immensely practical. He prays, and then he accepts Adonai's will, whatever that may be."

I carried Michal's story back to my empty chamber and sat on the bed, considering all that had happened in the last week. My son—the child I initially dreaded, a baby who should never have been conceived—had been born, and my hopeful heart rejoiced to hold him in my arms. I saw the same light of joy in David's eyes, and the cold place within me warmed to know that despite everything, the king wanted our child.

If the story Michal told could be trusted, David had honestly grieved for his sin and prayed for our son. Despite the brazen callousness he displayed nine months prior, the king still possessed a tender heart, one that remained sensitive to Adonai's discipline. To my knowledge, Uriah had never been brazen or cruel, but neither had he sought the Lord as earnestly as David. Uriah swore his loyalty to men, while David pledged his loyalty to HaShem.

I lay back on my pillow and felt a hot tear trickle from the corner of my eye. I had lost more than a son; I had lost faith in the prophecy that had given my life meaning and purpose. What kind of God bestows a promise and then withdraws it? Was I merely a plaything for Adonai's amusement? Did the Almighty enjoy tormenting women like me?

I wept, not only for the child I had lost but for all the hours and days I had spent trying to be the kind of woman who could raise a child intended for greatness. My mother's admonitions, my father's instruction—why had they been so foolish as to believe the prophet's words?

Their beliefs, their work, their aspirations . . . pointless! Meaningless! I had imagined myself chosen and special, but apparently I was nothing but an attractive woman who'd been brutalized by a powerful man. Since David apparently no longer found me appealing, I would be like Michal, condemned to live alone in a palace filled with people.

The thought of my loveless future drew bitter tears from some deep place behind my eyes, and I spent the rest of the night weeping.

❧

Thirty-three days after our son's birth, I took a spotless one-year-old lamb to the Tabernacle for my purification offering. And that night David the king sent for me. I went to him because I needed to confirm his conviction that we would indeed see our child again.

David invited me to sit on a cushion near the fire pit in his private chamber. Once I was settled, he sat next to me and asked what was on my mind.

I studied the fire to avoid his piercing gaze. "In truth, my lord and king, I have been thinking about our baby. I have come to believe that his death was my fault, for once I realized I was having a child, I hated him. I despised him for existing and I wanted him gone." Though I struggled to hold them back, tears began to flow again. "I thought God was punishing me, and on some nights when I couldn't sleep I went so far as to pray that he would die within my womb—"

"Bathsheba." David slid closer and tilted his head to better see my face. "You are not to torture yourself with these thoughts. The fault is not yours."

I hiccupped a sob, then looked him in the eye. "Why is it not my fault?"

"Didn't you hear what the prophet Nathan said? Before the entire court he announced the details of my sin against God. You were not to blame; I am the guilty one. Our baby died because of my sin, not yours."

I swiped tears from my cheeks. "But I was not innocent. Hate for you and the child burned hot in my heart, and I did not love him until I held him in my arms. You did wrong, I can't deny that, but Adonai could not have approved of my feelings. I questioned Him, I doubted Him—"

"The Lord is quick to forgive the repentant."

"Even when the rebel . . . even when she is angry at HaShem?"

The king's brows rose, then he smiled. "Even then. Especially then." He lowered his head to catch my gaze. "You hated me?"

I hiccupped again, then gave him the truth. "Very much."

He nodded. "Your hatred was not unrighteous. I sinned against you, Bathsheba, and I will understand if you can't forgive me. You wouldn't be the first wife to hate me, but you might be the first to . . ." He shifted his attention to the dancing flames, which painted his face with flickering light and shadows. "I would like for us to be friends. I know I cannot force you to love a man who has injured you so grievously, but I know who you are and I am honored to have you as my wife. I would be greatly pleased if you would give me an opportunity to be your husband."

Blinking my remaining tears away, I studied his profile. How did he know who I was? And what, exactly, did he expect of me? I was his wife and his subject already; my heart and body were his to command.

"My lord and king—"

"Please." He turned to me, his right hand lifting to thumb away the trace of a tear on my cheek. "When we are together like this, let me be David, and you shall be Bathsheba."

I stiffened, torn between a desire to lean into his palm and the urge to stand and run. "David." I swallowed hard. "I am your wife already."

"As is Michal," he said, his brow lifting, "yet she no longer desires my company, so I do not force her to endure it. I have wives aplenty, but I have few confidantes."

An image flitted through my mind, the memory of David embracing Abigail in the hallway outside my room. She was one of his confidantes, surely, because the connection between them had been almost palpable.

"I have a question," I said, strengthening my voice, "because I must find solace in my grief. I have heard that you said our son could not return to you, but you would go to him. How do you know this? That child was my reason for living, so I must know if I will see him again. I must be sure that Adonai's word is truth."

David's eyes widened, with an odd expression coming over his face, one of eagerness and tenderness mingled together. "You are the first woman to ever ask me such a question," he said, smiling. "But consider this. After Samuel died, Saul visited a witch in order to summon Saul's spirit from the place of the dead. We are commanded not to do such things, and Samuel rebuked Saul for the act that brought them together again. But Samuel remained *alive*, though not on earth. HaShem has set eternity in our hearts, so we know death is not the end. It cannot be.

"You can be sure, Bathsheba." David slipped an arm around me, and my skin tingled at his touch. "You can be sure of Adonai, and you can be sure of me. From this day forward, I promise to be a good husband to you. I will treat you with kindness, compassion, and gentleness. And if Adonai blesses us with another son . . ."

The words had barely entered my ears when a realization followed. David was speaking kindly to me; he did not regard me with disdain. If he could be trusted, if Adonai could be trusted, I could have *another son*.

My stomach knotted with anticipation. "Yes?"

"I will name your son as my heir. Before you and Adonai, I make this solemn vow."

He leaned toward me, but I placed my hand against his chest

in order to search his eyes. They did not burn as they had on our first meeting, but neither were they senseless from too much wine. David's gaze brimmed with sincerity and truth, so perhaps my prophecy would be fulfilled with another son, one who was not yet born.

I moved my hand to his neck as, with a soft sigh, the king settled his mouth on mine.

⁓✣⁓

Throughout the next several months, the king showered me with gifts. A heavy gold chain one week, a silk tunic and robe the next. He must have asked a servant to discover my favorite flower, for a bowl of lotus blossoms appeared on my dressing table one morning and every day afterward.

I hesitated to embrace these gifts because I knew the other wives would notice if I exhibited any signs of special favor. So the flowers remained in my room, and I wore the new garments and jewelry only when the king sent for me. He seemed to take pleasure from seeing me in silks and jewels, and to my surprise I took pleasure in our evenings together.

By the time I recognized the signs of pregnancy, I had come to terms with my marriage and my position in the palace. For reasons only He understood, Adonai had placed me in the king's house to bear a son who would do great things for Israel. The prophecy did not involve my first son, the child who suffered the consequences of David's sin, but my second. In His mercy, HaShem did not doubt me as quickly as I had doubted Him.

When the first three months of my pregnancy had passed, I answered the king's summons with a light step. We dined together in his chamber, but afterward, instead of following him to his bed, I took his hand and led him to the cushions around the fire pit.

"What's this?" His brow arched as he followed me. "Are you cold?"

"Not at all." I waited until he sat, then sat next to him. "I wanted to give you some news."

He reached out and wound a strand of my hair around his finger. "Do you want something? I will do my best to grant any request."

"This isn't exactly a request—at least, not yet." I exhaled in a rush, then caught another quick breath. "I am carrying another child. And if I bear a son, I beg you to remember your promise."

David grinned at me, joy shining in his eyes and bubbling in his laugh. "Adonai be praised for His goodness and mercy. He has given us another chance. And this son—this baby—will be king after me."

He clutched my shoulders, drew me to him, and kissed me, a gesture that began with joyful abandon and ended on a more serious note. Before the king's passion could fully ignite, however, I pulled away and pressed my fingers to his mouth. I wanted to deliver a bit of a speech, so I lowered my gaze and let the words tumble out. "Now that I carry another child," I told him, "you needn't send for me so often. I know you've lavished gifts and attention on me because you wanted to atone for the past. That is finished now, so you no longer have to pretend. I am quite content, and I wanted you to know that."

When David did not answer immediately, I lifted my gaze to search his face. The leaping light in his eyes had gone out.

"I see." David released me and turned to face the fire. When he spoke again, his voice seemed to come from a great distance. "So you want nothing else from me?"

"Only your grace and continued kindness, my lord."

"Then that is what you shall have." He tossed a polite smile over his shoulder. "Thank you for sharing your news. You may return to the harem."

I blinked, stunned by his swift change in attitude, but if he no longer wanted me . . .

I stood and bowed, then turned for the door. As I reached the threshold, he called out one final command: "Before you return to your chamber, send Abigail to me."

I paused, nodded, and hurried off to obey.

CHAPTER TWENTY-FIVE
BATHSHEBA

A YEAR AFTER DAVID AND I PAID A HORRIBLE PRICE for Uriah's death, I gave birth to David's tenth son, a baby every bit as handsome as my first. This chubby, well-formed child was ruddy like his father and exhibited no signs of illness. David and I rejoiced, and at the baby's circumcision on the eighth day I named him Solomon, meaning *his replacement.* David might have thought I was referring to the baby we lost, but I had proffered the name while thinking of Uriah.

Nathan attended our child's naming ceremony, and a cold hand slid over my spine when I saw the prophet approach the king's throne. I wanted to welcome my childhood friend, but I couldn't help wondering if he had received another dire message from Adonai.

The prophet caught my gaze and smiled with the easy grace that had always been a part of his nature. He came forward and lowered his head to study our newborn son. Then he looked at David and spoke in a voice pitched for our ears alone. "So says Adonai: 'Because you have killed many men in the battles you have fought, and since you have shed so much blood in my sight, you will not be the one to build a Temple to honor my name. But this son—this *Solomon*—will be a man of peace. I will give him peace with his enemies in all the surrounding lands. I will give peace and quiet to Israel during his reign. He is the one who will build a Temple to honor my name. He will be my son, and I will be his father. And I will secure the throne of his kingdom over Israel forever.'"

A thrill raced through my soul. Nathan had uttered the confirmation I had waited a lifetime to hear. *This* son, this baby boy, would not only do great things for Israel, he would be a great king. For this moment, I had been born and had waited a lifetime.

David silently absorbed the prophet's private message as Nathan looked into my eyes and raised his voice for the entire assembly to hear: "So says the Lord: 'This child is much loved of God.'" His voice boomed through the crowded hall. "'And I will give him another name: he shall be called Jedidiah, or *beloved of the Lord*, for Adonai's sake.'"

I felt the truth as if the Lord himself had whispered in my ear. I knew it as certainly as I knew the sun would rise on the morrow. I knew it down to the marrow of my bones and the innermost recesses of my heart. Samuel had not prophesied of my first son when he glimpsed the future at my mother's purification ceremony. He had spoken of this tenth son of David's. Solomon would be king—not because I schemed or plotted or flattered but because Adonai had willed it years before this baby's birth.

I remained silent, awed and thrilled by my new understanding. Before I came to the palace, I had lived a quietly prideful life, confident I had been somehow elevated from the women around me. Samuel's prophecy had filled me with an unmerited sense of worth, but HaShem destroyed my false self-image when He took my first son. For weeks I mourned the death of my self-centered dreams, but David had helped restore my faith in Adonai and His truth.

Though I knew I held the son of the prophecy in my arms, I would not consider him to be something I deserved, but an un-merited blessing from the Almighty. And because I lived in a harem teeming with jealous, suspicious women, I would remain quiet and do my best to raise my son to be a good man and a great king.

I would cling to God's promise until the crown rested on Solomon's head. Not because he deserved it more than any of David's other sons, but because Adonai loved him as He loved David. Nathan had assured me that my son would be *beloved of the Lord*.

As a ripple of approval passed over the assembled guests, I looked at the king's other children to see how they felt about their new brother. Eleven-year-old Amnon, ten-year-old Tamar, and nine-year-old Absalom stood closest to us, but only Tamar looked at the baby with any curiosity. The boys seemed bored and eager to be away.

But pretty little Tamar leaned closer and gave the baby her finger, which he promptly pulled to his mouth. She giggled softly and grinned while I gave her my warmest smile.

Unless I was sorely mistaken, Tamar would grow up to be a *tob* woman.

⌁

While my Shlomo was still a nursing infant, Joab sent a message to the king, reporting that he had captured the water supply for the city of Rabbah. The Ammonite stronghold, long under siege, had been severely compromised, so if David wanted the honor of capturing the city, he should assemble the rest of the army and hurry to Rabbah for what would certainly be the final battle.

The king sent for the baby and me to kiss us before he left. He did not summon any of the other wives, and I suspected that he thought of me only because Uriah lay buried somewhere in the fields outside that city. I couldn't blame David for wanting to be finished with this chapter of his life. God had forgiven him; now David wanted to conquer both the city and his past.

The king and his army rode out and merged with Joab's forces. Together, the armies of David and Joab fought against the men of the beleaguered capital and captured it. David entered the town, killed King Hanun, and took Hanun's crown from his head, a ceremonial action that proved to be unusual because the gold crown, set with dozens of precious stones, weighed more than seventy-five pounds. The warriors took a great deal of plunder from the vanquished city and set the survivors to work producing bricks, iron tools, and timber for Israel.

The people of Jerusalem would sing about the victory for years to come. Standing on the palace rooftop to watch the triumphant army's return to Jerusalem, I shifted the baby in my arms and realized that if I were still Uriah's wife, I would have spent the past two years waiting for his return. I would not have my beautiful baby, but neither would I have plumbed the depths of heartache and despair.

I shook my head and let a curtain fall on my imaginings. Life was a corridor with countless possibilities, and only Adonai knew the doors we would pass through. Sometimes He gave His prophets glimpses of the future, and sometimes they shared those visions and warnings with us.

Ever since my son's naming ceremony, I had been wondering why the prophet Nathan chose to lower his voice when he declared that Solomon would build the Temple and rule over Israel in a time of peace. My barely defeated pride wanted the world to know that my baby would rise above his brothers to rule the kingdom, but my conscience reminded me that I would be no better than the other wives if I flaunted my son's future.

And such an announcement might put my son's life in danger. David was a man of battle, and Israel was still surrounded by warring nations. If any of them came against Israel during my son's childhood, they would not only try to kill David but the heir apparent, as well.

Until David died, my task would be to remain silent and guard the future king with my life.

When David realized he would not be the one to build the Temple, he focused on expanding his palace, a project that became necessary as his family grew. Builders knocked down the wall surrounding the harem and built a small house for each wife, where she lived with her children and servants.

By the time I gave birth to Shammua and Shobab, David had arranged for me to have much larger accommodations. I loved being a mother and couldn't help taking pleasure in the knowledge that I had given David more sons than any other wife. As I suckled my beautiful twins, I began to understand that being a *tob* woman had advantages I hadn't realized. The king was attracted to beauty, and that attraction resulted in the blessing of children.

My mother was wiser than I had realized.

My fourth pregnancy was not as easy as the first three. My ankles swelled like an elephant's, and the summer heat drained my energy. After a difficult labor, I gave birth to another son—my fifth—and at his naming ceremony I smiled at a friend in the crowd and announced that he would be called Nathan.

Once the royal children reached the age of maturity, they were given homes outside the palace compound. By the time Solomon

reached his sixth year, Amnon, Absalom, Adonijah, and Shephatiah had houses in Jerusalem. Tamar remained with her mother
and would do so until the king arranged a royal marriage for her.

Though I was surrounded by noise and bluster in the harem, I
learned to be grateful for aspects of my new life. In the difficult
weeks after Uriah's death I would never have imagined that I might
come to admire David, but Nathan's public rebuke had indelibly
changed the king.

Before David's sin, Michal told me, he had been brash, cocky, and
frequently wild in his actions and conversations. After his confession and repentance, his brashness evaporated. The king remained
creative, poetic, musical, and unconventional, but Michal believed
he no longer considered himself infallible. Though HaShem had
granted David an eternal dynasty, the king now seemed to realize
that God's covenant promise did not make him immune to failure.
More important—and this the king confided to me himself—David
learned that his private sins had the power to inflict great suffering
on the people he loved.

Whenever I answered an invitation to join the king in his private
chamber, our conversations almost always centered on Solomon, an
amazing child and the light of my life. Though my judgment may
not have been impartial, I considered Shlomo the king's most attractive child, but David clearly favored Absalom, who had inherited
Maacah's thick hair and regal features. Maacah's daughter, Tamar,
was without question the most beautiful female in the palace. As
I watched her beauty increase with every passing week, I worried
about her and prayed that David would pay more attention to her,
and to all his children.

As David's children outgrew their interest in playing around
their father's throne, he left them to their tutors and focused on
the younger ones, who still loved to sit and marvel at his stories.
The king, I noticed, spent time with his children as long as they

looked at him with awe. When they had matured enough to realize their father was as human as any other man, he let them move into their own homes and rarely sent anything but generic invitations to mingle among the guests and dignitaries at court. Once grown, his sons were given the title of "personal priest to the king," but I never saw any of them participate in priestly duties or even visit the Tabernacle except during religious festivals.

The only royal wife who cared to befriend me was Michal. I'm not sure why we grew close. At times I thought we bonded because we had both suffered despair and grief on David's account. Neither of us hid the fact that we guarded our hearts where David was concerned.

Michal had never borne a child, but she had filled her life with the joys of mothering her five nephews. "I see my sister in each of them," she told me. "Elan, the oldest, has her smile. Boas has her nose and her sense of humor, while Hananel sings with her voice, the most beautiful thing I have ever heard. Phineas has her long feet—not a bad thing, since he has grown taller than his brothers— and little Ziv has her eyes. Every time I look at him, I see Merab smiling back at me."

Michal lived in one of the largest suites in the harem, and the space was constantly strewn with clothing, toys, and dusty sandals. The clutter would have driven me mad, yet she seemed to delight in the mayhem created by five active boys. I had active boys too, though mine were younger and calmer.

"HaShem has been good to me," she confided one day as we sat in the garden. "Just as Adonai opened unloved Leah's womb, He has opened my house and filled it with sons."

"How do you ever get any rest?" I ducked as Ziv threw a ball at Phineas and narrowly missed my head. "Do they ever get quiet?"

"Only at night." She gave me a rare smile. "Sometimes I sit awake and listen to the sound of them breathing, all in unison. They are close, these boys. When they first came to me, so soon after the loss of their mother, I wondered if any of us would ever be happy again. But our hearts healed, and we learned to lean on each other. Someday, when I am old and tired, I know they will bring their wives and children to visit me. Who knows? Perhaps David will allow me to go live with one of them, or maybe I will journey from Elan's house to Hananel's, then to Phineas's, Boas's, and Ziv's. I who never bore a child will be the most blessed mother in Israel."

I smiled at Boas, who had stopped to show my little Nathan a toy cart. Nathan had no idea what to do with it but clapped in excitement, a reaction that brought a wide grin to Boas's face.

"They are good boys," I told Michal. "You are blessed indeed."

On the afternoons we sat and watched our boys play together, Michal told me she had been madly in love with David when she first met him. "I wanted desperately to marry him," she said one afternoon, "but my father had heard about Samuel anointing David to be the next king, so Father didn't trust him. When David became renowned as a warrior, my father feared David would become more popular with the people than their king. So Father used my love against me and told David he could marry me if he brought one hundred Philistine foreskins as a dowry. He hoped David would be killed, and any other man probably would have been. But David could do no wrong in those days, for Adonai empowered him. He gave my father the foreskins of two hundred slain Philistines, so the king had to allow our marriage."

Her eyes misted at the memory. "We were happy in those days— or at least I was. The only threat to our marriage was my father's increasing paranoia, but it was enough to do damage. One night, when Father sought to kill my husband outright, I helped David slip away through an open window. I hid one of our household idols in the bed, and the next morning, when my father came to take David away, I said he was ill. The guards went barging into the room and discovered I'd deceived them. Father was furious with me, but I said what David had told me to say—that my husband had threatened my life, so I had to help him escape."

She tilted her head and looked at me, her eyes soft with the memory. "Odd, isn't it, that my father had no trouble believing that lie? I have learned that men have no difficulty believing their enemies are capable of doing what they themselves would do. If my father had actually known David—as I did, and as you do—he would have known that David could never have meant that threat. He can be fierce in battle, but he does not threaten his women."

I looked away as a blush burned my cheek. Michal had not been on the rooftop when David had me brought to him, but she did know him well. Would I ever know him that completely?

"After that," she went on, her voice flattening, "my father gave me to Palti, a man who couldn't seem to believe his good fortune in marrying a king's daughter, even if she arrived secondhand and slightly worn from wear. Palti was a good man, generous and kind, and I liked him well enough. But those were desperate times. My father became more paranoid and more intent on killing David, and as much as I wanted to spare Palti's feelings, I couldn't disguise the fact that I worried about the man I loved. The Philistines were bedeviling our army, my father was trying to protect his kingdom, and I knew the situation would not end well. When I heard that my father had visited a witch who summoned a ghost for him, I knew Saul's reign was over."

The mention of a witch strummed a shiver from me. I had heard the story from David, but still I could not believe that a king of Israel, a holy people, would resort to such a forbidden practice. "Your father really . . . I mean, he actually—"

"Samuel had died," Michal explained. "And the prophet, for better or worse, had always been my father's spiritual guide, as Father didn't seem to be able to talk to Adonai himself. So without the prophet"—she shrugged—"Father put on a disguise and sought out a witch, even though he had outlawed the practice of summoning spirits. He needed to talk to Samuel, and the witch was terrified when the prophet appeared and predicted that within a day my father and his sons would be handed over to the Philistines. They were. They died. And the entire army of Israel suffered defeat."

"Another prophecy." I whispered the words. "Sometimes I wish Adonai would remain silent about the future."

Michal's eyes became unreadable. "According to what I've heard, after Samuel's spirit disappeared, my father had no fight left in him, and that's perhaps the saddest part of the story. He had been a mighty warrior . . . once."

I remained silent, more than willing to hear more. I knew so little about my husband, but Michal's stories helped me understand who he was and where he'd come from.

"And you?" I finally asked when Michal did not continue. "You were with Palti, so how—?"

"David needed to bolster his claim to the throne." Her eyes narrowed. "Not all the tribes of Israel followed David at first, only the tribe of Judah. My brother, Ishbosheth, reigned as king over the other tribes, and Abner, a great warrior, commanded what remained of my father's army. Several times David led his men against Abner and his forces, and when he wasn't fighting he was living in Hebron with half a dozen of the women you've met here: Ahinoam, who had been one of my father's wives; Abigail, a woman he married because she seemed clever and diplomatic; Maacah, the snobby princess from Geshur; Haggith, Abital, and Eglah, who caught his eye for reasons I can't begin to understand. With so many wives, David didn't need me, but I was Saul's daughter, and his marriage to me helped legitimize his claim to the throne."

Her mouth spread into a thin smile. "Everything changed when foolish Ishbosheth charged Abner with sleeping with one of my father's women—a move that could have been interpreted as trying to push Ishbosheth from his position. Abner became enraged and went over to David's side. And David, no doubt smelling victory, said he would not negotiate with Abner unless the commander found me and returned me to David, as if I were a bushel of wheat that had been misplaced."

A cold expression settled on her face. "So Abner tracked me down, tied my hands, put me on a mule, and escorted me to David. Poor Palti followed us, weeping on the way, until Abner told him to go home, the marriage was over. When we finally arrived at David's camp, my former husband welcomed Abner warmly and sent me off to the women's tent without so much as a hello. I found myself in a tent filled with strangers, each of whom regarded me as an enemy. Only Abigail has ever had a kind word to say to me—probably because she is familiar with grief, too."

The repeated mention of Abigail piqued my interest. I barely knew the woman, but she seemed to spend a lot of time with the king. "What happened to Abigail?"

"Her little boy, Daniel, died of a fever just before David moved us to Jerusalem. She was most distraught."

"The king must have been upset, too. Abigail seems quite . . . close to him."

Michal shrugged, then reached over and squeezed my hand. "I should speak of happier things. You're probably tired of my stories."

"I'm not," I assured her. "And I'm glad you shared your history. We are all so different, and yet here we are, married to the same man."

"Adonai, they say, works in wondrous ways." She leaned forward, pushed her hair back, and looked over at me, her smile shadowed by sadness. Her lovely face wore the wrinkles of her age with serene elegance, and I realized she had to be beyond the age of child-bearing. The king would not send for her now unless he wanted her company. After hearing her story, I didn't think she particularly yearned for his.

"Do you ever miss David?" I asked.

She lifted one shoulder in a delicate shrug. "Sometimes I wish we were not estranged. I wish my father had not meddled in our marriage and given me to another man. I no longer see the sort of foolishness that caused me to hold David in contempt, and these days he seems to understand how a king should conduct himself. But no matter what he did or what he does, know this, Bathsheba: David is a better king than my father was. Because though he is far from perfect, David's heart longs to know HaShem. His love for Adonai will always set him apart from other men."

I opened my mouth to say that I hoped Solomon would grow to be like his father in that way, then I swallowed my words. I didn't want her to know that I held any particular ambition for my son.

Better that everyone in the harem think of my Shlomo as a harmless little boy.

⁓❧⁓

One afternoon in the palace garden, as Solomon studied with his tutor and I embroidered the sleeves of his new tunic, Tamar sidled over and sat beside me on my bench. She leaned forward, resting her head on her hand, then abruptly sat up and frowned. "I have to stop doing that," she said, casting me a sidelong glance. "Mother says I will ruin my face if I keep touching it."

Remembering my own mother's obsession with beauty, I resisted the urge to laugh. "Does your mother often give you beauty secrets?"

Tamar sighed. "All the time. She says my future happiness depends on marrying a rich and powerful king, so I must be *tob* beautiful lest I be scorned and left alone to grow old."

I gave her a sympathetic smile, remembering how I had been

similarly frustrated with my own mother. Samuel's prophecy should have been enough to assure her that I'd possess some degree of beauty, but she believed her duty lay in helping me be the most beautiful I could be. I was not allowed to play in casual clothing or step outside in anything but the finest garments my parents could afford. And I was never, ever to nibble my nails, pull at my hair, or play outside with bare feet.

Yet my mother wasn't the only woman concerned about her daughter's future. Almost from birth, all young girls were trained for their lives as wives and mothers. Failure to achieve either goal would be unthinkable.

"I do not think occasionally touching your face will mar your beauty," I told Tamar, keeping my voice gentle. "But perhaps I do not know as much about such things as your mother."

"Oh, but you must!" Tamar turned toward me, her brown eyes shining. "I have always thought you the most beautiful woman in the harem. Mother says I shouldn't make comparisons, but I can't help it. Your eyes are perfect, your skin flawless, and you have not allowed yourself to get fat like so many women here—"

"Thank you," I interrupted, not wanting to encourage her by saying anything that might be repeated or misconstrued. "I will agree that beauty does tend to catch a man's eye. But once you have captured his attention, then what? If you would be more than a beautiful frame, you must know how to hold a man's interest, entertain him, and understand him. If you want to bind him to your heart, you must offer a man more than mere beauty."

I stopped sewing as my thoughts returned to the previous night. David had called for me, and we spent the night talking about Shlomo, the grape harvest, and the competence of the new cook. He gave me a silk scarf, yet another gift, and then he played his harp until I fell asleep. Hardly the stuff of passionate romance, but a lovely evening nonetheless.

"So what do you offer the king?" Tamar asked, snapping me back to reality. "If beauty doesn't bind him to your heart, what does?"

I took a deep breath as a dozen different emotions pricked at my heart. David had not known me when he had me brought to his bed; I had been nothing more than a morsel to satisfy his appetite. But in the years since my arrival at the palace, we had developed an affectionate relationship. My feelings for him were not the all-encompassing and passionate love I had felt for Uriah, but neither were they simple friendship. I had seen David at his worst and at his best. I had seen him broken and triumphant. I had gone to him for strength and I had gone to offer comfort.

My feelings for David were nothing like my passionately protective love for Shlomo, but I respected him and wanted to honor him as my husband and king.

While David did not share everything with me, when he relaxed he would sometimes share stories from his youth, telling me about sights he'd seen and dreams he'd had. He did not often speak of the battles he'd fought or the men he'd killed, but he did share his poetry and his music. Sometimes, if I found him in the right mood, he would speak of HaShem with awe in his voice.

When he read verses he'd composed about his love and praise for God, I could almost see the King of the Universe high and exalted on His throne. Little wonder that I'd grown to love HaShem even more than I cared for His chosen king.

I stopped sewing and closed my eyes, sorting through the lessons I had learned since becoming David's wife. I had loved Uriah with the tumultuous passion of a bride consumed with the yearning to have her own husband, her own home, and her own children. Those yearnings had been torn away when I arrived at the palace cloaked in shame and fear. Within days I realized I would have nothing to call my own—I would share my husband with other

women, my home with other people, and my child with Adonai,
who quickly claimed him.

David and I had both been emotionally wrecked when we lost
our first baby, and in our emptiness we began a relationship that
eventually ripened to an understanding. Though he might never
admit it, I suspected that David sent for me often because we had
struck a sort of bargain. He had promised that Solomon would
inherit the throne, and I had promised not to make any demands
on him. Perhaps the feeling between us was simply affectionate
friendship, but at least we were at peace with each other.

How could I explain this to the king's starry-eyed daughter?

I sighed and folded my hands. "When you are young, Tamar, the
heart selfishly wants what it wants. When the heart grows weary
of wanting, it seeks a different kind of relationship, the support of
an understanding companion. This feeling is no less strong than
the first, but it is more constant because it is built on knowledge
and shared experience. This relationship is based on an effort to let
someone know they are important to you, that they are very dear.
For instance, do you love your mother?"

"Of course."

"Would you say she is precious to you?"

"Oh, yes."

"Then you love her. And she loves you, because you are undoubtedly dear to her."

I smiled at the understanding I'd stumbled across: I honestly
cared about David. He was precious to me because he was Solomon's father and because he seemed to delight in my company. His
delight brought me great pleasure.

"Is . . . ?" Tamar hesitated. "Is that how you feel about my father?"

I searched her eyes, curious about her choice of words. She had
not spoken of David as the king, but as "my father," so for her this
was about more than my feelings for David. This was personal.

"Why do you need to know?"

"Because Mother says I will be married to a king, so I must know how to please him. I want to be happy, but unless I please my husband, I know I will never find happiness. I look around the harem to see which wives are content and . . . well, you seem to be the only one. The others may be satisfied, but except for you and Abigail, I don't think any of them are truly happy."

I stifled a laugh, surprised by her astute observation. An atmosphere of serenity did seem to envelop Abigail, but why shouldn't it? The king sent for her even more often than he summoned me.

"You may be right," I answered, choosing my words carefully because I wasn't sure how much Tamar knew about my previous life. "I didn't like the king when I first came to the palace. I had to heal from some deep wounds, and I needed time to sort through my thoughts and feelings. But after spending time with the king and sharing experiences with him, yes, I have learned to care for him. But that sort of relationship takes time."

Tamar leaned against the back of the bench and sighed. "Oh, I hope I find that kind of love! Mother says I will be happy because I am beautiful and a king's daughter. But she is beautiful and a princess and she's not happy. I want to be as in love with my husband as you are."

I remained silent, not certain that what I felt for David was love, also knowing that it would not benefit Tamar if I told her everything. Furthermore, Tamar's mother had spoken the truth as she knew it. David married Maacah to form a political alliance, and he slept with her because he yearned to possess beautiful women. She'd given him two gorgeous children, and he was kind to her out of respect for her role in his household. But he did not seek Maacah when he wanted to talk. If Michal's gossip could be trusted, David never played the harp for her or told her stories about his childhood home in Bethlehem. She had never fully entered his heart.

I wanted Tamar to enjoy a more satisfying marriage than her mother's. As a good, kind girl, she deserved happiness, and at sixteen she was old enough to be betrothed.

I reached out and patted her hand. "The king will do what is best for you," I assured her. "And as much as it is in my power, I will ask him to find you a husband who will respect you as a friend and care for you as a wife. Do not worry, child."

She smiled, her eyes lighting, and before moving away she pressed a soft kiss to my cheek.

CHAPTER TWENTY-SIX

BATHSHEBA

THREE YEARS PASSED. My days revolved around Solomon, Shammua, Shobab, and Nathan—caring for them, clothing them, seeing to their education—and my nights revolved around the king. He did not send for me every night, of course, but as the sun drew down the sky I always made sure my hair was arranged, my skin perfumed, and my gowns appropriate for a visit to the king's bedchamber.

I kept my promise to Tamar and often spoke to David about her and his many sons. For a man who took great delight in his children, he did little to remain involved in their lives once they left their mothers' care. Though I urged him to devote an hour of each day to one of his many children, he would offhandedly reply that he had employed more than enough tutors, soldiers, priests, and counselors to take care of his sons. If I pressed, his temper would grow short, so I learned not to press him. "Why should I spend time with my children," he once retorted, "when the palace is overrun with servants and relatives who entertain them better than I?"

One evening, the king invited me to dine with him in the great hall. I entered at the appropriate time and found the chamber crowded as usual, with the king's older children, several captains from his army, a few counselors including my grandfather, and several guests from Judah. I bowed my head toward the appropriate dignitaries and made my way to a couch at the king's side. Tamar, I noticed, wore the brightly colored garment of a king's daughter and dined on a couch between two of her brothers.

David greeted me with a smile and then proceeded to preside over the gathering as best he could, ignoring the servants who continually carried in trays piled with fruit, vegetables, and various meats. He and a pair of Judean herdsmen launched a spirited discussion about sheep shearing, and although I had learned enough about sheep to converse with the king, I was not particularly interested in debating animal husbandry.

As I partook of the olives, grapes, and almonds the servants brought, I considered myself fortunate that I did not dine with the king every day. My grandfather once told me that Saul's meals were always loud, boisterous, unrefined affairs, more like warriors eating around a campfire than dignitaries in a king's household. David's banquets were not quite so raucous, but the male guests still laughed and joked loudly, and more than a few stripped the roasted meat from animal bones, then tossed the bones onto the floor. A trio of the king's favorite hounds prowled the room, searching for scraps, and several guests made a sport of tossing food into the air and wagering on which dog would snag it first.

Truthfully, I would have preferred to eat with my boys in the quiet of my room.

With no one clamoring for my attention, I turned to Tamar and her brothers. While the boys laughed and joked among themselves,

Tamar reclined gracefully on her sofa and nibbled at a dried fig as though her thoughts were far away. I would have wagered that she was dreaming of the young man who would one day be her husband. I reminded myself to urge David to accelerate his search for a suitable match. Tamar was nineteen, already older than I was when I married Uriah.

I studied her brothers. Amnon, still unmarried at twenty, had reached his full height and sprouted a beard thicker than his father's. Eighteen-year-old Absalom was also unmarried, though he too had attained the full measure of manhood. Adonijah was the youngest of the group at dinner, but at seventeen he was well on his way to surpassing his brothers in height. Also dining with the king's children was Jonadab, a son of David's brother, Shimea.

Watching the boys with an appraising eye, I thought it time for all the king's mature children to consider marriage. At fifty, David was more than old enough to be a grandfather. At twenty-nine, I was mature enough to engage in a little matchmaking.

Watching the older boys jeer and joke with each other, Amnon's behavior struck me as curious. For as long as I had known him, the spoiled young man had routinely intimidated his younger siblings, forcing me to delicately find ways to keep him away from Shlomo. But now, like Tamar, Amnon picked at his food as if he had no appetite. Yet he did not stare off into space but boldly focused his gaze on his half sister. Every time her head turned even slightly in his direction, he perked up as if she'd called his name.

A thin, sharp blade of foreboding nicked my heart. As a *tob* woman, I had often seen that look of burning desire on men's faces, but Elisheba had taught me to look away lest I encourage an unrighteous attraction. Tamar's mother, on the other hand, might have encouraged such looks, but surely not from one of the girl's brothers. Fortunately, Tamar was so intent on her thoughts that she seemed unaware of Amnon's interest.

I rested my chin on my hand and considered the possibilities. A marriage between Amnon and Tamar might be possible, but neither the king nor the girl's mother would find it desirable. Furthermore, Tamar would not want to marry one of her brothers. She had grown up in a herd of rowdy princes, and her dreams of romance would never include one of them.

My concern over what appeared to be a precarious situation diminished when I saw Amnon lean in Tamar's direction and inadvertently catch Absalom's eye. The sight of Absalom's chilly gaze must have alarmed Amnon, for he quickly turned his head, pushed his tray aside, and called out for the king's attention. When David looked his way, Amnon stood and asked to be excused, a request granted by a quick wave.

I reached out and squeezed David's arm, a silent signal that I wished to speak to him. He lifted his hand in response, wordlessly assuring me that he would turn as soon as he'd finished his conversation with the shepherd. I waited because I had no other choice, but clearly David needed to think about finding spouses for his older children.

~❦~

My grandfather never sought my company for idle reasons, so whenever he did ask to see me, I went at once to meet him. I never told him about David's promise to me, nor of the prophet Nathan's assurance that Solomon would one day sit on his father's throne. Samuel's prophecy was enough to convince Grandfather that one of my sons would do something great in Israel, but if he knew Solomon would be king once David died, I worried that he might try to rush my husband into the grave.

One hot summer afternoon, Grandfather asked to meet me in the palace garden, far from curious ears in the harem. I left

the younger boys with their nurse while Solomon and I went to
see him.

Grandfather stepped back to study Shlomo, who gave the king's
counselor a dignified nod. "You have grown!" Grandfather said,
his smile splitting his white beard. "And I understand you are as
smart as your tutors."

"Smarter than some of them," I couldn't help adding. "He can
name every animal that finds its way into the garden, yet some of
his tutors are helpless to identify many of the insects and birds."

Grandfather patted Shlomo on the shoulder. "Why don't you
run along and play with the other children? I need to talk to your
mother."

I lifted a brow, wondering what had motivated this rare meeting. Sometimes I thought Grandfather purposely avoided seeing
Solomon and me. I wondered if the sight of us awakened memories
of that dark time before I married David. Grandfather had always
adored my first husband, and the passing of years had not erased
his grief over Uriah's death or his anger about David's role in it.

As Solomon trudged off to find some way to amuse himself,
Grandfather took my arm and guided me to a balcony overlooking
the Kidron Valley. Standing at the balustrade, we could see nearly
all of east Jerusalem, the clear line of the fortified walls, the slop-
ing hills that curved to the valley below. I never tired of the sight,
because it reminded me of the many warriors who had given their
lives to help us claim our Promised Land.

"I have heard," Grandfather said, his voice light, "that David
has expressed interest in searching for any remaining sons of Saul.
Has he mentioned this to you?"

I blinked. "David rarely speaks of kingdom business when we're
together."

"Then what do you talk about?"

I tilted my head, annoyed by my grandfather's attempt to pry into a very personal relationship. "We talk about Solomon. Or he reads his poetry. Sometimes I listen to his writings."

Grandfather tipped his face to the sun. "You should make an effort to learn more about what is happening outside the palace. The mood in Jerusalem has changed. David is no longer universally loved by his people."

I crossed my arms and stared at the horizon. "David will always be the anointed king. Adonai has promised him an eternal dynasty."

"I didn't mean to irritate you. So let me ask this—have you heard of a man called Mephibosheth?"

"No."

"He is Jonathan's son. After David inquired about any remaining members of Saul's family, he sent for this Mephibosheth and welcomed him to the palace. The man is lame in both legs, but tomorrow he will eat at the king's table, just like David's other sons. Just like *your* son, when he is old enough to join his brothers."

My thoughts spun with bewilderment. Why did Grandfather think I would care about this news?

"Our king," I said, pronouncing each word carefully in case Grandfather had begun to go deaf, "is gracious, and he loved Jonathan. Why should anyone be concerned because David has been generous to a crippled man? Since I have a lame sister, I applaud what the king has done. The people of Jerusalem will do likewise."

Grandfather turned, his dark eyes pinning me to the ground. "Your king may appear to be kind and generous, but he is no fool. Any threat to his throne would arise from the house of Saul, so David is only keeping his enemy within arm's reach. Why do you think he has allowed Michal to raise her sister's sons? David wants to keep a tight rein on his enemies. If this Mephibosheth or any of his allies were to mount a campaign against David, they'd have to conspire beneath the king's very nose."

I took a quick breath of utter astonishment. "David's motives are entirely honorable. He would not even consider—"

"You have always been naïve, Bathsheba. That's why Uriah was such a good match for you. Though he converted to the worship of HaShem, he never forgot how the world operates."

"My husband the king," I said, keenly aware of the rage that had begun to boil beneath my skin, "acts out of a noble and loving heart. He loved Jonathan. They vowed that if one of them should die, the other would extend faithful love to the departed man's family. That is why he sent for this crippled man."

Grandfather paused, then gave me a one-sided smile. "Your husband is a heartless pragmatist," he countered. "And your defense of him, along with the flush on your cheek, reveals the depths of your feelings for the man. I wish HaShem had never brought you to the palace, because one day you will see the full extent of your king's ruthlessness." He patted me on the shoulder in a mocking display of sympathy. "May HaShem comfort you then, granddaughter."

CHAPTER TWENTY-SEVEN
NATHAN

I HAD JUST TRADED AHARON OF GILGAL four eggs for one pot of honey when a storm filled my head. As I winced beneath the sudden pressure, Aharon looked at me with concern. "Are you well, prophet?"

I waved away his sympathy and tucked the honey pot into the crook of my arm. "I need to go."

The storm continued to churn, whooshing in my ears and blurring my sight until I reached my small house. I had no sooner set the honey on a shelf than Adonai struck me blind, my vision blocked by a darkness that obliterated everything in sight.

"Nathan?" From a great distance, I heard Ornah's voice. "Husband, are you all right?"

I opened my mouth and found myself mute. I would have to surrender; let the *Ruach HaKodesh* consume my senses until I understood the vision or message Adonai wanted me to experience.

Groaning, I sank to the clay floor and stretched out on my belly, extending my hands in a position of supplication. *Adonai, have mercy on your servant. Let me see what you would have me see, hear what you would have me hear, but remember I am only dust. Spare me what can be spared, but let me face what I must in order to serve you.*

I had no sooner finished the thought than the event began. At first I heard nothing but a dull buzz in my ears, then I saw Tamar, the king's beautiful daughter, remove a pan of heart-shaped cakes from a clay oven. She wore a silk gown of many colors, a rich garment befitting a king's daughter. Humming to herself, she lifted the pan of cakes, inhaled deeply of their aroma, and smiled as if satisfied by her efforts.

Tamar walked through a small, well-furnished house to a room where a young man lay on his couch. I recognized him in an instant—Amnon, the king's oldest son, lay with the back of his hand pressed to his forehead, his expression flat, as if he were in pain. He gestured to his sister, and she approached with her tray. She brought it to his couch, knelt and offered it to her brother, but he shook his head. "Let every man leave the room," he said, sending the servants away. As the door closed, he stood and commanded her: "Bring the cakes into my bedroom and let me eat them out of your hand."

Tamar sighed, but rose and followed her brother to his bed, where he lay down and smiled. When she offered one of the cakes, Amnon pushed the tray aside and grabbed at her, catching a fistful of her tunic. As his eyes blazed with desire, he pulled her closer. "Come lie with me, my sister."

With terror etched into the lines beside her mouth and eyes, Tamar stared at Amnon. "No, brother, do not force me," she cried. "This scurrilous thing should not be done in Israel!" She lifted her hands and pleaded with him, but he continued to tug at her tunic, reeling her in.

"No, brother!" Panic filled her voice. "Don't do this to me! Where could I go in my shame? And you would sink as low as any beast in Israel. Please, just speak to the king. He will give you leave to marry me."

Deaf to her protests, Amnon rose up and pressed his mouth to hers. When she continued to plead, tears streaking her cheeks, the false invalid threw her onto his bed and climbed on top of her, silencing her cries with a hard slap.

Sweat beaded on my forehead and under my arms as I trembled. I had once witnessed the prelude to a similar scene—the night I saw David summon Bathsheba to the rooftop. Now I watched, unwillingly, as David's son took the same unwelcome liberties with his half sister.

I took a deep, quivering breath to quell the hammering pulse that pounded my ribs. Must I see all of this? When would HaShem have mercy and darken my sight again?

Tamar struggled throughout the ordeal, but Amnon did not relent until he had spent himself and lay next to her on the bed. Then David's daughter sat up and stared at her brother, tears streaming over her face. But instead of offering comfort, Amnon stood and regarded her with revulsion. When she did not move, he pulled her off the bed. She crumpled on the floor, bruised and dazed, then Amnon yelled for his servant. "You," he called, turning his back on the victimized girl, "get this thing out of here."

"No!" With what remained of her strength, Tamar clung to his leg. "Sending me away now, like this, is worse than what you've already done to me!"

Amnon kicked his sister aside. The manservant came and dragged the poor girl through the bedroom and out of the house and court-yard. When he reached the street, the servant released the king's daughter, returned to the house, and locked the door.

I watched with shuddering breaths as Tamar sat huddled in

the street. She then scooped a handful of dirt and held it over her head. As the earth slipped through her fingers, raining over her hair and clinging to the tracks of her tears, she opened her mouth and released a cry so heartrending that the all-seeing angels of heaven wept and covered their faces.

My stomach tightened. No one had ever seen the king's beloved daughter with disheveled hair, a bruised face, and a torn garment. She exhibited undeniable evidence of a violent attack, yet no one stopped to help as she sobbed in the road. Finally, swaying and stumbling, she struggled to her feet and lurched through the streets, not moving toward the palace but toward her brother's house.

At the sound of her cry the door opened, and Tamar fell into Absalom's arms. I saw his eyes—wide, shocked, and furious—and while he patted his sister's back and summoned a maidservant to help her, rage molded his face into a mask of fury.

Fear blew down the back of my neck when the vision finally faded and my senses resumed their proper functions. I did not know Absalom well, but life had given me a healthy respect for men embroiled in righteous rage.

As I sat, stunned and speechless, my mind burned with a memory. When Adonai sent me to confront the king for his sin in murdering Uriah, I told the story of a little ewe lamb, and then David decreed his own fate: *"Doomed is the man . . . he shall pay the poor man four times as much as he stole."*

Since that day, David had already lost one child, the baby with Bathsheba. Would Tamar be the second?

CHAPTER TWENTY-EIGHT

BATHSHEBA

WHEN THE BREATHLESS SERVANT WHISPERED that the king's counselor wished to see me at once, prickles of unease nipped at the back of my neck. "Which counselor?" I asked, hoping she would name anyone but my grandfather.

"Ahithophel."

My uneasiness swelled into alarm. Grandfather had made dire predictions the last time we talked, and I hadn't forgotten his slurs on David's character. Though I didn't want to hear any more comments about my husband's ruthlessness, Grandfather might need to discuss something truly urgent.

Still, I would leave the younger ones and take Shlomo with me. Perhaps his sweet innocence would remind my grandfather that David had much good in him.

"Shlomo?"

He looked up from the parchment he'd been reading. "Yes, Mother?"

"We're going to meet my grandfather. You can finish reading when we return."

Solomon did not complain, but took my hand and led the way out of the harem.

I found Grandfather waiting in the palace courtyard. With eyes as hard as granite and his mouth drawn into a disapproving knot, he gestured to the staircase that led to the garden.

So he wanted privacy.

Resigned to yet another difficult conversation with my only remaining kinsman, Solomon and I climbed the stairs and stepped out into the blinding midday sun.

Shlomo raced ahead of us. "Look, Mother," he called, pointing to something on a flowering bush. "That caterpillar has spots."

"Be careful," I warned. "Some of them sting."

"Not this one," he answered. "At least he won't sting me."

He scampered away, probably to search out some other form of animal life, and Grandfather smiled as he watched the boy run.

"He is bright," he said, his voice hoarse. "What is he now, ten?"

"Only nine." I squeezed Grandfather's arm. "Don't age him prematurely; he's already growing too quickly."

"Still, he is a good boy. And he will be a far better man than his father."

I gave my grandfather a reproving look. "David is not a bad man. And Adonai knows we are frail."

"Adonai also hates sin, and the king's house is filled with it."

I pressed my lips together, unwilling to revisit the past yet again. "Grandfather, if you sent for me only to talk about David's past failings—"

"I've not come to discuss the king. I've come to tell you about the king's son. Amnon has followed in his father's footsteps and

ruined his sister, Tamar. You must do something about it, for
if David cannot control his children, how can he control his
kingdom?"

I halted on the path as my feelings of uneasiness shifted to a
chilling fear. "What has happened?"

"Of all people, you should have no problem imagining what
Amnon has done." Grandfather stared down his nose at me, his eyes
cold and piercing. "He used the poor girl and left her in the middle
of the street, her gown torn, her face bruised, and her humiliation
complete. She is worthless now; no one will ever want her."

I snapped my mouth shut, stunned by his bluntness. Shock held
me motionless, and I realized I was crying only when I tasted tears
on my lips. "Oh, Tamar! That poor girl!"

In a rare moment of compassion, Grandfather guided me to a
seat inside a leafy alcove. He stood in front of me, glancing right
and left, allowing me a moment to grieve.

"I saw this coming," I admitted, swiping tears from my cheeks.
"I tried to warn David, but he didn't listen. I could see that Amnon
was infatuated—"

"The king's sons have been coddled and spoiled since infancy,
and the firstborn more than most," Grandfather said, his gaze
turned toward the garden. "David should have disciplined them,
but he would not. He left that to their mothers, and his women
are as spoiled as their children."

"I am one of those women!" I cried, realizing too late that Shlomo
might hear me.

Grandfather stepped away and waved at Solomon. "Go ahead,
son, all is well. Your mother and I need to talk a while."

I took a deep breath and tried to regain control of my emotions.
Amnon had committed a terrible sin, but surely he was not beyond
forgiveness. And Tamar . . . if she would come to me, I would tell
her she was not to blame for the shame and humiliation she had to

be feeling. I had felt that same shame, anger, and guilt, but Adonai salvaged my ruined life and set me on a new path.

"You must speak to David." Grandfather folded his hands. "His children have terrible reputations, and they have the potential to cause great harm. Do you remember how Eli's sons shamed Adonai? David's sons are equally sinful, yet he still refers to them as his personal priests." Grandfather shook his head. "This brings dishonor to the house of David. Someone needs to tell the king that his children will be his downfall."

I looked up, abruptly understanding. "You want *me* to speak to him? *You* are his chief counselor!"

"I *have* spoken to him, and he turns a deaf ear to my entreaties. He will not hear me on this subject, but perhaps he will listen to a wife he respects."

I nearly laughed aloud. "For years you have insisted that David could not respect me—"

"In the past, perhaps." Grandfather's mouth curled as if he wanted to spit. "But now you are the one wife who has well-behaved children. Go to him, Bathsheba, and tell him he must take a firm hand with his sons. Amnon must be called out for what he did to the girl, and—"

"Her name is Tamar," I interrupted, suddenly weary. "And she is not a piece of spoiled meat. She is a gentle young woman with many good years still ahead of her."

A shiver spread over me as a memory came rushing back—the long-ago night when I had curled up in the dust of our courtyard and decided that my life was over. I was treated as an object, and that callous treatment could have ruined my life, but it didn't. David went on to further complicate matters by committing terrible sins. In the end, however, he redeemed me. And for that, Adonai forgave him.

In a barely comprehendible flash, I realized a profound truth:

I had also forgiven him. If Amnon would confess and repent, perhaps in time Tamar could also forgive. David might even allow a marriage between the two, and Tamar's future would be restored.

I would speak to the king. The next time he called for me, I would open my heart and share these thoughts.

"Grandfather," I said, proceeding carefully, "the king is my husband and I care about him. Because we understand each other, I will speak to him about this."

"Good." Grandfather shifted his attention back to the garden. "And what do you think of our firstborn prince? Would you have Amnon, who violated his own sister and then abandoned her, rule over all Israel? How could he possibly be a righteous king?"

I blew out a breath. "For today, my duty is to raise my sons, protect them, love them, and teach them to love God as their father does . . . especially Solomon." I stood and stepped in front of Grandfather, forcing him to look at me. "You are the king's most trusted advisor. He considers you an oracle of God. Yet you do not seem to care for him at all."

Grandfather's jaw flexed. "Adonai's chosen people deserve a holy king."

"Is any of us truly holy? None of us can make that claim."

"I am loyal to the throne of Israel."

I shook my head. "I'm not talking about loyalty. I'm talking about *affection*. About *friendship*. Do you feel either of these for my husband?"

When he did not answer, I reached for his gnarled hand and held it with a firm grip. "If Adonai has forgiven David, why can't you?"

"David doesn't need more people to love him. He needs more people who will tell him the truth. I hope, Bathsheba, that you will be one of those people."

Grandfather's mouth spread into a thin-lipped smile as he bowed to take his leave.

⋇

Because David had so many wives and concubines vying for his attention, we women obeyed an unspoken rule and waited on the king's pleasure. We did not ask to see him; we waited for him to summon us. But with Grandfather's request ringing in my ears, I had a handmaid carry a message to the king: could he honor his wife and loyal servant by calling for Bathsheba at sunset?

I nearly wept in relief when I received a summons. My maid carefully applied my cosmetics and dressed me in a most appealing garment. Though I wanted to talk about important matters before the night was over, David was still a man of keen appetites, and age had not diminished his physical desires.

The guard had just opened the door to David's chamber when the king caught me up in a warm hug. "My lord!" I said, surprised by his enthusiasm. "I haven't even had time to bow."

"Why bow," David said, his eyes shining, "when you can kiss me?"

I wasn't sure what had sparked his ardor, but when at last we lay together on his bed, I sat up and pushed the damp hair away from his forehead. "My lord the king," I said, pressing my hand to his chest as I smiled down at him, "my grandfather came to see me today."

Groaning, David rolled toward me and propped his head on his hand. "And what did Ahithophel want with my most beguiling wife?"

I bit my lip, bracing myself to approach what might be a difficult subject. "He brought me sad news. I learned what happened between Amnon and Tamar. He bade me talk to you about that unfortunate situation."

My husband's smile vanished. "*That* is why you asked me to send for you? You wanted to talk about Amnon?"

Caught off guard by his reproachful tone, I floundered in search of a diplomatic reply. "I wanted to see you first, of course. But I also wanted to talk about Tamar."

David rolled onto his back and stared at the ceiling, his face blank and empty. "There is nothing to talk about. That episode is finished."

"But my lord the king—"

"It is over, Bathsheba." Irritation lined his voice. "The boy did wrong, but what can be done about it now? He is my firstborn son."

"But are you not upset? Do you feel no anger about this? He has ruined his sister's prospects—"

"Of course I'm angry!" David sat up, flushing to the roots of his hair. "I was furious when I heard about it. But what can I do? Amnon is a man now. I will not treat him like a wayward child."

Taken aback, I caught my breath and sought a different strategy. Clearly, David would not hear a word against Amnon, but he loved his daughter, too.

I softened my voice. "My lord and king, surely we must consider Tamar. She has been grievously wounded. If Amnon could be persuaded to confess his sin and ask her forgiveness—"

David laughed, but I heard no merriment in the sound. "Confess his sin? I hear that he refuses to admit any wrongdoing. I daresay the hatred he feels for the girl now is greater than any love fever that gripped him." David sat cross-legged and rested his wrists on his knees, then hung his head. "The boy was sick . . . and all I did was try to make him happy."

"My lord—" I halted, pained by a sudden thought. I gave my husband a deliberate, careful smile, knowing that an outright accusation might harden his heart. "I know you have always loved your children. What did you do to help Amnon?"

David blew out a breath. "The boy was ill. He was thin, wasting away, so great was his preoccupation. I couldn't help noticing that he wasn't hunting or participating in any of his usual activities. So when he took to his bed, I went down to see him. When he suggested that I send Tamar to him, well of course I wanted to please him. On my return to the palace, I called for the girl and told her to visit her brother."

The room seemed to grow dark as my mind buzzed with an ugly swarm of thoughts I dared not speak. David was many things, but he was not a fool. To send his virgin daughter, a *tob* woman, to his lust-crazed son was sheer madness. Anyone could have predicted the outcome, but I had to know all the facts before saying more.

"What did Amnon want Tamar to do? How was she supposed to be of service?"

David shrugged. "Amnon wanted her to prepare *lebibot* for him. A simple thing, really. A completely innocent task."

I turned away, unable to believe my husband and king could be so blind. *Lebibot* were heart-shaped cakes, a common symbol of love. The gift basket that arrived at my house when David tried to send Uriah home had been filled with *lebibot*. After Solomon's birth, David had the cook send me a basket of *lebibot*. Amnon's request had been far from subtle, so how could David not understand the young man's true intention?

I hugged my knees, deeply troubled. I knew Nathan had warned David that Adonai would punish him with a rod and blows if he strayed from the ways of the Lord. If a loving God disciplined His wayward children, shouldn't a loving father discipline his son? David had always doted on his sons, but had affection blinded him? If so, could I say anything to open his eyes? Or would he think I was being critical of his beloved offspring?

"Still," I said, knowing that I risked earning his displeasure, "as Amnon's father—"

"Bathsheba." His tone underlined my name with reproach. "I am the last man on earth who could speak to Amnon about forcing his sister. Did I not commit the same sin with you?"

What could I say to that? Nothing.

I lowered my head onto my folded arms, and after a moment a warm hand caressed my back. "If you did not come here because of mad love for me, at least keep me warm. The room grows cold."

Any other night I would have smiled and returned to David's embrace, but at that moment I had no smile for my king.

"Bathsheba?" Fingers tiptoed up my spine. "Has your affection grown cold, as well?"

"No, my lord." I sighed and turned to him. "As always, I am yours to command."

⁂

Walking in the shadow of a palace guard, I brought my veil up to cover most of my face and carefully stepped over the uneven stones. I kept my chin lowered, not wanting to see or be recognized by anyone who had known me as the wife of Uriah. A royal wife should not be walking the streets of Jerusalem without a full escort, but I did not want to create a spectacle.

Finally the guard paused at a courtyard gate. "This is the house," he said, disapproval in his voice. "If you insist on this folly of an errand—"

"Please wait in the courtyard," I told him, moving through the gate. "I will not tarry long."

I knocked on the door and, like a shy turtle, drew my arm back into the shelter of my robe and veil. After a moment, a servant opened the door and peered at me with narrowed eyes.

"I have come to see Tamar," I said.

The servant practically growled. "The king's daughter isn't seeing anyone."

"Please . . ." I reached out in entreaty. "Please ask if she will speak to Bathsheba."

The servant closed the door, leaving me outside, but after a few moments she returned and stepped aside so that I could enter.

Absalom's house was large and well furnished. The front room contained a couch and chairs, while the servants' area stood off to one side. Two doors opened off the main room, one to the right and one to the left. The servant gestured to the closest door. "Go on in."

I did. Shadows cloaked the room, and only after my eyes adjusted could I see a table, a carpet, and a couch piled with pillows. A woman lay curled up on that couch. She wore a dark tunic and veil, so all I could see was the faint shine of her eyes.

"Tamar." I moved to the couch and knelt on the floor. "How I have prayed for you over these past few days."

Dark lashes lifted, and the wide eyes fastened on me. "You have wasted your time. My life is over."

"Dear one." I searched for her hand amid the folds of her robe, found it and held it tight. "I know what happened to you, and I know it was horrible. When the same thing happened to me, I thought my life was over too, especially when I found myself with child. I cursed my beauty and faulted Adonai for making me a *tob* woman. I blamed myself, I blamed HaShem, and I blamed my parents for encouraging me to believe my beauty would result in a happy, productive life."

I studied her face, visible now in the shadows. Though she had to be hearing me, I couldn't tell if she was listening.

"I had been prideful," I went on, my voice breaking at the memory of my own foolishness. "I had trusted in my beauty instead of Adonai. And when my beauty led to the destruction of my pride, I could find no reason to live. When my husband died"—I did not elaborate because I wished to spare her more pain—"I wanted to end my life. But Adonai answered my prayers, and your father, David, redeemed me. Adonai will hear your prayers too, Tamar. You must give Him time to redeem your life and make it new."

She laughed—a bitter, broken sound that seemed to come from a much older woman.

"I have heard your story," she said. "Absalom told me everything, so I know that my father is as much a monster as my brother. My father will not redeem me; he has not even sent escorts to take me back to the palace. I have become an object of loathing in Israel."

"It's not so, Tamar!"

"Isn't it?" Her eyes searched mine, and I couldn't deny her truth.

"I am not completely without hope," she said, tears glistening in the dark wells of her eyes. "Absalom has spoken of sending me to my grandfather in Geshur. There I will be an old, unmarried princess, but perhaps I can find a new reason to live."

I nodded, then squeezed her hand again. "You may be right. But whatever you do, Tamar, do not lose faith in the God of our fathers. He is ever faithful, all-seeing, and all-knowing. And He loves you."

She nodded, too, then reached out to me. I opened my arms, and she buried her face in my shoulder and quietly sobbed her heart out.

As I held her, I prayed that Adonai would send someone to redeem her life . . . and realized anew just how much the Lord had done for me.

CHAPTER TWENTY-NINE

BATHSHEBA

WITH MINGLED PLEASURE AND SADNESS I watched my first-born take his first steps toward manhood. At eleven, Solomon stood nearly as tall as my shoulder, and his interests shifted from bugs and plants to people and nations. Since he read every scroll and parchment his tutors could procure for him, my living quarters overflowed with baskets of reading material.

His brothers weren't far behind him. Shammua, Shobab, and Nathan were beautiful little boys, and I loved them dearly, but I had to admit that Solomon was uniquely gifted. As the prophet had said, Shlomo appeared to be "greatly loved" by Adonai.

David continued to indulge Shlomo, praising his growth, his quick mind, and his knowledge of nature. In order to provide a bit of balance, I did not approve of everything my son did, but was quick to correct him for disobedience, thoughtlessness, and ingratitude. "You may have been born a king's son," I frequently reminded him, "but your mother is a soldier's daughter and your father was once a shepherd. Adonai promotes some people, while He keeps others humble, and we have little choice in the matter. Never forget that everything you have, even the breath in your body, comes from the Almighty One, so be grateful for all you are given."

Solomon had many reasons to be proud of himself, but given my history, I was especially quick to correct even the mention of the word *pride*. "Pride is evil," I told him repeatedly, "for it compares one man to another, and both men are Adonai's creations. If you are happy with the work of your hands or the lesson you have learned, do not say you are proud. Say you are *pleased* with the result or you take *pleasure* in what you've studied. But never, my son, never say you are proud."

While David and I often talked about Solomon, Shammua, Shobab, and Nathan, I no longer felt free to mention my husband's other children. Since Amnon's attack on Tamar, the king behaved as though Amnon had never done anything worthy of discipline or censure. Because I worried that Absalom might do something to avenge his sister's ruined innocence, I fixed a watchful eye on him when he came to the palace. He kept to his usual routines, yet on several occasions I caught Absalom staring through Amnon as if the firstborn did not exist.

As her brothers lounged around the palace with nary a change in their lives, Tamar remained secluded in Absalom's house. Her life as the king's daughter had ended. The beautiful girl who had once enlivened the king's court disappeared and not even her mother dared ask about her. Like a hand leaves no imprint when it is removed from a basin of water, every trace of Tamar vanished from the palace.

One day my boys and I were invited to a wedding—that of Nathan's daughter, Yael, to a farmer who lived near Nathan's family. With David's permission, my sons and I mounted donkeys and rode to the newlyweds' small house outside the city walls. The feast had already begun by the time we arrived. Nathan's wife, Ornah, welcomed us warmly and offered us sweet wine. "The bride and groom are inside the house," she said, arching a brow, "but we will eat when they step outside."

The simple celebration, complete with farmers and plowmen and shepherds, felt as familiar as my precious sons' faces. I lifted my cup and drank as a memory, a safe one, brushed past me like a gentle breeze. My wedding had been like this—happy and relaxed and brimming with the congratulations of friends and neighbors.

"Bathsheba?"

I looked over and saw Nathan, his hair now veined with white, threading his way through the crowd. "You came?"

"We were invited, weren't we?" I smiled at him over the rim of my cup, then nodded at my youngest son. "Your namesake and I were pleased to accept."

"My house is honored by your presence." Nathan bowed, then turned his dark eyes on Solomon. "You have certainly grown, young prince. I was present at your naming ceremony. You let out quite a scream when the knife did its work."

Color flushed Shlomo's cheeks. "I . . ." He glanced at me. "I don't know what to say."

Nathan and I both laughed. "You don't have to say anything." The prophet clapped Solomon on the shoulder. "It happens to every son in Israel, so you are in good company."

"We met your wife," I offered. "She seems a wonderful woman. And that girl—is she your youngest daughter?"

Nathan followed my gaze and nodded at a pretty girl who appeared to be fourteen or fifteen. "Ah yes, that's Nira, my youngest. I expect to be arranging her betrothal soon."

Nathan and I talked a few moments more about the weather and the king's health. While we talked, I couldn't help noticing that

Shlomo's gaze never left young Nira. Apparently he had inherited more than reddish hair from his father. From all appearances, he had also inherited David's appreciation for a lovely face.

"Bathsheba!"

A familiar cry interrupted my musings. I turned to see Elisheba and Amaris at the edge of the crowd, their faces wreathed in smiles. I thanked Nathan once again for his hospitality and moved toward Elisheba, halting when I realized Shlomo had not come with me.

He remained rooted to his spot, his face lit with a grin, his eyes fastened to Nathan's youngest daughter. I frowned. Nira was at least four years older than Shlomo and would probably be betrothed before the year was up. But if he wanted to indulge his fancy, what would be the harm . . .

I closed my eyes, wondering if David's mother had ever shared those thoughts. I turned again and called my son's name in a sharp voice: "Shlomo! Come greet your aunt Amaris!"

He obeyed reluctantly, but at least he obeyed.

⁓❊⁓

One day not long after Passover, I was among those in the king's hall when Absalom entered and approached the throne. The whispering crowd grew silent as the king's handsome son knelt before his father. When David bade him rise, Absalom smiled and extended an invitation for the royal household to join him at Baal-hazor near Ephraim. "The sheepshearers are now at work on my flock," he explained, speaking of the transient workers who celebrated the completion of each shearing job with a feast. "Would the king and his servants please come celebrate with me?"

The king gave his favorite son an affectionate smile. "Thank you, Absalom, but we don't want to be a burden to you."

"Won't you please reconsider?" Absalom propped a foot on the

edge of the king's elevated throne, then leaned forward on his knee
and grinned. "The herd is especially large this year, and I want to
honor you. Come see the magnificent beasts I've bred. Their fleece
is exceptional."

David chuckled. "You honor me with your invitation, but I really
shouldn't go. However, I will give you my blessing. Invite someone
else to help you celebrate."

A frown flitted across Absalom's features. "If you won't come,
will you at least send my brother Amnon?"

"Amnon?" David lifted a brow. "Why him?"

Absalom shrugged and casually scanned the assembly. "Why
not? We're brothers. If the king will not honor my feast with his
presence, let the firstborn come in your stead."

David sighed and looked at me as if searching for a sign of reas-
surance. Startled by this wordless appeal, I looked again at Absalom's
guileless face, then glanced at my grandfather. He watched the king's
son with a tight mouth and narrow eyes, and instinctively I knew
he sensed something peculiar about Absalom's invitation. But what?

I sat motionless as Grandfather's prediction about David's children rose in my memory. In his insistence that David's sons would
be his undoing, Grandfather had been as certain as a prophet, but
he had never claimed to speak for Adonai. He could be wrong. And
the awful business with Tamar lay two years in the past.

But Grandfather unreservedly believed in Samuel's prophecy
about *my* son, and he had to be thinking about Solomon. He would
want to protect him because he didn't trust or approve of Absalom.

Yet what could I do? To speak against my husband's favorite
would only cause David to distrust *me*.

My gaze moved back to my husband, and I lifted one shoulder
in a barely perceptible shrug.

"All right." Laughing, David leaned forward to wrap his hands
around his handsome son's head. "Go with my blessing. Amnon

shall go with you, and so shall the others. Take all your brothers, eat, drink, and celebrate. And may your yield be even more bountiful next year."

Absalom grinned and turned away as David settled back in his chair, smiling, no doubt, at the thought of his sons gathering to celebrate their brother's success.

I slipped out of the chamber to search for Solomon and spotted my grandfather in the hallway outside the throne room. I tugged on his sleeve and pulled him into an alcove for a private word.

"I saw your expression as Absalom made his request," I said, looking up into his eyes. "You don't often reveal your emotions on your face, but at that moment you seemed worried. Why?"

My grandfather inhaled deeply and then closed his eyes. "Do not let Shlomo attend that feast."

"Surely he's too young," I answered, grateful for my boy's tender age. "But why shouldn't he go with his brothers?"

"Because, child"—his words rode on a tide of exhaled breath—"revenge is a dish best served cold."

CHAPTER THIRTY

NATHAN

WHEN I ROUNDED THE HILL and recognized the silvery sheen of the lake known as the King's Pool, my eyes misted with relief. I had been walking for days, returning from a settlement where a false prophet had stirred up trouble and led the people to worship an idol. After correcting their error and destroying the false image, I reminded the people that any prophet who spoke falsely could not be from Adonai, for the Lord did not—could not—lie.

Now the sight of water refreshed my weary body and soul. I lengthened my stride and planned to linger by the lake for a while. I would drink my fill and wash the desert grit from my hands, feet, and face. Once I had rested, I would pick up my pack and staff and continue on my journey, happy to be heading home.

I fell to my knees when I reached the lake, ignoring the young shepherd who watered his flock nearby. The mild wind cooled my body as it flapped the folds of my tunic, and for one wild instant I wanted to fall into the lake and float, motionless, until my weariness eased.

But I was not alone, and a prophet should show some dignity. So I drank and washed and splashed like a child in the shallows, then picked up my sandals and retired to the shade beneath a terebinth tree. The young boy cast a curious glance in my direction, then waved a greeting and led his flock away. I sat in a happy daze, staring at the lake's glassy surface until a sharp pain shot through my temple.

The pain was a warning, for it eased as the familiar darkness rolled in, quickly replaced by a scene of great revelry. I saw two banquet tables in a field, the first lined on each side by working men in sweat-stained tunics. Some of the workers raised their cups and offered toasts while others passed dishes of venison and succulent roast lamb. At the second table, another group of men wore the colorful robes of high-ranking dignitaries. Absalom, the king's son, stood at the head of the second table, his cup raised. The other men lifted their cups, as well.

I peered more closely at the scene. The man standing closest to Absalom was none other than Amnon, the king's firstborn.

Sheer fright raced through me when I realized exactly who and what I beheld.

Absalom looked at the king's firstborn. "Is your heart merry, brother?"

Amnon grinned the wide, sloppy grin of a man who had tarried too long in his cup. "It is. You set a—" he patted his chest and burped—"bountiful table."

"Good." Absalom tossed his thick hair as he lifted his glass again. "To our father the king, may he live forever. And to our beautiful sister, Tamar, who baked you heart-shaped cakes before you despoiled her!"

Amnon staggered slightly and blinked, continuing to hold his cup aloft, but his glassy eyes narrowed as he met Absalom's accusing glare.

"Now!" Absalom commanded, still staring at his half brother. "Take him down!"

At this, the working men at the first table pulled daggers from their belts and rushed at Amnon, catching and stabbing him before he could gather his wits. At the hired murderers' approach, the king's other sons rose from their places and fled, calling for their servants and running for their mules in a confused melee.

I watched, my heart in my throat, as Absalom stood over his bleeding brother. "Thus shall it ever be with lecherous fools." Smiling at his dying brother's gasps, he overturned his cup and poured the dregs of his wine onto Amnon's face.

The scene faded from my consciousness. Paralyzed by astonishment and sorrow, I did not move for quite some time.

Adonai's words to David, spoken through me, returned on a flood of memory. *"Here is what Adonai says: 'I will generate evil against you out of your own household.'"*

Sadness pooled in my heart as I recounted David's losses. One infant son. One daughter. One firstborn prince.

Adonai had given me the dire task of telling the king about the consequences of his sin, yet He had given me no words to comfort the king when the sword over David's house struck once again.

Chapter Thirty-One
BATHSHEBA

I DID NOT WANT SHLOMO TO ATTEND Absalom's feast, but when David heard that Solomon would not be making the trip, he sent a message that my oldest son should join the travelers at once. I had no time to convince the king that Shlomo should remain behind, so when the caravan departed, Solomon went with them.

I watched them go with a lump in my throat, telling myself everything would be fine. Of course, the king would expect Solomon to travel with his brothers. I didn't want David to think I was being overprotective, did I? Nor did I want to insult him by implying I didn't trust the king's favorite son.

And I had faith in the prophecy. My son would greatly influence Israel. I could only pray that influence would not be the result of an untimely and undeserved death.

The next day I attended the king's court and sat with Michal behind the throne. I had just leaned over to tell her the great hall seemed unnaturally quiet without David's older sons when a great hubbub from the courtyard interrupted my thoughts. Distracted from a merchant who had asked him to judge a property case, David pointed to a guard at the door and commanded him to determine the reason for the disturbance.

A moment later, a red-faced, perspiring servant rushed into the room, pushed the merchant aside, and fell on the carpet before David. "My lord and king," the man said, not lifting his head, "forgive the bearer of this news, but Absalom has killed all the king's sons, and not one of them remains."

The throne room swelled with silence as every person present tried to make sense of the messenger's words. A loud wail then shattered the silence, which ended only after the king stood, ripped his robe, and fell facedown on the floor.

Horrified, I looked from the king to the messenger and back again, unable to believe what I'd heard. More wailing and shrieks of grief echoed through the throne room, piercing my heart. Only then did I realize that "all the king's sons" meant *my* son, too.

My first thought was that Michal had been blessed. Her five sons were not David's, so they had not attended the deadly feast. I thought then of Solomon lying on the ground with a knife in his chest, and a suffocating sensation tightened my throat.

Unable to speak, I looked for Grandfather and spotted him slumped in his chair, horror plainly visible in his wide eyes and waxy skin. My hands were damp and trembling, though my mind had sharpened like the blade of a knife. Where was Adonai? HaShem had promised David an eternal dynasty, yet in one afternoon all his sons—and my precious Solomon—had been wiped out. How could this be? Did Adonai speak truth or was Nathan a false prophet? Was Samuel a false prophet, too? Did—could—anyone really speak for Adonai?

Had I been wrong about Samuel's prophecy yet again?

Another messenger ran into the throne room. My pounding heart stuttered when I recognized Jonadab, David's nephew, a young man I had never trusted. He went immediately to the prostrate king and, falling on his knees, shouted in David's face, "No! Do not believe that all the king's sons have been killed! It was only Amnon! Absalom has been plotting this ever since Amnon raped his sister, Tamar. No, my lord the king, your sons are not all dead! Only Amnon is dead."

Tension filled the air as David lifted his head and stared at his nephew. I clutched the neckline of my garment, ready to rend it in sorrow. Did I dare hope Jonadab was telling the truth? Did any of us?

Then we heard a distant cry from the lookout, and a guard hurried into the chamber. "It is true!" he said, gesturing out the door as if we could all see from the lookout's perspective. "A great crowd is coming around the side of the mountain from the road behind it."

"My lord," begged Jonadab, still on his knees, "there they are now! Rise, look and see that the king's sons are coming, just as I said."

I dropped into my chair, and only when the tension ran out of my body did I realize that every muscle had been stretched as tight as a bowstring. Solomon was safe, and in a few moments he and his manservant would come running in to assure me that he had not been harmed. Solomon was alive, and the king's other sons, too.

A smile of pure relief curved my lips, and when I looked across the room I saw that though Grandfather had tilted in his chair like a listing ship, he appeared to be at peace.

My smile vanished when I glanced at David. He knelt on the floor, one arm draped over his head, the other pounding his chest as grief tore at him.

Amnon, his beloved firstborn, was dead.

CHAPTER THIRTY-TWO

BATHSHEBA

I lie in the dust;
  revive me by your word.
I told you my plans, and you answered.
  Now teach me your decrees.
Help me understand the meaning of your commandments,
  and I will meditate on your wonderful deeds.
I weep with sorrow;
  encourage me by your word.

Psalm of David

DAVID HAD LOST ANOTHER SON, but his reaction to this death was far different from his reaction to the loss of our baby. This death had come swiftly and unexpectedly, so the king had no opportunity to fast and beg Adonai to save his son's life. Amnon was gone, and by giving Absalom permission to invite his brother to the feast, David had practically placed a sword in his other son's hand.

Just as he had placed Tamar in Amnon's house.

Knowing that my husband felt himself morally unqualified to rebuke his oldest son, at times I wondered if he had allowed Absalom to enact the justice he could not bring himself to impose on his unrepentant firstborn. David was not foolish, nor could he have believed that Absalom had forgotten the crime inflicted upon his sister.

Regardless of David's reasons, I realized that another prophecy was being fulfilled before my eyes: Nathan prophesied that the sword would not leave David's house, and it had not. When would it strike again? Whatever happened, I could not let it strike Solomon.

I walked through the palace hallways and felt death bearing down on us with a slow and stately tread. Our baby boy was dead, Amnon was dead, and Absalom and his family had fled to Geshur, where they would be protected by their maternal grandfather. The chorus of youthful voices that always enlivened the king's banquets had been greatly diminished.

The king spent more and more time in his chamber writing, playing the harp, and struggling to put words to the emotions and troubling thoughts that assaulted him. He did not speak openly about his feelings, but his poetry and music revealed them as plainly as if he'd given us a knife and let us open his heart for examination.

In the hours when I read his poetry and listened to his music, I saw a side of David I had not seen before. So many of us thought of HaShem as exalted and holy, which He certainly was. But David cried out to God as a man who had an actual *friendship* with the Lord Most High. As a man opens his heart to an intimate friend, he agonized before Adonai, confessed his feelings, shared his heartbreak, admitted his failures. Then he turned to the Lord for comfort and correction even as he praised the God of heaven and earth for His glory and majesty.

My father had been devout, but he had never spoken to Adonai that way. I had watched dozens of priests go about their duties in the Tabernacle, and I had never seen any of them approach the Lord as anything like a friend. Among all the men I knew, only David loved Adonai in such a down-to-earth way.

During those dark days, I rarely saw my husband, for he spent many of his evenings alone. When he did send for me, instead of asking about Solomon or inquiring after my thoughts, he tended to vent his grief over Amnon and Absalom.

Though I understood his grief for his sons, I could not forget that Solomon was his heir by promise and prophecy. The king had not lost Shlomo, but he spent little time with him. Now that the older princes lived outside the palace, I had hoped that David would call for Solomon and begin to appreciate what an intelligent and virtuous boy he was. But the king preferred to spend his time in his chamber, writing or staring out at the site he had selected for Adonai's Temple.

Remembering Elisheba's advice about storing up good memories for bad days, when summoned to the king's chamber I did everything within my power to cheer him. I talked about Amnon, glossing over his glaring failures, in the hope that David would celebrate the young man's charms and put his memory to rest. When that approach failed, I reminded David that Amnon had been the cause of much strife among his brothers, and that he had purposefully intimidated the younger ones.

I attempted to distract David with music and dancing; he turned away as though the merry tunes rubbed salt into a wound. I dared to speak of Absalom and praise his attractiveness, and the mention of that son brought tears to the king's eyes. After a while I surrendered the care of my husband to his other wives and concubines.

I hated to admit it, but I slept better with Amnon gone. If David had died and Amnon tried to seize the throne, I suspected that his first act would have been the execution of his half brothers. I had never cared for the spoiled boy, and my distrust had increased as the king's firstborn developed into a young man. While he honored HaShem with sacrifices and pretty words when called upon, I never saw any evidence of genuine reverence in his heart. He had spent hours by his father's side in worship, and yet I never saw any trace of humility on his face. How could a child of David remain cold to the things of the Lord?

Yet David had always taken great pleasure in his firstborn, and to hear him talk one would think Amnon gilded every morning and sprinkled the nighttime with stars.

When I could no longer bear my frustration over David's inattention to Solomon, I spoke to Grandfather about my feelings. He listened, nodded gravely, and tugged on his beard as I vented my exasperation. Since I knew Grandfather held no great love for my husband, I was surprised when he answered my emotional outburst with a story.

"When Adonai sent Samuel to Bethlehem to anoint one of the sons of Jesse as the next king," he began, "Jesse assembled his seven sons to stand before the prophet. Each one passed before him, and each time Adonai told Samuel that the lad before him was not the one He had chosen. Then Samuel said to Jesse, 'Are these all your sons?' And Jesse said, 'There is another, the youngest, who watches the sheep and goats out in the field.'"

I had heard the story before and frowned as Grandfather looked at me as if waiting for a reply. "The eighth son was David," I said, shrugging. "So Samuel anointed him."

Grandfather shook his head. "Bathsheba, do you not see? David was easily overlooked, a child whose name barely entered his father's thoughts. Jesse didn't summon him to stand before the prophet, and he certainly didn't esteem him highly, if at all. The child who lives unseen by his father will perform outlandish feats, anything to be noticed. And the man who matures outside his father's attention will not know how to be a father to his own children."

Understanding crashed into my consciousness. David wasn't a good father because he never *had* a good father. A wave of pity for my husband threatened to engulf me, but I held it at bay. While David might not have had a worthy example to follow, he still needed to teach his sons.

A mother could only do so much.

❧

A servant told me that Elisheba waited to see me. I sent the servant to escort her to my apartment, where I embraced my old friend. "I saw Solomon riding his mule in the courtyard," she said, smiling. "He has grown so tall!"

"He has a house of his own now," I said. "I miss him, but I am pleased with him, and so is the king."

"I wish I had been able to come sooner." Elisheba held my forearms as her chin trembled. "But everything happened so quickly." She halted, her eyes filling. "Please do not be angry, but your sister, Amaris, has married."

Somehow I remained upright, though I couldn't seem to stop blinking. "Married?"

"She met a shepherd from Bethlehem," Elisheba went on, her words running together. "He was taken with her and presented me with a betrothal contract. I didn't know what to do, so I sent him to your grandfather at Giloh." A tear rolled down Elisheba's lined cheek. "I am so sorry, child. I knew you would want to come to the wedding, but Amaris didn't want to wait, and your grandfather couldn't believe that someone wanted to marry her. So he gave his permission, the groom came for the bride, and they left yesterday for Bethlehem. Forgive me for not letting you know before today."

I sank to a bench and felt my heart contract. Amaris was my only sibling. I had loved her deeply, and I'd always imagined she'd remain in my house with Elisheba. Now she was gone to Bethlehem to be a shepherd's wife. I pressed my hand to the spot where my chest ached. Is this what David felt when they told him Absalom had fled?

I bowed my head. "She is happy?"

"She is overjoyed. Her new husband has two children from his late wife, so Amaris will have her hands full."

"Do you think she will manage? She's always had your help."

"She will manage very well. Amaris has always been able to cope with whatever came her way."

"I can't believe she's gone."

"Don't fret, child. She and her husband will be coming to Jerusalem for the festivals. You'll see her then."

I pressed my lips together and quietly adjusted my perspective. For so many years Amaris had been the baby of the family, the helpless one, but now she was twenty-eight and quite capable of being a wife and mother. Which meant that Elisheba was fifty-five and living alone—

My thoughts came to an abrupt halt. "I'm so glad you came." I gripped her worn hands. "You have seen both of us girls safely married, and now you must come live with me. You shouldn't live alone. I need you—I still have Shammua, Shobab, and Nathan to care for."

Elisheba's forehead crinkled. "How are the dear boys?"

"As fine as young boys can be. They miss Shlomo, of course. He keeps to himself these days, as Absalom remains away and his older brothers stay busy with their own affairs."

"And his father?"

The question grated against my nerves, reminding me of the

unhappy reality I kept trying to forget. "The king is . . . often pre-occupied." I forced a smile. "He does not hunt or go out as much as he used to. He is no longer a young man, and lately . . . well, he tends to dwell on memories, and not all of them are pleasant."

Elisheba smiled, then waved my offer away. "Thank you, child, but I can't live in the palace. I am a common woman."

"So am I." I caught her hand again and pressed it to my cheek. "Elisheba, I need you. My boys need you. We will sell the house, and you will be welcome to spend the rest of your life with me."

A smile gathered up the wrinkles of Elisheba's weathered cheeks, and her eyes filled with tears again as she nodded.

After she departed, I sent a servant to help her pack her possessions. I would move her into my suite, where she could indulge herself in the pretense of looking after me and the boys, but I would assign servants to look after her. After a lifetime of faithful service to my family, she deserved a time of rest.

And I needed a friend.

❧

The earth itself seemed to mourn in those days. The seasonal rains did not refresh the ground that year, and everyone casually remarked that we'd had a dry season. When the rains did not fall the next year, the king's advisors said the situation was certain to improve. During the third year, when the seasonal rains did not fall and the crops did not grow, the king's seer reminded David that Adonai had promised to send rain at the proper time only if the people followed the Lord's commands and walked in His ways.

From my conversations with David, I knew he feared that he had done something to displease the Lord. So as the people of Israel struggled and starved, he went to the Tabernacle to ask Adonai the reason for the famine.

The high priest, wearing the ephod with the Urim and Thummim, went into the holy place and prayed. Within a few moments, the engraved stones on the breastplate flashed, spelling out the Lord's answer. "Famine has come upon the land," Zadok the priest told the king, "because Saul put the people of Gibeon to death."

Swamped by a wave of relief that *he* wasn't the guilty party, David carried Adonai's answer to his counsel room and consulted his advisors. One of the counselors reacquainted David with the history of Israel's relationship with the people of Gibeon. When Israel began to conquer the Promised Land, the people of Gibeon heard about the destruction of Jericho and Ai. Fearing for their safety, a group of men from Gibeon pretended to come from a great distance and went to meet with the leaders of Israel. Joshua, speaking for the Israelites, met with the wily Gibeonites and entered into a treaty with them, promising that they would not be destroyed as the Israelites entered the Promised Land. In return, the Gibeonites would live safely within the territory and serve the Israelites as woodcutters and water carriers.

Years later, however, in his zeal to conquer the territory for the children of Israel, Saul set out to exterminate the Gibeonites and very nearly succeeded.

"Everything you have heard is true," Grandfather told David. "The reason for the famine lies with Saul and his thirst for blood. The murder of the Gibeonites has polluted the land."

David sent mules and a messenger to Gibeon, inviting the tribal leaders to Jerusalem. When the delegates entered the throne room, my weary husband asked what he could do to make things right.

I was seated in the great hall when the representatives from Gibeon stood before the king. David regarded them with a look of defeat, opened his hands, and confessed the nation's guilt. "How can I make atonement so you will be able to bless Israel?"

The Gibeonites conferred among themselves, then their leader stepped forward. "Our dispute with Saul is a blood dispute that cannot be resolved with silver or gold. But as foreigners in your land, we don't have the right to put anyone to death."

David frowned. "Then what can I do for you?"

The leader tightened his grip on his staff. "The man who ruined us, who schemed against us so that we would cease to exist anywhere in Israel's territory—have seven of his male descendants handed over to us. We will put them to death before Adonai in Gibeon, on the mountain of the Lord."

I expected a horrified whisper to ripple through the great hall, but the Gibeonite's reply was met with an almost tangible silence. The atmosphere in the royal court had changed since Amnon's death—no trace of bravado or certainty remained. Those attitudes had been replaced by resignation and sorrow.

David nodded, his countenance sober. "It shall be done." He gestured to my grandfather, who rose from his seat and came forward to confer with the king. They whispered for a moment, then Grandfather stepped back. David looked at me, and in his eyes I saw regret and determination. He had made up his mind . . . to do what?

"On account of the oath Jonathan and I swore before Adonai," David said, his voice heavy with sorrow, "I will spare Mephibosheth, Jonathan's son. But I will give you Armoni and Mephibosheth, sons of Rizpah, Saul's concubine. I will also give you the five sons of Saul's daughter Merab."

My breath caught in my lungs. Merab's sons were now Michal's. She was not in the throne room at that moment, so she would not understand what was happening when guards showed up to take her sons away. And even though I had heard the entire story, I struggled to understand why those young men had to die. Michal lived for those boys, and she had reared them as her own sons ever since their father brought them to the palace. If someone came to take *my* boys away . . .

I brought my hand to my mouth, then lowered my head lest anyone see my look of distress. I did not want to contradict or question the king, and I would never dare to question Adonai, but what was David thinking? How could this be just? Perhaps Adonai had reasons I couldn't comprehend. Still, how was Michal supposed to endure this?

I looked at my grandfather, whose eyes flashed a warning. So I quickly slipped out of the throne room. But as my sandaled feet skimmed the stone floor, I found myself running toward Michal's chamber.

༺❦༻

As swift as I was, I was not swift enough. By the time I reached Michal's quarters in the harem, the sound of her heartrending screams filled the air.

A squad of elite warriors had formed a circle outside her door, and Michal's much-loved sons stood at its center—Elan, Boas, Phineas, and Hananel. Only Ziv, the youngest, was absent, but within a moment a guard approached with that young man, who had obviously been working outside. Still covered in dust and sweat, with wide, questioning eyes he looked from Michal to his brothers.

Elan stood stoically while Boas and Phineas wept openly. Hananel, who had inherited his mother's talent, had begun to sing a mournful tune, and the sound of his voice quieted Michal's screams.

I gathered her into my arms, then kept one arm around her as she turned to watch her sons being led away. Tears rolled down her face, trails of loss and fury, yet despite her grief she managed to ask me a question: "What has David done this time?"

A tear trickled down my cheek, but I swiped it away. "He dispensed justice for the Gibeonites, whom your father slaughtered."

She closed her eyes as her body shook with sobs. Her knees gave way and she collapsed like a woman speared. As I tried to help her up, two of her handmaids hurried forward and lifted her, then carried her into her chamber.

Anger lit a fire in my belly, and if David had stood before me in that moment, I would have pummeled his chest with my fists and demanded to know how he could be so cruel. Every pleasant feeling I'd come to feel for him melted away in a hot tide of disbelief and righteous fury. How could his action be just? Adonai was punishing Israel with a rod and blows, but because she was married to David, Michal would bear all the bruises.

No wonder she despised him.

I turned, frustrated and heartbroken, and saw my grandfather standing outside the iron gate that protected the harem. With determination in my stride I hurried toward him, then grabbed hold of the bars and spat words at him. "Why?" I demanded. "Michal is devastated. How can this be just?"

"Murder pollutes the earth," he said, frowning at my display of temper. "Thus says the Lord: 'Blood defiles the land, and in this land no atonement can be made for the blood shed in it except the blood of him who shed it.'"

I stared at him, the words rattling in my head.

"David's decision was right," he continued. "The Gibeonites deserve legal restitution, and now they will have it. And the land will be cleansed of Saul's evil."

I shook my head, unable to reconcile my grandfather's judgment with the grief-stricken wail coming from Michal's rooms.

"You may never understand Adonai's reasons." Grandfather gentled his voice. "As a woman, you need not concern yourself with such things."

"Just because I am a woman doesn't mean I don't *feel*! I feel only a small part of what Michal is enduring, and I am heartbroken. I cannot understand how or why—"

"Suppose," Grandfather interrupted, moving closer, "one of those young men were to decide to reclaim his grandfather's throne. Suppose he waged war against David or against one of your precious sons. Such things happen, Bathsheba. Men are prone to covet power and position, and those desires are magnified when a legitimate claim exists."

I shook my head. "Michal has not raised those boys with pretensions to power. They wouldn't want—"

"You don't know what they will want, child. You can't know. And the king, though still not himself, is wise enough to realize that meeting the Gibeonites' demands protects his own dynasty from potential rivals. That's why he didn't hesitate to accede to their terms. But whether he acted out of prudence or the need to see justice done, he made the right decision."

I snapped my mouth shut, overwhelmed once again by my grandfather's logic.

⁂

My thoughts were still centered on Michal's loss the next day when I crossed the harem's courtyard. Every time I thought of my friend in her empty apartment, my hands clenched and my stomach tightened. My mind roiled with thoughts about what I would do if I were a man and David had decided to offer our sons to the Gibeonites. I would pick up a sword. I would take my sons and flee to some high mountain. I would sell every trinket the king had ever given me and hire an army to defend my beloved boys.

But I wasn't a man, and neither was Michal. And she had been blindsided by the news, so she had no time to prepare for the loss of her sons.

I wanted to scream with fury—at David, at the Gibeonites, at Adonai himself, for requiring such bloody vengeance. Grandfather's

explanation made sense to some rational part of my brain, but I was
too overcome by sorrow and rage to listen to reason.

I walked with my head down, so I did not see Abigail until she
was close enough to touch my arm. When her fingers lightly brushed
my skin, I looked up and recoiled as though the devil himself had
crossed my path.

"I'm sorry." She stood tall and graceful, yet in her posture I saw a
trace of timidity, as if she had come forward reluctantly. I couldn't
think of any reason she would hesitate to approach me—she was
older, more authoritative, and clearly David's favorite. "I would
like to speak to you," she said, offering a small smile. "In your
living quarters?"

I glanced around. We were alone in the courtyard, but anyone
could come along at any moment. If Abigail wanted to speak in
my quarters, she clearly wanted privacy.

"Forgive me, I am exhausted," I answered. "I've been with Michal all morning—"

"Please." Abigail gestured toward my chambers. "I wouldn't ask
if it weren't important."

I gritted my teeth and led the way, then stood back as she entered my suite. My living quarters had changed very little since
Nathan's birth, the only addition being an extra bed for Elisheba.
She had been resting when we entered, but when she saw that I
wasn't alone, Elisheba mumbled something about going for water
and slipped out the door.

I pulled out a chair for Abigail. "Would you like to sit?"

"Thank you." She sat on the edge of the seat and waited until I
sat on the bed. We were as close as we had ever been, our knees a
mere hand's breadth from each other.

Abigail leaned forward and looked into my eyes. "I have come
to see you because you should know how deeply the king loves you.
I know Michal's situation has made you angry, but please don't

harden your heart toward David. If you become as bitter as Michal, you will destroy a man who loves you very much."

I sat back, stunned. "The king doesn't love me. If he loves anyone, he loves you."

Abigail gave a gentle laugh. "That's where you're wrong, my dear. David and I are friends, so I listen to his thoughts and keep his secrets. This is why I know he loves you more than life itself, and why I know he has promised that Solomon will inherit the throne."

With numb astonishment I realized she was privy to things no one else knew. I was certain David hadn't told anyone about his promise to me, because he wanted to protect Solomon from his scheming older brothers and anyone else who might covet the throne. Yet Abigail knew . . . and no one else. She had kept our secret.

"David loves you," she said again. "He has tried to demonstrate his love in a hundred ways. Yet he is a man, so he will not risk rejection. And he is a king, so he cannot grovel."

She stood and placed her soft palm against my cheek. "If you cannot love him as he loves you, at least be kind to him. Do not let your anger break his heart."

She moved toward the door and opened it, then turned back to look at me. "Do not let him know that we have spoken. He is proud and would not appreciate knowing I've made an entreaty on his behalf."

I nodded slowly, unwilling to commit to Abigail's truth. For all I knew, she could be spinning some sort of malicious web, and I did not want to be caught in it.

⌇⌇⌇

At the time of the barley harvest, as we observed the Feast of Firstfruits, the Gibeonites executed Saul's seven descendants by

having them climb a mountain and then step off a cliff. I did not
see Michal's sons die, but according to reports, all seven young men
joined hands and fell together to the earth below.

Afterward, Rizpah, Saul's concubine and mother of two of the
men, spread sackcloth on a rock near the corpses and remained
outdoors for nearly six months, intent on preventing the vultures
and wild animals from tearing at their bodies and scattering their
bones. She stayed at her post throughout the harvest season.

When I heard what Rizpah was doing, I carried the news with
me into the king's bedchamber. As the king and I shared a meal,
I tried to behave as though everything was fine, but not even for
David's sake could I pretend that nothing troubled my thoughts.
When he asked why my countenance was downcast, I told him what
Saul's devoted concubine was doing for Saul's sons and grandsons.

David did not respond immediately, but later I learned that he
went to the people of Jabesh-gilead, who had the skeletons of Saul
and Jonathan, and retrieved their bones, as well as the bones of
the seven men who had died at the hands of the Gibeonites. He
ordered that the bones be buried in the tomb of Saul's father, Kish,
in the territory of Benjamin.

After David's wishes had been fulfilled, Rizpah left her lonely
post, and Adonai blessed the land with autumn rains. So ended
the famine in Israel.

And I began to think that perhaps Abigail had spoken the truth.

⚜

Because David had been kind enough to honor my concern and
see to a proper burial for the bones of Saul's relatives, I wanted to
do something for him. The years after Amnon's death had been
hard on him, and though he seemed resigned to Amnon's loss, he
still fretted over Absalom. That young man had taken his family,

including Tamar, into exile with him, cutting himself off not only from David but also his grandchildren. At every meal, every court appearance, and even on the occasions when the king invited me to his bedchamber, Absalom remained the most frequent topic of David's conversation.

Unable to bear my husband's discontent for another month, I took Elisheba as an escort and went in search of Joab, David's nephew and the commander of the king's army. I found him at the royal stables and suggested that he employ a bit of artifice in order to influence the king and persuade him to end his fixation with Absalom. Nathan had done something similar when he confronted David with the sin of murdering Uriah, so why shouldn't Joab use the same approach?

"Find someone who is skilled in speech," I said, "someone who can move others with dramatic words. Weave a story, plan a play, and use it to motivate the king. But whatever you choose, you must not breathe a word of my involvement."

Joab considered this, then pinned me with a piercing look. "And what would you have the king do?"

"Consider the Gibeonites. Adonai sent a famine because a grave injustice was never addressed. Now consider Absalom, who murdered his brother. Perhaps the king has agonized so long because justice was never served. The king should either go to Geshur and confront his son, or he should have Absalom brought back to Jerusalem to face the king's judgment. Though it would be painful in the short term, confronting Absalom might bring an end to David's mourning."

Joab listened attentively—a rare thing for a warrior—then tugged on his beard. "I will think on it," he said, nodding. "And I appreciate the suggestion, for the king's grief has affected the entire nation. It is time David behaved like a king again."

Chapter Thirty-Three
NATHAN

HAVING COME TO THE KING'S COURT for no other reason than a prompting from the *Ruach HaKodesh*, I sat on a bench against the wall and studied the men around me. The Spirit of God had given me no message, no truth to tell or future to reveal. Sometimes, I had learned, Adonai simply wanted me to use my eyes to see and ears to hear.

So I mingled with other onlookers as petitioners stepped forward to praise, petition, or placate the king. One man complained of a foul odor coming from his neighbor's home. David told the offending neighbor to clean his house and move his chickens to the communal pen down the hill. "Your problem," the king told the malodorous offender, "is that you do not trust your neighbors with your livestock. Become more trusting, so you and your neighbors can live in peace."

A woman from Tekoa stood next in line. When the king granted her permission to approach, she crept forward, gray tendrils escaping the scarf tied around her head. Falling to the floor, she said, "Help me, O King."

The king leaned back in his chair. "Rise and tell me what troubles you."

The woman lifted her head but remained on her knees. "Alas, I am a widow, O King. Your servant had two sons, and they quarreled in the field. Because no one was around to part them when they fought, one struck the other and caused his death."

The king straightened and gave the woman a look of chilling intentness. "Go on."

"What happened next was even worse," the woman said, "for my whole clan rose against me and said, 'Give over the one who struck down his brother, so we may put him to death for taking his brother's life. It matters not that he is your dead husband's sole heir.' They want to take my last son from me, quench my last remaining ember, and leave my husband no name or remnant on the face of the earth."

Every eye in the court shifted from the impassioned woman's face to the countenance of the king. He closed his eyes, his face rippling with anguish, then a hoarse cry burst from his lips: "Leave it to me. Go home, and I'll see to it that no one touches him."

The woman lowered herself to the floor in gratitude. "Thank you, my lord the king. If you are criticized for helping me, let the blame fall on me and on my father's house, and let the king and his throne be guiltless."

"If anyone objects," David responded, "bring him to me, and he will never complain again."

"Please," the widow continued, apparently not willing to leave, "swear to me by Adonai your God that you won't let anyone take vengeance against my son. I want no more bloodshed."

"As the Lord lives," the king declared, his face flushing, "not one of your son's hairs shall be disturbed. No one shall touch him."

I expected the woman to rise and slink away at this, but apparently she had not finished.

She lifted her head. "May I add one more word, O King?"

David sighed. "Speak."

The woman from Tekoa rose and stood before the king. "Why don't you do as much for the people of God as you have promised to do for me? You have convicted yourself in making this decision, because you have refused to bring home your own banished son. All of us must die eventually. Our lives are like water spilled out on the ground, which cannot be gathered up again. But God does not just sweep life away; instead, He devises ways to bring us back when we have been separated from Him.

"I have come to plead with my lord the king because people have threatened me. I said to myself, 'Perhaps the king will listen to me and rescue us from those who would cut us off from the inheritance God has given us. Yes, my lord the king will give us peace of mind again.' I know that you are like an angel of God in discerning good from evil. May the Lord your God be with you."

After this audacious and prolonged statement, silence filled the throne room, a silence like the hush after a storm when nature seems to call for a Sabbath rest. I gaped in pleased surprise. Whoever this woman was, she had more courage than most men of my acquaintance. Someone had surely sent her, either Adonai or—

"Is the hand of Joab behind you in this?" David shouted, his voice splintering the silence.

I snapped my mouth shut. Of course. The king's cousin was one of few men with the confidence to attempt such a brazen manipulation.

"My lord the king, how can I deny it?" the woman answered. "No one can hide anything from you. Yes, your servant Joab had me do this, and he put in my mouth every word you have heard me say. Your servant Joab did this in order to bring about some change in the situation. But my lord is wise; he has the wisdom of an angel of God when it comes to understanding anything going on in the land."

The king turned toward Joab, who stood near the throne, ostensibly on guard. "All right, Joab," David said, staring at his army's commander. "I am granting your request. Go to Geshur and bring back young Absalom."

Joab prostrated himself and blessed the king. "Today," he said when the king bade him rise, "your servant knows I have won your favor, my lord and king, because you have granted me this request."

I leaned forward, eager to study the king's countenance. The marks of grief were apparent, etched in the lines beside David's mouth and eyes, highlighted by a ribbon of sunlight that poured from a window high on the wall. The corners of his mouth were tight with distress, his eyes shiny with unshed tears.

David had not publicly mentioned Absalom's name in over three years, but through this clever ruse, Joab had ripped the scab off the king's grief-stricken heart and made us all see that the wound had not healed.

"You may go," David added in a trembling voice, "and you may bring young Absalom back to Jerusalem. Let him return to his own house, but he is not to appear in my presence. He is not to come to court."

Joab bowed again, then took the woman of Tekoa by the arm and led her away from the throne.

I leaned back and considered the scene with mixed feelings. Everyone who frequented the king's court knew the king had not been himself since Absalom's bloody feast, but most of us thought David mourned for Amnon. Yet Absalom had always been a favorite, no matter his misdeeds, so was the king actually pining for his murderous son?

From personal experience, David knew that murder was a serious crime against Adonai. David had repented of his sin, but to my knowledge, Absalom had not repented of his wrongdoing. In bringing his son back to Jerusalem, David would be ignoring Adonai's requirement of blood for blood: "Whoever sheds human blood, by a human being will his own blood be shed; for God made human beings in his image."

If David did not administer justice to Absalom, Adonai would.

With the eerie sense of detachment that precedes an impending disaster, I watched Joab leave. Absalom's return could mean trouble, for the other sons, perhaps, but especially for Bathsheba and Solomon if Absalom ever learned that both Adonai and the king had already promised the throne to Bathsheba's son. A man who had not hesitated to kill the king's firstborn might not hesitate to kill again.

Adonai had decreed that the sword would never depart from David's household. For the king's sake, I hoped the decision to bring Absalom back to Jerusalem would not put the sword in enemy hands.

CHAPTER THIRTY-FOUR
BATHSHEBA

WITH JOY SHINING FROM HIS EYES, the king had me sit on the edge of the bed while he explained that Joab had gone to Geshur to bring Absalom home. He told me about the woman from Tekoa, her fearlessness in artifice, and her insistence that Absalom not be harmed.

"When she told the story, she said *her* son's life was at risk," David said, pacing before me. "But I recognized her story as a ruse almost immediately. She was referring to Amnon and Absalom, and she was begging for Absalom's life, pleading that no one harm him no matter how many people insisted he pay for Amnon's death. So I have given the order. Absalom and his family are to be brought home, and my son is not to be harmed in any way."

I clung to the edge of the bed and closed my eyes, unwilling to look at the king for fear he'd see the guilt in my countenance. Thoughts of Absalom living near Solomon sent a tremor of terror and dread through me. At fourteen, Shlomo was much younger than Absalom, but among the king's sons, Shlomo sparkled like a ruby among rocks. What would happen if Absalom began to view Solomon as a rival? What would happen if he learned of David's promise to me, and Adonai's assurance that Solomon inherit the king's throne?

I clenched my jaw, silently ruing the day I pulled Joab aside to express my concerns. I had wanted to end David's sorrow, but I had not expected *this* outcome.

"When?" I managed to whisper. "When will Absalom return?"

"As soon as possible." David stepped forward, clasped my shoulders, and planted a kiss on my forehead. "Bathsheba, it does my heart good to know my son will be home in Israel, where he belongs. I cannot have him at court, of course. People would think I was somehow condoning murder, and I could never do that. But it does my heart good to know he will be nearby. How I have missed seeing that boy!"

I stared at him, wondering if he realized what he had said. He'd missed *seeing* Absalom, missed taking pride in his handsome appearance and manly form. But he hadn't missed *being with* Absalom, for if he had spent any real time with the young man, he might have realized how ambitious Absalom was.

The king sat beside me, looped an arm around my shoulders, and turned my face to his. Though I tried to disguise my apprehension, apparently I wasn't successful.

"What's this?" His mercurial brown eyes sharpened. "Are you not happy about Absalom?"

"May it please the king"—I forced a smile—"I am always pleased when you are happy. But I cannot help thinking of my boys . . ."

"Do not worry, wife." He tapped my nose, then kissed me again, this time on the lips. "I'm sure Absalom has matured in his time away. Didn't you hear me say that he won't be allowed at court? Your sons will be safe, as will all my sons. And Absalom will be *home*."

He leaned back on the mattress, searching my face as he waited for my reply. I nodded, reminding myself that I was only a woman, only one of many wives. "May Adonai prosper and protect my lord and his sons, wherever they are."

He gave me an indulgent smile and ran his finger down my neck until it tugged my garment from my shoulder. "Now—" he pressed his lips to my bare arm—"let us celebrate this good news. I have been melancholy far too long, and I have missed you, my love."

"I have missed you," I replied truthfully. But as I caressed his face with gentle fingertips, I couldn't help remembering the prophet's curse. A sword hung over the house of David, and rather than let Absalom harm my sons, I would throw myself in front of that sword. I would do anything to preserve my sons' lives, even if it meant conspiring against the husband I was trying to honor and obey.

CHAPTER THIRTY-FIVE

NATHAN

WHEN I DID NOT HAVE TO WORK IN THE FIELD or help Ornah make cheese, I enjoyed following the road to David's palace. As a prophet, I had been given leave to sit in the great hall and watch as the king and his counselors governed Israel. David was now in his mid-fifties—an old man, according to many. Though he could be as fierce as ever, at a glance anyone could tell that he no longer possessed the wild courage of his younger days. Yet those of us who made a habit of studying David noticed a definite improvement in his disposition immediately after Absalom's return to Jerusalem. While the king refused to visit his son or permit Absalom to come to the palace, David seemed content to know that Absalom and his family were once again living within the walls of Jerusalem.

Absalom brought more than his family and his flocks when he returned; he also brought the sad news that his sister Tamar had died in Geshur. The report spread throughout the city like a contagion, and those who told the story whispered that the girl had taken her own life. Soon all who lived in Jerusalem mourned for the king's lovely daughter and praised Absalom for caring for his sister.

On the day of Absalom's return, public opinion considered him the king's wayward son. A week later he had become an avenging hero. Six months after that, he was quietly cheered as Israel's future king.

In his mid-twenties, Absalom was a prime example of youth and virility. Everyone in the city fawned on his wife, three sons, and two young daughters, whom he'd named Maacah, after his mother, and Tamar, after his sister. According to all reports, the young Tamar's beauty would one day equal or surpass her namesake's.

Certainly no man in Israel was more celebrated for attractiveness than Absalom. I heard young women praise him as I walked the streets, declaring they could find "no defect on him, from the sole of his foot to the crown of his head." The crown of his head was adorned by unusually long and thick hair. Seeking an explanation for such a wonder of nature, several learned men claimed the king's son had been blessed with the hair of Adam, the first man of creation, making it a supernatural gift.

Absalom cut his hair only once a year, and the only reason he cut it then, he claimed, was because its weight slowed him down. After the annual haircut, the barber swept up trimmings that weighed over five pounds. At Absalom's second annual haircut, the barber charged an admission fee for those who wished to watch.

As Absalom's popularity grew after his return to Jerusalem, I wondered if Adonai had permitted David's son to come home because Amnon's murder might be considered justifiable. After all, the king's firstborn had committed a serious sin against Tamar, and Tamar had subsequently gone to her grave in sorrow. The people of Jerusalem adopted this theory and held it firmly, but I was not a judge, and Adonai had never spoken to me about Absalom.

One day as I walked the path to the barley fields where each
Jerusalem household maintained a plot, I spied a young family.
Three boys were running through a newly planted acre while two
little girls remained close to their mother. The father, a well-built,
sturdy fellow, was calling directions to his servants, and he turned
when he heard my footsteps on the rocky path.

I gasped, recognizing Absalom. If he hadn't been recently shorn,
I would have known him by his shining mane, but the striking face
left no room for doubt. Holding my gaze, the young man finished
his directions to his servants, then walked toward me.

"Wait, please." His voice rang with authority. "I would have a
word with you."

I leaned heavily on my staff as I watched him approach with the
sure grace of a forest creature. Adonai had blessed me with good
health and an adequate body, but I would never command attention the way Absalom did. Some of HaShem's creations—Absalom,
Tamar, Bathsheba, and even David—had been blessed in a way
I never would be, and I had never coveted that quality until that
moment.

"You are the prophet, are you not?" Absalom smiled when I
nodded. "Good. Perhaps you would be good enough to perform
a service for me." The shining dots of perspiration beading on his
forehead only served to highlight his hair. "I have twice sent mes-
sages to Joab, and he has refused to acknowledge them. I would
like to speak to him, but if I went to his house, I don't think I'd
be welcome." Absalom tilted his head and grinned, every tooth in
perfect alignment with the others. "I can't search for him at the
palace, so would you be good enough to tell him to come see me?
He is a kinsman, after all."

I hesitated, torn between good intentions. Ordinarily I wouldn't
hesitate to do a favor for another man, especially one of the king's
sons. Yet by refusing Absalom's requests, Joab had made his wishes

clear. If I were to do this favor, I'd be inserting myself into a situation that had nothing to do with my calling from Adonai.

I bowed as a sign of respect, then returned the prince's grin, though mine was nowhere near as charming. "I am sorry, but I cannot do what you ask. If the captain wishes to speak to you, he will seek you out."

A flash of irritation flitted across that handsome face, then Absalom heaved a sigh and gave me another shining smile. "Well said, prophet. I see you are as wise as you are circumspect." He took a step backward, lifted a hand in farewell, turned and went back to his family.

Two days later, I heard that Absalom had commanded his servants to set Joab's barley field afire. If that didn't result in a conversation with the king's commander, nothing would.

∽✢∾

Lying beside Ornah in our small house, I dreamed.

In spirit I floated into King David's room, where a harp lay on a table beside his bed. A wind blew over the strings, and the rippling tones woke the king, who stirred, sat up, and got out of bed to begin composing a new psalm. Bemused, I smiled at the busy king. Then the scene shifted. I was standing in a shadowy forest, the area dominated by a gigantic terebinth tree. The massive limbs spread toward the north, east, and west, its canopy effectively blocking the sunlight. The musical wind played here as well, moving the leaves until they applauded in praise to HaShem. Only then did I notice an object hanging from a low branch.

I moved closer. The object, which turned and twisted in the wind, was a man, and for a moment I didn't recognize him. Then I realized I was staring at Absalom, the king's son. His thick hair had become tangled within the tree, and Absalom had pulled a dagger from his belt and was attempting to cut himself free.

I stared as surprise siphoned the blood from my head. The sight of Israel's best-known prince dangling by his hair was so unexpected, so absurd, that I nearly laughed aloud. Though I saw no sign of a mule, somehow the prince had lost his royal seat.

As I watched Absalom struggle, a great ripping sound shook the forest, and the ground split beneath the prince's feet. He looked down into a breach filled with steaming red mud and hissing black stones that moved and melted in the fissure.

Without being told, I knew I was looking into the abyss of Gehinnom. From the expression of stark terror on his face, Absalom had recognized the place, too. He dropped his dagger, no longer willing to fall free of the tree, and then his panic-stricken eyes met mine. They widened and filled with wordless appeal, but I could do nothing to save him.

And then I woke.

Chapter Thirty-Six
BATHSHEBA

I SHOULD HAVE EXPECTED IT TO HAPPEN—knowing David as I did, and knowing of his obsession with his most handsome son, I should have been prepared.

But I had relaxed during the years Absalom lived as an exile from the king's court, and the palace walls had sheltered me from the outside world. Because Elisheba lived with me, she was no longer a source of gossip about daily life in Jerusalem.

So when the king asked all his wives and children to attend court one spring morning, I dressed with care, thinking we were about to celebrate a treaty, a birthday, or some gift the king wished to bestow on one of his soldiers. Shlomo, tall and thin at sixteen, met his brothers and me in the palace courtyard, and together we walked through the central doorway to the throne room. We bowed before David, then made our way to the area where members of the royal family sat in attendance on the king.

When we had all assembled, David nodded, lifted his hand, and gestured to Joab. At this signal, the army commander, looking unusually grim, threw open the double doors and announced his guests in a loud voice: "Presenting Absalom, son of the king, his wife, and his children."

Something cold trickled down my spine at the sight of the young man who had murdered the king's firstborn. Absalom seemed to have grown bigger in the five years he'd been away from the palace, wider somehow, and more robust. He strode majestically forward until he reached his father's throne. He bowed, pressing his forehead to the floor, until David rose, walked forward, and touched his shoulder. Absalom stood, his eyes glowing with anticipation. I saw his hands move as if he would embrace his father, but David did not open his arms to his son. Instead, the unsmiling king caught Absalom's left hand, kissed it, and turned, offering his back to the son who had returned.

The empty air between David and Absalom vibrated, the silence filling with disappointment so bitter I could almost taste it. Absalom swallowed hard as his father again took his throne. The prince stepped to the side and introduced his family. "My wife," he said, smiling at the crowd, "and my children."

I stared at David, baffled. For three years he had pined for Absalom, and then the young man had returned. But even though Absalom lived in Jerusalem, David had not once confronted or counseled his son, yet Absalom still managed to find a way back into the palace. Clearly, however, David was not eager to welcome him. Resigned? Perhaps. Happy? Not at all.

If this had been staged as an act of public reconciliation, only those who had not witnessed it would believe that any sort of reconciliation had taken place.

Absalom turned toward us, the king's family. He caught my eye and dipped his head in acknowledgment, though his gaze lingered on Solomon. I wanted to throw myself in front of my son and shout that Absalom should never look at, never even *think* about Shlomo, but that sort of behavior would not please my lord the king. So what could I do? David had allowed his scheming older son to return to court, and I could do nothing but accept Absalom's presence. I would be expected to smile at him, honor him, and perhaps even obey him.

In that instant, I realized I did not have the power to protect any of my sons.

I closed my eyes and wished I could shout out a message for the world to hear. *My Solomon will be the next king!* But David had not mentioned making the news public, and I understood why. At sixteen, Solomon was still a youth, and anything could happen to him—a hunting accident, a slip of a sword, a poisoned dish. Even in the guarded halls of the palace, plots and schemes developed, any one of which might prove dangerous for my son.

By remaining silent, however, David allowed his other children to dream of power. With Amnon gone, Absalom would be the presumptive crown prince, and over the next few years he could forge alliances that might prove fatal even to his father. Absalom was old enough to be king, and Adonijah, Shephatiah, and Ithream also waited in the shadows.

Blood pounded in my ears as Grandfather stepped forward and invited Absalom and his family to a banquet. I closed my eyes, fervently hoping that Solomon and I would not be expected to attend. Or, if we were, that we would be seated far across the room, away from the attractive man I could neither admire nor trust.

Chapter Thirty-Seven
NATHAN

STANDING WITH OTHER OBSERVERS in the king's throne room, my mouth twisted with the acceptance of a terrible knowledge: history was repeating itself before my eyes. A son who yearned for acceptance and approval from his father had found none.

I lowered my head out of respect as Absalom and his family walked away from David. Absalom would probably smile falsely for the rest of the day, making much of his return to the king's court and the bosom of his family. But in truth, the king had greeted enemies with far more cordiality, and other members of the royal family—especially Bathsheba—had looked at Absalom with fear in their eyes.

I slipped away from the crowd and left the throne room, wandering toward a quiet seat in a stone alcove. Soldiers and visitors occasionally walked through the hallway, but for the most part silence reigned here, allowing me to be alone with my thoughts. If

Adonai wished to speak to me in this place, I would be ready and quick to hear His voice.

Sitting in the alcove, I was filled with remembering. When David fled from Saul, he came to see Samuel, my teacher. While staying with us, he wrote one of his *tehillim* and read it to the prophet:

> For your sake I suffer insults,
> shame covers my face.
> I am estranged from my brothers,
> an alien to my mother's children,
> because zeal for your house is eating me up,
> and on me are falling the insults
> of those insulting you.

He had written much more, but those lines remained with me because I'd been startled by David's confession that he felt no connection to his seven brothers. When I asked Samuel about it, my teacher quietly explained that since David felt cut off from his own family, he began to consider Saul his father and Jonathan his brother. He might have considered the king's daughters, Merab and Michal, his sisters until the king offered one of them in marriage. In the end, David married Michal because Saul wanted him to. David would have done anything to please the king he so admired.

In the same way, Saul loved David . . . until he began to fear him. Then that fierce love turned to fierce hate, and Saul's hate nearly destroyed the young shepherd.

"The lad has a sensitive soul," Samuel had finished. "And that is why he is here now. He has been hurt, and his soul needs time to heal. When a cry for love is met by hate or indifference, the one who begged for love will become hard as a seed of bitterness grows. We will pray with David and encourage him to seek Adonai so his heart will remain tender."

I closed my eyes and again saw Absalom's handsome face as he looked at the king, his eyes alight with hope, his fingers fluttering in anticipation of embracing his father in reconciliation and forgiveness. He had been silently, earnestly seeking love and approval, and David had not granted it. David had given ceremonial kisses on both cheeks to former enemies, yet to his son he could only bestow a chilly kiss on the hand.

I groaned. Oh, Absalom. After being his father's favored child for so many years, this sort of public humiliation would do nothing to keep his heart soft and tender toward the king. After waiting two years for the king to do something about Amnon's sin, Absalom had boldly avenged his sister, and what had been the result? Exile. Disinterest. And now, public humiliation.

No, Absalom's heart would not be softened by David's welcome today. And seeds of bitterness thrived in the hard ground of anger and resentment.

⁓✢⁓

One day it occurred to me that David treated his son Absalom in the same way he'd treated Michal, the daughter of Saul. He had sought his wife when she lived with another man, but after she dared rebuke him, he'd kept her at arm's length. In the same way, David had pined for Absalom and allowed him to return to Jerusalem, but then he forbade the young man to appear at court.

So just as Michal had invested her life in raising her nephews, Absalom began to invest his life in the people of Israel.

After he'd been officially welcomed at court by his father the king, the citizens of Jerusalem were no longer shy about praising and admiring the supposed heir. In return, Absalom indulged in princely perks no son of Israel had ever claimed. He expected free food at the market, the lending of servants to tend his fields, and volunteers to care for his animals. No longer content to travel by mule like others in the royal family, he bought a chariot and horses and hired fifty men to run in front of his conveyance to announce his approach.

Unlike some wealthy men, Absalom was not a sluggard. He rose early to ride out in his chariot and station himself beneath a shaded tent near the approach to the city gate.

Since I lived in the last house at the outskirts of Jerusalem, he often set his tent across the road from my home. Each morning I rose at sunrise only to find that Absalom had risen in the dark. As I sat beneath the shade of my fig tree, Absalom greeted every traveler on the road, hailing them with a smile and friendly questions: "What city are you from? What business have you in Jerusalem?"

If someone from a neighboring tribe was bringing a case to the king for judgment, Absalom would run his fingers through his thick hair in a thoughtful gesture, then lean forward to say, "Look, your cause is good and just, but the king hasn't deputized anyone to hear your case. If I were made judge in the land, anyone with a suit or other cause could come to me. I would see to it that justice was meted out fairly."

When anyone, visitor or neighbor, approached and prepared to prostrate himself before Absalom, the prince would put out his hands, hold the person upright, and kiss his cheeks as if they were close kinsmen and not prince and servant.

Whenever I witnessed the prince's effusive greetings, I couldn't help remembering what I'd observed on the morning Absalom returned to court. Since he did not receive a warm welcome from the king, he seemed determined to offer it to anyone who crossed his path.

After four years of this behavior, Absalom had thoroughly stolen the hearts of those who lived in Jerusalem and those from neighboring tribes who had met him on visits to the capital city.

Because he acted with fierce intention and bold rashness, many of the king's counselors dared to call the king's attention to Absalom's overweening ambition.

David's only response was to offer a polite smile. "And why shouldn't Absalom win the people's hearts?" he would ask. "He is a prince of Israel. Let him be, and do not disturb him."

I didn't know what to make of David's answer. I believed he loved his son, but why didn't he show it? Did he not know how, or did he worry that any display of support for Absalom would appear to be support for a murderer?

I didn't know what Ahithophel and the counselors said to the king about his son or if they said anything at all. But I did know this: though many of the king's officials felt uneasy with Absalom's intentions, nothing they said could sway the king's opinion that Absalom should be allowed to do as he pleased.

~❧~

One day I was working in my family's field when I looked up to see a familiar form in the distance. The prophet Gad, the king's personal seer, was approaching on the road, and within a few moments I realized he had come to see me. I dropped my hoe, washed my hands, and greeted my guest with water and a seat in the shade.

From the line between his brows, I knew something troubled the man, so I sat and waited for him to speak. After a few moments of apparent soul-searching, he did. "David has taken a census," he said. "Months ago the king sent Joab's men throughout the tribes to count the number of people in the land."

I blinked. I had heard nothing from Adonai about a census, but the Lord did not tell me everything. "Well," I said, "the offering will be good for the priests. The Tabernacle may need repairs—"

"They are not collecting an offering," Gad interrupted, his face grim. "They are only counting men twenty and older."

I smoothed my beard, troubled by this news. HaShem told Moses that whenever a census of the people was taken, each man was to pay a small piece of silver as a ransom for himself so that no plague would strike the people as they were counted. The payment was intended to purify the populace and confirm their commitment to the care of the Tabernacle. If David's men weren't collecting an offering, why were they counting heads?

Gad must have read the question in my eyes. "It would appear this census is being taken to satisfy the king's curiosity. Perhaps he has been tempted to take pride in the strength of his army or the number of his people."

"We are at peace," I pointed out. "David doesn't need to know the strength of his army." I paused to search my thoughts. "As a rich man foolishly places his trust in the number of silver coins he has, perhaps the king has placed his trust in the number of his soldiers."

"I don't know what David is thinking," Gad said. "And Adonai has not told me. But even Joab tried to persuade the king to forget the idea, but David insisted. The commander's men have been traveling through Israel for nearly nine months and will soon return with an answer for the king."

"And after that?"

Gad's dark brows slanted in a frown. "Then we shall see what Adonai says."

Days passed before I heard from Gad again. When I met him at the palace, he told me that Joab's men had returned and reported their findings: Israel had eight hundred thousand men capable of swinging a sword, and Judah five hundred thousand.

After hearing the report, David realized the extent of his sin almost immediately. "I have offended greatly in what I have done," he told Joab. Then he addressed Adonai, saying, "And now, Lord, pardon the guilt of your servant, for I have been foolish."

Gad went to David early the next morning with a question from HaShem. "'For your sin in taking the census, will you choose three years of famine throughout your territory, three months of fleeing from your enemies, or three days of severe plague throughout your land?' Think this over and decide what answer I should give Adonai."

"I am in great distress," David told his seer. "Please let us fall into the hand of the Lord, for His mercies are great, but do not let me fall into human hands."

So for three days a plague smote the people of Israel. From Dan in the north to Beersheba in the south, seventy thousand men died, along with women and children. As the angel of death prepared to destroy Jerusalem, Adonai relented and told the angel to stop.

At that moment David looked up and saw the death angel hovering over a threshing floor that belonged to Araunah the Jebusite.

Gad told David to go to the threshing floor and build an altar there. The king went as the seer had instructed, then purchased the threshing floor and oxen for a sacrifice of burnt offerings and peace offerings. After David prayed, Adonai answered by sending fire from heaven to burn the offering on the altar. David was filled with the *Ruach HaKodesh* and declared, "This will be the location for the Temple of the Lord God and the place of the altar for Israel's burnt offerings."

Gad looked at me when he finished his story. "Were any sick in your house?"

I shook my head. "None. Though I heard about many who died in other villages."

"I do not always understand the ways of Adonai," Gad said, "but He makes His plans in the heavens while we make ours on earth. We may not understand His ways, but we must trust that they are right."

The census and its grievous consequences affected David's own family, though the king did not realize it right away. The next day, while he sketched out plans to build Adonai's Temple on the former threshing floor, Absalom and his wife dressed in sackcloth and led a procession of mourners to the King's Valley, where the king's son buried four of his five children and piled rocks on the grave, inviting other mourners to do the same. When the pile of stones reached higher than a man's head, Absalom addressed those who had come with him. "I have built this monument," he said, placing his hand on his chest, "because I have no son to carry on my name. Only my daughter, Maacah, still lives."

When he had finished, he returned to his post at the city gate. Though he had buried four of his precious children that morning, he stood stoically beneath his tent, unsmiling and red-eyed. On that day the visitors who entered the City of David kissed and comforted *him*, for word of his loss had spread throughout the land, proving beyond doubt that he was a man of the people.

The citizens of Jerusalem wept over those dead children, not for their grandfather David's sake but for Absalom's.

CHAPTER THIRTY-EIGHT
BATHSHEBA

AFTER WATCHING MY SONS TRAIN with Abishai and other members of the Thirty, I left the practice field and walked back to my apartment. The afternoon was bathed in honey-thick sunshine, and it felt good to stretch my legs.

I smiled when I thought of my boys. Solomon was a fair swordsman, but he had inherited my father's height and my lean frame, so he would never be known for physical strength. The twins, Shammua and Shobab, were stocky and square like their father and would make good soldiers when the time came. At seventeen, they were older than David had been when he killed Goliath, yet Israel did not conscript soldiers under the age of twenty.

My youngest, Nathan, was fifteen, and though he might have to fight one day, I prayed he would not. He had inherited the sensitive side of David's nature, so I hoped he would spend his days serving

Adonai as a musician or a poet. Like all princes, he had to train in the art of warfare, but it did not suit his nature.

I nodded at the guard posted at an inconspicuous gate in the palace wall, then slipped through the opening and crossed the harem courtyard. Few of the king's women would be stirring at this hour unless they covered themselves with scarves and veils to protect their skin from the hot sun.

I paused at a fountain when I saw three men leaving Abigail's chamber. I recognized two of them as royal physicians, but the third was a stranger. I let the fountain spray my fingers as I considered the unusual guests. Who was sick in Abigail's quarters? One of her maids or the lady herself?

I ran my wet fingers over the warm skin at my neck, then decided to seek my own answers. I hadn't seen Abigail in several weeks, and we usually crossed paths at least every few days. But nearly all of David's wives attended worship at the Tabernacle on feast days, and lately I hadn't seen Abigail at those ceremonies, either.

The door was slightly ajar when I approached, so I knocked softly and pushed it open. "Hello?"

Before anyone had time to answer, I saw Abigail seated on the edge of her bed, her hair piled on top of her head and her chest bare. Her handmaid was struggling to wrap a wide linen strip around her mistress's chest, and with one downward glance I saw why. Abigail's left breast was malformed, distorted with purple lumps, one of which had broken open to reveal a suppurating tumor.

"Oh!" Upon seeing me, Abigail raised her hands to try to hide her disfigurement, discomfiting the handmaid all the more. The poor girl broke into tears, and after a speechless moment in which every word left my head, I stepped forward and said the only words that came to mind: "I'm so sorry."

Abigail released a heavy sigh, then dropped her defensive posture and gave me a sad smile. "Sometimes it happens," she said simply.

"The physicians have no answers, but they do give me herbs for the pain."

A wave of guilt washed over me, slumping my shoulders and leaving me weak-kneed. I had envied this woman so many times—her pleasant features, her charming smile, her open countenance. Most of all, I had envied the relationship she shared with David. Even though she had only given him one son, she knew things about him that I might never know, because they were friends.

"Abigail." I sank to a stool, then rose on impulse and took the linen strip from the weeping handmaid. Dismissing the girl with a nod, I held the edges and looked into Abigail's eyes. "I'm sorry this has happened to you," I told her. "But let me help. If you would raise your arms . . ."

She did, and with the skill I'd gained from dressing rambunctious little boys, I wrapped the linen around her breasts, careful not to cause her pain. I padded the festering area with loose cotton, then wrapped another layer over the first. When I had finished, I dropped a silk tunic over her head, helped her stand, and gently tied a fabric belt at her slender waist.

"Mirza means well," Abigail murmured, speaking of her maid. "But the sight of my disfigurement frightens her."

"What does David say?"

"I have not seen him since . . ." She looked away as her words trailed off.

The sight of such an awful wound was enough to shock anyone, but what could a woman do? In this, as in all things in which we were powerless, we could only trust Adonai to help us endure what must be endured.

I helped Abigail back to her bed, lifted her feet onto the mattress, and propped her up with pillows. "I wondered why I hadn't seen much of you," I offered in a pitiful attempt to make conversation. "Now I understand."

Anyone with a festering sore was unclean according to our law and had to be separated from others. Abigail could not attend worship or visit David, and anyone who touched her would have to wash their clothes, bathe in water, and be unclean until evening—including me.

Abigail moved a pillow over her chest and wrapped her arms around it. "Actually, I'm glad we have this time to talk alone. I know my days are numbered, and there is much I want to say to you."

"I remember," I assured her, "what you said the last time we spoke. At first I wasn't sure I could trust you, but now I know you had only good intentions."

"The king and I—" a coughing spasm interrupted her—"are the same age. We are friends. And as his friend I have always tried to rejoice when he rejoices and weep when he weeps. I have also cared for those he loves. And the woman he loves most, Bathsheba, is you."

I moved to the stool by the bed. "I care a great deal for him. I hope you know I would never hurt him."

"I worried about you in the beginning." A glaze seemed to come down over her damp eyes. "You were so beautiful, and experience has taught me that beautiful women are dangerous. Their beauty gives them power over men, and some of them use it against the king, or try to."

She gave me a secretive smile, and I knew she was talking about Maacah, mother to Tamar and Absalom. Maacah had always demanded the best for herself and her children—the best garments, the best tutors, the best mounts, the best accommodations. The woman did not know the meaning of the word *humility*.

"I would never—"

"I know you wouldn't; such selfishness is not part of your nature. But I didn't know you at first. I only knew David was smitten with your beauty. He brought you to the palace because he knew what would happen if he abandoned you. And because you were so devastated and grief-stricken because of what he'd done to your husband, he determined to do anything in his power to make you happy. And in doing so, he began to love *you*, the woman beneath the beautiful face and form."

Her expression softened into one of fond reminiscence. "I knew my lord and king had finally found a woman worthy of his love. Yet with all you had endured, I wondered if you could really care for him. I still wonder, but at least I know you will not be cruel to him. You are not cruel by nature."

"I . . ." I floundered in a desperate search for words. I wanted to give this woman an answer that would set her at ease, but what could I say? I respected David, I cared for him greatly, and I enjoyed his company. But did my heart leap at his approach like it did when I waited for Uriah to come home?

No. I did not love him that way.

I reached across the empty space between us and took Abigail's hand. "I will always care for him," I promised her. "He is the father of my sons, my lord and my king. You can be sure I will never harm him."

She drew a deep breath and smiled, though I saw the gleam of disappointment in her eyes. She had hoped for more, and I could not give it.

But at least Abigail and I now understood each other.

⋘⊱

Absalom did not often come to court, but when he did I frequently felt the pressure of his gaze on me. He would sit with other tribal leaders in the throne room, usually across from the area members of the royal family occupied. Frequently I looked up and caught him staring at me; once or twice he even smiled. When he was not looking at me, I noticed he watched his father, and his expression grew more alert whenever David looked at me to share a smile or some other unspoken communication.

Once I leaned over and whispered in Michal's ear, "Is it my imagination or does Absalom seem unusually interested in the king's wives?"

She watched in silence for a moment, then confirmed what I'd been too discreet to verbalize. "It's not the king's wives that interests him. It's you. He watches you, then looks at the king, then returns his gaze to you. It is almost as if he would test the bond between you and David."

When Absalom stopped coming to court, I dismissed the matter from my mind. But one day my servant came in from outside, closed the door behind her, and dropped to her knees.

"My lady, forgive me if I am being intrusive."

I put down the garment I had been sewing for Solomon, now quite the man at twenty. "What is it?"

The woman kept her eyes downcast. "I am acquainted with a man who stands guard at the king's bedchamber. We were speaking in the garden, and he remarked that one of Absalom's servants had been asking him questions. I'm sorry to bother you with this, my lady, but I thought you ought to know."

My nerves tightened. "Go on."

Her cheeks flushed crimson. "Apparently the servant from Absalom's house inquired as to which woman the king sends for each night, who is summoned most often, and who is the king's favorite. My friend said he tried to avoid giving a direct answer, but the man became quite persistent."

I waited, but my servant appeared uncertain about proceeding. "Persistent in what way? Please, speak freely."

She lifted her gaze to meet mine. "The man from Absalom's house finally asked if you were the favorite wife. The guard was put off by the question, but when the man invoked his master's name and insisted on an answer, he admitted that you spent more time with the king than any other woman. Then Absalom's servant departed."

I thanked my servant for her honesty and dismissed her, then sat in silence and sorted through a maze of troubling thoughts. Absalom wanted to know if I was the favorite wife. I could think of only one reason that might cause a prince to care about which wife the king favored. He wanted to know if David had promised that wife that her son would ascend to the throne. If he truly believed I was first in the king's heart, Absalom would be certain to draw a target on my eldest son. On Solomon.

A few days later, my handmaid was arranging my hair when a messenger pounded on my door. I gave my servant leave to answer, and a moment later she returned with news that the king's chief counselor wanted to see me at once. "Is it so urgent?" I tugged at a wayward curl. "I will be leaving my chamber before long—"

"The counselor said he'd be waiting in the garden," my maid answered, clearly flustered. "Please, my lady, he seemed most anxious. Do not keep him waiting."

What could Grandfather be worried about now? I thanked my handmaid for her efforts, then pulled a mantle over my sleeveless tunic. I did not like to go outside in the brutal afternoon sun, but Grandfather would not be put off.

I found him seated by a fountain, his forehead dotted with perspiration and his bony foot tapping with impatience. "Bathsheba!" Despite his obvious irritation at my delay, he stood, took my hands, and kissed my forehead. "Come, let us walk. I want to extend an invitation to you—and to your sons."

I lifted a brow. "An invitation?"

"Please." Grandfather gestured to the path that led to the balcony. "Let us walk."

I took his arm and noticed that my grandfather seemed intent on getting us away from the shaded areas where we might be overheard by servants or gardeners. His lined face offered no clues, so I walked slowly, keeping pace with his unsteady stride. By my calculations, Grandfather was seventy-seven years old, yet still as quick and stubborn as he had ever been.

"I have made plans," Grandfather said, "to spend the summer at my farm in Giloh."

"Good. You always enjoy your time there, don't you?"

"Why shouldn't I? It is a restful place. This year I would like you and your boys to join me there. I am not long for this world, Bathsheba, and before I join my fathers I would like to spend some time with my granddaughter away from the palace. Please say you'll join me in Giloh."

I halted, caught off guard by his suggestion. "I appreciate the invitation, but I can't leave the king for such a long time."

"Can't you?" He turned to face me. "The king is an old man, Bathsheba, and he doesn't need a woman every night. Even if he did, he has a harem."

My mouth fell open as indignation poured through my veins. "He's younger than you! And as it happens, sometimes the king enjoys talking to me. I am his wife; I belong by his side."

"I am your flesh and blood. I have only two granddaughters, and by my count David has seventeen wives and even more concubines. He doesn't need you."

I drew a breath, about to argue, but Grandfather had a point. David didn't *need* me, but still . . . the thought of leaving him felt disloyal. He was my husband, and I his wife. I belonged with him.

I placed my hand on my grandfather's arm. "I will ask the king if the boys and I can visit for a few days."

"Not a few days." Sweat beaded on Grandfather's forehead. "Three months. I want you with me. If you won't come, you must send the boys. If you can't send all of them, send Solomon. He should spend the summer in Giloh."

"Our place is with the king. But he is not unreasonable, so if you want us to visit for three or four days—"

"When are you going to see that he is not worthy of you?" Grandfather caught my wrist as his mood veered sharply to anger. "Look outside the palace and see what is happening in the city! You live in a protected suite, but tremors are shaking the foundation of David's house, dangerous quakes that will destroy his kingdom, and you along with it. Come to Giloh, with or without the king's permission. Bring Solomon, meet me in the palace courtyard, and I'll take you out of here. I can hire a wagon—"

"No!" I pulled out of Grandfather's grasp and backed away, horrified by the words pouring out of him. "We will not leave the king."

"Then I cannot be responsible for you." Grandfather radiated disapproval like a heat wave. "Samuel's prophecy about your life— we can all see what being a *tob* woman has done for you. But your sons, your precious boys, are not going to survive David's bloody history. If you care about them, if you care about your own life, you will come to Giloh with me."

A scream of frustration clawed at the back of my throat. Grandfather always felt his opinions were more correct than anyone else's, and I knew he would not soften his position. Still, I could not obey him because he could not be right. David had been promised an eternal dynasty, and Solomon had been promised the throne. Adonai could not lie. If David were to encounter any kind of trouble, I should be with him, not hiding on Grandfather's farm.

I lifted my chin and met my kinsman's gaze head on. "I am not yours to command. I will remain with my husband because this is where Adonai has placed me. So go if you must, but do not worry

about me or my children. I will protect my sons with my life, and
Adonai will protect us *and* His anointed king."

Grandfather's eyes rested on me, then narrowed as he lifted his
hands and backed away. "Ignore my counsel if you will," he said.
"But know that you are ignoring a man considered to be an oracle
of God. When God speaks, you should listen."

"When Adonai speaks, I will," I snapped. "Though I love you,
Grandfather, you are not a prophet, and you are not Adonai."

He turned and moved away, rocking from side to side on his stiff
hips, and I flushed with momentary victory. I had stood up to my
strong-willed grandfather, and that was no small feat.

Yet a niggling doubt hovered at the edge of my thoughts. Grandfather never sounded an alarm without cause, so why did he feel so
strongly that my sons and I were in danger? Did he have knowledge
he hadn't shared, and did this knowledge have anything to do with
Absalom?

I walked to the edge of the balcony and scanned the valley
beyond, half expecting to spot the fires of an enemy camp on the
horizon. I saw nothing, but anxiety squeezed my heart and then
slithered lower to twist in my gut.

Trouble stirred somewhere nearby, of that I was certain.

⸙

"Nathan the prophet wishes to see me?" I stared at the servant
who huddled on the ground. "Are you certain?"

The young girl nodded, then sat up and jerked her thumb toward
the harem gate. "He waits out there. He said I should find you at once."

Perplexed and feeling a little guilty—had I done something to
displease Adonai?—I left my bench in the harem garden and walked
toward the gate. I could not recall Nathan ever coming to see me,
or any of the king's other women, for that matter.

His eyes lit when he saw me, then he bowed. "Rise, please," I told him, smiling. "I am not of royal blood."

"But you are the mother of our future king," he said, keeping his voice low as he rose. "And I have come here to discuss Solomon."

Tension nipped a nerve at the back of my neck. "Have you heard something? Has Adonai spoken of him?"

The prophet shook his head and gestured toward a path that led toward the Tabernacle. "Shall we walk? I will remain a discreet distance away, since I am not willing to entrust my words to a chaperone's ears."

I pulled my mantle over my hair and set out for the Tabernacle, walking slowly so we could speak without becoming winded.

"I have not come in the service of Adonai"—he kept his eyes on the cobblestones at our feet—"but in your service, my lady. For some time I have believed that Adonai would have me be your protector."

I laughed softly. "I live in a royal harem, prophet. I am surrounded by guards."

He chuckled too, and for an instant his gaze crossed mine. "I understand. If you needed a protector, surely the Lord would not send an unarmed prophet, eh? But still, for years I have felt a strong urge to protect you, and recently I have sensed danger from a nearby quarter. I do not believe you are in immediate danger, but I fear for your son."

His verbalization of my own anxieties sent a drop of perspiration streaming down my spine. I turned to face him, my face burning. "Who would dare harm Shlomo?"

Nathan lowered his head, folded his hands behind his back, and seemed intent on the pathway. Realizing I had broken out of our small charade, with difficulty I turned to walk forward again, keeping my head and my voice low.

After a moment, Nathan spoke. "I daresay you know the answer to your question. I have been watching Absalom long enough to know that he plans to sit on his father's throne. He has already killed

Amnon. Before he wantonly kills any other brothers, he would certainly want to determine which son the king considers his heir."

I forced a smile. "Perhaps we do not need to worry. Only you and I, Abigail and the king know that both David and Adonai have promised the throne to Solomon. The boy himself does not know because I've never told him."

Again, the prophet's gaze crossed mine. "What about Ahithophel?"

I tilted my head, admitting the truth. "Grandfather bases his conviction that Solomon will reign on Samuel's prophecy. But he could easily be persuaded that Samuel's prophecy meant something else. After all, it only promised great influence for one of my sons. It didn't specify which son or what that influence would be. Grandfather is, however—" I hesitated, remembering his last visit—"he is very concerned about me and my sons. The other day he tried to get me to take the boys and go with him to Giloh."

Nathan stopped. "Perhaps that is not a bad idea."

I stopped as well and glanced back at him. "Do you really think the threat so serious?"

Nathan nodded. "Absalom has been nursing his wounds for four years. Most young men are not so patient, but even Absalom's patience will eventually run out."

We had stopped near a fork in the path. To the right lay the Tabernacle; to the left lay the king's stables and the road that would take us out of the palace and into the city.

I gestured to the left. "Let us find a guard and a horse. Let's go to Solomon's house and speak to him. Perhaps I can convince him to go to Giloh for a while."

Nathan shook his head. "You should not leave the palace without the king's permission, so I will go. I will speak to your son and bring him to you. Perhaps it is time we had an honest talk with him about his future."

With my hand at my throat, I nodded, hoping Nathan was right.

Chapter Thirty-Nine

NATHAN

THE LORD GAVE ME STRENGTH, opening a path for me amid hordes in the streets, throngs near the palace gate, at the market-place, and at the crowded well. In time I found myself in the street where Solomon's house stood, and the sight of a donkey tethered to a pole eased my frantic heart.

I knocked on the door and bowed to the servant who opened it. "Nathan the prophet," I said, snatching a breath. "To see Solomon, the young prince."

The servant stepped forward and peered left and right. "I don't see him."

"But . . ." I gestured to the donkey. "Isn't that his mount?"

"Oh." The servant laughed. "His brother Absalom came by and offered one of his animals for Solomon to ride. They have gone hunting."

My pulse, which had begun to slow, increased its speed as my thoughts scampered like wild rabbits. "Do you know . . . do you know where they are hunting?"

The servant shrugged. "The wilderness?"

I wiped perspiration from my forehead and resisted the urge to box the young man's ears. Of course they were hunting in the wilderness! Clearly, the lad had no idea where to find his master.

I waved him away and stood at the courtyard gate for a moment. I had no idea where Absalom hunted, but one thing was certain—he would not choose a place frequented by other hunters. If he meant Solomon ill, he would leave the city and go to some desolate spot.

I gripped my walking stick and plunged into the street, dodging people and donkeys and carts, threading my way through the crowd, intent on getting out of the city. I could only trust Adonai to reveal the princes' whereabouts.

Chapter Forty

Bathsheba

I RETURNED TO MY APARTMENT and sat at my dressing table, my eyes fixed on a small carved pendant Shlomo had given me when he was five years old. He had been so proud of himself, so confident, but even then he had been wise enough to answer my thanks with a careful answer: "It gave me great pleasure to make this for you, Mama."

My son. My pleasure and purpose, but never my pride.

I loved all my sons, but Solomon was not mine alone; he belonged to Adonai and to Israel. Hadn't Samuel foreseen the moment when Solomon would step onto the dais that held his father's throne? Hadn't the prophet foreseen the glory and peace Nathan mentioned at Solomon's circumcision?

If the Word of God was true, I told myself, then Solomon was not in danger. If God wanted him to sit on the throne of David, then Absalom could do nothing to thwart that plan. Nothing.

Yet God had never promised that Solomon would not be a wounded king or a crippled king, crawling from table to bed like my sister, Amaris. God had never said that Solomon would never be sick, or disfigured, or gravely injured—

"Help!"

The worst burst from my lips without conscious thought, startling the maid who was sorting linens in the next room. She rushed forward and stared at me from the doorway. "Do you need something, my lady?"

I need my son. I need assurance that he is safe.

I couldn't speak those words, so I gave her a tight smile and inquired about the other boys. "Where are they?"

"Still with their tutor," she said. "Shall I send for them?"

"No, leave them. They are fine."

I waited until she went back to her work, and then I picked up the carved pendant, wrapped my fist around it, and pressed it to my heart as I begged Adonai to keep Solomon safe.

Chapter Forty-One

NATHAN

My chest rose and fell like a human bellows as I jogged over the road that led out of the city. I had asked several hunters, farmers, and travelers if they had seen Absalom or young Solomon that day, but no one had.

I had run quite a distance past my own house when I collapsed on the side of the road and rested my weary back against a huge stone. My attention drifted away in a mist of fatigue as my lungs redoubled their efforts at breathing. I drank in great gulps of air and asked myself if I was behaving like a fool.

Adonai had not commanded me to visit Bathsheba, but the Lord knew I had not gone to the palace to fulfill a selfish desire. I had gone out of conviction, certain that danger loomed before the young prince. I couldn't say if that conviction rose from my own common sense, logical conclusions, from HaShem—or perhaps a combination of all three. I only knew I had to see Bathsheba, and now I had to find young Solomon.

I pressed both hands over my eyes as they burned with weariness. If I went home with my mission unfulfilled, Ornah would wonder if I'd lost my senses. What if I'd alarmed Bathsheba and run myself past the point of exhaustion for no reason?

With my eyes closed and my eyelids shaded, I stood in darkness, and then I heard a sound I'd missed. A groan. Frantic breathing, so close it might have been on the other side of the rock I leaned upon.

I opened my eyes and turned. The scrubby land behind me was empty, populated with small shrubs, a few scattered trees, and boulders. I ventured into it, straining to listen, and when I heard nothing I covered my eyes again.

"Le me hear, Lord," I whispered, blind in the shimmering desert.

I heard the sounds again. A groan, accompanied by frantic breaths. And farther away, the clumsy *clip-clop* of a wandering donkey.

I kept my eyes closed and trudged forward, pulling back when I ran into a bush, pressing through the shrubs and occasionally stumbling over a rock. When the sound had become so loud I knew I could not miss the source, I opened my eyes and found myself in the shade of a terebinth tree. I lowered my gaze and there, to the right, I saw a pale hand on the sand.

"Solomon!"

With a certainty borne of conviction, I rounded the tree and found the young prince lying on the ground, an ugly bruise and cut at his temple. The wound would certainly not be fatal, but I could not understand who or what had inflicted it. Holding the unconscious prince's wrist, I glanced around, and spotted a brightly feathered arrow in a shrub some distance away.

I glanced back at the young man's wound. The arrow had grazed him, no doubt. A hunting accident, one that might have proved fatal had I not arrived to stop a second arrow.

"Solomon." I patted his cool cheek. "Solomon, wake. I have promised to take you to your mother."

His eyelids fluttered, then opened. For a moment he stared at me, confused, then a slow smile quirked his mouth. "You're the prophet."

"I am. And I believe Adonai sent me to fetch you today."

"What about Absalom? He sent me after a buck—"

"Did you see the buck?"

Solomon's smile went sheepish. "No. I was following a rabbit."

"Perhaps the buck was behind you, then. Your brother's arrow struck your head—forcefully, I'd wager, since you're lying on the ground. But not forcefully enough to do any permanent damage."

Solomon snorted, then attempted to sit up. I extended my arm, offering assistance, and he gratefully accepted it. "What's this about my mother?"

"She would like to talk about your future. When we find your donkey, we'll ride back to Jerusalem."

We separated to look for the beast, but I did not allow Solomon to leave my sight. I was circling the terebinth, looking for hoofprints in the soft sand, when a shadow fell across my path. I looked up in time to see Absalom standing on a ridge, his bow upheld, an arrow on the string. Solomon, oblivious to his brother's appearance, stood downhill, his attention focused on the ground.

"Well met, Absalom," I called in my loudest voice. "You are a most blessed man today."

The older prince startled and hastily lowered his bow. With wide eyes he looked from Solomon to me, then back to Solomon again. "I thought . . . I thought I saw a deer."

I smiled and came out from behind the tree. "Apparently there are many deer in this area. I have not been fortunate enough to see one today, but then I am not a masterful hunter, only a prophet of Adonai."

Absalom came down the ridge, his attention shifting to his brother. "Solomon! Is that blood on your ear?"

"And my head," Solomon said, grinning. "Your aim is off today, brother."

Indeed it was.

I motioned to Solomon. "Come, my boy. Let us walk to the palace and leave Absalom to find his donkey. We should not keep your mother waiting."

CHAPTER FORTY-TWO
BATHSHEBA

My nerves grew tighter with every passing moment. As the shadows lengthened and the day sped away, I worried that Nathan would not find Solomon; that my son had already ventured into the grave.

Should I go to David? What could I tell him? That Nathan had experienced forebodings and I suspected Absalom of murderous mischief? I might have gone. I might have run to him but for one realization: David loved Absalom, too.

I fell to my knees and pressed my forehead to the floor. "Adonai," I whispered, "there was a time when I counted your word a curse, but now I cling to it. Being a *tob* woman, hard as it was, brought me Solomon, and I love him desperately. I confess that my heart is fickle and my spirit more eager to embrace comfort than struggle, but please, Adonai, be faithful to your word. Bring Solomon home safely."

I had just finished uttering my prayer when I heard footsteps in my courtyard. My servant stood at the door, pointing toward the hallway outside the harem. "The prophet has returned, my lady, with Solomon. They are most eager to speak to you."

Without even pausing to check my appearance, I hurried out to join them. I cried out when I spotted the cut and bruise on Solomon's temple, but both men assured me that the wound was not serious. "He might have a headache, though," Nathan added, looking pleased to have completed his task. "But Adonai has kept him from real danger."

If Solomon had any idea of the heavy meaning behind the prophet's words, he gave no sign of it. Instead, he looked at me, a question in his eyes. "You wanted to speak to me, Mother?"

"Nathan and I," I replied, gripping his upper arm. "But not here. Let's go to the garden where we can speak freely."

In the garden, I listened while Nathan shared the words he had uttered at Solomon's first public appearance in the throne room. "You will be king one day," he finished, his voice calm and neutral, "not because of anything you have done, but because it is Adonai's will to place you in that position. Adonai has great love for your father, and also has great love for you. David's house is an eternal one, and of his kingdom there shall be no end."

Solomon, still much a boy even at twenty, looked from the prophet to me. "You knew of this, Mother?"

I nodded.

"Why did you never say anything?"

"Why did you need to know?" I allowed myself to smile. "I would not have burdened your youth or inflated your ego. Even now, I would charge you to say nothing of this to anyone else, especially your brothers. Loving them as you do, I'm sure you would not want to say anything that might incite them to jealousy."

He lifted a brow as if surprised that any of his brothers could fall prey to that dangerous emotion, then he nodded. "My father the king will live a long time still," he said, leaning forward with his elbows on his knees. "I will try to put this information out of my mind."

"No," Nathan said. "You cannot forget where your destiny lies. For the rest of your father's life, you must observe life as it happens around you. Take note of what people do and what they say. Learn all you can about the royal court, for it is a treacherous and often dangerous sea of ambition and pretense. If you would be a good king, a wise king, you must know how to detect undercurrents and conspiracies. You must learn to see the motivations behind a man's eyes; you must learn to see the truth behind their words. So watch, young prince, and learn all you can before Adonai elevates you to your father's place."

Solomon's expression stilled and grew serious. "All right."

"One more thing," Nathan said as he leaned forward on his staff. "No more hunting with Absalom, or anxiety will be the death of your mother."

Solomon glanced at me for confirmation, and I nodded.

"All right, then," he said.

I gave Solomon a reassuring smile, and when he stood to leave for his own house, a part of my heart went with him.

Chapter Forty-Three
NATHAN

THE JOY OF TRAGEDY AVERTED endowed me with the strength to walk home. I passed the city gate and neared my house, walking slowly and carefully with nothing but moonlight to guide my path. I had just sung one of David's songs of praise to encourage my exhausted limbs when the moon grew so large as to fill the horizon, brightening the earth like the sun. The unexpected brilliance forced me to lift my arms and shield my blinded eyes.

"So be it," I told the Lord. "I am listening."

I sank to the side of the road, leaned upon my staff, and waited. The brightened road before me faded, and a moment later the backs of my eyelids filled with a view of the interior of a well-furnished home. A man sat at a table. Even though I could see only the back of his head, I knew I was watching Absalom.

"What do you mean, you grazed him?" A woman's sharp voice cut into the silence. "And a prophet saw you?"

"Not till later," Absalom muttered, both hands in his dinner bowl. "He didn't see anything."

"I don't know why you're messing with that one anyway," the woman said. "Why spend your energy ridding yourself of a future rival when you could take the throne now? Four years, husband! Four years you've been cultivating the hearts of the people. They love you. They are ready for you to be their leader."

"But what about Solomon? There are rumors about an old prophecy—"

"Forget the son who bedevils you. You can rid yourself of him and his mother once you are king."

The woman entered my field of vision. She moved closer to Absalom and draped her arms across his shoulders. She bent to whisper in his ear. "Promise me, husband. Promise me that you'll forget the commoner's son. Time enough to clear the field when you sit on the throne of Israel."

She kissed the top of her husband's head, and the scene faded from my view.

I exhaled a heavy sigh and gripped my staff. So . . . Solomon and Bathsheba would be safe, at least for a while. But David faced oncoming danger.

Chapter Forty-Four

NATHAN

ONE MORNING ABSALOM REAPPEARED in his father's court. I was sitting in the assembly when he, a mature man of thirty, stepped forward and bowed to his father.

"Absalom." Though David's face remained composed, I thought I detected a wistful note in his voice. "What can I do for you?"

The prince straightened himself. "If it pleases my lord and king"—he smiled his most charming smile—"allow me go to Hebron and fulfill the vow I made to Adonai."

"A vow?" David tilted his head. "What sort of vow was this?"

"Your servant made a vow while I was staying at Geshur," Absalom explained. "I vowed that if Adonai would bring me home to Jerusalem, I would sacrifice to the Lord in Hebron."

I had felt uneasy about Absalom ever since his return to Jerusalem, but at the mention of Hebron my unease gelled to a lump in my stomach. Hebron was the capital city of Judah, David's tribe.

David had first reigned as king in Hebron, so he had friends and family in that city. Despite all he had done in Jerusalem, the people of Hebron considered their town the *real* City of David.

I could think of no innocent reason for Absalom to make a sacrifice in Hebron.

The king seemed to weigh the matter. He studied his son for a long moment, then said, "Go in peace, my son."

I sat motionless as a wave of déjà vu swept over me. Absalom had appeared in court once before, asking for permission to take a different journey. That one had ended in disaster and death.

Had the king forgotten so soon?

Absalom spun on the ball of his foot and addressed the assembly in the throne room. "Who will go with me?" He lifted his hand in a welcoming gesture. "Come help me observe my vow to thank Adonai for His graciousness in returning me to Jerusalem."

I watched as leaders and counselors shot sharp looks at one another. I knew some of them had succumbed to Absalom's charm, but others were staunchly loyal to the king. Yet hadn't the king just given his blessing to Absalom's sacrifice? Surely it would please the king if they journeyed with his son to Hebron, if only to keep an eye on the ambitious prince.

By the end of the day, two hundred of the king's men had agreed to accompany Absalom. I later learned that Absalom even sent a special envoy to invite Ahithophel, the king's counselor, who was resting at his home in Giloh.

Should I go? I briefly considered making the journey, but in the end, the *Ruach HaKodesh* prevented me.

CHAPTER FORTY-FIVE

BATHSHEBA

I DID NOT SOON FORGET my grandfather's hurtful words, nor could I forget Nathan's warning. I frequently went up to the palace rooftop to look for signs of trouble in the city, but saw nothing. I talked to Michal, but she was still so grief-stricken she wouldn't have noticed if our water turned to blood. I finally told myself that Grandfather had become old and unstable, and Nathan had handled the problem with Absalom.

My boys had just returned from a hunt one afternoon when my servant rushed in and said a messenger waited to see me. Judging from the woman's breathless state, I surmised that Grandfather had returned to needle me again.

"Who waits outside?" I asked.

The servant bowed. "Nathan the prophet."

Twice . . . in so short a time? The thought of another warning for Solomon dropped into the pool of my heart and sent ripples of fear in every direction.

I asked the servant to have the prophet join me in the palace garden.

"Nathan wants to see you again?" Solomon, who was visiting his brothers, released a baritone chuckle as he propped his feet on a small table. "Perhaps he has a prophecy for you."

"I've heard enough prophecies for one lifetime." I glanced at my other sons. Shammua and Shobab were intent on devouring the lunch Elisheba had prepared for them, and young Nathan had picked up a scroll to read.

I smiled at Solomon. "Please, will you come? I'd feel better about meeting him if you were with me."

Solomon escorted me to the garden, then sat on a bench at my side as the prophet crossed a graveled path and bowed before us.

"Nathan." I greeted him with a sincere smile. "What brings you to us again?"

The prophet did not smile in return. "I have heard a report that should concern you," he said, his features hardening in an expression of disapproval. "You may have heard that more than two hundred men from Jerusalem—many of whom are devoted to the king—are with Absalom in Hebron. In addition to removing those loyal men from the city, the king's son has circulated a message throughout the tribes of Israel. As soon as his followers hear the ram's horn, they are to shout, 'Absalom has been crowned king in Hebron' until the entire land has heard the news."

I stared at him in dazed exasperation. "What are you talking about?"

"My lady." Nathan leaned toward me, desperation in his eyes. "Absalom has stolen the hearts of the people, so you must warn the king before it's too late. If David remains in the city, its walls will become a deathtrap. You can be sure Absalom will return here

with a military force. He will kill the king and anyone who is loyal
to him. He will kill your sons . . . all of them."

My heart seemed to stop beating in my chest. I stared at the
prophet, struggling to make sense of his words, and then I remembered the urgency in my grandfather's voice. He had wanted me
away from the city, not to protect Solomon but to flee danger from
within. He had warned that my sons' lives might be in danger.
When he uttered the warning I could not imagine anyone wanting
to harm my children, but he had not mentioned Absalom.

After seeing the wound on Solomon's temple, I knew Absalom
would not hesitate to kill Solomon if he knew David had promised
him the throne.

"Mother," Solomon said, straightening his spine, "I can handle
Absalom."

I nearly laughed aloud. Like many young men, Solomon had
buckets of bravado, but he did not have an army. Apparently Absalom had both.

I reached for Shlomo's arm and held it tight. "Why are you telling *me* this?" I asked the prophet. "The king does not come to me
for military advice. He will not listen to warnings from a woman."

"And he is not the sort to listen to me when my words concern
Absalom." Nathan pressed his lips together, then gripped his walking stick. "We shall go together. Bring Solomon with you, and
perhaps the sight of the young man will convince David that he
cannot surrender to Absalom. But we must go at once. The prince
and his army will soon be on their way."

Responding to the urgency in the prophet's voice, I stood, gripped
Solomon's hand, and begged Adonai to honor His word.

Chapter Forty-Six
NATHAN

I THINK IT WOULD HAVE BEEN EASIER to erase a leopard's spots than to convince the king to set aside his lethargy and escape the oncoming threat.

"We are not in danger," David insisted. "Ask Joab. Ask Ahithophel."

Bathsheba, Solomon, and I stood in the king's dining hall, nearly deserted except for a few servants, a handful of military men, and three of the king's quiet sons—Adonijah, Shephatiah, and Ithream.

"My lord and king." Bathsheba stepped forward and bowed, but she didn't wait for the king's permission to speak. She rose almost immediately and boldly took a step closer to his chair. "If you try to summon your chief counselor, you'll find he is gone. A few days ago he tried to convince me to leave the palace with him. He was most insistent that I leave you for my safety's sake, and the safety of our sons." A deep worry line appeared between her delicate brows.

"My lord, I believe he knew what Absalom was planning. And I wouldn't be surprised if he was in Hebron now, celebrating with your absent son."

Lines of concentration deepened under the king's eyes, though he was not yet ready to believe. He lifted his hand and gestured to the guard at the door. "Summon Joab."

The guard had no sooner disappeared than we heard the shrill sound of a shofar—a sound out of place and time. In Israel, the shofar was blown as a call to war, a warning of war, or at the anointing of a king.

When I heard it in David's dining hall, the shofar seemed to signify all three.

"That is the appointed sign," I told the king, eyeing him steadily. "The ram's horn has been blown, and even now your people are shouting, 'Absalom has been crowned king in Hebron.'"

The piercing blast of the shofar seemed to stir the king from his complacency. He lifted his head, closed his eyes for a moment, and then rose from his chair. With an energy I had not seen him display in years, he strode across the dining hall shouting orders. "We must flee at once!" he said to the military men who stood guard at the door. "Hurry! If we leave Jerusalem before Absalom arrives, both we and the city will be spared from disaster."

Bathsheba, Solomon, and I followed the king to his throne room, where men from his personal guard had gathered at the sound of the shofar. Joab also stood there, his face tense and anxious, and he spoke for the others, saying they would do whatever David wanted them to do—even stay and fight, if necessary, to defend the city.

But David had no heart for war against his handsome son. "No, we must leave," he said, absently looking around for members of his household. "We must all go."

"All?" a servant asked.

"All but . . ." Pressing his fingers to the bridge of his nose, the king seemed to sort through a mental list of the people who depended on him. "All but ten of my concubines. Leave them behind to look after the house."

The servants responded with quick obedience, and within the hour a caravan of warriors, servants, and members of the royal family streamed out of the palace, carrying baskets packed with food, clothing, and whatever else they could find. Since the king did not know whom to trust—the realization that Ahithophel had joined Absalom both shocked and hurt David—he did not muster soldiers from Israel's army but allowed the foreign troops of his bodyguard to accompany him. Six hundred Philistines, Kerethites, and Pelethites filed out of their barracks and strapped on their swords. They loaded donkeys with supplies and kept order as the king's household fled the palace and walked away from Jerusalem.

As we neared my house, the last before a wide stretch of wilderness, I approached the king and asked if he wanted my wife to bring water. He cast me a look of gratitude and nodded, so the sad travelers halted while Ornah drew water from our well. My wife and daughters stared at David in abject horror. Though surprised to find the king at their door, they were astounded to see him bent and broken, with thinning hair, a gray beard, and wearing a defeated expression.

Most of the travelers remained in line, but Bathsheba left Solomon with his brothers and came forward to help Ornah at the well. Ornah poured while Bathsheba held a pitcher, then Bathsheba carried water to the thirsty people in line. When one of the guards protested that the king's wife should not do common work, Bathsheba gave the man a wry smile and said that hauling water was not new to her.

I was standing near the king when David turned to Ittai, a leader of the men from Gath. "Why are you coming with us?" he asked, his voice brimming with uncertainty. "Go back, stay with the king, for you are a guest in Israel. You arrived only recently, and why should I force you to wander with us? I don't even know where we will go. Go back and take your kinsmen with you, and may Adonai show you His unfailing love and faithfulness."

I flinched when David referred to Absalom as "the king." Had he completely given up? Absalom might have had himself proclaimed king, but until Adonai proclaimed it as well, I would never refer to the upstart by that title.

Apparently Ittai agreed with me. The warrior thrust out his chest and answered David, "I vow by Adonai and by your own life that I will go wherever my lord the king goes, no matter what happens—whether it means death or life."

And so David left Jerusalem in the company of women, children, servants, and foreigners. At the rear of the procession, Zadok led a priestly contingent of Levites, who carried the Ark of the Covenant. But when David spied the Ark, he told Zadok to take it back to the Tabernacle. "If I find favor in Adonai's sight, He will bring me back and let me again see the Ark and the place where it is kept. But if He says, 'I am displeased with you,' then here I am. Let Adonai do to me whatever seems good to Him."

Though David sent the priests away, he was not above using them for political purposes. I for one was glad to see that the king had not forgotten the lessons he had learned in warfare. Clearly he remembered the value of a good spy.

As Zadok turned to leave, David caught the priest's sleeve. "Look," he told the man, "you and Abiathar should return quietly to the city with your son Ahimaaz and Abiathar's son, Jonathan. I will stop at the shallows of the Jordan River and wait there for a report from you."

The priestly contingent turned and walked back to Jerusalem, with Zadok and Abiathar carrying the Ark back to the Tabernacle. They would remain in Jerusalem to wait for Absalom and his army.

Meanwhile, those of us who followed David felt our hearts break as the aging king set out for the Mount of Olives. Weeping as he went, his shoulders hunched in defeat, the king covered his head with his prayer shawl and walked with bare feet over the dusty road. The men and women from the settlements we passed wept as well, horrified and aggrieved to see the pride of all Israel, the king who had unified our nation, brought so low.

By the son he had loved above all others.

I followed David, of course. Leaving my family to wait at home, I remained with the king, traveling a few steps behind Bathsheba, Solomon, and Elisheba, the old woman. And as we walked, my thoughts centered on the prophecy I had shared with the king so many years before. Adonai had promised to discipline David with blows, but I had never imagined a blow as hard as this one.

David's glorious kingdom lay in shambles at his feet, but if he had remained within the city, Jerusalem might have been destroyed by sword and fire. And yet Adonai had promised him an eternal dynasty. . . .

At a moment like this, Ornah would have asked me how I managed to cling to my faith.

⚜

After crossing the Kidron Valley on the eastern side of Jerusalem, David began a long, slow climb up the Mount of Olives. He moved woodenly, like a man whose heart is broken, so it was easy for a mounted messenger to catch him and confirm that Ahithophel, the king's chief counselor, had aligned himself with Absalom.

I stood close enough to hear David's brief prayer: "Turn the counsel of Ahithophel into foolishness, O Lord."

As David walked, he poured out his heart in a spontaneous psalm:

Adonai, how many enemies I have!
How countless are those attacking me;
how countless those who say of me,
"There is no salvation for him in God."

But you, Adonai, are a shield for me;
you are my glory, you lift my head high.
With my voice I call out to Adonai,
and he answers me from his holy hill.

I lie down and sleep, then wake up again,
because Adonai sustains me.
I am not afraid of the tens of thousands
set against me on every side.
Rise up, Adonai!
Save me, my God!
For you slap all my enemies in the face,
you smash the teeth of the wicked.
Victory comes from Adonai;
may your blessing rest on your people.

When we reached the summit, we encountered Hushai, who
had been a loyal counselor to the king. Ordinarily a well-dressed
and commanding figure, Hushai wore a torn garment, and he had
poured dirt over his head and beard. He, too, was mourning a king
dethroned. But David seemed to take courage from the sight of a
counselor who had not deserted him.

Moments after greeting Hushai, David suggested that the man
clean himself up and return to Jerusalem. "If you cross over the
river with me, you will be a burden to me," David gently explained.
"But if you return to Jerusalem and tell Absalom you will be his
loyal servant, you can overturn any counsel Ahithophel gives to
the young man. Won't Zadok and Abiathar the priests be there
with you? Whatever you hear from the king's house, tell Zadok

and Abiathar. They will tell their two sons, Ahimaaz and Jonathan, and they will come and tell me whatever you have heard."

The king did not have to persuade Hushai, who promptly rose, gave the king his solemn vow, and took the path that led down the Mount of Olives. He was a younger man and swift of foot, and I had every reason to believe he would soon appear in Absalom's throne room looking every bit like an advisor prepared to transfer his loyalties.

Watching him go, I had to smile. David had asked Adonai to thwart Ahithophel, and a moment later we spied Hushai, the perfect man to serve as an answer to David's prayer. Sometimes, I reflected, HaShem worked His will through the service of faithful men.

CHAPTER FORTY-SEVEN

BATHSHEBA

NOT KNOWING IF WE WERE BEING PURSUED, we dared not tarry long on the Mount of Olives. We set out again, traversing the opposite slope, and in the distance we spotted a caravan of donkeys led by a man with several servants. One of the king's soldiers rode ahead to determine whether the man was friend or foe, and in a short time we had an answer. The man was Ziba, the servant of Jonathan's son Mephibosheth. On those saddled donkeys Ziba had loaded two hundred loaves of bread, a hundred fluffy cakes, pounds of fruit, and a large jug of wine. He was a most welcome sight, as we were exhausted from hunger, travel, and heartbreak.

When David asked what the provisions were for, Ziba prostrated himself before the king. "These donkeys are for the king's household to ride on, the bread and the summer fruit are for the lads to eat, and the wine for the exhausted to drink in the wilderness."

David looked around for Mephibosheth. When he did not see the young man, he asked Ziba about his master.

Ziba hung his head. "My master is remaining in Jerusalem. I heard him say, 'Today the house of Israel will return my father's kingdom to me.'"

I covered my mouth when I heard this, for despite what Grandfather had said about David helping Mephibosheth only because he wanted to keep his enemy close, I could not imagine anyone repaying the king's kindness with such brazen disloyalty. David must have had the same thought, for he clasped Ziba's shoulder and said, "Today, everything of Mephibosheth's has become yours."

The servant prostrated himself yet again. "May I find favor in your eyes, my lord the king."

I sat on a rock, my head spinning with the day's bizarre events. Men I would have considered forever loyal had turned on us, including my own grandfather. Worse yet was the realization that Grandfather had known about Absalom's plans for some time. He had been involved in a conspiracy of treason, and why? He could not believe that prideful Absalom would be a better ruler than Adonai's anointed king!

After eating and drinking to fuel our weary bodies, we walked on, desperate to find a place where we could set up a defensible camp. I insisted that Abigail ride one of the donkeys and I walked beside her, knowing that each jarring step caused her pain. Her young handmaid had disappeared, probably losing herself in the crowd so she would not have to witness her mistress's suffering.

People poured out of their settlements as we passed by, some of them weeping, others cursing. A man called Shimei cursed David, calling him a "bloodstained fiend of hell" and claiming that the king's sorrow was punishment from the Lord for spilling the blood of Saul's house. "The Lord is paying you back for all the bloodshed in Saul's clan," Shimei ranted. "You stole his throne, and now the

Lord has given it to your son Absalom. At last you will taste some of your own medicine, for you are a murderer!"

Better than anyone, I knew my husband was guilty of murder, but I also knew he had been forgiven. But forgiveness did not eliminate the consequences of bloodshed, not in our family, nor in the kingdom of Israel. David had killed scores of men in his struggles against Saul, and when it came to spilled blood, people had long memories.

When Abishai, the leader of the Thirty, asked for permission to lop off Shimei's head, David gave him a weary smile and said, "If the Lord has told him to curse me, who are you to stop him? My own son is trying to kill me. Doesn't this relative of Saul have even more reason to do so?" He stopped walking and used his sleeve to mop his brow. "Leave him alone and let him curse, for the Lord has told him to do it. And perhaps the Lord will see that I am being wronged and will bless me because of these curses today."

So we kept walking, accompanied by the curses and stones Shimei and his clan threw in our direction. I looked over at David, my husband and king, and wondered if he truly believed that Adonai had led this man and so many others to curse him. Curses, like blessings, were powerful when issued in Adonai's name.

We did not stop again until we reached the banks of the Jordan River.

⁓⋇⁓

We were resting near the Jordan when two men approached on foot, breathless and drenched with sweat. Abishai stopped them at the edge of our encampment, questioned them, and then promptly escorted them into the royal tent, where David, Solomon, Joab, Abigail, and I had sought shelter from the sun.

David recognized the two young men, Ahimaaz and Jonathan,

sons of the priests Zadok and Abiathar. They had received a report from Hushai. As soon as I saw the messengers, I knew that Absalom had taken his father's city and his throne.

"We were spotted leaving the house where we were stationed," Jonathan said, breathlessly explaining their delay to the king. "We got as far as Bahurim before we realized we were being pursued, so a woman there hid us in her well. When Absalom's man asked where we had gone, she sent them in the wrong direction, which allowed us to escape without notice."

David's eyes flashed, and in that moment his countenance filled with the spirit of a younger man. In his fighting days he had been as clever and slippery as these two.

"And what is the state of affairs in Jerusalem?" he asked.

Ahimaaz stepped forward. "If it please my lord and king, the young Absalom asked advice of two counselors, Ahithophel and Hushai. Ahithophel advised setting out in pursuit of you tonight, while you and the people with you are weary and weak. He promised he himself would lead the army. He said he would so frighten the people that they would desert, so he would have to kill no one but you."

Despite the heat, a tide of gooseflesh rippled up my arms and neck. Ahimaaz did not glance in my direction as he repeated my grandfather's words, and neither did David. But Solomon looked at me with questioning eyes. How could I explain his great-grandfather's bloody offer?

"But," Jonathan added, "the king's friend Hushai advised Absalom to wait until he had raised an army from every tribe of Israel. He said Absalom should have an army as numerous as the sand on the seashore, and that Absalom should personally lead the troops, and that they should kill everyone in the king's party and destroy any town that might give sanctuary to the king and his household."

I shivered again, for Hushai's advice had been far bloodier than Grandfather's. Kill *everyone*? Even innocent women and children?

David looked from Ahimaaz to Jonathan, his brows knitting. "And what did Absalom decide?"

Jonathan glanced at his companion before answering. "My lord and king, Absalom and his men decided to wait and take Hushai's advice. But you should cross the Jordan tonight in case he changes his mind."

David exchanged a look with Joab before giving his reply: "We will cross immediately and set up our camp at Mahanaim."

⚜

Mahanaim proved to be an oasis in the desert. We crossed the Jordan in the middle of the night—a task not without perils of its own, especially when the king's household included the young, the sick, and the old—and walked until we reached Mahanaim, a fortified city. Friends of the king warmly welcomed us: Shobi, from Rabbah, the city where Uriah had died; Makir, from Lodebar; and Barzillai from Rogelim. They took one look at our wet, weary group and urged us to come through the city gates, where we could rest in safety. "You must all be very hungry, tired, and thirsty after your long march through the wilderness," Barzillai said, extending his hand. "Please, come inside and be comforted."

I clutched Solomon's hand and entered the city, then stared at the supplies they had hastily assembled for us—sleeping mats, cooking pots, serving bowls, wheat and barley, flour and roasted grain, beans, lentils, honey, butter, sheep, goats, and cheese. They brought servants to help us establish a camp, and pack animals to help us transport additional supplies for our military men.

At some point in the moonless night, we slept, stretching out in whatever empty space we could find. I lay near Solomon so I could keep an eye on him, and I saw that Joab stood watch over the king. Good. With Joab standing guard, I knew I would be able to sleep.

I doubted that David would sleep at all.

The next morning, while we women set about the tasks of feeding, clothing, and supplying our refugees, David assembled his commanders and focused on the work of reclaiming his kingdom. He divided his foreign troops into three groups, naming Joab, Abishai, and Ittai as the company commanders, and then announced he would strap on his sword and venture out with the army.

"No, you won't," Joab objected, echoing the concerns of the other two commanders. "If we are overcome, if we have to run, it won't matter because they are looking for you. If they find you, the battle is over. You are worth ten thousand of us, so you must stay in town where you will be safe."

Sitting in my quiet corner, I watched David reluctantly accept this hard truth. Something came to life within him at the thought of sallying forth with his men, and for a brief moment I could see inside his heart. I saw confidence there, a quick spark of excitement, and then I saw that spark flicker and die.

"If you think that's the best plan," he said, once again wearing the face of an aging, exhausted king. "I will agree."

He stood aside as his men collected and strapped on their weapons; he watched them divide into companies and fill the open area inside the walls of Mahanaim. Before he sent the warriors out, he called the three commanders to stand before him, speaking loudly enough for every soldier to hear. "For my sake," he said, his voice trembling more like a father's than a king's, "deal gently with young Absalom when you find him."

And then the shofar blew. Mahanaim opened its gates as the armies of David marched toward the forest of Ephraim.

As the army battled, Elisheba and I did our best to help the women of Mahanaim handle the care and feeding of so many refugees. While David's other wives lounged beneath makeshift sun shades, we hauled water, served food, and distributed blankets for the coming night. I had just given a blanket to Abigail when I heard a familiar voice call my name. "Bathsheba!"

I whirled around and saw Amaris hobbling toward me and clinging to a man's arm. From the look in his eye and the careful way he helped her, I surmised he was her husband.

I left Abigail and flew into my sister's arms, then called for Elisheba. "Come see who's here!"

Despite the dire circumstances, we shared a joyful reunion. "We left Bethlehem as soon as we heard what Absalom was planning," Amaris's husband, Efrayim, said. "My mother is with the children—"

"Children?" Elisheba's face split into a wide grin.

"Twin girls," Amaris said. "As alike as two sparrows in a nest. They are of toddling age now."

I turned back to my sister's patient husband. "You were on the road to Jerusalem?"

"When we heard the king had already left the palace," Efrayim said. "We support the king, of course, and decided to follow, hoping we would be able to serve our king in some way."

"Efrayim wanted to march out with the army," Amaris said, color rising in her cheeks, "but I reminded him that I would be lost without him."

"You can still serve," Elisheba pointed out. "There is much work to be done. The king's younger children need to be watched, or you can sit and catch up with your sister while she prepares food. You can even help."

I smiled at the thought of sitting with Amaris. As long as our hands remained busy, our work-minded Elisheba would not mind.

"Come," I told Amaris and Efrayim. "My boys are in a tent over there. Let's keep our hands occupied while the men battle. We can talk while we wait."

"And pray," Amaris said.

"And pray," I agreed.

‧⋲᪥⋼‧

I am not a soldier. A woman's weapons are words and smiles and the careful arrangement of the folds in a garment, so I do not know how to fight with swords or pikes or spears.

After two or three hours of sitting in my children's tent, the king sent for me. I left Amaris and Efrayim and walked to his tent, prepared to give him silent support for as long as he needed me.

I do not know what happened out in the forest that day, but I can tell you what David endured in the hours of waiting. Inside the royal tent, the king paced. He looked at the delicious foods our hosts had prepared for him, but he could not eat. Occasionally he stared at me with a bewildered expression, and I knew he was thinking of my grandfather and wondering how Ahithophel could give Absalom good, solid advice while thoroughly betraying his king.

Though most of David's children had accompanied us into exile, only two of the king's sons waited with us: Solomon, who remained close to me, and twenty-eight-year-old Adonijah, Haggith's quiet son. Shammua and Shobab waited with Amaris, Elisheba, and Efrayim, and I'd asked Nathan to watch over Abigail.

Both Solomon and Adonijah wanted to accompany the army into the fray, but David had refused to allow either of them to fight. Now they sat silently and watched their fretful father, and from my perspective it was hard to tell whether David agonized more over his broken kingdom or his traitorous child.

The crisis must have stirred the king's memories, for occasionally he would interrupt our quiet vigil with a story. He told us about slaying the giant Goliath when he was merely a lad in Saul's camp. He chuckled when he told us about how he had pretended to be insane, scratching and drooling down his beard, when he had to face King Achish of Gath, a fierce Philistine.

He grew serious when he related the story of how he and his men had come home and discovered the Amalekites had raided their town and carried off the women and children. "We stood and wept until we could weep no more," he said. "My men were so unhappy about losing their families that they began to talk about stoning me. But I found strength in Adonai. I asked Abiathar to bring me the ephod, and then I asked the Lord if I should chase after the raiders. The Lord said I should. He said I would recover everything that had been taken from me."

David fell silent, and I knew he was wondering if Adonai would make that same promise today. But Solomon, who did not know his father's moods as well as I did, wanted to know the end of the story. "What happened, sir?"

Brought back to the present, David looked at Solomon. "I went after them—with six hundred men. When we reached a brook, two hundred were too exhausted to cross the waters, so I continued on with four hundred. During our pursuit we found a starving Egyptian slave left to die in a field and learned that he had belonged to one of the raiders. With his help we found the Amalakites and spent the next night and day slaughtering them.

"We rescued every soul who had been taken from us, including Ahinoam and Abigail, two of my wives. We received our flocks, our herds, and more plunder besides. And we used the plunder to send gifts to the elders of Judah. Let that be a lesson to you: never forget to honor your friends."

"If we have any," Adonijah said with a weak laugh, but I did not care for his joke.

Ignoring Adonijah's comment, David reached out and placed his hand on Solomon's head. "Do not fear, son. Adonai is with us."

"Is there anything," Solomon asked, "you regret, Father?"

"Many things," David said, his gaze moving to me. "Too many to count. But chief among them is the day I stopped to ask for help at Nob, where Ahimelech the priest lived. The priest did not know that Saul fancied I wanted to kill him, and I didn't tell the priest that Saul wanted to kill me. The priest gave me holy bread to eat because I was starving, and the sword of Goliath the giant because I had no weapon. I left and spared no thought for the priests at Nob until Abiathar, one of Ahimelech's sons, caught up to me. He told me that Saul had followed me to Nob, learned that Ahimelech had given me aid, and ordered his men to kill all the priests of Adonai. When they refused, Doeg the Edomite killed eighty-five priests of the Lord. Then he killed their families—men and women, children and babies, even the cattle, donkeys, sheep, and goats. Only Abiathar managed to escape."

David turned toward the tent opening, and in that hard light I saw the face of an old man.

"I would urge you never to risk innocent people's lives," David said, looking back at Shlomo. "But more than that, I would urge you to be a man of peace."

The sound of a shout broke the tension, and a moment later a runner stumbled into our presence. "My lord, I bring you—" he placed his hands on his knees as he struggled to catch his breath— "news of the battle."

David seemed not to notice that the man hadn't bothered to kneel. "How fares our army?"

A broad smile crossed the man's flushed face. "The forest favors your men, my lord. Absalom's force is too large, and his men have not been trained to fight among trees and rocks. Your army is more nimble. Your men scamper over stones while Absalom's force struggles to make headway in the woods. The forest and wild beasts are claiming more of his men than the sword."

David crossed his arms. "And Absalom?"

The runner shook his head. "No word of him, my lord."

David pressed his lips together, then stepped forward and clapped the man on the shoulder. "Thank you. Now get some water and take a moment to rest. Then go back and be sure to bring word if you hear news of my son."

The runner nodded his appreciation, bowed, and hurried away.

Chapter Forty-Eight
NATHAN

I AM A PROPHET, NOT A WARRIOR, so I did not leave with David's army. I am no diplomat, either, so instead of lingering near the king's tent, I found a shady spot beneath a tree outside the city walls. Here I'd be able to pray in silence and I wouldn't bother the citizens of Mahanaim, who were busy preparing food and drink for the refugees from Jerusalem.

I stretched out beneath my tree and studied the faces of Mahanaim's women, older men, and children. None of them seemed to resent the burden of caring for the king and his household, and many actually smiled as if they were thrilled to be so close to the king they had admired from afar. I found it ironic that they should be so pleased, because Mahanaim had been the city from which Saul's son Ishbosheth reigned ever so briefly after his father's death. The passing years must have eradicated the residents' loyalty to Saul, for they now worked diligently for David.

A hush fell over the city as the afternoon sun climbed high in the sky. My eyelids grew heavy. I folded my hands, ready to avail myself of some much-needed sleep, when a familiar darkness settled behind my eyes, one that had nothing to do with exhaustion or slumber.

A thrill of anticipation chilled my spine. The city of Mahanaim and the king's tent vanished from my sight, replaced by a shadowed, woody realm. Tall trees canopied the area, while lush undergrowth carpeted the floor and covered the rocks that had tumbled from a mountain generations before. A dead tree, rotting and terraced with fungus, lay on the forest floor, its massive girth impeding the progress of the soldiers who cursed and struggled to make their way through the woods.

Then I saw Absalom astride his mule, sword in one hand, reins in the other. He shouted at his men and slashed at tangled vines that hung like spider webs, but the forest swallowed up his words. His mule balked at the dead tree even as soldiers clambered over it, so Absalom kicked the animal and urged it to go around the fallen log. Separated from his men, Absalom rode parallel to his faltering front line, abruptly driving the mule into the forest. Half blind with panic, the animal spied an opening and ran like a hen dodging the ax, dragging his rider into a tangle formed by the low-hanging branches of a giant terebinth tree. The mule ran on, leaping over stones and shrubs, while Absalom dangled helplessly, his prized, much-admired hair caught in the tree limbs.

With a shiver of vivid recollection, I stared at a scene I had viewed before. I had dreamed of this, and in my dream I had seen hell open before Absalom's feet.

I took a wincing breath, stunned beyond words by the new vision playing on the backs of my eyelids. Absalom twisted and jerked and roared in frustration as the branches kept him suspended between heaven and earth. He pulled his dagger from his belt and began to cut his hair.

His voice was no more than a hoarse whisper when the nearby shrubbery rustled and one of Joab's men stepped out. The soldier stared up at the captive prince, his face blank with shock, and then he disappeared. Absalom roared in frustration, doubtless aware that the man had gone for help. But by the time the bushes rattled their leaves again, he hung quiet and still.

Surrounded by ten armor bearers, Joab stepped out of the devouring woods and stared up at Absalom, his kinsman, his prince, and the man who would forever be a threat to David and the kingdom of Israel. The commander held three sticks in his hand, one for each company of David's small army, and with little effort he reached up and thrust the sticks into the heart of the man who had burned Joab's barley fields, betrayed his king, and brought turmoil to Israel. As the prince gasped his last breaths, the armor bearers pulled him down, closed in, and finished the kill.

Joab pulled a ram's horn from his belt and blew it, signaling every man on the field.

The battle was finished, the victory won.

The rebellion was over.

Chapter Forty-Nine

BATHSHEBA

At the sound of the shofar, David straightened and stared out the doorway of his tent. "It's finished," he whispered, so faintly I could barely hear him.

Solomon and Adonijah stood, but waited for their father to lead the way to the city gate. Bloodied warriors began to trickle in, exhausted and covered with sweat, yet all but the most severely wounded were smiling as they reported the flight of the enemy.

I closed my eyes and silently thanked Adonai for His grace and mercy. If Absalom had reached our camp, he would have killed David and all of David's children. And he would have killed me, because I would have forced him to go through me to reach my sons.

My thoughts shifted from my sons to my husband, who stood alert and hopeful between the inner and outer gates of Mahanaim. He watched the returning troops with bright eyes, but his gaze barely skimmed the soldiers, his eyes searching for one man with long, thick hair.

Fear tightened my stomach as the king began to question warriors, pulling them away from their comrades to ask if they had seen young Absalom. David, David . . . why did he have such great love for the son who least deserved it?

A watchman on the walkway above the gate let out a shout. "A runner! A man is running toward the city."

David turned and caught my eye. "If he is alone, he has news."

The watchman cried again, "Here comes another runner! And the first runs like Ahimaaz, the son of Zadok."

"Ah." David smiled at me, the light of hope shining from his eyes. "He is a good man and comes with a good report."

A moment later the priest's son bowed before David and lowered his face to the ground.

"Up, son," David urged. "Tell me everything."

"Everything is all right," Ahimaaz said, rising to his knees. "Praise the Lord your God, who has handed over the rebels who dared stand against my lord the king."

"What about young Absalom?" The king searched Ahimaaz's face. "Is he all right?"

The messenger flinched almost imperceptibly, but the slight movement caught my eye. The young man cleared his throat, then met the king's earnest gaze. "When Joab told me to come, many men were milling about in the area. I didn't know what was happening."

David squeezed his arm. "Wait. Another runner comes."

Ahimaaz moved aside, blending into the growing crowd around the king. When the young man's gaze crossed mine, he looked away—and that was when I knew Absalom's fate.

The second runner, an Ethiopian mercenary, approached and fell to his knees before David. "Rise, man," David said. "Stand and deliver your news."

"I have good news for my lord the king," the man said, scrambling to his feet. "Today the Lord has rescued you from all those who rebelled against you."

"And what about young Absalom?" David's eyes gleamed. "Is he all right?"

A bright smile split the Ethiopian's dark face. "May all of your enemies, my lord the king, both now and in the future, share the fate of that young man!"

Time stopped in that moment. The Ethiopian's words echoed in the stillness. Somewhere a baby cried, a dog barked, and swords slapped against leather armor. David staggered at the man's words, toppling sideways toward Adonijah, and I reached out, too late, to comfort the king. Bewildered by his father's unusual display of weakness, Adonijah stepped backward, forcing David to land on the packed earth of the gateway. Other men helped him to his feet, someone murmured soothing words, and I finally reached his side. I slipped my arm around his waist, and someone put David's arm around my shoulder. Together we moved toward the narrow stairway that led to a small room over the fortified gate.

Once we were inside the watchman's room, David sank to the stone floor and wept as I had never heard him weep before. Not even on the sorrowful walk to the Mount of Olives had he wept with such passion. I held him, allowing him to bury his face in my lap as I draped my arm around his trembling shoulders. From what David said, I gathered that he wept not only for the loss of his son's life but also for his indifferent treatment of the young man.

"Oh, my son Absalom! My son, my son Absalom! If only I had died instead of you! Oh, Absalom, my son, my son . . ."

I caressed his face, felt his tears burn my fingers like hot wax as a memory ruffled through my mind. My grandfather might have sided with the wrong man in this war, but at least he had understood the problems between David and his sons. *"The child who grows up unnoticed by his father will perform outlandish feats,"* he had told me, and Absalom had been such a child, as had David. *"And the man who grows up outside his father's attention will not know how to be a father to his own children."*

I smoothed stray hairs from David's damp forehead and gently whispered his name. He had been more king than father to his sons, but still, he loved them. Even though he never knew how to show it.

I heard a timid rap at the door. David tightened his grip on me, so I answered. "Who is it?"

The door creaked, and in the narrow opening I saw Nathan the prophet. He glanced at the king, then turned to me. "My lady," he said, bowing slightly, "we have received news that concerns you."

My pulse quickened. "Solomon?"

"No, your grandfather. After Absalom spurned his advice yesterday, Ahithophel saddled his donkey, went home to Giloh, and set his affairs in order. They found him this morning, hanging from a tree."

I blinked. Suicide? Grandfather was not a quitter, but having betrayed one king and finding his advice ignored by another, he probably thought he had no further reason to live.

Either that or he put the noose around his neck with quiet satisfaction, content that he had finally avenged Uriah's murder.

Tears streamed over my cheeks, but I wasn't really crying—they were the result of an overflow of feeling, too many emotions compressed in too short a time.

"Thank you for telling me," I whispered.

In the prophet's eyes I saw understanding, compassion, and something that looked a little like love.

CHAPTER FIFTY
NATHAN

As a father, I knew David would grieve over his son Absalom, but all of us who were with him were surprised that he mourned so publicly, so loudly, and for so long. Like blood out of a wound, word of the king's distress flowed out of Mahanaim, and returning warriors crept back to the city as though they had committed some unforgivable sin. From his room over the fortified gate, David wept and cried and wailed, refusing to be silent until Joab climbed the stairs to confront his kinsman and king.

All of us waiting in the area heard his rebuke through the open window. Sparing nothing, Joab raised his voice and rebuked David as few men would dare.

"We saved your life today," he began, his voice brimming with contempt, "and the lives of your sons, your daughters, and your wives and concubines. Yet you act like this, making us feel ashamed of ourselves. You seem to love those who hate you and hate those who love you. Today you have made it clear that your commanders and troops mean nothing to you. It seems that if Absalom had lived and all of us had died, you would be more pleased. Overjoyed, in fact."

Below the gatehouse we listened in silence. If David made a response, we didn't hear it.

"Go out there and congratulate your troops," Joab shouted. "If you don't, not a single one of them will remain here tonight. Then you will be worse off than before."

A few moments later, our pale king came down the staircase, trailed by Joab and Bathsheba. Someone produced a makeshift throne and set it on a raised platform near the city gate. David seated himself, and word went out that he was waiting to congratulate his people. Knowing that the king sat in the traditional place for judges and priests to exercise the powers of their office assured the populace that order had been restored. The brief and bloody civil war was over.

Ahimaaz, the young man who had not found the courage to tell the king about Absalom, elbowed me as we stood at the periphery and listened to the king answer his petitioners. "Are we able to go back to Jerusalem?" he asked, his forehead creased with worry. "After all, Absalom was anointed king in Hebron. Even though David is from Judah, the people of that tribe may not be willing to accept him so soon after crowning his son. They might send men—"

"The king has already sent a message to the elders of Judah," I answered. "He said that until his own tribe recognizes his right to reign, he will stay away from Jerusalem."

Judah capitulated a few days later, and David gave us leave to plan our return to the capital city.

On the journey, we encountered the same people we had met on the way to Mahanaim, only this time they greeted us with far different tidings. Ziba, the servant who had claimed that Jonathan's son Mephibosheth wanted the throne for himself, met us at the

Jordan River. He was in such a hurry to greet David that he waded into the water to meet the king's boat.

Shimei, who had cursed and thrown rocks at David, met us on the road. He prostrated himself before the king and begged for his life with his face pressed to the sand. Abishai, one of David's captains, spoke before the king could answer, saying that Shimei was guilty of cursing the Lord's anointed and should die for his sin. Showing mercy, David replied that the day was not made for execution but celebration. Shimei was spared.

Mephibosheth, Jonathan's crippled son, arrived on his donkey to greet the king. The man explained his disheveled appearance by saying he was so upset by the news of David's exile that he had not washed his feet, trimmed his beard, or changed his clothing since the day the king left Jerusalem. He further reported that Ziba had slandered him by giving a false report, for he had never intended to claim the throne.

"I know my lord the king is like an angel of God, so do what you think is best," Mephibosheth told the king, bowing to the ground. "All my relatives and I could expect only death from you, my lord, but instead you have honored me by allowing me to eat at your own table. What more can I ask?"

Rather than choosing between one man and the other, David decided that Mephibosheth and Ziba should divide the family property equally. But Mephibosheth, his features relaxing in visible relief, declared, "Give Ziba all of it. I am content just to have you safely back again, my lord the king."

Those who had been kind to the king reappeared as well, and the king rewarded them for their kindness. He invited Barzillai, one of the men who had provided food for the king's household, to live in Jerusalem. Barzillai declined, saying he was too old to relocate. "But here is my son Kimham," he said. "Let him go with my lord the king and receive whatever you want to give him."

David agreed. "Kimham will go with me, and I will help him in any way you would like."

The journey home was not without difficulties. After we crossed the Jordan, rivalry sprang up between Judah, David's tribe, and Israel, men from the other tribes. The men from Israel claimed that men from Judah had stolen the king and not given the men of Israel the honor of helping the king cross the Jordan. The men of Judah argued that the king was one of their own, so why should the men of Israel be offended? The men of Israel declared that since Israel consisted of ten tribes, they had ten times as much right to the king as Judah did, and hadn't they been the first to speak of bringing him back to his throne in Jerusalem?

Then a troublemaker named Sheba, from the tribe of Benjamin, blew a shofar and began to shout, "We have no share in David, no inheritance in the son of Jesse. Come on, you men of Israel, back to your homes!"

So the men of Israel who had been with David since his departure from Jerusalem went home while the men of Judah escorted the king from the Jordan River to Jerusalem.

I listened to these arguments with rising dismay. Had we learned nothing from the tragic episode we had just survived? Were we still so intent on our tribal differences and loyalties that we could not work together as a nation? How long would Adonai tolerate our jealousies and stubborn pride?

I watched silently as Bathsheba wept, hugged her sister, Amaris, and said farewell to her brother-in-law. The couple departed outside Jerusalem, for Bethlehem lay farther south. Though Bathsheba wept until the pair disappeared on the dusty road, I knew that her heart had been greatly cheered by her sister's visit. Visiting with Amaris, she told me in a fleeting encounter, reminded her of her former life, when she did not have to worry about plots or schemes designed to destroy everything she held dear.

With a glad heart I spied my own home as we approached the city. Ornah must have seen the dust from our approach, for she and my daughters and their husbands stood by the side of the road, waving colorful veils in celebration. I threaded my way to the front of the procession and ran forward to meet them, embracing my wife and each of my daughters and sons-in-law. David smiled at my growing family as he rode by, and I gave Ornah a grateful kiss as the last soldier passed our house.

"I am going forward with the king," I told her, taking pleasure in the familiar scent of her hair, "but I will return tonight. Since I began this journey with David, I want to see it through."

She nodded, tears shining in her eyes, and I kissed my daughters again before jogging forward to catch the king's caravan.

So many emotions assailed me as we covered the familiar road. Indignation flooded my heart when we approached the spot where Absalom had erected his canopy to flatter and cajole those who entered Jerusalem. But my indignation faded to compassion when I saw the path that led to the valley where the king's son had heaped stones over the graves of his children.

If Absalom had realized how deeply his father loved him, perhaps he would not have hungered so for the approval of other men. I prayed the other fathers of Israel would hear the tale of Absalom and David and heed its message.

Men and women lined the top of the city wall and cheered as David approached. Children waved palm branches and shouted "Hosanna" as the king returned to his rightful place, and women fluttered colorful flags above the wide stone gate. I lifted my face to the heavens and felt the caress of the sun like a kiss. Adonai had restored His ordained king to Jerusalem, and I hoped the kingdom of Israel would be stronger for the trial we had endured. I didn't know what, if anything, this war had accomplished, but I prayed it would help the people of Israel learn to place their faith in God's sovereign king. I also hoped the struggle had convinced David to shake off his grief and behave like the king he had been called to be.

By the time I stepped through the palace gates and stood in the courtyard, most of the animals were on their way to the stables and the warriors were returning to their barracks. I knew Bathsheba would be safely tucked into her suite with Elisheba. And David would be . . . where?

On a whim I stepped through the open doors of the throne room. The place had been thoroughly ransacked—hangings ripped from the walls, chairs broken into splinters, scrolls tossed into the center of the room and burned. David's throne was intact, however, probably because Absalom had coveted it—and David sat on it now, surrounded by several of the chamberlains whose job it was to care for the king's household. They were reporting on the condition of the palace, since only a handful of concubines had been left behind to care for it.

"The kitchen supplies are a mess, yet food remains," one man said, bowing before the king. "I will have a meal ready soon."

"Your personal chamber is ruined," another servant said, flinching as though he expected to be punished for a bad report. "Someone rifled through the trunk with the king's robes, and few are intact."

"The stables are fine," the stable master reported. "We took most of the animals with us, and they will be put away with fresh hay. Nothing was burned."

"The Tabernacle?" David looked through the crowd. "Has Zadok arrived?"

"Yes, my king." The venerable priest stepped out of the crowd. "As you commanded, we returned the Ark to its place and it is safe. Neither Absalom nor his men ventured near the Tabernacle."

The king lifted a brow, then called on the eunuch who oversaw his harem. "And the women? The concubines who stayed behind?"

The eunuch stepped forward, his hands locked together behind his back. "My lord the king, your servant is sorry to report that the concubines, all ten of the women . . ." His voice broke as he faltered. He took a deep breath and began again. "My lord, not long after his arrival to the palace, your son Absalom erected a tent on the rooftop, and there, within full view of anyone who cared to look, he ravished the ten concubines you left behind. I am sorry, my lord. The women are deeply grieved by what happened."

David's lips thinned with anger, but what could he say? Absalom had done what any conquering king would do. To prove that the kingship had passed to him, Absalom had taken possession of everything that belonged to his father. And he had done it publicly, in plain sight, so no one would refute his right to rule. He had raped the king's women, worn the king's robes, and occupied the king's throne. He had not only committed treason with his actions, he had also violated the Law of HaShem.

I stood silently in the crowd of onlookers as my heart twisted with regret. Years before, I had stood in this very spot and told David that Adonai would generate evil out of his own household. The Lord of Israel would give his women to someone who would possess them publicly so that everyone would know of it. He would do it before all of Israel in broad daylight.

David rubbed his hand hard over his face, then nodded at the eunuch. "Let the women be set apart in housing of their own, and let them live in peace and safety from this day forward. They will be as widows; I will never sleep with them again."

With a heavy heart, I turned and left the great hall. Outside, servants had begun to clean the courtyard, repair the broken furnishings, and remove damaged objects from the palace. Weary warriors were bedding down in quiet corners, and I knew the king's house would be restored within a matter of days.

I was about to leave the palace and go home when I spotted Bathsheba approaching, her head veiled and her eyes downcast. I hesitated, wondering if she meant to speak to me, and felt my heart constrict when she caught my gaze and motioned for me to wait.

She gave me a fleeting smile. "Is there anything else?" she whispered, her voice pitched for my ear alone. "You have seen and foretold so much, Nathan. Is there anything else I should know in order to help the king and protect my son?"

I closed my eyes and listened for the voice of Adonai, but heard nothing.

"Adonai does not tell me everything." I opened my eyes and met her gaze. "In my experience, no prophet hears from God every day."

She gave me a smile I would accept as my last glimpse of earth. "But the sayings of the prophets," she said, "have guided my thoughts and actions in every hour." She stepped back and lifted her hand. "Thank you, Nathan. For your service to the king, and to me."

On the road home, I walked as if the blood of a younger man filled my veins.

CHAPTER FIFTY-ONE
BATHSHEBA

ABIGAIL—WHO, LIKE ME, HAD COME TO DAVID as a widow—died shortly after our return to Jerusalem. David mourned her, as did I. Remembering her advice, I opened my heart to the broken-hearted king, determined to do anything in my power to make him happy. In doing so, I hoped I might learn to better serve him . . . and love him.

Nine years passed—years in which David, my lord and king and husband, grew old. From his wives and concubines he no longer sought pleasure but warmth, yet we were growing old with him. To better care for the aging king, one of his servants suggested that the palace seek out a young woman, a virgin, who would become his handmaid. She would care for him, feed him, and keep him warm at night.

The king's counselors searched throughout all the territory of Israel and settled on Abishag, a Shunammite, and brought her to the king's house. Lovely and gentle, with childlike innocence and an infectious laugh, she cared for the king and slept with him, but she remained a virgin.

I never felt one spark of jealousy regarding Abishag. The girl who slept with my husband knew little about life or love or suffering, but David and I had experienced all those things over the years. Our relationship had been forged by sorrow and grief, and pain had brought us together and kept us dependent upon Adonai.

I smiled gratefully at Abishag whenever I happened to see her in the palace and frequently asked her to let me know if I could do anything to help her.

During the passing years, Solomon took a wife, a lovely Ammonite girl called Naamah. David was able to hold Solomon's firstborn son, a handsome boy they named Rehoboam.

I smiled at my little grandson and whispered my secret in his tiny ear: his father would one day be king, so little Rehoboam might well wear a crown himself. "But you are not to fret," I told him, "because these things are not accomplished by men but by the will of the Lord."

Life was pleasant for me and my precious sons, but as the days passed and David grew weak and forgetful, I began to hear rumors about Adonijah.

According to servants who lived in the city, Adonijah had followed Absalom's example and hired chariots, horsemen, and men to run before him to announce his approach. A quick trip to the palace rooftop allowed me to witness this spectacle for myself, so I sent a message to Joab and urged him to warn the king of his fourth son's preening ambition. I thought Joab would not hesitate to speak to the king, for no one in David's household wanted to endure another princely rebellion.

Day after day passed, and Adonijah continued to extol himself throughout Israel. I didn't know what to do next. Since his decline, the king rarely summoned me to his chamber, and even if he did, experience had taught me that he didn't like to discuss his sons.

Why hadn't Joab taken action?

I spent hours praying over the situation, then one day an old friend came to visit. "The prophet Nathan," my servant told me, "waits for you in the palace garden."

My blood seemed to flow faster. Had Adonai answered my anguished prayers? Had He sent another warning through the prophet?

I pulled my veil over my graying hair and hurried outside, then slipped up the stairs to the elevated garden. Nathan sat in a shady alcove, but he rose and bowed when he saw me.

"Friend." I greeted him with an outstretched hand, which he held only a moment. "I hope you are well."

"And you, my lady." A smile showed briefly in the thicket of his beard. "I have come to you on a matter of some importance."

"I am glad you are here." I nodded, taking care lest desperation show on my face. "Solomon is to be king, yet from the rooftop I've seen Adonijah parading through the city like the heir apparent—"

"That, my lady, is why I am here." Nathan gestured to a bench beneath a pergola. "Shall we talk?"

I glanced around. Nothing but gossip could come from a man and woman meeting alone without witnesses, but several gardeners were working in the vicinity, enough to bear witness that we were merely talking.

I sat, expecting Nathan to sit beside me, but he remained on his feet, standing before me with a concerned expression on his face. "You know about Adonijah's princely parade through the streets, but do you also know that today he has planned a feast and a sacrifice by the stone of Zoheleth? He has invited his brothers, Abiathar the priest, Joab, and all the men of Judah."

I stiffened. The stone of Zoheleth, commonly known as the

Serpent's Stone, was a rocky plateau near the spring at En-rogel. The place was within walking distance of Jerusalem.

The mention of sacrifices and a feast made me shiver. Absalom had planned a similar venture, and that excursion had resulted in disaster.

"He did not invite Solomon to this feast," I told Nathan. "But if he had, I would have urged Shlomo not to go. His life would be in danger."

Nathan tugged on his beard. "A wise choice. But not only did Adonijah not invite Solomon, he also neglected to invite the king's mighty men, Zadok the priest, or Benaiah. The court has divided, my lady, into two camps: one for Solomon and one for Adonijah. But Adonijah is not waiting for the king's death. Like Absalom before him, he has already begun to live as a king. Some have whispered that today's feast and sacrifices are part of a coronation."

Rage rose within me, flushing my face and heating my skin. I had stood at David's side when Absalom tried to take the throne, and I watched my husband's heart break. Truth to tell, David had not been the same since. Though he had returned to power, he had never stopped grieving over Absalom's brazen rebellion, and nothing I said seemed to comfort him.

I turned to the prophet. "Do you think Adonijah plans to attack the palace?"

Nathan shook his head. "He may emulate some of Absalom's tactics, but he will not make the mistake of attacking the king. He will wait until David dies, and then he will seize what is nearly his already. My lady, if you will save your life and your son's life, you must take action at once. You must go to the king and have him declare Solomon his heir. You cannot wait."

I pressed my hand to my forehead as my thoughts swirled in a haze of questions. Absalom's actions had been reprehensible, and so were Adonijah's, but I did not want to talk to David

about the inevitability of his death. Even broaching the subject
felt abhorrent.

What if my concern angered him? What if he had forgotten his
long-ago promise and now favored Adonijah? I had not seen David
in weeks, and I had no idea how he would receive my concerns.

"Are you sure we must take action before . . ." I allowed the
thought to remain unspoken. "After all, if the king's mighty men
are for Solomon—"

"And therein lies the problem, my lady. Joab, commander of the
army, is for Adonijah. The king must declare his choice, and he
must do it today. He must do it in a way that leaves no room for
doubt. Only then will your son be assured the throne. Only then
will you both be safe."

I clasped my hands and stared at the paving stones beneath my
feet. What should I do? With my grandfather gone, I had few allies in the palace. Even after all these years, the powerful men who
swayed the king could not speak my name without thinking of the
shameful circumstances that brought me to the king's household.
They would not hear my plea.

I looked up at Nathan. "What do I do?"

Slowly, he knelt on the stones before me. "You go immediately
to the king. You must ask why Adonijah has become king when he
promised that your son would sit on the throne. Then, while you are
still talking with David, I will come in and confirm your words."

I considered the prophet's idea, my heart racing, then reached out
and gripped his hand. "I will do it," I said, standing. "As soon as—"

"You need to do it now," Nathan interrupted. "Adonijah and his
allies are feasting at this hour. Do not delay, my lady. I am here to
support you, so do it immediately."

I stared at the prophet for a long moment. I had told my little
grandson that Adonai made kings, and yet it appeared that Adonai
wanted me to take a hand in placing Solomon on the throne. Could

a mere woman play a role in bringing the will of HaShem to pass? My grandfather would have scoffed at the idea, and my father, as well. But I had been praying, begging Adonai to fulfill His word . . .

And the Lord sent Nathan, who told me what must be done.

"I am doing this only because I believe it is Adonai's will," I told the prophet. Then I lifted my chin and led the way out of the garden.

꩜

I found David in his bedchamber, propped on pillows as Abishag cleared away the bowl and tray she had used to feed him. I greeted the girl with a nod and knelt beside the bed. My husband's cheekbones looked like tent poles under taut canvas, and his lips had thinned to pale blue lines in his beard. David appeared to be sleeping, but the fingers of his right hand twitched as if he were playing an invisible harp.

"My lord and king, live forever," I said, my heart breaking at the sight of my frail husband. "Your wife, Bathsheba, begs to speak to you."

David stirred, lifting his head to peer at me. His lined face brightened as he smiled. "My beautiful Bathsheba. Rise and speak freely."

I sighed in relief, then placed a stool near the bed. "My lord, I have come on a matter of some urgency."

"Speak, lady. I am listening."

I sat and stretched my arms toward him, fighting tears. "My lord, you made a vow before the Lord your God when you said to me, 'Your son Solomon will surely be the next king and will sit on my throne.' But instead, Adonijah has made himself king, and my lord the king does not even know about it. Adonijah has sacrificed many cattle, fattened calves, and sheep, and he has invited all the king's sons to attend the celebration. He also invited Abiathar the priest, and Joab, the commander of the army. But he did not invite your servant Solomon. And now, my lord the king, all Israel is waiting for you to announce who will become king after you. If you do not act, my son Solomon and I will be treated as criminals as soon as my lord the king has died."

"What's this?" David stretched his gaunt arm toward me. "What are you saying?"

At that moment Nathan stepped into the room and prostrated himself on the carpet. Overcome with emotion, I stood and backed away, more than willing to let the prophet carry the conversation forward.

"Nathan?" David's voice, though weak, held a note of surprise. "Come you to support Bathsheba?"

Nathan rose. "My lord the king, have you decided that Adonijah will be the next king and that he will sit on your throne? Today he has sacrificed many cattle, fattened calves, and sheep, and he has invited all the king's sons to attend the celebration. He also invited the commanders of the army and Abiathar the priest. They are feasting and drinking with him and shouting, 'Long live King Adonijah!' But he did not invite me or Zadok the priest or Benaiah or your servant Solomon. Has my lord the king really done this without letting any of his officials know who should be the next king?"

David spoke again, his voice stronger than before: "Bring Bathsheba to me."

I stepped out of the shadows and moved into his field of vision.

"As surely as the Lord who has rescued me from every danger lives"—David lifted his hand toward heaven—"your son Solomon will be the next king and will sit on my throne this very day, just as I vowed to you before the Lord, the God of Israel."

Overcome with gratitude and relief, I knelt on the carpet and pressed my face to the floor. "Let my lord King David live forever!" Never had I spoken more heartfelt words.

Something in my voice must have struck the dying man.

"Bathsheba—" his voice broke—"are you still there?"

I sat on the stool by his bed. "Of course, my lord."

He shook his head, then patted the blanket by his side. "Come closer."

Never had I sat so close to him with other people in the room, but I set aside my self-consciousness and sat on the bed, then leaned forward so our faces were only a hand's breadth apart.

"There you are." His compelling brown eyes found and held mine. "Tell me, wife—in all our years together, have you ever been able to love me?"

The question caught me off guard. A king's wife came when summoned, departed when dismissed, and freely bestowed false smiles and words of flattery. In all our years together, I had never once told David that I loved him. A king's wife did not need to love; she only needed to obey.

Laughter bubbled up from my throat as I found his trembling hand and held it steady. "After so many years, why do you speak of such things? Is it not enough that we have both loved the son who will inherit your kingdom?"

"I know what people say," David went on, ignoring my question. "They say that I do not easily open my heart to anyone but Adonai, and for the most part, they are right. But I have opened my heart to you, Bathsheba, and loved you more than the others."

"My king." I bit my lip, unsure how to respond. "I have always been grateful for your kindness—"

"I loved you most," he continued, his voice trembling, "because you forgave the most."

I watched, stunned and perplexed, as a tear slipped from the corner of his eye and rolled into the gray fringe of his hair. "I loved you . . . because you grieved over our baby when you could have hated him. I loved you because you loved Solomon. I loved the look on your face when I sang songs of praise to Adonai. I loved your kindness to my bitter Michal. I loved your gentleness with Tamar. And I knew . . . I knew I would love you forever when I saw your tender care of Abigail. You are more than a *tob* woman, Bathsheba. You are Adonai's blessing to me."

His eyelids fluttered and closed, and the hand within mine relaxed.

"Is he . . . ?" I asked.

"He naps." Abishag shifted her gaze from the king's face to mine. "He tires easily when he has visitors."

Aware of the many watchful eyes in the room, I struggled to maintain control of my emotions. I had to think about Solomon; I had to fulfill the king's command to place my son on the throne.

But beneath the surface of my composure, I could feel a hidden spring trying to break through. *I loved this man.* The feeling was not like what I felt for Uriah; it was deeper and more powerful. I had simply never recognized it for what it was.

Gently I slid my hand from the king's, then stood and turned. Nathan remained in the room, watching with a small smile on his face. I smoothed the wrinkles from my tunic and stepped toward the doorway.

The prophet caught my sleeve. "He meant it, you know."

"What?"

"I don't know that he has loved any of his other wives, but he loves you, Bathsheba. Just as Samuel prophesied."

"What are you saying?"

"I was there." Nathan moved to the door, and I followed, caught by his reference to the prophet whose words had shaped my early life. "I was only an apprentice when your parents brought you to the Tabernacle. But I saw Samuel look at you, and I heard his prophecy: 'This child shall grow to be a *tob* woman. She will be mother to a great man in Israel, and the heart of her husband will incline toward her alone.'" Nathan's smile turned to a chuckle. "I memorized his words. In my youth I hoped I would be the husband in question, but realized my error soon enough."

Overcome, I stared at the prophet.

"Know this, my lady—no pain exists without purpose, no grief without comfort. You have been more than David's wife; you have been his consolation, his joy, and his one love. Your forgiveness redeemed him. Don't ever forget that. Now go," he said, abruptly changing his tone. "I will stay with the king and assist with Solomon's coronation. You must summon your son and bring him to the palace. We haven't a moment to waste."

Spurred by our urgent reality, I left the king and hurried away to find Solomon.

Chapter Fifty-Two

NATHAN

AFTER BATHSHEBA LEFT THE KING'S CHAMBER, I woke the king and asked what must be done to crown Solomon. David summoned Zadok the priest and Benaiah to stand with me in his presence. Then he gave us direct and explicit instructions: "Take my son Solomon and my officials to the Gihon Spring. Solomon is to ride on my own mule. There Zadok the priest and Nathan the prophet are to anoint him king over Israel. Blow the ram's horn and shout, 'Long live King Solomon!' Then escort him back here, and he will sit on my throne. He will succeed me as king, for I have appointed him to be ruler over Israel and Judah."

"Amen!" Benaiah replied. "May Adonai, the God of my lord the king, decree that it happen. And may Adonai be with Solomon as He has been with you, my lord the king, and may He make Solomon's reign even greater than yours."

So the three of us, accompanied by the king's bodyguard, put

Bathsheba's son on the king's mule and led him over the streets of Jerusalem, through the gate, and to the Gihon Spring. There Zadok took the flask of olive oil from the sacred tent and anointed twenty-nine-year-old Solomon. We sounded the ram's horn, and all the people with us shouted, "Long live King Solomon!"

The crowd followed Solomon back into Jerusalem, playing flutes and shouting hosannas. The celebration was so joyous and noisy that the earth shook with the sound.

I smiled, knowing Bathsheba would hear the celebration from within the palace walls. Perhaps she was with David now, holding his hand as they smiled in relief that Adonai's will—and the king's—had been carried out.

Adonijah and his fellows would hear the sound too, and their reaction would determine their futures. If they stood and fought, we would have another bloody revolt to quell, but at least it would be confined to Jerusalem. If they scattered and accepted David's decree, perhaps Jerusalem would indeed be a city of peace.

A few hours later, I learned that Adonijah's followers had run like a herd of startled deer. Adonijah himself had been so frightened by the thought of his younger brother's vengeance that he ran to the sacred tent of the Tabernacle and seized the horns of the altar, a traditional place of sanctuary. Clinging to the horns with all his strength, he begged anyone who would listen to carry a message to the new king: "Let King Solomon swear today that he will not kill me!"

When Solomon heard his brother's request, he sagely replied, "If he proves himself to be loyal, not a hair on his head will be touched. But if he makes trouble, he will die."

Solomon sent for his brother. The royal guards had to peel the upstart prince from the altar. Then Adonijah walked through a thick, expectant silence into the throne room and bowed respectfully before his brother the king.

Solomon's reply was simple and terse: "Go home."

Chapter Fifty-Three
BATHSHEBA

ON ONE OF HIS LAST DAYS, David sent for Solomon. Solomon asked that Elisheba and I join him, so the three of us met in the ailing king's bedchamber.

"My son, I wanted to build a Temple to honor the name of the Lord my God," David said, reclining against his pillows. "But the Lord said to me, 'You have killed many men in the battles you have fought. And since you have shed so much blood in my sight, you will not be the one to build a Temple to honor my name. But you will have a son who will be a man of peace. I will give him peace with his enemies in all the surrounding lands. His name will be Solomon, and I will give peace and quiet to Israel during his reign. He is the one who will build a Temple to honor my name. He will be my son, and I will be his father. And I will secure the throne of his kingdom over Israel forever.'"

Standing in the back of the king's bedchamber, I watched the weight of David's words settle on Solomon's broad shoulders. My son had been given a great responsibility and a great blessing, for David's kingdom had known only fleeting periods of peace.

"Now, my son," David continued, "may Adonai be with you and give you success as you follow His directions in building the Temple of Adonai. And may the Lord give you wisdom and understanding, that you may obey the Law of the Lord your God as you rule over Israel. For you will be successful if you carefully obey the decrees and regulations the Lord gave to Israel through Moses. Be strong and courageous; do not be afraid or lose heart."

Solomon nodded, then found his voice. "I will, Father."

Something that looked like a smile twitched in and out of David's gray beard. "I have worked hard to provide materials for building the Temple of the Lord—nearly four thousand tons of gold, forty thousand tons of silver, and more iron and bronze than can be weighed. I have also gathered timber and stone for the walls, though you may need to add more. You have a large number of skilled stonemasons and carpenters and craftsmen of every kind. You have expert goldsmiths and silversmiths and workers of bronze and iron. Now begin the work, and may the Lord be with you!"

David then had a scribe transcribe an edict, ordering all the leaders of Israel to assist Solomon in the project. When the scribe had finished, David lay back on his pillows, placed his hands in his lap, and slowly exhaled. "Solomon?" he asked, not lifting his head.

"I am here, Father."

"Stand, please. Come where I can see you."

Solomon rose and sat on the edge of the bed, leaning over his father's shrunken frame. David blinked, seeming to focus his vision, then lifted an age-spotted hand and placed it on the crown of Solomon's head.

"The Lord your God is with you," David declared. "He has given you peace with the surrounding nations. He has handed them over to me, and they are now subject to Adonai and His people. Now seek the Lord your God with all your heart and soul. Build the sanctuary of the Lord God so that you can bring the Ark of the Lord's Covenant and the holy vessels of God into the Temple built to honor the Lord's name."

"I will, Father."

David sighed again and lowered his hand to his chest. "Thank you, my son."

Watching David bless Solomon assured me that at long last David had learned something about being a father. The overlooked, unseen shepherd boy had finally learned to see and trust his son.

I buried my face in Elisheba's shoulder and wept in a spontaneous overflow of gratitude and love.

⚜

With Solomon safely installed on the throne, my concern shifted to my dying husband. Having successfully passed the kingdom into the hands of the man Adonai had chosen, David approached the end of his days. On some afternoons I sat with him, wanting to keep him company.

One day, after he had finished scratching out a verse on parchment, I stood and went to his side. Motioning for Abishag to remain in her place, I removed the tray, pen, and parchment, then lifted the blanket and slid into the space next to him. Lying close to him, my head propped on my hand, my breath brushing his face, I studied the man who had been my husband and king.

My gaze rested on his wide forehead, the bearded cheeks and chin, the lips that had so often caressed mine. As I watched him rest in deep and peaceful slumber, the bitter memories of the past fled away. Long ago I had forgiven him. In that moment I wanted to forget everything but his love, his friendship, and his willingness to defend our son. I had never felt for David what I felt for Uriah, but my feelings for David far overwhelmed my adolescent yearnings.

My hand moved under the blanket and came to rest against the tender flesh of his chest. I sighed and rested my cheek against his now-bony shoulder, my sorrows and joys blending seamlessly in the myriad intricacies of love.

⌘

The next day, David sent for Solomon, and as he often did, Solomon invited me to come with him. Together we went to the king's bedchamber and knelt on the carpet by the side of the bed.

As David struggled to sit upright, Abishag arranged pillows to support his head. "Solomon, my son," David began, "I am going where everyone on earth must someday go. Take courage and be a man. Observe the requirements of the Lord your God and follow His ways. Keep the decrees, commands, and regulations written in the Law of Moses so you will be successful in all you do and wherever you go. If you do this, the Lord will keep the promise He made to me. He told me, 'If your descendants live as they should and follow me faithfully with all their heart and soul, one of them will always sit on the throne of Israel.'"

While David spoke, I stood and quietly slipped into the shadows. This moment existed for David and his son, and I had no part in it.

"There is something else," David continued, wheezing. "You know what Joab did to me when he murdered my army commanders Abner and Amasa. He pretended it was an act of war, but the murders were committed in a time of peace, staining his belt and sandals with innocent blood. Do with him what you think best, but don't let him go to his grave in peace.

"Be kind to the sons of Barzillai of Gilead. Make them perma-

nent guests at your table, for they took care of me when I fled from
your brother Absalom.

"And remember Shimei, the man from Bahurim in Benjamin.
He cursed me with a terrible curse as I was fleeing to Mahanaim.
When he came to meet me at the Jordan River, I swore by the
Lord that I would not kill him. But that oath does not make him
innocent. You are a wise man, and you will know how to arrange
a bloody death for him."

I stared, shocked and dismayed, as David delivered his final
charge to Solomon. We had lived through so much bloodshed that
I'd hoped David's thirst for war had been slaked. But he wanted
peace for his son, and even in his final moments he was determined
to achieve justice and remove unfaithful men.

David drew a deep breath, his chest rising and falling with the
effort. "This is the speech of David, the son of Jesse, the speech of
the man who has been raised up, the one anointed by the God of
Jacob, the sweet singer of Israel. The Spirit of Adonai spoke through
me, His word was on my tongue. The God of Israel spoke; the Rock
of Israel said to me, 'A ruler of people must be upright, ruling in
the fear of God; like the morning light at sunrise on a cloudless day
that makes the grass on the earth sparkle after a rain.'

"For my house stands firm with God. He made an everlasting
covenant with me. It is in order, fully assured, that He will bring
to full growth all my salvation and every desire. But the ungodly
are like thorn bushes to be pushed aside, every one of them. They
cannot be taken in one's hand; to touch them one uses a pitchfork
or spear shaft, and then only to burn them where they lie."

He might have gone on, but David's next breath ended in a bout
of coughing. When he had finished, he lay back and remained quiet.

Solomon stood and reached for his father's hand. Curious, I
stepped into the light and saw that David's eyes had closed. He rested
against his pillow, one hand in his son's, the other limp at his side.

When I heard the sound of Solomon's sobs, I realized that David, our shepherd king and my royal husband, had gone to the place where our infant son waited. Where he would find Samuel, his teacher, and Jonathan, his best friend. And where one day he would find me.

~※~

A few days after David's funeral, I was surprised to find Adonijah waiting for me in the palace garden. I blinked when he approached and bowed, then lifted a brow. What did this shifty, scheming prince want now?

"Do you come with honorable intentions?" I asked, forcing a smile.

"Yes." His mouth twisted in a way that reminded me of Absalom's charming grin. "I come in peace, my lady. In fact, I have a favor to ask of you."

"Can't you ask your own mother?"

He smiled as he shook his head. "I have a favor to ask the king, and who better to represent me than you?"

I folded my hands. "What is it?"

"Please speak to King Solomon on my behalf, for I know he will grant anything you request. Ask him to let me marry Abishag, the girl from Shunem."

I stared, too startled by the request to offer any objection. Was he *insane?* To claim a king's wife or concubine, virgin or not, was to claim the throne. If by some folly Solomon allowed his brother to marry the girl, Adonijah might not claim the throne immediately, but he would do it. At some opportune moment he would point out that he had David's wife, so surely he was the son who ought to have inherited the throne.

I tilted my head and studied the young man before me. Handsome, yes, but definitely not the brightest of the king's many sons. Or, if he was not as thick as a plank, he must have believed I was.

"All right," I told him. "I will carry your request to the king."

My thoughts burned as I hurried to the throne room. Despite David's resolute action, Adonijah had not been able to bury his ambition. Haggith's son had proven to be a thorn in David's side, and I would not let him needle Solomon. I would pass on Adonijah's request, and I would trust Solomon to take the right action.

A dozen counselors bowed as I entered the king's hall and moved immediately to the open area before my son's throne. Solomon rose from his seat and bowed before me, a gesture that brought unexpected tears to my eyes. When he sat again, he asked a servant to bring a throne for me, as well.

Completely taken aback, I timidly took the chair by his right side and looked over the crowd assembled for the king's attention. Men in armor, merchants in fine apparel, priests in their woven white tunics—in all my years I had never seen the throne room from this elevated perspective.

"What is it, my mother?" Solomon asked, keeping his voice low as he looked at me. "You know I won't refuse any request."

I gave him a guileless smile. "My king, I would be pleased if you would let your brother Adonijah marry Abishag, the girl from Shunem."

In a flash, Solomon realized the motivation and the threat behind the request. "How can you possibly ask me to give Abishag to Adonijah?" His brows rushed together. "You might as well ask me to give him the kingdom! You know he is my older brother, and he has Abiathar the priest and Joab on his side."

"I know, son." I allowed my gaze to leave his face and move over the crowd, which certainly included several men who quietly supported Adonijah. "I am only passing on your brother's petition."

Solomon stared at me for a moment more, then understanding lit his eyes.

He stood, his face flaming, and lifted a fist in midair. "May God strike me and even kill me if Adonijah has not sealed his fate with this request. The Lord has confirmed me and placed me on the throne of my father, David. He has established my dynasty as He promised. So as surely as the Lord lives, Adonijah will die this very day."

I pressed my lips together, knowing that after this, none of David's other sons would have the courage to challenge Solomon for the throne.

Solomon wasted no time carrying out the last of his father's instructions. He told Abiathar the traitorous priest to go back to his home in Anathoth. "You deserve to die for your treason," he said, "but I will not kill you because you carried the Ark of the Sovereign Lord for David my father and shared all his hardships. But you will no longer serve as priest of the Lord at the Tabernacle." Zadok the priest replaced Abiathar.

Because David's commander Joab had joined Adonijah's rebellion, Solomon dispatched Benaiah to execute him. The wily commander also ran to the sacred tent of the Tabernacle and clung to the horns of the altar, but Solomon ordered Benaiah to kill him anyway to remove the guilt of Joab's senseless murders from David's family. Benaiah was then named commander of the army.

As for Shimei, the man who had foolishly cursed David on his way to Mahanaim, Solomon told him, "Build a house here in Jerusalem and live in it safely. But the day you step outside the city, you will die and your blood will be on your own head."

For two years Shimei lived in his house, but when two of his slaves ran away, he saddled his donkey and traveled to Gath to find them. When he returned, Solomon had him executed.

Shlomo, my precious son, had inherited my peaceful nature, but

he also possessed his father's iron will. And though the ruthless requirements of kingship often made me flinch, in Solomon's resolute
actions I saw a strength and courage I had never possessed. Truly
he was the best of me and the best of David, wrought together in
order to fulfill Adonai's will for His people Israel.

Epilogue
BATHSHEBA

MORE THAN TWENTY YEARS HAVE PASSED since David's death, but I have never forgotten the prophet's reassuring words. Nor have I forgotten that David paid dearly for his sins, losing four children: our baby, Amnon, Absalom, and Tamar.

In my youth I was a *tob* woman. I am a *tob* woman still, but one must look deep into my eyes to see the beauty and strength that once made me desirable. My sons have seen it, as have their wives.

David came to see the *tob* woman within, and in doing so, taught me how to love him.

I am now an old woman of seventy years. I have laughed in a small house and wept in a palace. I have loved two men and lost them both. But throughout the winding length of my life, I have been pulled and directed by words that sprang from prophets' lips after being breathed by the *Ruach HaKodesh*.

Adonai created me a *tob* woman . . . and I am content.

DISCUSSION QUESTIONS

1. The story of David and Bathsheba has probably been told thousands of times. How is this story different from other versions you've heard? How is it similar?

2. At one point Nathan thinks, *Surely Adonai had not given His promise in order to lull David into complacency. A complacent man would eventually neglect the Lord because he would depend upon HaShem's promise and not HaShem.* Many who claim to be Christians today have fallen into this same trap. They place their faith in something they did for God, whether it's joining the church or being baptized or making a donation, instead of placing their faith in God himself. In your view, what is the difference?

3. What do you think of Absalom? Is he a misunderstood and neglected son or a scheming opportunist with royal ambitions?

4. Did Bathsheba love David? If you were in her position, would you have been able to love him?

5. What did David mean when he said he loved Bathsheba most because she forgave the most?

6. What struck you most about the time period of the story? How would this situation have played out in contemporary times?

7. What, if anything, did you admire about Bathsheba? What about her personality did you find less than admirable?

8. Has a prophecy—or some words uttered by someone you respected—influenced the course of your life? Who said them, and how have those words affected you?

9. This story would not be complete without prophets, who still exist today. Most preachers, for instance, have the gift or the calling of prophecy in that they speak God's truth to people, and sometimes that truth can be hard to hear. Do you think most pastors are exercising the gift of prophecy today, or are they saying things most people want to hear?

10. History tells us that Solomon was the greatest king in the history of the world, the wisest and the wealthiest. After his death, however, the nation of Israel split down its fault line, dividing into Judah and Israel. Does this historical fact surprise you? What contemporary examples exist of nations or groups that seem to coexist better when they are separated?

11. The author has said that she takes great pains not to contradict the biblical record. With that in mind, did anything in *Bathsheba: Reluctant Beauty* surprise you?

12. Beauty is a theme in this series—how it can influence the course of a life. In *Esther: Royal Beauty*, the first book of the series, beauty places a Jewish girl on a pagan throne and gives her the power to save her people. In *Bathsheba*, beauty causes a girl to be raped by a king and then forced into his harem. In what ways did beauty harm these women, and in what ways did beauty become one of their strengths?

AUTHOR'S NOTE

I'M WELL AWARE that this novel might raise as many questions as it answers, so I wanted to take a page or two to explain why events in this story unfolded the way they did.

First, I have taken pains not to purposely contradict anything in the Bible. If it happened a certain way in the Scripture, I wrote the events as the Bible said they happened. But because biblical writers only give us the "big picture" of events, as a novelist, I feel free to fill in the canvas with logical details, feelings, conversations, and settings.

When I first began to write this story, I tweeted a few comments about my progress and almost instantly became aware of a prejudice against Bathsheba. One man tweeted a reply to the effect of, "Boy, she really did a number on David," and I was stunned when I read it. How in the world had Bathsheba become the *aggressor*? Are we so enthralled with the man "after God's own heart" that we cannot see that he was as fallible as any other human?

I mentioned my work-in-progress on my blog and sparked an interesting conversation in which even women remarked that Bathsheba must have played some role in what was considered a "seduction" of the king. After all, she was taking a bath outdoors, and perhaps she intended to tempt David.

But homes in ancient Jerusalem did not have indoor plumbing. The word *mikvah* means "large container of water" and came to be associated with the ritual bath women had to take after their menstrual cycle. Where would a family put this *mikvah*? Out in the courtyard, of course. Bathsheba's bathing outside was not unusual; most women in Jerusalem would have bathed outdoors unless they watered their livestock inside the house.

David had an excellent view of Bathsheba (and everyone else), because not only was the palace located at a higher elevation than the rest of the city, he was also on the *rooftop*. Perhaps he went there to survey his kingdom; perhaps he wanted to enjoy the sunset. In any case, he was on the roof at sunset, and sunset marked the end of one Hebrew day and the beginning of another. It is therefore logical and normal that Bathsheba or any woman would have been bathing outdoors around sunset at the end of her menstrual cycle.

I have also considered the point that Bathsheba's experience couldn't qualify as rape because she had options. Deuteronomy 22:23–26 asserts that if a woman is raped out in the country, she is always considered innocent, for it can be assumed that she screamed and no one was around to come to her defense. If a woman is raped in the city, however, and does not scream, then she was judged guilty of adultery.

That passage was written in the days before Israel's kings, and the establishment of Israel as a kingdom changed many aspects of everyday life. The king held the power of life and death over his subjects, so I do not think any woman assaulted by the king would endanger her life by screaming. His power and authority were a metaphorical gun at her head, and his use of force was a threat not only to her life but to her reputation.

To be fair, I asked myself, *could* Bathsheba have been in love with David from the start? The Bible tells us very little about what she thought or felt, and she speaks in only two recorded instances (2 Samuel 11:5 and 1 Kings 1). So in order to gauge her feelings about the men in her life, I considered the parable Nathan told David. The poor man and his "ewe lamb" represented Uriah and

Bathsheba, and from the parable it's clear that the poor man and the ewe lamb shared a tender relationship. The violence in the story springs solely from the rich man, while the poor man and his lamb are completely innocent.

That parable, therefore, is the biblical basis for my portrayal of Bathsheba and Uriah's relationship.

Why do I often refer to God as HaShem? *HaShem* literally means *the name* in Hebrew, and it is used instead of the word we would translate *Jehovah*. Many Jews still use *HaShem* to refer to God, because His name is considered too holy to speak or write.

Did Samuel utter a prophecy about Bathsheba? That prophecy is a fictional invention, but the prophets prophesied many things, and Scripture records only a few of them.

Did Nathan predict all the trials that would befall David's house? That prophecy is found in 2 Samuel 12.

Did Uriah know what David had done to his wife? We cannot know for certain. Some people in the palace definitely knew, for David used palace messengers to find out who she was and then to fetch her to the rooftop, so it's entirely possible Uriah knew his wife had been ill-used by the king. But one thing is clear—whether or not Uriah knew, he was a man of honor, so he was determined to do his duty even if his king and master sent him to his death. I chose to exercise this option, because the story is far more dramatic if Uriah knew and walked willingly—sacrificially—into the trap David set for him.

Did Michal really raise her older sister Merab's sons? Second Samuel 6:23 tells us that Michal remained childless all her life (after she mocked David's dancing during the Ark's arrival to Jerusalem). Yet in 2 Samuel 21:8–9, the Masoretic Text (and the *King James Bible*) says that Michal had five sons who were handed over to the Gibeonites. Most likely the substitution of *Michal* for *Merab* was a copyist's error, but I chose to have Michal bring up her deceased sister's sons. (Biblical inerrancy refers to the fact that the Bible is without error *in the original texts.* Copyists have made errors over the years, and many Bibles will point those out in margin notes.)

Did David really sit up on his deathbed and charge Solomon with taking care of his enemies? Yes. Somehow I am reminded of Marlon Brando in that scene.

Did Absalom really cut his hair only once a year? Did the trimmings really weigh five pounds? Yes, and yes (2 Samuel 14:26). Was his hair really the hair of Adam? That's a Jewish legend. Did he really get his hair caught in an oak (terebinth) tree? Yes.

Did Absalom have children? Yes (2 Samuel 14:27, 18:18; 2 Kings 15:2). Did four of them die in the plague? I don't know how they died, but only Maacah is ever mentioned in Scripture again. Some scholars believe that 2 Samuel 14:27 actually means that Maacah is Tamar's daughter and Absalom's granddaughter (who later married Solomon's son Rehoboam). I chose the literal rendering, though I believe either alternative is plausible.

Did Bathsheba really have five sons, four of whom survived? Yes (1 Chronicles 3:5).

I found it interesting that the Gospel of Matthew traces Jesus' lineage through Solomon, while Luke traces it through Nathan, Bathsheba's youngest son. The two genealogies do not agree, and here's an explanation as to why they differ:

A. The lists of ancestors found in Matthew 1:1–17 and Luke 3:23–38 do not agree. There are two major theories for the discrepancies:

1. Matthew wrote primarily to a Jewish audience and recorded Joseph's lineage to satisfy Jewish legal practices, while Luke wrote to Gentiles and recorded Mary's lineage. Both trace Jesus back to David, yet Luke goes further, all

the way back to Adam (probably because he was writing for Gentiles).

2. Matthew recorded the lineage of the kings of Judah succeeding David (or after the Exile, those who would have succeeded), while Luke recorded the actual ancestors.

B. This lineage would serve the purpose of proving Jesus' tribal identity and showing the fulfillment of prophecy (cf. Genesis 49:8–12 and 2 Samuel 7). Fulfilled prophecy (cf. Matthew 1:22; 2:15, 17, 23; 4:14; 8:17; 12:17; 13:35; 21:4; 27:9; 35) is strong evidence for a supernatural Bible and for God's control of history and time.

C. Matthew 1:17 gives the key to understanding why some ancestors are not listed. The author was using a numerically structured, three-tiered "fourteen generation" approach to Jesus' lineage.[1]

If you'd like to read the supporting Scriptures for this novel, you'll find most of them in 2 Samuel and 1 Kings.

I hope Bathsheba's story, like Esther's, has encouraged you to pick up a Bible and read the historical accounts of how they lived and how God used them. I love to hear from readers, so if you have any questions or comments, feel free to drop me a note at Angie@angelaelwellhunt.com.

---

1. Robert James Utley, vol. 9, *The First Christian Primer: Matthew*, Study Guide Commentary Series, 6 (Marshall, TX: Bible Lessons International, 2000).

REFERENCES

————. 1975. *Bible and Spade,* Volume 4, 1, 27. Ephrata, PA: Associates for Biblical Research.

Alter, Robert. *The David Story.* New York: W.W. Norton and Company, 1999.

Beeching, M. "Bathsheba," in *New Bible Dictionary,* ed. D. R. W. Wood, I. H. Marshall, A. R. Millard et al., 3rd ed., 125. Leicester, England; Downers Grove, IL: InterVarsity Press, 1996.

Believer's Study Bible. Ed. W. A. Criswell, Paige Patterson, E. Ray Clendenen et al., electronic ed., 2 Sa 1:1–24:3. Nashville: Thomas Nelson, 1991.

Brisco, Thomas V. *Holman Bible Atlas.* Holman Reference, 110–13. Nashville, TN: Broadman & Holman Publishers, 1998.

Day, Colin A. *Collins Thesaurus of the Bible.* Bellingham, WA: Logos Bible Software, 2009.

Dockery, David S., Trent C. Butler, Christopher L. Church et al. *Holman Bible Handbook,* 235–41. Nashville, TN: Holman Bible Publishers, 1992.

Drazin, Israel. *Mysteries of Judaism.* Jerusalem: Gefen Publishing, 2014.

Edersheim, Alfred. *Sketches of Jewish Social Life in the Days of Christ,* Bellingham, WA: Logos Bible Software, 2003.

Eisenberg, Joyce, Ellen Scolnic, and Jewish Publication Society. *The JPS Dictionary of Jewish Words,* 14. Philadelphia, PA: Jewish Publication Society, 2001.

Elwell, Walter A. and Philip Wesley Comfort. *Tyndale Bible Dictionary.* Tyndale Reference Library, 36. Wheaton, IL: Tyndale House Publishers, 2001.

Halpern, Baruch. *David's Secret Demons: Messiah, Murderer, Traitor, King.* Grand Rapids, MI: W. B. Eerdmans, 2001.

Hancock, Omer J., Jr. "Nathan," in *Holman Illustrated Bible Dictionary.* Ed. Chad Brand, Charles Draper, Archie England et al., 1175–76. Nashville, TN: Holman Bible Publishers, 2003.

Jeffrey, David L. *A Dictionary of Biblical Tradition in English Literature.* Grand Rapids, MI: W. B. Eerdmans, 1992.

Jenkins, Simon. *Nelson's 3-D Bible Mapbook.* Nashville: Thomas Nelson, 1995.

Josephus, *Jewish Wars.* Loeb Classical Library: Harvard University Press.

Kaiser, Walter C., Jr., Peter H. Davids, F. F. Bruce, and Manfred T. Brauch. *Hard Sayings of the Bible*, 228–29. Downers Grove, IL: InterVarsity Press, 1996.

Kirsch, Jonathan. *King David: The Real Life of the Man Who Ruled Israel.* New York: Ballantine, 2000.

KJV Bible Commentary. Ed. Edward E. Hindson and Woodrow Michael Kroll, 221–23. Nashville: Thomas Nelson Publishers, 1994.

Klein, William W., Craig Blomberg, and Robert L. Hubbard. *Introduction to Biblical Interpretation*, 193–94. Nashville, TN: Thomas Nelson Publishers, 2004.

La Bossière, Camille R., University of Ottawa; David L. Jeffrey. *A Dictionary of Biblical Tradition in English Literature.* Grand Rapids, MI: W. B. Eerdmans, 1992.

Lagassé, Paul and Columbia University. *The Columbia Encyclopedia*, 6th ed. New York; Detroit: Columbia University Press; Sold and distributed by Gale Group, 2000.

Long, Thomas G. "Preaching in the Prophets" in *Handbook of Contemporary Preaching*. Ed. Michael Duduit, 306–08. Nashville, TN: Broadman Press, 1992.

MacArthur, John. *The MacArthur Topical Bible: New King James Version*, 1198. Nashville, TN: Word Publishing, 1999.

MacArthur Study Bible, The. Ed. John MacArthur, Jr., electronic ed., 441–52. Nashville, TN: Word, 1997.

Manser, Martin H., Natasha B. Fleming, Kate Hughes, and Ronald F. Bridges. *I Never Knew That Was in the Bible!* electronic ed., 165. Nashville: Thomas Nelson Publishers, 2000.

Martin H. Manser. *Dictionary of Bible Themes: The Accessible and Comprehensive Tool for Topical Studies.* London: Martin Manser, 2009.

Much, Terry C., *Sins of the Body: Ministry in a Sexual Society*, vol. 19. The Leadership Library, 141–47. Carol Stream, IL; Waco, TX: Christianity Today; Word Books, 1989.

Myers, Allen C. *The Eerdmans Bible Dictionary*, 33. Grand Rapids, MI: W. B. Eerdmans, 1987.

Nelson's New Illustrated Bible Dictionary. Ed. Ronald F. Youngblood, F. F. Bruce, R. K. Harrison, and Thomas Nelson Publishers. Nashville, TN: Thomas Nelson Publishers, 1995.

Open Bible: New King James Version, The, electronic ed. Nashville: Thomas Nelson Publishers, 1998.

Packer, J. I., Merrill Chapin Tenney, and William White, Jr. *Nelson's Illustrated Manners and Customs of the Bible*, 498–503. Nashville, TN: Thomas Nelson Publishers, 1997.

Radmacher, Earl D., Ronald Barclay Allen, and H. Wayne House. *The Nelson Study Bible: New King James Version*, 1 Ki 1:12–27. Nashville: Thomas Nelson Publishers, 1997.

Rice, Gene. *Nations Under God: A Commentary on the Book of 1 Kings.* International Theological Commentary, 16–18. Grand Rapids, MI: W. B. Eerdmans, 1990.

Richards, Larry. *Every Man in the Bible*, 150. Nashville: Thomas Nelson Publishers, 1999.

Richards, Lawrence O. *The Bible Reader's Companion*, electronic ed., 203–08. Wheaton, IL: Victor Books, 1991.

Richards, Sue Poorman and Larry Richards. *Every Woman in the Bible*, 128–31. Nashville, TN: Thomas Nelson Publishers, 1999.

Robinson, Gnana. *Let Us Be Like the Nations: A Commentary on the Books of 1 and 2 Samuel.* International Theological Commentary, 208–15. Grand Rapids, MI; Edinburgh: W. B. Eerdmans; Handsel Press, 1993.

Rosenberg, Joel W., Ph.D.; Associate Professor, Hebrew Literature and Judaic Studies; Tufts University; Medford, Massachusetts, quoted in *Harper's Bible Dictionary*, 1st ed., 1035–36. San Francisco: Harper & Row, 1985.

Rust, Eric C. "Preaching From the Minor Prophets," *Biblical Preaching: An Expositor's Treasury*, 133. Ed. James W. Cox. Philadelphia: Westminster Press, 1983.

Schley, D.G. "Joab (Person)," vol. 3, *The Anchor Yale Bible Dictionary.* Ed. David Noel Freedman, 852–54. New York: Doubleday, 1992.

Smith, James E. *The Books of History*, Old Testament Survey Series, 2 Sa 11:26–12:25. Joplin, MO: College Press, 1995.

Spirit Filled Life Study Bible. Ed. Jack W. Hayford, electronic ed., Dt 18:1. Nashville, TN: Thomas Nelson Publishers, 1997.

Sproul, R. C. *Essential Truths of the Christian Faith.* Wheaton, IL: Tyndale House, 1992.

Stern, David H. *Complete Jewish Bible.* Clarksville, Maryland: Jewish New Testament Publications, Inc., 1998.

Strong, James. *Enhanced Strong's Lexicon.* Bellingham, WA: Logos Bible Software, 2001.

Thomas Nelson, Inc. *The Woman's Study Bible.* Nashville: Thomas Nelson, 1995.

Thomas, Robert L. and The Lockman Foundation. *New American Standard Exhaustive Concordance of the Bible: Updated Edition.* Anaheim: Foundation Publications, Inc., 1998.

Tyndale House Publishers. *Holy Bible: New Living Translation*, 3rd ed., 1 Sa 19:18–1 Sa 20. Carol Stream, IL: Tyndale House Publishers, 2007.

Unterman, Alan. *Dictionary of Jewish Lore & Legend.* London: Thames and Hudson, 1991.

Utley, Robert James. Volume 9, *The First Christian Primer: Matthew*, Study Guide Commentary Series, 6. Marshall, TX: Bible Lessons International, 2000.

Von Rad, Gerhard. *The Message of the Prophets*, 101. London: SCM Press, 1968.

Wiersbe, Warren W. *Be Restored*, "Be" Commentary Series, 132–34. Colorado Springs, CO: Victor, 2002.

————. *Be Worshipful*, 1st ed., "Be" Commentary Series, 194–97. Colorado Springs, CO: Cook Communications Ministries, 2004.

Wilson, Robert R. "Prophet," *Harper's Bible Dictionary*, 829. San Francisco: Harper & Row, 1985.

Wolpe, David. *David: The Divided Heart.* New Haven: Yale University Press, 2014.

Angela Hunt has published more than one hundred books, with sales nearing five million copies worldwide. She's the *New York Times* bestselling author of *The Tale of Three Trees*, *The Note*, and *The Nativity Story*. Angela's novels have won or been nominated for several prestigious industry awards, such as the RITA Award, the Christy Award, the ECPA Christian Book Award, and the HOLT Medallion Award. Romantic Times Book Club presented her with a Lifetime Achievement Award in 2006. In 2008, she completed her doctorate in Biblical Studies and is currently completing her Th.D. Angela and her husband live in Florida, along with their mastiffs. For a complete list of the author's books, visit angelahuntbooks.com.

If you liked *Bathsheba,* you may also enjoy...

After she is forcibly taken to the palace of the king, a beautiful young Jewish woman, known to the Persians as Esther, wins a queen's crown and then must risk everything in order to save her people...and bind her husband's heart.

Esther by Angela Hunt
A DANGEROUS BEAUTY NOVEL
angelahuntbooks.com

In this series, Lynn Austin brings the biblical books of Ezra and Nehemiah to vivid life, capturing the incredible faith of these men and their families as they returned to God after the Babylonian exile. This story of faith and doubt, love and loss, encompasses the Jews' return to Jerusalem and their efforts to rebuild both God's temple and the city wall amid constant threat.

THE RESTORATION CHRONICLES: *Return to Me, Keepers of the Covenant, On This Foundation*
by Lynn Austin
lynnaustin.org

More Fiction From Bethany House

Experience the gritty, action-packed story of two biblical heroes! For the sake of his new God and his loyalty to his friend Joshua, Caleb will battle the enemies of God's people until his dying breath. From his early days as a mercenary for Pharaoh in Egypt to his flight with the Hebrews through the Red Sea, Caleb recounts, with graphic detail, the supernatural events leading up to the Exodus.

Shadow of the Mountain: Exodus by Cliff Graham
SHADOW OF THE MOUNTAIN #1
cliffgraham.com

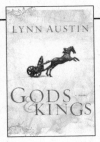

Encounter the history and promises of the Old Testament in these dramatic stories of struggle and triumph. When invading armies, idol worship, and infidelity plague the life and legacy of King Hezekiah, can his faith survive the ultimate test?

CHRONICLES OF THE KINGS: *Gods and Kings, Song of Redemption, Strength of His Hand, Faith of My Fathers, Among the Gods* by Lynn Austin
lynnaustin.org

Journey to an Old Testament–style world full of action and intrigue! An unlikely prophet, a headstrong judge, and a reluctant king are called by their Creator to fulfill divine destinies akin to those of their biblical counterparts. All three face unforeseen challenges as they attempt to follow the Infinite's leading.

BOOKS OF THE INFINITE: *Prophet, Judge, King* by R. J. Larson
rjlarsonbooks.com

⬥ BETHANYHOUSE